What Happens in the Highlands

Books by Anna Bradley

The Sutherlands
LADY ELEANOR'S SEVENTH SUITOR
LADY CHARLOTTE'S FIRST LOVE
TWELFTH NIGHT WITH THE EARL

The Somerset Sisters
MORE OR LESS A MARCHIONESS
MORE OR LESS A COUNTESS
MORE OR LESS A TEMPTRESS

Besotted Scots
THE WAYWARD BRIDE
TO WED A WILD SCOT
FOR THE SAKE OF A SCOTTISH RAKE

The Swooning Virgins Society
THE VIRGIN WHO RUINED LORD GRAY
THE VIRGIN WHO VINDICATED LORD DARLINGTON
THE VIRGIN WHO HUMBLED LORD HASLEMERE
THE VIRGIN WHO BEWITCHED LORD LYMINGTON
THE VIRGIN WHO CAPTURED A VISCOUNT

Drop Dead Dukes
GIVE THE DEVIL HIS DUKE
DAMNED IF I DUKE
THE DUKE'S CHRISTMAS BRIDE

Castle Cairncross
WHAT HAPPENS IN THE HIGHLANDS

Published by Kensington Publishing Corp.

What Happens in the Highlands

ANNA BRADLEY

kensingtonbooks.com

KENSINGTON BOOKS are published by

Kensington Publishing Corp.
900 Third Avenue
New York, NY 10022

All Kensington titles, imprints, and distributed lines are available at special quantity discounts for bulk purchases for sales promotion, premiums, fund-raising, educational, or institutional use.

Special book excerpts or customized printings can also be created to fit specific needs. For details, write or phone the office of the Kensington Sales Manager: Kensington Publishing Corp., 900 Third Avenue, New York, NY 10022. Attn. Sales Department. Phone: 1-800-221-2647.

ISBN: 978-1-4967-5523-0 (eBook)
ISBN: 978-1-4967-5520-9

First Kensington Books Trade Paperback Printing: July 2025

10 9 8 7 6 5 4 3 2 1

Printed in the United States of America

The authorized representative in the EU for product safety and compliance
is eucomply OU, Parnu mnt 139b-14, Apt 123
Tallinn, Berlin 11317, hello@eucompliancepartner.com

What Happens in the Highlands

Prologue

Dunvegan, Isle of Skye, Scotland
September 1775

In the end, it was the lightning that saved them.

It was there and gone again in an instant, a single streak tearing a jagged hole into the sky above the shoreline below the castle.

If it hadn't been for the lightning, Cat never would have seen the boat.

It wasn't unusual for boats to sail the waters of the Little Minch on their way east toward Portree, but it was rare for them to venture into Loch Dunvegan, especially so close to the shoreline, where sharp rocks loomed just under the water's surface, ready to sink their teeth into the hull.

But this was no ordinary boat. It was a lugger, compact and quick, painted black, its dark sails billowing in the sudden brisk wind that had come with the lightning strike.

The lugger's crew didn't light a lamp to warn of their approach. She waited for a tinderbox spark, or a flash from a flintlock pistol, but they continued their stealthy approach, gliding silently through the waters of Loch Dunvegan, all but invisible on a moonless night.

A night like tonight.

It was a smuggler's boat, and their destination was unmistakable.

They were coming toward the castle.

Straight toward her home.

She turned and ran then, the wind whipping her skirts into a frenzy and tearing her hair from its tidy bun, hairpins scattering in her wake as she flew from the rock's edge toward the castle, through the door and past the grandfather clock on the landing to the winding stone staircase clinging to the inside walls of the turret.

"Freya!" She burst through the low, beamed door that led to the pitched roof of the castle. "Sorcha!"

Freya was in her usual place, scribbling something in one of her notebooks. Beside her was a chair, and atop it another notebook, the pages covered with her sister's tight, cramped handwriting flapping in the wind.

Beside the notebook lay a thermometer, and beside that a rain gauge.

"Cat?" Freya's head jerked up at the crash of the door slamming, her pencil slipping from her fingers. "My goodness, what is it? You look positively wild."

"There's a boat." Cat leaned over, clutching her knees, and tried to catch her breath. "Where's Sorcha?"

"Round the other side, with her birds." Freya waved a hand toward the opposite side of the turret. "All this fuss over a boat, Cat? It's just a fishing boat on the way to Portree."

"It's not a fishing boat. Come with me. Quickly, Freya!"

Freya scrambled to her feet with her notebook still clutched in her hand. "But what kind of boat would—"

"Sorcha!" Cat caught her skirts in her fists and tore around to the other side of the roof, nearly losing her balance as she skidded around the narrowest edge of the turret. "Sorcha, we need you at once!"

"For pity's sake, Cat, will you cease that shrieking? You're frightening my birds."

"I beg their pardon, but we're about to be overrun by smugglers." The three of them were alone here, and there was no telling how many men were in the boat below. Half a dozen? More?

"Smugglers!" Freya grasped the sleeve of Cat's cloak. "You're scaring me, Cat."

"There's a boat near the shoreline, just below." Cat leaned over the edge of the stone wall that surrounded the turret and peered down into the Loch. "A lugger."

"A *lugger*!" The color drained from Freya's cheeks. "But why? The rocks are treacherous, and there are no caves to hide their contraband. It doesn't make any sense, Cat."

But it did. Alas, it made perfect sense.

The smugglers hadn't come here to leave something. They'd come to *take* something.

Freya and Sorcha crowded around her, peering out into the dark waters below. "I don't see any boat. I daresay it was only Mr. Alpin in his fishing boat you saw."

If only that were true! "It wasn't Mr. Alpin, Sorcha. I'm telling you, there's a lugger just off the shoreline. I'm certain of it."

"How can you be? It's as dark as midnight out there!" Sorcha squinted into the inky blackness surrounding them. "I can't see a blessed thing."

"Wait."

They stood there, shoulders touching as they gazed into the impenetrable darkness, Cat counting off the seconds in her head.

One, two, three—

A spiky bolt of lightning pierced the sky, setting Loch Dunvegan alight for an instant, just long enough to catch the flutter of a dark sail in the rising wind and the prow of the boat drawing silently closer, like a snake slithering through the grass.

Dear God, it was close. Far, far too close.

A low curse left Sorcha's lips. "That's a lugger, right enough. But what do they want here?"

The same thing smugglers always wanted. Gold coins. Jewels. Treasure.

But Sorcha didn't expect an answer, and Cat didn't give her one. It didn't matter what they wanted. The only thing that mattered was keeping them far away from the castle. "The lightning, Freya. You said earlier that there's a storm coming?"

"Yes." Freya tipped her head back and searched the sky. "I've been tracking it all day."

It was coming out of nowhere, too. Today had been a glorious summer day, the sky as blue as she'd ever seen it, and the fading glow of the sunset had ushered in a calm evening with the promise of moonlight and stars.

But they hadn't appeared. The temperature had dropped, and dark clouds had come roaring in from the west, snuffing the light from above, just as Freya had predicted.

Cat never questioned Freya's predictions, any more than she did Sorcha's "inklings" as she called them, or her own telltale flutters and twitches. They'd long since accepted it as a part of having their mother's Murdoch blood flowing through their veins.

They didn't even talk about it. It just *was*.

"It's going to be a bad one, this time." Freya's brow creased as her gaze moved across the sky. "The wind is already picking up."

Good. The worse it was, the better. Their only hope was it would be bad enough to send the lugger careening into the rocks, splintering the hull. "When? How long do we have until it descends on us, Freya?"

"I'd thought not until morning, but it's coming much faster than I anticipated—"

"How long, Freya?" Cat asked again, biting back her impatience.

"I can't predict exactly."

"Your best guess then." Cat's tone was sharper than she'd meant it to be, but panic was clawing at her now. They were wasting time.

"An hour, maybe?"

An hour! That was too long. The lugger would reach the shoreline in a matter of minutes, and from there, there was little standing in the way of them breaching the castle.

The rocks were their best hope.

"Quickly, Freya, run and fetch Father's pistols."

"You can't shoot into the dark, Cat," Sorcha said as Freya fled for the door.

"We don't have any other choice." Cat reached for the oil lamp at Sorcha's feet, turned up the wick, and set it on the top edge of the wall, but the weak flicker was no match for the deep darkness. "Unless you have a better idea?"

Sorcha didn't reply at once but stood staring out into the darkness. "My birds," she said at last, turning to Cat.

"The birds? What of them?"

"Perhaps we should send them down to greet our guests." Sorcha glanced up into the sky, which had grown darker still, the clouds amassing as the wind whirled around them. "The storm is coming on quickly. I daresay my girls could keep our visitors, ah, occupied until it does."

Sorcha's "girls" were a pair of sparrowhawks she'd rescued after their mother was killed by a fox. She'd trained them to do all manner of things, from eating from her hand to returning to their box perches on the roof every night.

But attacking on command? "You mean a bird attack?"

"I wouldn't say *attack*, exactly, but they can make rather a nuisance of themselves, yes. It could gain us some time."

Below them, the boat was now so close Cat could make out male voices, an occasional laugh, and the swish of oars moving through the water. They were out of time. "Do it."

"Come here, darlings," Sorcha cooed as she donned her thick leather gauntlet. Athena hopped onto her arm, and Sorcha carefully removed her hood. "No need to mind your manners this time, lovey."

Athena hovered over the ledge for an instant, then in one smooth movement she was off into the night, her beautiful brown striped wings spread wide. Artemis quickly followed her sister, the pair of them swooping low over the water.

A door slammed behind them, and Freya appeared, breathless, another lantern in one hand and their father's pistols stuffed into the pockets of her apron. "I've got them!"

"I think—" Cat began, but she was interrupted by a splash. A panicked shout rang out below them. "We may not need them."

Freya turned to her, wide-eyed. "My goodness. What was that?"

"It's Artemis and Athena!" Sorcha braced her elbows on the ledge, barely able to contain her glee. "They're entertaining our callers!"

They couldn't see a thing in the dark, but it was clear a battle was taking place from the shouts and curses coming from below.

It didn't last long.

A streak of lightning illuminated the darkness, followed by a deafening roll of thunder. The skies opened, and a heavy rain came lashing down on them, bringing with it a gusty wind that tore at their skirts and tossed their hair.

"A squall." Freya held a finger up in the air. "The wind's turning west."

"Thank God." Cat caught her sisters' hands in hers and squeezed with all her might. "Thank God."

The lugger never made it to shore. The wind turned, just as Freya predicted, and drove the boat back out toward the Little Minch, the smugglers' curses echoing in the darkness. Artemis and Athena returned to their perches, and soon afterward, Freya and Sorcha went to their beds, and the castle was quiet once again.

But Cat didn't go to her bed.

She stood at one of the arched windows inside the turret and searched the darkness.

It was a miracle they'd made it through the night unscathed.

But there would be a next time. It was as certain as the changing of the tides, as the sun setting every evening and rising again in the morning.

What would become of them, then?

CHAPTER 1

Six weeks later.

She'd had the dream again tonight. The one where she was being chased.

Cat rested her palms on the rough stone edge of the window casement, sweat cooling on her skin, and stared blindly into the darkness surrounding her, searching for stars in the darkness over Loch Dunvegan.

How many times had she stood here as a child, gazing into the night sky?

More times than she could count.

Back then, she'd imagined the stars were winking a greeting for her alone, but there were no stars tonight, not even the faintest gleam of light in the sky to relieve the surrounding darkness. If it wasn't for the whoosh of the waves against the shore below, she might have imagined the world had somehow slipped away—as if the sea, the castle, and the floor under her feet had tumbled into an abyss while she'd slept, leaving her alone.

Alone atop an ancient castle clinging to a bit of rock suspended over Loch Dunvegan, nestled between Dunvegan and Kilmuir, on the Isle of Skye.

Just her, and the endless approach and retreat of the waves below.

There'd been a time when she'd found the rhythmic rush of water soothing, a lullaby that would send her off into a dreamless sleep, but these last few months, it had turned ominous, like a lie whispered in her ear.

But that wasn't what had woken her.

Not tonight, or on any of the dozens of nights before this.

It was the dream. The same one, every time.

In the dream, she was running from something.

No, not something, but *someone*, their heavy footfalls close behind her and growing nearer with every step, the heat of their ragged breaths stirring the hairs on the back of her neck to panicked attention.

No matter how nimbly she darted through the trees, she couldn't elude them. She could do nothing but fly through the woods, the branches snatching at her skirts and tearing long, bloody scratches into her arms and face, and wait for the awful moment when a heavy hand would land on her shoulder and pull her down to the ground in a tumble of tangled limbs.

Thankfully, that moment had never come. Not yet.

Just as she'd give herself up to her fate, she'd wake, shaking and drenched in perspiration, her heart shuddering like a wild thing trapped against her ribs. She'd lay awake for hours afterward, every limb taut and her frantic heartbeat echoing in her ears as she struggled to put a face or a name to her pursuer.

But they were nameless, faceless, and silent, a hulking presence that loomed over—

Stop. She squeezed her eyes closed, shaking her head to dislodge the images threatening to unfold behind her eyelids, and turned away from the window and back to the comforting familiarity of her workroom.

It wouldn't change anything to dwell on it, and goodness knew she had plenty to keep her busy while she waited for the sun to crest the horizon. It would be best to get it done now before her sisters awoke.

There would be fewer questions, that way.

She turned up the wick on the lantern sitting in the middle of the scarred table until it threw a bright circle of light over the clutter of shallow bowls, mismatched mortars and pestles, and a battered set of brass scales. Bits of torn leaves littered the floor underneath her, and the thick scent of black licorice hung in the air.

To one side of the table stood a row of four glass bottles, each with its own label, neatly printed in her handwriting.

MacLeod's Maidenhair Syrup.

And, in smaller print underneath, *Relieves Cough and Inflammation.*

The maidenhair fern was a useful little plant, and pretty, too, with its feathery, palm-shaped fronds. Ancient legend had it that any lady who could hold a branch of maidenhair fern without making the leaves flutter was as yet untouched. Over the years it had come to represent purity and innocence, and to symbolize the bond that tied two lovers together.

It was a sweet legend, but for all that maidenhair fern worked miracles on a trifling cough, there was nothing terribly intriguing about it. It was handy enough, but it was simple, humble.

Not like hemlock or foxglove. Aconite. Arsenic, Deadly Nightshade, or Cantarella.

Take foxglove, for instance. One ounce of fresh, ground foxglove leaves boiled in a pint of water, then strained, distilled, and sweetened with cinnamon oil made an admirable treatment for dropsy, but if one went a touch too heavy on the foxglove?

It could stop the heart.

They were fascinating things, toxic plants, requiring a light touch and an exquisite sense of balance. The delicacy of them appealed to her, the conundrum of a thing that was both useful and deadly at once.

That could preserve life or end it, depending on the slip of a hand.

Arsenic, for example, could be used as a preservative. Hemlock was often used as a dye, and in the proper doses, it offered a cure to those who suffered from breathing problems. Aconite made an admirable numbing agent as well as a sedative, and Deadly Nightshade could be taken to cure a cough or to treat melancholy.

But any one of them taken in excess?

Fatal. As for Cantarella, one needn't look any further than the French nobility in the mid-seventeenth century for proof of its effectiveness as a poison. Those French courtiers had been a murderous bunch.

Her skills wouldn't have gone unappreciated at Versailles.

But while the toxic plants were a great deal more interesting than simple curatives, she didn't have much of an opportunity to indulge her interest in them. There wasn't a demand for the trickier remedies in Dunvegan, and even less so for poison.

Oh, the villagers had their secrets, much like everyone else did, but these tended more toward the usual minor squabbles than they did the murderous. Livestock theft, land disputes, drunken belligerence, and on one notable occasion . . .

A bewitching.

Or so the villagers claimed, but the less said about that, the better.

She took up the glass flask that held her maidenhair extract and gave it a little shake. She'd hoped to make up half a dozen bottles tonight, but there wasn't enough left for even one more bottle, much less two.

No matter. There was time enough yet to make another batch of extract before her sisters rose for the day. It was a painstaking process, but with any luck, the good citizens of Dunvegan had been so troubled with the cough this fall, Glynnis would take all six bottles she'd prepared.

She'd pay a nice sum for each bottle, and goodness knew, they could use the extra—

"You said you wouldn't do this anymore, Cat."

Cat jumped, dropping the flask with her maidenhair extract. It hit the old wooden worktable and the delicate glass shattered with a pop, the thick extract oozing into the cracks in the worn surface. "For pity's sake, Freya!"

Her sister emerged from the shadows near the door and approached the worktable, her night rail billowing around her. "You *promised* you wouldn't spend your nights up here in this drafty old workroom anymore." Freya wrapped her arms around herself with a shudder. "You'll catch your death."

She had promised, but in her defense, she hadn't thought she'd get caught. "That doesn't excuse you sneaking up on me like that. It took me the better part of an hour to prepare that syrup, and now it's ruined."

"This is ill done of you, Cat." Freya's forehead creased with the disappointed frown she always wore whenever she caught one of her sisters doing something they oughtn't to be doing. "I am sorry about your . . ." She waved a hand at the broken glass scattered over the worktop. "Your tubes and things."

Cat glared at her sister, but she bit back the ill-tempered retort hanging on the edge of her tongue. She'd sooner berate the birds for singing than snap at her sister. Freya was a sweet, gentle soul who hardly ever had an unkind word for anyone, and when she did offer a reproach, it wasn't ever out of anger, only concern.

"Are you having trouble sleeping again?" Freya slid one of the stools out from under the table and plopped herself down on it. "Did you have another nightmare?"

Not another one, no, but the *same* one, repeatedly, and each time it was more vivid, more frightening than the last. But it would only worry Freya if she said so, and there was nothing to be done about it, in any case. "No. I'm just restless, I suppose."

"Restless," Freya repeated, one eyebrow arched. "I see."

Freya *did* see, and far too much, too. How was a lady meant to keep her secrets with such troublesome sisters about?

"Did we not agree, Cat, that you'd give up spending all hours of the night locked up in this dark room with your potions?"

Cat took up a cloth and tried to soak up the extract, then threw it aside in disgust when she only succeeded in smearing it across the table. "They're not *potions.*"

At least, not this time.

If she *did* occasionally dabble with a toxin here and there, it was merely out of a thirst for knowledge, and it was no one's business but her own.

"I seem to recall you promising you'd confine your experiments to the daylight hours," Freya went on. "But perhaps that was a figment of my imagination?"

Had she promised? Yes, in a fit of misguided optimism, she'd made that foolish promise.

She should have known better.

By now, one would think she'd have learned that promises were ephemeral things and apt to dissolve the instant one's circumstances shifted.

Well, they'd shifted, and not for the better.

Freya took up one of the glass bottles and lifted it to her nose. "Cucumber, with a hint of black licorice. My goodness, Cat, why are you up here in the wee hours of the morning making maidenhair syrup? I daresay no one's going to expire of a trifling cough anytime soon. Couldn't this wait until morning?"

"No, because . . ." Cat blew out a breath. She'd hoped to have this business settled without either her sisters knowing about it, but it seemed not one of the three of them could take a step inside these castle walls without the other two finding out about it.

"Because?"

There was no use trying to hide it now. Freya would persist until she had the whole of it. Despite her gentle nature, Freya was still a MacLeod, and she had a stubborn streak as deep and wide as Loch Dunvegan.

"Because I sent a note to Glynnis yesterday that I'd deliver the syrup today."

Freya sucked in a breath. "Glynnis! You mean to say you're going to the village today?"

A sharp rebuke rose to Cat's lips—something about dramatics and making such a fuss over nothing, but once again, she bit it back.

As much as she hated to acknowledge it, Freya was right. It was no longer a comfortable thing, visiting with Glynnis, because as dear a friend as she was to them—Glynnis was one of the only friends they had left in Dunvegan—it always caught the villagers' attention when they were seen in each other's company.

A pair of peculiar women, their heads bent together, whispering.

No good could come of *that*.

"You can't go, Cat. What in the world are you thinking, even considering it?"

"It's only a brief visit, just long enough to—"

"Cat, please." Freya reached across the table and gripped her hand. "You remember what happened the last time?"

Oh, she remembered. She wasn't likely to forget it anytime soon.

Or ever. A lady didn't forget the day the street emptied when she appeared at one end of it, or the echo of a dozen doors slamming shut, one after another, as she passed.

It wasn't an experience she was eager to repeat, but there was no help for it. A review of her account books earlier this evening had told her that plainly enough. She'd counted and calculated until her head was wobbling on her neck, but no matter how many times she tallied her columns, the result was the same.

They were down to their last few pounds.

It was no wonder she'd slept ill and woken with her heart pounding and her lungs on fire in her chest, startling awake at every creak of the heavy wooden shutters, every crash of a wave on the rocks below her window. It was no wonder she'd dreamt of a mob of crazed villagers with pitchforks in their hands, chasing her and her sisters through the cobbled streets of—

No! It was a dream only. Just a dream.

Still, dream or not, there'd been no chance of sleep after that.

"Come now, Freya. There's nothing to worry about." Cat gave her sister's hand a brisk pat. "Why, I'll be there and then gone again before any of them even realize I came."

"They *will* realize it, Cat. They always do, now."

If only she could argue the point! More than anything she wished she could tell her sister it was nonsense, that none of the good citizens of Dunvegan cared a whit for what they did, but Freya knew as well as she did that it was a lie. Even Sorcha, for all that she did her best to ignore anything having to do with the villagers, knew it.

"I'll be as quick as I can be. I promise it."

Silence. Freya's cheeks had gone pale, but she said nothing, only stared at Cat with an expression that made her squirm. "Please, Freya, don't look at me like that. Say something, will you?"

"Say something? All right then, since you demand it. I'll say that it looks as if you intend to break the second promise you made, just as you did the first one."

"We need the money, Freya."

Freya gave her a stricken look, then glanced away, biting her lip.

The silence stretched between them until at last Freya let out a long, slow breath. "You'll only go to the apothecary? And you won't speak to anyone aside from Glynnis?"

Alas, it wasn't that simple. "I can't promise I won't be obliged to speak to Bryce, but you can be sure I won't seek out his company. Indeed, I'll do my best to avoid him."

She always did, but Bryce Fraser *was* the apothecary, at least officially. Everyone in the village knew it was Glynnis who had all the medical and scientific knowledge, but naturally, it wouldn't do for her to act as the village apothecary.

She was a *woman*, after all.

A brilliant one, with a great many unusual talents, including an exhaustive knowledge of plants and their medicinal uses that rivaled Cat's own, but when had *that* ever mattered?

So, it was left to Bryce, a man without the faintest trace of his sister's talents or intelligence, and if that weren't awful enough, he was one of the few unmarried gentlemen in Dunvegan and fancied himself quite dashing, indeed.

God above, just the thought of those bulging blue eyes wandering over her made a shudder dart up her spine.

Freya's lips turned down at the mention of Bryce Fraser's name, but she didn't offer any further objections. Instead, she caught Cat's hand between her two cold ones. "You'll see that you're not left alone with him, won't you? Not even for a moment, Cat. Promise me."

"I promise it." It was an easy promise to make, and unlike the others she'd made so recklessly, easy to keep, as well. She wouldn't ever make the mistake of being alone with Bryce Fraser again.

Freya still didn't look pleased, but she rose from the stool and crossed the room to the door, turning back to glance over her shoulder when Cat didn't follow her. "You need to sleep, Cat. Come to bed. You can finish this in the morning."

"I'd just as soon finish it, now I've begun." There'd be no sleep for her tonight, in any case. There never was, after the dream.

Freya sighed. "Very well, if you must, but this is the last time."

"The last time. I promise it."

Dear God, what a liar she'd become! The truth was that promises were a luxury she could no longer afford. Still, she'd just as soon keep the worst from her younger sisters for as long as possible. She gave Freya what she hoped was a reassuring nod. "Go on, then. Off to bed with you."

The workroom felt dreadfully cold and empty once Freya had gone with the darkness and silence pressing in on her. But she set to work, and by the time the sun peeked over the edge of the horizon, she had six bottles of maidenhair syrup waiting to be packed into her marketing basket.

She had no excuse for putting off her foray into the village now, but perhaps it was just as well. She couldn't avoid it forever, and the sooner she went, the sooner she'd be back.

She paused at the window again before going downstairs, watching the hazy fingers of light struggling against a sky thick with gray clouds. From up here, the loch appeared as smooth as a sheet of dark glass, like the kindest of friends, tempting you to dip a toe in and refresh yourself.

To look at it now, one would never guess the treachery that lay beneath the calm waters, the swirling currents that caught you around the ankles and jerked you down into the deep, the rocky bottom falling out beneath you as the water closed over your head.

If the currents didn't finish you, the jagged rocks you hadn't noticed at first would do the trick. That, or the cold. It was a convenient reminder never to forget that danger lurked beneath the most harmless of surfaces.

It was rather like poison that way.

She closed her eyes, shutting out the sight of the deceptive waters below, and ran a hand over her eyelids. Had it only been a matter of months since a visit to the village had become something to dread, instead of a pleasure?

Perhaps it had been inevitable, the villagers turning on them as they'd done. If her father hadn't been an infamous smuggler, or her mother a Murdoch daughter, it might have been different. If their Great-great-aunt Elspeth hadn't met her end at the hands of a mob who'd lashed her to a stake and watched her burn, the villagers might have had more patience with them.

But so much wickedness in one family? There was no overlooking *that*.

She turned away from the window and made her way down the narrow stone staircase to the low door that led into the main part of the castle. From there, she emerged into the portrait gallery and hurried down the staircase to the entryway, but she came to a dead stop at the bottom of the stairs.

It was deserted.

Even now, weeks later, it still felt like a fist to her stomach to come downstairs and find Duffy's usual place by the door empty. For as long as she could remember, his craggy face was the first thing she saw when she came down the stairs in the mornings, his stern expression softening into a smile when he caught sight of her.

She'd ask after his health, and he'd launch into his usual complaint about the damp making him "a wee bit achy" in the joints, and she'd smile because Duffy's troublesome joints were as much a fixture at Castle Cairncross as the sixteenth-century suit of armor that stood in the alcove to one side of the staircase.

Then she'd tell him he mustn't stay in this drafty hallway all morning, as it would only aggravate his joints, and he'd wave a hand and tell her that one room in the castle was as drafty as the next.

Over the years, this exchange had become something of a ritual of theirs.

But Duffy had been gone these past few weeks, and with him Mrs. Duffy, who'd been their housekeeper for as long as she could remember. She'd pensioned them off because she couldn't in good conscience allow them to continue in the castle once the boats started coming.

If they'd stayed, it would only have been a matter of time before the villagers turned on them, as well.

She remained frozen at the bottom of the stairs, staring at the place where Duffy had once stood. The castle had never felt as lonely as it did now, not even after their mother had died.

"Cat?" Freya wandered into the entryway but paused on her way up the stairs when she saw Cat standing there, staring at nothing. "What are you doing?"

"Nothing, I . . . is Sorcha about?"

"No. She's gone off on one of her adventures." Freya waved a hand in the direction of the woods, which was the scene of most of Sorcha's adventures.

"Ah. She's wasting no time this morning, I see." Goodness only knew what she got up to out there, but there were some things best left unasked, and Sorcha's comings and goings was one of them. "You're on your way up to the roof now, I imagine."

"Yes. I felt a bit off this morning. I think a storm is approaching."

For all her warnings to Cat about catching her death, Freya spent an inordinate amount of time on the chilly roof with her notebooks, thermometers, and rain gauges. "Don't linger up there if it starts to rain like you did last time. You were in bed for a week."

As scoldings went, it was a mild one. Freya's mysterious aches were much like her own flutters and twitches, although in Freya's case, it signaled an impending change in the weather.

Freya had the same connection to the elements their poor Great-great-aunt Elspeth had had, which was rather worrying when one considered Aunt Elspeth's fiery end. Still, Freya's talents had proved extraordinarily useful these past few months, perhaps even more so than Cat's, though Freya's particular skills didn't line their pockets the way Cat's potions and unguents did.

Yet they'd proven the difference between life and death, for all that.

"I won't stay out for long. I don't like that wind." Freya regarded her in silence for a moment. "Perhaps you'd better put off your trip to the village for another day?"

"It can't wait, I'm afraid." Cat buttoned the front of her cloak and settled the deep hood over her head so it covered most of her face.

All the better to hide her from the prying eyes of the citizens of Dunvegan.

"I don't like this, Cat."

"Nonsense. I'll be back before you know it, I promise it." She drew her basket over her arm, taking great care to avoid her sister's concerned gaze.

Freya let out a soft huff, but she said only, "See that you are."

It would take an hour, perhaps a little longer. Really, it was hardly any time at all. Why, she'd be back before Freya had a chance to miss her. It was a walk into the village, nothing more. She'd done the same walk dozens of times before.

There was no need to fall into hysterics over it, for pity's sake.

It wasn't as if the villagers were *really* going to chase her into the woods. It was just a dream, nothing more. It meant nothing. She'd found the castle to be much the same this morning as she'd left it the night before, and her sisters engaged in their usual pursuits.

All was well.

But the uneasiness in her belly persisted. Her eyebrow was

twitching most insistently, and there was an ominous tingle underneath her breastbone. As she made her way down the rocky pathway that led to the village, a spray of gooseflesh rose on the back of her neck.

She knew better than to dismiss her telltale tics and flutters.

Something was amiss. She couldn't see or hear it, but she could sense it, the air around her alive and crackling with portent.

She'd long since learned to heed these sorts of warnings.

They were signs of ill-tidings yet to come.

Chapter 2

Of all the cold, gray villages tucked into Scotland's darkest, most desolate corners, Dunvegan was the dreariest Hamish had ever encountered.

Although, did the term "village" really apply here? It seemed a generous description of this tiny, rain-soaked shred of muddy earth. If Dunvegan held more than three dozen crofts within its borders, he'd eat his hat.

Well, perhaps not his hat. It was rather a nice one. A black silk jockey, of course, as the latest fashion in London dictated, but he'd much better have left it at home, as it would be a miracle if his cockade survived this incessant drizzle.

He emerged from the inn—the Merry Maiden by name, incongruously enough, as there was a shocking lack of both maidens and merriment in Dunvegan—and onto the High Street.

If one could call it that. The apothecary's shop crouched at one end of it, and Baird's Pub at the other, with little to be found in between them aside from a joinery, a stonemason, and a tiny bakery, which admittedly did make a nice barley cake.

And just beyond the High Street . . .

He turned and shaded his eyes from the pale November sunlight filtering through the clouds. There it was, looming over the village like a hulking giant.

Castle Cairncross, the source of all his frustrations.

Like most things in Dunvegan, it was misnamed. It boasted

neither cairn nor cross, and neither was it named after Clan MacLeod, though it had been theirs since the dawn of time.

There was some sort of trickery there, no doubt. The MacLeods were a wily lot.

It was a horror of a place, done in rough, dark stone with a narrow turret to one side that was too tall for its width, jutting into the sky like a broken bone. The few muted rays of gray light that passed for sunshine in Dunvegan were no match for the shadows that atrocity threw over the village.

Beyond it, a gray horizon stretched to infinity.

If the MacLeod sisters had been anyone else—or, more accurately, if they'd had any other father—he might have felt a twinge of pity for them. It was unfair that three women should be doomed to spend their lives trapped inside that monstrosity.

But Rory MacLeod's daughters were no concern of his, or they wouldn't be, soon enough. He'd save his pity for those who deserved it, and from what he'd heard about the MacLeod sisters, they *didn't*.

Not even one of them had appeared in the village this past week. That was reason enough for him to despise them, but their absence was the least of their rumored sins.

The worst of their sins? Why, that they were wicked, treacherous crones, of course.

Or so the gossips would have it. Some claimed the MacLeod sisters were simply doing the best they could to survive, while others maintained they were wily enough, but not dangerous. But there were those who insisted that the sisters were positively Machiavellian, redheaded mythical beings—sirens or sorceresses—with the power to cast spells and curses.

A shame, that. He was partial to both redheads and wickedness, but a man didn't want to take a witch to his bed, did he?

To be fair, that bit about the spells had come from his cousins Dougal and Clyde, who'd made such a mess of this whole business weeks earlier that he'd been obliged to come to Dunvegan himself to separate the truth from the figments of their overly fertile imaginations. They were good lads, Dougal and Clyde, but perhaps not the brightest of the Muir bloodline.

Sorceresses, for God's sake. Hideous harpies, too, if Clyde and Dougal's hysterical ramblings could be trusted, all bent and gnarled, with bulging eyes and wiry red hair protruding from their heads like a nest of snakes.

It was utter bollocks, no doubt. At least, the sorceress part was. The sisters may well be as ghastly as Clyde and Dougal claimed.

One thing was certain. They were maddeningly elusive.

He'd been in Dunvegan for a week on an errand that should have taken no more than a day or two. He couldn't laze about here for months on end, waiting for some vixen to make up her mind to go shopping. If they refused to come to the village, how was he meant to charm them into inviting him into their castle?

If one of them didn't appear sooner or later, he'd be forced to either stroll up the front drive or storm the castle from Loch Dunvegan like a proper brigand. Neither approach was advisable, as they'd see him coming from a mile off from the top of that blasted turret of theirs.

That wouldn't do. The MacLeod sisters may not be sorceresses, but they were shrewd, guileful lasses, and sure to rain hellfire down upon him if they saw him coming. If he'd learned anything from Dougal and Clyde's failure, it was not to attempt to approach the castle directly.

At least, not without an invitation.

No, he'd much better wait for one of them to appear in the village, introduce himself, and simply explain—logically, rationally, and above all, charmingly—that he'd come to Dunvegan to relieve them of the fortune their father had stolen from his father.

Of course, that discussion was bound to be a trifle unpleasant. If he'd been anyone other than the ruthlessly charming, diabolically captivating Hamish Muir, the Marquess of Ballantyne, it might have proved a rather thorny problem, but if there ever was a gentleman who could coax his way into the good graces of a recalcitrant lady, it was *him*.

But alas, without a MacLeod witch to charm, his talents were utterly wasted.

It was all excessively trying.

He eased away from the doorway of the Merry Maiden and made his way down the street toward Baird's Pub. If a man wanted information, the pub was the best place to find it, inebriated men being, upon the whole, much less discreet than sober ones. Drunken louts were worse than women when it came to telling tales. If he hadn't yet learned all there was to know about the MacLeod sisters, he'd find it out here.

The door let out a rusty squeal when he entered. The place smelled strongly of ale and whisky, as if the dark, heavy beams in the ceiling had been soaked in it, the stone walls bathed in it. Half a dozen long, rough wooden tables were scattered about, and a handful of men lounged upon the benches, glasses of ale clutched in their fists.

Every eye in the place turned his way, all of them narrowed, none of them friendly. He'd ventured into Baird's twice before, earlier in the week—there was little else for a visitor to do in Dunvegan but go to the pub—but these sorts of tiny villages didn't always take kindly to strangers in their midst, and no one had spoken to him.

No matter. They'd all be best friends soon enough.

He strode across the room and sat himself down at a table in the corner near the window, where he had a clear view of the High Street. If one of the MacLeod sisters did venture into the village today, she'd have to pass by Baird's to get to any of the other shops along the street.

He waved a hand at the barkeep. "Two pints of ale. One for me, and one for my friend here." He raised an eyebrow at the man seated at the other end of the table.

"Name's Munro," the man grunted.

"Munro." Munro was a big one, with a headful of black hair and huge, meaty fists. "How do you do, friend?"

The man stared at him for a moment, taking his measure. "Haven't seen you around here before this week."

He'd expected this. Dunvegan was too remote a place for an unfamiliar face to pass unnoticed. "I've never been here before this week."

"Aye? What brings you here now, then?"

Hamish almost smiled. These tiny villages were all the same. Scotland, England, Ireland—it didn't matter where he was. He'd yet to come across one where everyone wasn't salivating over their neighbors' business.

"I had a matter to see to in Portree." Portree was the largest town on Skye, and a busy port town, at least by Scottish standards, so this was a believable enough lie. "Since I was so close, I figured I'd stop and visit Rory MacLeod. He was a friend of my father's."

That part was true enough.

Munro grunted again. "Mayhap he was once, but not anymore. Rory's dead."

Yes, he was, and thus not at all likely to contradict Hamish's story.

Useful, that.

"He is, indeed." Hamish raised the pint glass the barkeep had set before him. "To Rory MacLeod, Heaven keep him."

Or hell, more likely. The best that could be said of Rory MacLeod was that he was good and dead, but there weren't many Scots who'd fail to raise a glass to him. The man had been a smuggler and a thief, but he'd been good at his trade. Rory's exploits against the English had made him something of a legend in Scotland.

Hamish waited with his glass raised.

Three, two, one . . .

"To Rory MacLeod, the scourge of England." Munro raised

his own glass and knocked it against Hamish's with such enthusiasm ale sloshed over the sides.

"A scourge, indeed. God rest the old devil."

Munro looked him over, his eyes narrowed. "You English?"

"Half. My father was a Muir." This was also true. It was best to stick as closely to the truth as possible when telling lies. It made them more believable.

As for the other half, well . . . best not to mention his English mother, or the title he'd inherited from his maternal grandfather. If there was one thing the Scots despised, it was an English nobleman.

Understandable, really. English noblemen were useless creatures.

"Ye sound English to me. Ye look English, too."

"I drink like a Scot, though." Hamish drained his pint in one swallow, then waved to the barkeep. "Two more pints for me and my friend Munro here."

There. That should do it.

Munro ran a hand over his grizzled jaw, but the appearance of a fresh pint in front of him went a long way toward easing his suspicions. "We don't get many strangers up this way. Not much to interest visitors in Dunvegan."

"What about the castle?" Hamish jerked his chin toward the window. The long shadow cast by the turret was slowly advancing as the morning marched on, darkening the already dim interior of the pub. "They must allow visitors."

"You want some advice, friend?" Munro set his pint on the table and turned a pair of bloodshot blue eyes on Hamish. "You'll stay away from that place if ye know what's good for ye."

Ah. Now they were getting to it. "Why is that? Is it one stiff wind from toppling into the sea?" Hamish cocked his head as if considering it. "It doesn't look terribly sturdy."

"Nay, that's not it. That castle's been hanging on to that bit of rock these two hundred years or more. I reckon it'll stay as it is for another two hundred." Munro contemplated his pint glass, his expression thoughtful. "Mayhap it's all gossip, but there are those that say there's some dark doings up there. Dark doings, indeed."

Doings so dark, so evil they'd drive a man to drink apparently, because no sooner had Munro uttered this warning than he brought his pint to his lips and tipped the whole of it into his mouth, as if he were cleansing the wickedness from his throat.

"Another?" Hamish nodded at the empty glass. "Unless you prefer something else?" Preferably something that would loosen the man's tongue more quickly than ale would.

Munro shrugged. "Arthur has a nice whisky back there behind the bar. You fancy a taste?"

Hamish hid his wince. Whisky, of all godforsaken swill. But it was no use asking for claret here. "I don't see why not."

"Fetch us that Glenturret, Arthur," Munro called to the barkeep.

Arthur rummaged underneath the bar, then approached the table with a dusty bottle of amber liquid and two glasses in his hands. Hamish slid the bottle toward Munro, who wasted no time relieving it of its cork and pouring two deep measures into each glass.

"We'll keep the bottle, Arthur." Hamish slid a banknote into the man's hand, then turned his attention back to Munro. "I hear tell there's three women living in that castle."

"Aye. Three sisters."

"Well, what sort of bad doings can a handful of women get up to? Not much, I'd wager." It would have been a sound enough wager if the three women in question hadn't been Rory MacLeod's progeny, and thus more apt to be the troublesome sort.

"Depends on who ye ask. I don't credit gossip, ye ken, but there's those in Dunvegan who'll tell ye those women get up to plenty of no good up there in that castle of theirs. They're redheads, you know. All three of them." Munro gave him a significant look, as if the red hair somehow explained everything.

Ridiculous, of course. It wasn't a mystery, that red hair. Rory had been a redhead, too.

Yet it was as good an opening as he was likely to get. "Redheads? How curious. I haven't seen any redheaded women wandering about. Do they ever come into the village?"

"The eldest one, Catriona, used to come often enough. Not so much now. It's been weeks since the last time." Munro leaned over the table, lowering his voice. "Devil only knows how those three occupy themselves, but the old women in the village say as they're up there summoning spirits."

Hamish choked on the whisky he'd just swallowed.

Spirits? He'd never heard such nonsense. The only spirits he believed in were the kind that came in a bottle. "Surely not."

"Who's to say?" Munro leaned closer. "That Catriona? The eldest? She's ah . . . what do you call it? Them that know how to mix up potions and whatnot."

"Potions? You mean a chemist?" How intriguing. He would have said he'd heard every rumor there was to hear about the MacLeod sisters, but he hadn't heard *that*.

"Aye. Those that make up witch's brews, ye ken? That one? Catriona? You go see Mrs. MacDonald, friend, and she'll tell you Catriona's got a cauldron hidden up there in that castle."

A *cauldron*? Good Lord, had he traveled back to the previous century?

Dunvegan was a tedious little village, but at least he was getting somewhere. What other useful secrets could he squeeze from Munro's loose tongue? "A cauldron, you say? And what does she brew in this cauldron of hers, do you suppose?"

"Eh, who knows? She's a healer, is Catriona, so maybe it's medicines and whatnot, but there's plenty in Dunvegan who'll tell you she's up to no good. She used to come and spend hours with Glynnis Fraser, up at the apothecary's shop. She and Glynnis are as thick as two thieves, they are." Munro held up his hand, his fingers crossed.

Hamish widened his eyes as if there were something inherently suspicious about a young woman visiting an apothecary. "Do you suppose she was procuring the ingredients for her next potion?"

"I couldn't say, but mayhap she was. Always up to something, those two. They're both right clever. Hard to say what they might get up to if left to it, but Bryce Fraser doesn't put up with any nonsense. He keeps that sister of his well in hand."

Kept her well in hand, did he?

That sounded rather menacing, but Glynnis Fraser wasn't any more his concern than the MacLeod sisters were. He'd come here for one purpose only—to fulfill his promise to his father and put an end to any rumors about his family's association with Rory MacLeod.

He may be the Marquess of Ballantyne now, with a London townhouse, a country estate, and a seat in the House of Lords, but he was also a Muir, and the Muirs weren't smugglers, by God.

Once he'd settled this absurd business about the stolen treasure, he'd leave Dunvegan, its castle, and its witches behind without a backward glance.

He peered out the window, but there were no stray women about, redheaded or otherwise, so he turned his attention back to Munro, who seemed to know more than he should about the MacLeod sisters and hadn't the least compunction about sharing it.

And people claimed it was the old women who were the gossips.

"Do the three sisters live alone up there in that huge castle?" In other words, were there dozens of burly footmen he should know about?

"Aye. Old Duffy used to live up there with them. He was butler there when Rory was still alive, and his wife, Mrs. Duffy, the housekeeper, but the sisters dismissed them both some weeks ago."

Not a single servant, then? That *was* welcome news.

Munro eyed him over the edge of his glass. "Were you a friend of Rory MacLeod's?"

"I can't say I was." It wasn't a lie. He'd never laid eyes on Rory MacLeod, but one could argue he knew him as well as one man could know another through the stories his father had told him. In a way, he'd grown up with Rory.

"Ach, well, he's been dead these four months now, but he was an adventurer, ye know." Munro leaned over the worn table, lowering his voice. "A smuggler, some say."

"A smuggler? How shocking." Or it might have been, if Hamish hadn't already been aware of Rory's criminality.

"Aye, a smuggler, and a thief, but not just any thief, ye hear? They say he went east on that last run of his, the one right before he died, and when he returned . . ." Munro cast a stealthy glance around the pub, but no one was paying any attention to them.

"Yes? When he returned?"

Munro took a healthy swallow from his glass, then set it aside, wiping his arm across his mouth. "He didn't come home empty-handed, if ye ken."

Oh, he kenned, all right. He kenned far better than Munro could ever guess. "No?"

"Nay." Munro dropped his voice to a whisper. "They say as he found a fortune in treasure down Penicuik way, and the lot of it worth a pretty penny, by the sounds of it."

Penicuik? More like Lochaber, but Hamish kept that bit of information to himself. "Really? Why, how utterly fascinating. What kind of treasure?"

"As to that, I can't say for sure, but coins and jewels, I expect." Munro gave a wise nod and poured another measure of whisky into his glass.

"I see. And what's become of this treasure, do you suppose?"

"Can't say for sure, friend. Mayhap those three women are hiding it up there in the castle. I don't stick my nose into things that don't concern me, ye ken, but there's some people in the village who are none too happy about it."

"Why should it matter to them? I don't see that it's any of their business."

"Aye, and mayhap it wouldn't be, but a month ago a smuggler's lugger came calling at the castle for their share of the treasure, and there's some in town who don't want that sort here in Dunvegan."

"Did they get their share of the treasure?" They hadn't, of course, damn them.

Munro cackled. "Nay. They couldn't find their way around those sisters. Ye ask me, and I'll tell ye the truth." Munro beckoned him closer. "No one's ever going to get past those women."

"I don't see why not." Hamish leaned back in his chair and let a mocking smile drift across his lips. "What are three old maids going to do to stop them? Nothing, that's what."

"Mayhap you'd be right if they were your ordinary old maids, but they're not." Munro pointed a finger at him. "They're cunning ones, make no mistake. That lugger that came? It disappeared, never to be seen again."

Disappeared? Hardly. Clyde and Dougal and that creaky old lugger of theirs were still in existence, and no wiser from their experience with the MacLeod sisters, either. "Nonsense. Boats don't just vanish into the air."

"This one did. I reckon those sailors met their end right there on the rocks below the castle." Munro ran a hand over the scruff on his chin. "Like as not they got what they deserved, but mayhap the less said about it, the better."

Oh, no. That wouldn't do.

Hamish scoffed. "It all sounds like bollocks to me. I don't believe a word of it."

Munro snorted. "That's as you please. Maybe it's all just stories, but they say as how that middle one—Freya MacLeod, her name—conjured a wild storm out of a clear sky as soon as the lugger approached, only to get smashed to bits on the rocks. Or how the youngest one, Sorcha by name, and the wickedest of the three, if you ask the villagers—set a horde of birds loose on them, like to scalp them where they stood."

And there it was. The same outlandish story he'd heard from Dougal and Clyde.

Useless, those two, coming back as empty-handed as when they left, their mouths full of extravagant tales about three witches guarding the castle. To hear those fools tell it, the MacLeod sisters could cast spells and curses, control the weather, and command birds and other animals.

But it wasn't just Dougal and Clyde telling tales about the MacLeods. In the six weeks since the lugger had been driven from the waters of Loch Dunvegan below Castle Cairncross, the rumors had traveled from mouth to mouth into every corner of Scotland.

Violent storms conjured out of thin air. Massive attack birds with grotesquely long, sharp beaks, strange lights flickering inside the castle, and three redheaded sorceresses sending innocent young sailors to watery graves with a wave of their magical hands.

But he knew better. Far from perishing, Dougal and Clyde had made their way back to London, and nearly every fool at the Lamb and Fig in Covent Garden had been standing them drinks on the strength of that tale ever since they—

"There she is."

"Who?" Hamish paused with his drink halfway to his lips. Across from him, Munro was staring out the window behind him, his eyes wide.

"Catriona MacLeod." Munro jerked his chin toward the window.

Hamish turned, expecting to find an enormous, raw-boned harridan with a crooked walking stick in her bony hand and an aura of evil surrounding her.

But that wasn't what he found.

A man would be hard-pressed to describe either of the two women on the other side of the glass as threatening. The elder was a withered, sour-faced old crone, but she was far too advanced in years to be one of Rory MacLeod's daughters.

As for the other . . .

No. There had to be some mistake.

"Where is she?" He turned back to Munro. "I don't see any witch."

"Are ye blind, friend?" Munro nodded at the window again. "She's right there, plain as day."

"What, you mean that tiny little thing there? The chit wearing the flour sack?"

"Aye, that's her."

Hamish turned toward the window again, blinking.

That dainty little thing? *That* was Catriona MacLeod?

She was draped in a coarse brown cloak from the top of her head to the toes of her boots. It did an admirable job of hiding her, but there was no disguising those narrow shoulders or the slender line of her back.

She was no bigger than a hummingbird, for God's sake.

"*That's* one of the infamous sorceresses?" Why, a stiff wind would send her sprawling. "She doesn't look as if she's up to summoning so much as a butterfly."

Still, there was no denying she was a MacLeod.

The ridiculous hood hid her face, but a wayward curl had escaped, and it gave her away as surely as if she'd shouted her name.

It was as red a curl as he'd ever seen.

Munro pointed a finger at him. "Don't let her fool ye. I tell ye, there's those in Dunvegan who swear Catriona MacLeod is as wicked as the devil himself."

Wicked? Perhaps. Cunning? Certainly.

If she and her sisters hadn't been as devious as a trio of foxes with their eyes on a henhouse, they never would have come up with such an ingenious scheme to frighten off their attackers. They'd put on some sort of performance, that was certain, but it was merely that—a performance.

Whatever it was they'd done, they hadn't done it with witchcraft. He couldn't say how they *had* done it, precisely, but it seemed they'd inherited their father's wiliness, his intelligence, and his creativity.

His ruthlessness, as well. They were his daughters, after all, and his father had always said that a man underestimated Rory MacLeod at his own peril.

Damned if their scheme hadn't worked, too.

He watched through the window as the girl made her way down the High Street toward the apothecary's shop at the other end, her shoulders hunched and her head down, as if she could pass unnoticed if she only made herself small enough.

Not likely. The MacLeod sisters weren't destined to live quiet, anonymous lives, any more than their father had been.

Clever, clever little witches.

But this time, Catriona MacLeod had met her match.

CHAPTER 3

"Just what do you think you're doing, Catriona MacLeod?"

Cat froze in front of the large window of Baird's Pub, the click of her boot heels over the cobbles falling silent. Saints above, that voice, like the ominous crack of rotted ice underfoot right before the frigid waters of Loch Dunvegan closed over your head.

She'd know it anywhere.

Why, oh *why*, of all the people she might have encountered today, did it have to be *this* one who'd sneaked up behind her? Perhaps if she remained still, the odious woman would go on about her business without—

"Well, girl? What have ye got to say for yourself?"

Cat muttered a curse at the thump of a walking stick striking the cobbles behind her. She knew that thump, and what it meant. She'd heard it dozens of times before.

Mrs. MacDonald was in a temper, and Cat was one of the woman's favorite targets.

There was no avoiding the unpleasantness that was coming, so she sucked in a calming breath and turned, lifting her chin. "Mrs. MacDonald. How do you do?"

That question was, alas, destined to remain forever unanswered.

A pair of gray eyes icier than the leaden skies above narrowed on the lock of hair that had escaped Cat's hood, the grizzled chin beneath them quivering with disgust, and a touch of fear.

A mark of the devil, that red hair. Only a century earlier the subtlest hint of it was enough to arouse suspicion, and it was a mere half a step from suspicions to accusations. Her Great-great-aunt Elspeth could attest to that, although if family legend could be trusted, Aunt Elspeth hadn't been entirely innocent.

But then the Murdoch women had always been a peculiar lot. Just ask anyone in Dunvegan. And she, Freya, and Sorcha had always been more Murdoch than they were MacLeod.

Aside from their red hair, of course. That was pure Rory.

But Rory was dead now, and her mother, as well, and not many of the villagers seemed to remember her mother's kindness to them or the respect they'd once shown her father.

That had been before the *incident*. Since then, there wasn't a soul in Dunvegan who hesitated to repeat the gossip and rumors about them or describe in breathless detail all the "strange doings" up at the castle.

It was astounding how quickly people could turn on you. Terrifying—

"You've not been in the village much, Catriona MacLeod." Mrs. MacDonald's cold gray gaze swept over her. "Weeks, by my reckoning."

Weeks, yes. Eight of them, to be precise, although it felt as if a dozen lifetimes had unfolded since then. Eight weeks wasn't long enough for Mrs. MacDonald, however. Not if the ugly twist of her lips was any indication.

But Cat dredged up a smile and nodded down at the marketing basket looped over her arm. "I've business with the Frasers."

"Glynnis Fraser," Mrs. MacDonald repeated, her tone flat.

Cat flinched. For pity's sake, would she never learn discretion? It wasn't as if she owed Agnes MacDonald an explanation for her business here.

Especially not when her business involved Glynnis Fraser.

Glynnis was a bit peculiar herself and occasionally roused the suspicions of the more distrustful among the good citizens of Dunvegan. No one dared breathe a word against her, as her brother was a well-respected gentleman who attended the Sunday service every week.

But even that wouldn't stop Mrs. MacDonald from envisioning Cat and Glynnis getting up to all manner of wickedness together, from concocting deadly potions to casting curses and spells.

It wasn't true, of course. At least, not about the spells and curses.

The potions, however—

"Are your sisters about?" Mrs. MacDonald cast a wary glance around them as if she expected Freya and Sorcha to appear out of thin air, leap upon her, and drag her off to the underworld, where a dozen devils with pitchforks awaited her.

"No. Not this time." Not ever again, if she had her way, especially not Sorcha. She never brought her youngest sister to Dunvegan if it could be avoided.

It was only asking for trouble, as Sorcha was not known for her even temper.

"Mayhap you'll want to get back to them soon." Mrs. MacDonald glanced over Cat's shoulder at the castle looming behind them, and a visible shudder ran through her. "Rain's coming."

Rain was *always* coming in Dunvegan, but Cat didn't say so. What was the point?

Instead, she offered Mrs. MacDonald a cursory nod before she stepped around her and continued down the High Street, the heels of her boots sliding on the slippery cobbles.

But the damage had been done. Mrs. MacDonald had snatched away any hope she'd had of conducting her errand in privacy as soon as she'd stopped Cat in the street.

Dozens of eyes were following her now, the gazes heavy on her back. Mrs. MacDonald's eyes, yes, but others as well, peering through windows as she made her way down the street, past Mr. Murray's fishmonger's, with Mrs. Murray's nose pressed so tight to the glass as Cat passed that she risked a sliver in her nostril, and from there past Mr. Wood's mercantile, and onwards to Fraser's Apothecary at the end of the street.

Had it truly only been a handful of months since she'd enjoyed coming into the village and looked forward to marketing day? Only a handful of years since she'd skipped along at her mother's side as they made their way down the High Street together?

There was precious little skipping these days. She was like a ghost now, creeping down the street, her hand wrapped so tightly around the handle of her basket that her fingertips had gone numb.

This was what came of tucking oneself into the darkest corner of one's castle like a timid mouse, pink nose twitching in panic at the slightest disturbance from the terrifying world beyond the tight confines of its own safe little corner.

Wee, sleeket, cowran, tim'rous beastie, indeed.

She'd loved that poem, once upon a time, but that was before she'd become the quivering mouse. One would never guess to look at her now, with her hood pulled low over her face and her heartbeat thudding in her ears, that she'd once been fearless.

She'd been the cat, not the mouse, with her claws extended and a fierce hiss upon her lips.

But then cowardice begat cowardice, didn't it? The longer one spent shrinking into the shadows, the greater the threat of the light became. Not that there was much light to be had in Dunvegan, especially at this time of year. She'd lived all her twenty-three years on this island, yet she couldn't recall a single winter as dark and dull as this one.

It was fitting, really.

She glanced neither right nor left but stared straight ahead as she made her way toward the apothecary at the end of the street, her face hidden inside the deep hood of her cloak.

It took ages, decades, but at last her trembling fingers closed around the iron doorknob, and then she was inside, the dim, cool interior closing blessedly around her, hiding her from all those prying eyes, and for a moment—an instant only—she let herself slump against the door at her back with a ragged sigh.

"Cat." Glynnis emerged from behind the long wooden counter with her usual serene smile, but it dimmed as she came closer, and got a better look at Cat's face through the gloom. "Oh, dear. Who was it this time?"

"Mrs. MacDonald." Cat straightened and attempted a proper smile for Glynnis. "She wasn't pleased to see me, I'm afraid. Eight weeks is not, it seems, a long enough absence if one is a MacLeod sister. It's lucky I didn't bring Sorcha with me, or else that confrontation may well have ended with a stoning."

Or a burning stake.

"Ach, well, never mind her." Glynnis took her arm. "I've all sorts of delightful things here, yours for the asking."

Cat allowed herself to be led inside, her dark thoughts falling away as Glynnis led her toward the counter, underneath the dozens of herbs hanging in bundles from the ceiling beams to the rows upon rows of small drawers and the flasks and glass jars lining the shelves, each containing their own little store of magic.

She drew in a deep breath. Mrs. MacDonald and all the prying eyes that had followed her here faded away as the scents of piney amber, sweet clover, and the bitter bite of wormwood all crowded into her nose at once.

Goodness, how she loved the apothecary! She always had done, even as a child. Some of her first memories were of standing at her mother's side at this very counter, her fingers fisting her mother's skirts, the acrid scent of camphor tickling her nose.

Of course, as a child, she hadn't known why she was so drawn to this place—why it should feel as if she were coming home when she passed over the threshold.

But her mother had. She'd known it at once.

Peculiar, those MacLeod women—

"Now then, Cat." Glynnis gave her a sunny smile. "What have you got for me today?"

"Some of my marigold tincture. I daresay you're nearly out by now." Cat rummaged in her basket and withdrew a few small, squat jars, along with a bundle of long, spiky leaves with a string tied around the stems. "I brought you some aloe leaves, as well. This is likely the last batch I'll have for you this season."

"Yes, I'll have those." Glynnis bustled about behind the counter, opening drawers and peering inside. "Do you have any of your maidenhair syrup? The cough has been rather bad this year, and the matrons in the village have been demanding the syrup."

"I do, indeed. I flavored this batch with licorice extract. I can never get Sorcha to swallow anything bitter without sweetening it with licorice first."

Glynnis laughed. "Miss Sorcha and her sweet tooth."

Cat withdrew the half dozen bottles of syrup she'd prepared last night and set them down amid the little pile of leaves on top of the counter. "One of these is a gift for you, as I know you're often troubled by a cough in the winter."

"Thank you, Cat. That's good of you." Glynnis took the bottles and the bundles of herbs and deposited them under the counter. "Now, I daresay there must be something I can do for you, in return?"

Their eyes met, and Glynnis didn't need to say anything more.

They had an understanding, she and Glynnis.

It was best for them both if certain of their transactions remained unobserved.

Cat darted a glance around the room. Ah, what luck! There were no other patrons about. She could hear Bryce Fraser moving about in the workroom at the back of the shop, but for once, he'd left Glynnis to her own devices.

It was a rare opportunity.

Cat leaned over the counter, lowering her voice. "Pennyroyal oil."

Glynnis darted a look over her shoulder toward the workroom in the back. Bryce was visible through the half-open door, bent over the workbench, writing something.

There was nothing inherently suspicious about pennyroyal, of course. The leaves made a lovely tea, and it was safe enough if used in moderation. Pennyroyal oil, however, would be a trifle more difficult to explain, particularly for her.

It wasn't as if she had anything nefarious in mind. They were troubled by mice at the castle, and the oil took care of them. No doubt dozens of other households in Dunvegan used it for the same purpose, but they weren't *her*, were they?

Glynnis knew the risks as well as she did. "You're quite sure about this, Cat?"

No. She wasn't sure about anything, even something as simple as pennyroyal oil, but wasn't it bad enough she could hardly bear to set foot in the village anymore? Were they to be overrun with mice, as well?

Cowardice begets cowardice . . .

She nodded before she could change her mind. "I'm sure. If anything should go awry, I promise your name will never come into it."

Glynnis nodded and dragged a stepstool out from under the counter. She slid it over to a shelf in a far corner, climbed up, and reached for a round jar of dark brown glass. Cat held her breath as Glynnis slid the brown jar aside and rose to her tiptoes, reaching for something behind it.

"Glynnis."

Glynnis froze, her hand suspended in midair, but she gathered herself quickly, and when she turned and looked over her shoulder at her brother, her face was composed. "Yes?"

Bryce Fraser stood in the doorway of the workroom with his arms crossed over the barrel of his chest. "What are you about? Come down from there."

"I'm fetching the ginger for Miss MacLeod." Glynnis snatched up the brown glass jar and pulled it from the shelf. "Poor Freya has been suffering from a nervous stomach."

She climbed down from the stool, the jar in her hands.

Bryce Fraser glanced from Glynnis to Cat, his blue eyes narrowed.

Dear God, those eyes. They were the iciest blue imaginable, and his skin was so unnaturally pale she couldn't even look at him without a shiver darting down her spine.

Bryce Fraser was cold, down to his marrow. He'd done an admirable job of hiding it at first, but a person's true nature would out, sooner or later.

Sooner, in Bryce's case, and it had taken precious little to reveal it.

She'd known, of course, that there was a certain type of man who turned ugly when a lady declined his advances, but until recently, she'd never imagined Bryce Fraser was one of them. Looking at him now, she couldn't understand how she hadn't seen it at once.

Her mother had always told her a lady could read everything she needed to know in a man's eyes. The worst of him, and the best of him. She'd used to delight in telling the story of how she'd agreed to marry Rory MacLeod after one look into his eyes.

Before Bryce Fraser, Cat had admired blue eyes, but he'd put her off them entirely.

Finally, Bryce let out a grunt. "Get on with it, then."

He returned to the workroom in the back, shaking his head.

"If you've a mind to go hunting in the woods for some heather, I could use some of your liniment." Glynnis set the ginger aside. "Poor Mrs. Douglas has been in twice already this week searching for it, and she won't be the only one, as it's meant to be a damp winter. I don't like to do without it."

"There's not much heather to be found this late in the year."

"Aye, that's so, but if you could find some and see clear to making up a batch, I'll make it worth your while." Glynnis braced her hands against the counter. "Say, half a pound per bottle?"

"Half a pound!" The liniment wasn't worth that, and they both knew it. Indeed, Glynnis was perfectly capable of making up her own batch of the liniment. She didn't need Cat's help at all.

A lump rose in her throat. "You're too good to us, Glynnis."

"Nonsense." Glynnis reached for the twine, avoiding Cat's eyes. "It's not charity, Cat. I'll sell it to Mrs. Douglas for half again that amount, and I don't have the time to go digging about in the woods for heather."

Glynnis didn't fool her for a minute, but she wasn't in any position to say no to half a pound per jar of liniment. Goodness knew they needed the money. "Very well, then. I'll see what I can find."

It wouldn't be easy, but if there was any heather to be had this late in the year, she knew where to find it. Her mother had shown her long ago how to find what she sought in the forest. From there it was simply a matter of cleaning the fresh plants, grinding them into a paste, then pressing it and extracting the valuable liquid.

"Very well. Here's your ginger." Glynnis held Cat's gaze as she took a small portion of ginger root from the jar and dropped it in a neat mound in the center of a length of brown paper.

There'd be no pennyroyal oil changing hands today, then. It was too risky with Bryce watching their every move through the open door. She'd have to come back for it. Her heart sank at the thought of yet another trip into the village with all those staring eyes following her down the High Street, but she gave Glynnis a smile. "Thank you."

"Of course." Glynnis tied off the packet with a length of twine, then withdrew a handful of coins from a small wooden box under the counter, and held them out to Cat as payment for the maidenhair syrup.

But when Cat reached out to accept the coins, instead of dropping them in her palm, Glynnis gripped her wrist.

Cat looked up, startled, but Glynnis put a finger to her lips and jerked her head toward the workroom, where they could hear Bryce moving about.

"Out back, in the mews." She pressed the coins into Cat's palm and closed Cat's fingers around them. "Wait for me there, and I'll bring the oil to you."

The MacLeod chit didn't *look* like a witch.

To be fair, he'd only gotten a glimpse of the side of her face—the curve of a pale cheek, the tip of an upturned nose, and that lock of startling red hair—but it was plain to see she was far from the monstrosity Dougal and Clyde had described.

Bloody Dougal and Clyde, with their nonsense about grotesque figures with long chins, sunken cheeks, and a dusting of hair on their upper lips.

Although that was how witches were meant to look, according to the paintings he'd seen. The paintings were always dark affairs, with half-dressed crones prancing round a fire and small horned devils leering in the background.

It was all rather alarming.

He hadn't believed for a single moment that the MacLeod sisters were witches, of course. The very idea was absurd. But he had suspected they'd at least *look* the part.

How could anyone in Dunvegan mistake the dainty little thing that had just darted into the apothecary's shop, with her wee basket over her arm and her cloak pulled low over her head like a turtle hiding inside its shell, for a witch, for God's sake?

Although that cloak did make her look as if she had something to hide.

It was pure folly on her part to imagine she could disappear underneath that cloak. There was no way to disappear in a tiny village like Dunvegan. That was the trouble with these sorts of places. One couldn't set a toe onto the High Street without every bloody citizen for miles around knowing about it.

Cloak or not, within an hour all the villagers would know she'd come here this morning.

But if the young lady who'd just hurried down the cobbled street couldn't be mistaken for a witch, neither was she a figment of his imagination. No, she was as much flesh and blood as he was, and thus as much of a problem as she'd ever been.

Chaos would find poor, timid little Catriona MacLeod soon enough.

But first things first.

"I'd best be off, friend." Hamish rose from his chair, glancing down at the half-full bottle of whisky on the table. "You'll do justice to the rest of that whisky, eh?"

"Aye." Munro curled his arm protectively around the bottle. "Kind of ye."

Hamish reached into his pocket, tossed a handful of coins onto the table, and made his way out the door, but in the brief time it took for him to emerge onto the High Street, Catriona MacLeod had disappeared.

"Damn it." She was just here. Where could the chit have gotten to?

At the other end of the street, a door creaked on its hinges, and he glanced up just in time to see the hem of a brown cloak disappearing behind the door of the apothecary's shop.

Catriona MacLeod. Who else?

She vanished into the dim interior.

He waited until the door closed behind her before he eased away from the wall at his back and strolled down the High Street, as cool as you please, and took up a position at the corner of the alleyway adjacent to Fraser's Apothecary.

Yes, this would do nicely. Unless the chit really was a witch and could make herself invisible, there was no way she could return to the castle without him seeing her.

He'd simply wait here.

But a minute slid by, then another, then a half dozen, and Catriona MacLeod didn't appear. He poked his head out, but the apothecary's door remained closed, and the street outside it was deserted.

For God's sake, how long did it take to visit the apothecary?

Was it possible she'd caught sight of him in the pub's window? She wouldn't have recognized him even if she had, of course, but given how rare strangers were in Dunvegan, just a glimpse of an unknown face might have been enough to spook her.

But where could she go, aside from out the door she'd gone in? Unless . . .

Was there a door around the back?

He turned and slipped down the alleyway and had just come out into the mews behind it when one of the back doors opened. He ducked out of sight, but the lady who emerged from the gloomy depths of the shop wasn't Catriona MacLeod. It was another lady, young and fair-haired, with a large apron covering a plain, blue cotton dress.

Ah, that must be Glynnis Fraser, the apothecary's sister.

He'd made it his business to find out her name.

He knew *all* their names. Every single shop owner in the village of Dunvegan.

Glynnis Fraser didn't venture far but remained just outside the door, looking this way and that, as if she were waiting for someone.

Curious. If he didn't miss his mark, the lady was up to something.

Sure enough, a few moments later there was a click of boot heels against the cobbles, then Catriona MacLeod rounded the corner and hurried to the back door of the shop, the hem of her cloak fluttering in the wind. He edged a little closer and peeked around the side of the building, but even now, with her facing in his direction, he couldn't see more than the barest outlines of her face.

That bloody cloak was doing its job.

Instead of ducking out of sight, as a proper spy would have done, he lingered at the corner. It was risky, but he wanted to get a better look at her. For informational purposes only, of course.

A man liked to know what he was up against.

Unfortunately, the mews behind the apothecary shop were as gloomy as a haunted churchyard. Between that and the hood she was wearing, he couldn't make out a single feature of Catriona MacLeod's face.

It wasn't so gloomy, though, that he couldn't see her creep up to Glynnis Fraser. They spoke briefly, their heads bent together. He couldn't make out a word of what they said from where he stood, but he saw Glynnis pull something from her apron pocket and hand it to Catriona.

It looked like a parcel, wrapped in brown paper and tied with several lengths of twine.

It had been a furtive exchange, each of them glancing over their shoulders the entire time like a pair of thieves exchanging a bit of contraband.

Neither lady lingered, after that. Glynnis slipped back into the shop, closing the door behind her. As for Catriona MacLeod, she shoved the item Glynnis had handed her into her basket.

He'd give a pretty penny to know what it was, but there was no time to ponder it now because as soon as she'd secured her prize, Catriona MacLeod scurried away like a small redheaded mouse with a bit of cheese clutched in its paw.

He followed, taking care to keep a half dozen or so paces between them, but he may as well not have bothered, for all the notice she paid him. Whatever mischief Miss MacLeod was getting up to, it had all her attention.

She didn't return to the High Street, as he'd expected, but instead darted behind the row of shops, onto a rutted path that led up a steep hill, and into a wooded area at the crest.

The woods? He glanced up at the sky, where the first of a mass of threatening gray clouds were gathering. God above, what did the girl think she was doing, scampering up into the hills—alone, no less—with a storm brewing?

Damn it, he despised being caught in the rain. Despised climbing hills, too, and that was to say nothing of the healthy dislike he now felt for Catriona MacLeod.

But there was no help for it. If he wanted to know what the chit was about—and he *did*—there was only one way to find out.

And that was to go after her.

Chapter 4

The wood smelled the same as it always had, like pine needles and damp earth.

The thick canopy of branches swayed above Cat's head, the stiff breeze coming off Loch Dunvegan rustling her hair. There was something reassuring about it, comforting, like stepping into a private world of shadows, with the wind whispering through the trees, the ground soft with matted leaves and moist soil, and the muted gray light filtering through the leaves above.

The hush of it, the silence.

Wandering through the woods with the scent of soil and growing things tickling her nose had always been one of her favorite things, but she rarely came here now. She hadn't ventured into the woods since her father's death and the arrival of the first of the smuggler's boats at the shores of Loch Dunvegan.

Not since the dreams started.

Everything had changed, after that. The world had shifted beneath her, and she had yet to regain her footing. Even the woods, with the pungent scent of rotting leaves tinged with a trace of salt from the breeze, had changed.

She had changed.

What had once been a welcome silence was now ominous, the shadows surrounding her no longer comforting, but threatening, the rustle of the branches in the wind and the snap of every twig under her feet making her jump.

How disappointed her mother would be if she could see her now! But after Cat's father's death, her eyes had been opened to the worst the world had to offer, and once that happened . . .

Well, there was no closing them again, was there?

But these woods had always been a second home to her. She'd already let her fears poison the peace she'd once felt inside the castle. Was she really going to let the same thing happen here?

No. It was ridiculous. She'd walked this path dozens of times before, and nothing unpleasant had ever happened to her. Why should it be any different this time?

She threw her shoulders back and raised her chin. Surprisingly, it helped, the little show of bravado. Her steps became less hesitant as the air around her grew heavier and wetter, the light waning as she made her way into the deepest part of the woods, pushing aside the branches as she passed.

If there was any heather to be had this late in the year, it would be further back, closer to the center of the wood, where the ground was wetter, and the plants were somewhat protected from the harsher rays of the sun.

Freya would be worrying about her by now, wondering where she'd gone, but it was already late in the season for the heather, and she didn't want to leave it any longer. She'd just nip in, search out whatever plants may have survived the autumn cold snap, and get them safely tucked into her basket.

Then she'd be on her way back to the castle, quicker than anything.

It was the easiest thing in the world. She'd done it dozens of times before.

It would take her almost no time to extract the oil from the plants and make the liniment. She could have it finished by the day after tomorrow.

Of course, delivering it to Glynnis would mean another trip into the village. There was no use in pretending she didn't want to avoid that, but for half a pound per jar, she'd risk the hostile stares, the ugliness of people like Mrs. MacDonald.

No good would come of dwelling on all that unpleasantness now, however. No, she'd much better think of positive things, like Glynnis, who remained as steadfast a friend as she'd ever been. Yes, she'd think only of cheerful things, until she was free of this oppressive wood, and tucked inside the castle with her sisters, where it was safe.

Mostly safe.

With any luck, she'd find enough heather to produce a half dozen or more jars of liniment. Then there'd be no need to return to the village for months, perhaps even into the winter. The more time that passed between her visits, the better.

She hadn't liked the way Bryce Fraser had looked at her today, like . . . like he knew something she didn't, and was biding his time, waiting for a chance to spring it on her.

A shudder tripped down her spine at the thought of those watery blue eyes roving over her, both cold and hot at once. But Bryce hadn't been the only one staring at her. There were others, those she hadn't seen watching her from behind the shop fronts as she'd made her way down the High Street.

But hadn't she just told herself she wouldn't think of it now?

She kept on, her footsteps silent against the soft ground, breathing the scent of damp earth deeply into her lungs.

Her basket had grown heavy on her arm and the toes of her boots were soaked through by the time she found what she sought, the bright lilac-colored flowers, with their tiny petals with the strange black tips.

She stopped and lowered her basket to the ground before stepping closer. Dash it, it was so dim this deep in the woods it was difficult to see, but heather did tend to grow in clumps.

She inched closer, taking care where she stepped, and squinted at the ground.

Yes, there it was. There wasn't much left, and the flowers

were somewhat faded, but there were a dozen or more plants with their prickly, brownish-green stalks. There didn't seem to be another patch nearby, but there were more than enough plants here to make a half dozen jars of the liniment.

She squatted down and began digging, unearthing the plants carefully from the soil, keeping as much of the root intact as possible, which was rather difficult, as she hadn't brought any gardening implements, and was forced to dig with her hands.

But they came up easily enough, and soon she had a nice pile of them tucked inside her basket, and another half dozen stuffed into the pockets of her cloak. Freya would scold about the dirt, but it couldn't be helped.

There. It was done.

She straightened to her feet, ready to be on her way back to the castle, but just as she bent to take up her basket, she caught a flash of a dark purple plant behind her, tucked further back into the deeper shade directly under the trees.

It looked like . . . no, surely not.

Aconitum napellus thrived in southwest England and parts of southern Wales, but not in Scotland, especially this far north. It was too wet.

It couldn't be, yet those smooth, palm-shaped leaves with the deep lobes, that distinctive shade of bluish-purple, the five sepals curving downward like a monk's cowl . . .

She drew closer, breath held, until she was standing in the middle of the patch, the hems of her skirts brushing the tall stalks.

By God, it *was*. Monkshood, growing right here in her own woods.

Was it possible her mother had planted it? Monkshood was a slow-growing species, one that took years to reach flowering maturity, but her mother had always been a patient gardener, especially when it came to a plant as powerful as this one.

It was pretty with its lovely deep purple leaves, but its beauty was deceiving. Ingesting monkshood was fatal, yes, but the toxins could be absorbed through the skin, as well. Even the merest brush of any part of the plant against bare skin could result in poisoning.

Yet in the proper doses, monkshood was an effective treatment for nerve and joint pain, breathing difficulties, various swellings and inflammation, and heart arrhythmia.

Of course, it could also stop the heart entirely, if used improperly.

It was a tricky little plant, one where the margin between useful and deadly was exceedingly narrow. The challenge was to reduce the toxicity of the plant while still retaining its healing benefits.

She'd never had a chance to work with monkshood—had never imagined she'd ever have the chance, either, but here were more than a dozen stalks, right at her feet, just waiting to be plucked from the ground.

Did she dare?

Silly question. Her courage might have dwindled over the past few months, but when it came to plants and medicines, she'd never been a coward.

She knelt in the center of the patch, taking care not to let her skin touch any part of the plants, and fetched her gloves from her basket. She tugged them on, then pulled the sleeves of her cloak down so that the bare skin of her wrists was protected.

Then, she started picking. Carefully, of course. One didn't just snatch at stalks of monkshood as if they were plucking daisies. Not unless they had a perverse desire for a prolonged, painful death.

Monkshood poisoning was no small matter.

As she picked, gray clouds gathered over Loch Dunvegan, darkening the sky above her head. The storm Freya had predicted was coming quickly. She'd never make it back to the castle before the heavens opened, so she'd end her day with a cold drenching.

Drat it, she'd thought she'd have more time, at least until late afternoon, but it couldn't be helped. She reached for her basket, looped it over her arm, and rose to her feet.

It was well past time she returned to the castle.

The hill hadn't looked quite so steep from the bottom, but then hills never seemed to be steep until one tried to climb them.

Hamish leaned an arm against a rotted tree trunk, his breath sawing in and out of his lungs, and glanced back at the tiny village crouched below, the stone cottages with their neatly thatched roofs huddled in the castle's shadow.

He wasn't even halfway there, for God's sake.

This was the trouble with becoming a marquess. Titles generally came with money, and with money came luxuries like warm beds, roaring fires, and exceptionally good port.

It made a man soft.

There'd been a time when he could have scaled a hill this size without a second thought, but here he was, one arm braced against a tree trunk, gasping for breath, while Catriona MacLeod scampered up like a mountain goat.

He wiped the sweat from his eyes, cursing under his breath as he squinted at her rapidly retreating figure. How could such a tiny bit of a woman move so quickly? She was nearly at the top of the hill already. In another moment she'd disappear among the towering Scottish pines, and he'd never find her.

Meanwhile, he was clinging to this bloody tree as if he were about to fall into a swoon.

It was humiliating, damn it.

Above him, Catriona MacLeod had just breached the tree line at the crest of the hill and vanished into the woods. Well, that was just splendid, wasn't it? The best he could hope for now was that she'd trip over a tree root and sprain an ankle.

He straightened, sucked a deep breath into his abused lungs, and with another muttered curse, began once again to trudge up the hill after his quarry.

It wasn't pretty, but he managed to stagger up the steep incline, the heels of his boots sinking into the soft ground with every step. They'd never be the same, after this.

At last, he reached the tree line, and as it happened, luck was on his side today, because there she was, only a short distance from the top of the hill, her face still hidden by that hood.

She stood there, one dainty hand braced on the trunk of an enormous tree, breathing in great gulps of the crisp air, her gaze on the branches swaying above their heads.

The chit hadn't the vaguest idea she was being followed. Perhaps she wasn't so wily after all, despite the extravagant rumors about her cunning.

She didn't rest for long. Soon enough, she was off again and leading him on a merry chase deep into the heart of the woods. The trees grew denser with every step until the branches shut out the sun, plunging them into near darkness.

The dimness didn't seem to slow her down any, though.

She shimmied under branches and clambered over fallen logs as if she knew every inch of this wood, until at last, she made her way to a small clearing where wildflowers bloomed in a chaos of color.

He ducked behind a tree, then immediately felt ridiculous for doing so.

Was he *hiding* from her? A chit less than half his size? There was no reason he shouldn't stroll up to her this instant, explain the circumstances—that is, that her dead father had been a thief and a scoundrel who'd stolen part of a treasure *his* dead father had promised to someone else, and he would like it back, please.

That was simple enough, surely?

Instead, here he was, hiding behind the massive trunk of a towering pine, spying on her like a naughty little boy peeping through the keyhole into the serving maids' bedchamber.

Not that he'd ever done that, of course.

To be fair, she was rather fascinating to watch, although he couldn't say why, precisely. He still couldn't see her face—that absurd cloak was doing an admirable job of hiding her—but there was something about the way she moved through the woods, without making a sound, or even so much as setting the branches aflutter.

She was careful—reverent, even—as if she were in the private home of someone she admired, and they'd done her a great honor by welcoming her. She reminded him of the fashionable churchgoers in London, except her reverence wasn't feigned, as theirs was.

He edged around the tree trunk to get a better look at her as she hesitated in the small wildflower clearing. It was illuminated by a muted patch of sunlight, and she stood there for a long moment before she set her basket aside on the ground and dropped to her knees next to a patch of spiky heather and started digging.

He watched, waiting, as she filled her basket and the pockets of her cloak before rising to her feet again and taking up her basket.

At last! He readied himself to follow her, but just as she was turning back toward the pathway, she paused, her gaze lingering on something she'd seen behind her.

Over her shoulder, he could just make out a small gathering of bright purple flowers growing in a patch of shade beyond the clearing.

She stood there staring at it for some time, then, for some inexplicable reason, she withdrew a pair of gloves from her basket and pulled them on before ducking under the hanging branches and kneeling in the shady patch.

He drew closer, taking care to remain hidden among the tree trunks, and watched as she began loosening the soil around the base of the purple flowers and plucking them from the ground. She held each stalk carefully and set them down beside her gently, one by one, as if she were fearful of bruising them.

Picking flowers? She'd clambered to the top of that steep hill—his thighs were still burning from that climb—*alone*, under a sky that grew more ominous with every moment that passed—to *pick flowers*?

For God's sake, didn't the girl have any sense at all?

Hadn't she noticed the unfriendly eyes following her down the High Street? Had it somehow escaped her notice that the villagers of Dunvegan were distinctly hostile toward her? She was alone in a remote wood, well out of shouting distance of the village, should she feel a need to call for help.

A sitting duck, really.

Any one of the ruffians in the pub could have followed her up here, intent on doing her some mischief.

Indeed, someone had.

Him.

Not that he intended to do her any mischief. He was a gentleman, after all.

For the most part.

He wouldn't do her any harm, but if she happened to catch sight of him lurking behind a tree trunk, she wasn't likely to see it that way. Tiny young ladies were, at a guess, generally opposed to being followed into a dark wood by a strange gentleman, no matter how gallantly it was done, or how politely that gentleman introduced himself.

He *would* gain entrance into her castle, one way or another, and once he was there, he wouldn't hesitate to relieve her of the fortune she was hiding behind those thick stone walls, but perhaps accosting her in a darkened wood wasn't the best way to endear himself to Catriona MacLeod.

The treasure didn't belong to her, any more than it had belonged to Rory MacLeod, and he'd have it back, one way or another, but not now.

Not *here*. No, for now, it would be best if she didn't see him.

He leaned a shoulder against the tree trunk and let out a long, slow breath, watching her as she knelt in the patch of shade, her slender back bent over her work, and liberated one flower after the next from the soil.

Then another, and another, and another, and . . .

What in the world did she need with so many flowers? At this rate, he'd be obliged to spend the night in these woods.

By the time she rose to her feet at last, the sun had dipped below the horizon. She'd filled her basket with the Scottish heather and tucked what wouldn't fit into the pockets of her cloak, so she was obliged to carry the purple flowers in her hand.

She caught the basket up in the other hand and headed back toward the pathway, but instead of turning back toward the village, she headed away from the hill and the village spread out below it and made her way deeper into the woods.

Where was she going *now*? Not back to Castle Cairncross, unless she was approaching the castle from a different direction—

Wait. Was there another way into the castle? A back way, known only to the MacLeod sisters? Yes, of course, there must be. Why hadn't he thought of it before? Castle Cairncross was ancient—Munro said it had been clinging to that bit of rock for centuries.

There must be dozens of different ways into the old place, and it looked as if Catriona MacLeod may be about to lead him directly to one of them.

He hadn't the vaguest idea why the girl had taken it into her head to take a stroll through the woods with a storm coming. It seemed like an awful lot of bother just to pick a bouquet of flowers, but it was certainly a stroke of good luck for him that she had.

If things with the MacLeod sisters should become, ah . . . *contentious*, his knowing another way into the castle could mean the difference between fulfilling his promise to his father and leaving Dunvegan empty-handed. Fate had handed him a gift this afternoon, and a gentleman didn't toss a gift back into a lady's face.

He eased out from behind the tree and followed her, but he took care to tread softly and keep to the shadows. It wouldn't do to make his move too—

Snap!

He froze for an instant, then looked down. There was a broken branch under his boot heel, and the sound of it snapping in half had just echoed through the trees with all the subtlety of a pistol shot.

Ahead of him, Catriona MacLeod's head jerked up.

Then, in the next instant, she froze. He could see the sudden tension in her body, the precise moment she realized she was no longer alone.

Chapter 5

Snap!

Cat jumped, her head jerking up. That had sounded like a twig snapping under someone's boot heel.

She stilled, listening, but aside from the sigh of the breeze rustling the branches above her, it was silent, and the gloomy woods revealed nothing. Not the faintest movement, a hint of a footstep, or the twitch of a branch.

But someone was there, nearby. She could sense them, hiding just out of sight, waiting, and watching her. She scrambled to her feet with the half dozen stalks of monkshood she'd liberated from the patch tucked carefully into her hand.

It was eerie, too much like her dream, and all at once, she couldn't get out of the woods quickly enough. The first few drops of rain began to fall as she hurried back down the pathway, startling at every sound and seeing a hulking shadow lurking behind every tree trunk.

But there was no one there. Just her and the birds flitting from branch to branch and the flutter of the leaves in the wind.

Was it possible she'd only imagined the sound, her fevered brain conjuring it from thin air? Goodness knew she was as nervous as a cornered mouse. Her eyebrow had been twitching and her belly quivering since the nightmare last night.

Perhaps her imagination was simply running away with her.

Yes, that was it. Of course it was. It wasn't as if anyone would be out here in the woods so late in the day, and with a storm coming, too. Even in the best of weather, the villagers tended to avoid the woods, and today was not the best of days.

There wasn't anyone in Dunvegan who would have braved the steep hill and the dim woods on such a day as today. She was the only one in the village aside from Glynnis who took any interest in plants.

Really, it wasn't as if Mrs. MacDonald was going to scramble up the hill after her, was it?

No, she couldn't think of a single person who'd venture into the woods, unless . . .

Unless someone followed her here.

But who would follow her? Ever since that business with the boats, the villagers kept their distance from her and her sisters. One didn't consort with sorceresses, lest one find themselves on the receiving end of a curse.

Or worse, be accused of sorcery themselves.

It had been weeks since any of the villagers had spoken a word to her, except for Mrs. MacDonald, Glynnis, and—

Bryce Fraser.

Bryce Fraser, with that smirk on his lips, as if he knew something she didn't, and those strange, cold blue eyes. Bryce Fraser, who had more reason than most to dislike her.

All at once, the air grew closer, the damp chill of it pressing against her. A shudder rushed over her, drawing a spray of goosebumps to the surface of her skin. She turned around in a circle, eyes narrowed as she peered into the gloom, but if there was someone there, they were keeping as still as the towering trees surrounding her.

Silent, as well. Watching?

Oh, dear God, this was just like the dream, except this time it was happening.

This time, it was real.

She glanced around again, panic clawing at her throat. She was miles away from the village. There wasn't a soul nearby to help her. Not that it was at all certain anyone there would help her, anyway. She might be flying down the High Street with a crazed madman at her heels, threats pouring from his frothing lips, and every door would slam in her face.

Aside from Glynnis, there wasn't a single person in Dunvegan she could truly count as a friend any longer.

Dear God, things had come to a sad pass, hadn't they?

But if there was someone in the woods with her now—Bryce, or someone else—then she couldn't simply stand about, waiting for them to pounce.

The entrance into the castle's cellars was closer than the village, but even if she cut through the woods and came to it from the eastern corner, it was still a good half an hour's walk from here, and most of that through the thickest part of the woods.

It was only an hour until sunset, perhaps a bit more.

Well, then, she'd best get on with it, hadn't she?

She hiked her basket higher on her arm, the stalks of monkshood she'd gathered still clutched in her other hand, and crept along the rough pathway that led into the deepest part of the woods.

One step, another, each one bringing her closer to the castle. It wasn't all that far, only a half an hour's walk, nothing more.

What could possibly happen in half an hour? But her mind refused to calm, insisting instead on tormenting her with dozens of distressing scenarios.

Hordes of villagers with pitchforks at the ready—

No, don't think on it, don't think of anything . . .

She shook her head to banish the thought of a mob of angry villagers and took a hesitant step forward, then another, then paused, listening, her heart crawling into her throat, but there was no rustle of branches, no footsteps.

Perhaps she had imagined it, after all.

Still, the air around her had grown thicker, more threatening somehow, and it took every bit of self-control she had not to go tearing through the woods like a madwoman. Her every instinct was urging her to flee whatever—or whomever—was watching her and run headlong through the dark tunnel of trees until she'd reached the safety of the castle.

But that wasn't what she did.

Once she ran, the chances that whoever was following her would chase her increased rather alarmingly, and if there truly wasn't anyone there, if this was all just a figment of her imagination . . .

She drew the line at fleeing from ghosts.

So, she picked her way over fallen logs, venturing deeper into the woods with every step. The occasional branch snatched at her as she passed, but her steps were sure, her face set resolutely forward, and her breath steady.

There wasn't anything to be afraid of. She'd walked through these woods dozens of times and knew them as well as she knew the patterns of lines crisscrossing her palms.

Yet it was no use.

She could feel him behind her, sense those watery blue eyes on her back, and soon enough she could hear him, too, his footsteps clumsier than they had been initially, the snap of twigs and the rustle of branches as he pushed them aside. It seemed as if he were no longer even trying to be quiet, as if he wanted her to know he was there behind her, following her.

He was toying with her, as a cat did with a trapped mouse.

Yet there was nothing she could do but keep on, keep moving forward, her gaze darting right and left as she passed tree after branch after bush.

If she could find a weapon—a stick, perhaps, a heavy one, with a sharp end . . .

But she could tell by his solid tread on the ground that he was a big man. Almost certainly large enough to overpower her. Could she outrun him, then? If she tore off through the woods now, could she clear the tree line and make it to the eastern entrance of the castle before he caught her?

Please, please . . .

He was getting closer. She could hear the rustle of his clothing, the soft thud of his boot heels, and she could almost feel the rush of his breath against the back of her neck.

Dear God, what was she to do? Oh, she should never have gone to the village at all today! Freya had tried to warn her, but she'd been too foolish to listen, too caught up in believing the lie that all was still well with the villagers, or that it could be made right again.

Now she was about to find out how wrong she'd been because he was advancing on her, inching closer with every step, and what would become of Freya and Sorcha if something happened to her?

And it *would* happen, was *about* to happen, and there wasn't anything she could do to stop it but keep going, her lungs burning now and her steps clumsy, her basket so heavy she was nearly staggering under the weight of it.

The dream was coming to terrifying life right before her eyes.

It hadn't been a dream at all, but a premonition.

The breathing was closer now, the thud of his footsteps quickening, her own ragged, panting breaths harsh in her ears. He'd have her soon, his massive hand reaching for her, mere seconds from landing on her shoulder and yanking her down, tumbling her headlong into the dizzying blur of the ground under her feet, but she could see the castle now, the turret rising into the leaden sky, still so far away, but closer with each of her hurried steps.

Closer, closer, two dozen paces away, a dozen . . .

Please, please.

Yes! She was going to make it! The door leading into the cellars below the castle was right there, nearly within reach of her straining fingers, so close she could almost feel the cold iron doorknob pressing into her palm—

But just as she reached for it, her boot heel caught the hem of her cloak. She opened her mouth, a scream building in her throat and rushing toward her lips, but just as the desperate cry turned from breath to sound, she began to fall.

Her basket flew from her arm, her fingers going slack around the monkshood clutched in her fist as the ground rushed up to meet her. She squeezed her eyes closed, her body tensing for an impact that would certainly knock the air from her lungs.

But it never came.

A thick arm caught her around the waist and jerked her backward, off her feet, the gray sky spinning over her head as they both slammed into the ground in a tangle of limbs.

Oh, God, he had her now. He had her, and he was going to murder her not a dozen footsteps away from the door of her own home!

She couldn't breathe. She couldn't *breathe*—

Darkness hovered at the edges of her vision, lovely and cool and quiet, tempting her to give in, to let it take her. The pounding of footsteps and the throb of her heartbeat faded into silence as the darkness fell over her, but she struggled against the encroaching blackness, sucking in great gulping breaths until the tunnel receded.

This wasn't how the dream ended. It ended with her waking up.

In the dream, she never gave up, and she wouldn't give up now.

Catriona MacLeod had torn through the woods like a wild thing, her brown cloak whirling around her ankles and a waterfall of ringlets streaming out behind her.

That ridiculous hood had finally yielded its treasure, and quite a treasure it was, too, that glorious crown of tumbled russet curls, but there was no time for him to stop and admire it.

Of all the things she might have done, running from him was the very worst one she could have chosen, and not because he wasn't the sort of man who let his quarry escape him.

That is, he *was* that sort of man, but he would have been

content to let Catriona MacLeod go about her merry way, provided she led him to the hidden entrance of her castle first.

Alas, they were still a quarter of a mile from the castle when she chose to take to her heels. So, he was obliged to run after her, and once the chasing began, well . . . the chances this would end with a cordial understanding between them had just dwindled down to nothing.

There would be no agreement between them *now*.

No, now he was obliged to behave like a perfect savage and chase a tiny, terrified woman through the woods. Once he caught her, as he inevitably would, there was likely to be some scuffling, as scuffling did tend to go hand in hand with a chase.

None of which was likely to endear him to Catriona MacLeod.

But she'd left him no choice. The instant she burst into motion, he was after her, tearing through the woods like a wild boar after a defenseless squirrel.

It was rather an unsavory image, for a man who considered himself a gentleman.

If he'd paused for even an instant and given himself a chance to consider it, he would have just let her go and found some other way to achieve his ends, but his instincts worked against him.

He shot after her, and by God, she was *fast*, faster than any woman as petite as she was had a right to be, and the chase seemed to go on forever, until at last, there was a break in the gloom ahead of them.

They were nearing the tree line at the edge of the woods, and as the trees thinned, he caught a glimpse of Castle Cairncross's turret. They were close now, yet still she ran like a thing possessed, her cloak flying out behind her.

But she wasn't fast enough. He doubled his pace, his chest heaving, his harsh breaths echoing in his ears, his gaze fixed on the hems of her cloak, almost within reach . . .

It was the cloak that proved to be her downfall. Her heel got caught up in the voluminous skirts. She threw her hands out in front of her just as she pitched forward in a confused tumble of red hair and brown skirts.

He was only inches away from her by then, and he instinctively reached out a hand to catch her and . . . there! He grabbed her around the waist and jerked her backward against him, her slender shoulder blades slamming into his chest.

Her basket flew from her hand, the purple flowers scattering on the ground at their feet.

But Catriona MacLeod never made a sound.

She didn't gasp, or scream, or cry out in any way. There was no squirming, no flailing, and no cursing. She didn't attempt to jerk free, nor did she strike out at him.

The instant he touched her, she went utterly, unnaturally still.

It was, once again, the worst thing she could have done, and the last thing he expected. It was too late for him to stop, by then. His momentum hurled him forward, and he crashed into her, his chest striking her directly in the back, and then they were falling, falling, and he was going to crush her beneath him.

The ground came toward him in a sickening rush, her body tumbling like a rag doll in his arms as he wrapped his other arm around her shoulders and somehow—God only knew how—he managed to turn them so he hit the ground first. She jolted against his chest, and her breath left her lungs in a pained whoosh as they struck the ground with a bone-shattering thump.

Smack!

His back hit the ground, and she came down on top of him.

For a long, agonizing moment he couldn't draw breath, his lungs frozen.

Oh, good Lord, what had he done? Something unforgivably stupid.

She was as still as a corpse on top of him, but her chest was moving in short, hard pants against his, and her warm breath drifted over the arm he'd wrapped around her shoulders.

Not a corpse, then, thank God. She must have fallen into a swoon.

The rain was coming down hard now. He blinked and reached up to wipe the water from his face. There was something stuck to his cheek, the edge of it tickling his bottom lip.

He peeled it off and frowned down at the crushed green stalk in his hand.

It was one of the purple flowers she'd picked earlier. The basket had flown from her hand when she fell, and the flowers had burst free of it in a shower of pink and purple petals. He sat there for a moment, staring at it, and that was when everything got strange.

His chest tightened as if an iron band were squeezing it. His breaths became short, labored, and there was the strangest tingling sensation in his fingertips.

What the devil? What was wrong with him? Had he hit his head? He reached up with an oddly unsteady hand to check for blood, but before he had a chance to draw another breath he was swamped with dizziness.

He lay there, unable to move, the branches above him swaying in the breeze, the leaves blurring together into an indistinct smear of dark green.

What was happening? The fall had knocked the wind out of him, but he'd taken dozens of falls in his lifetime, and it had never felt like this before, as if his head were floating away from his body. His lips were numb, as well, and his stomach was roiling with nausea.

Suddenly, the branches swimming in his vision were gone, and in their place was a pale, heart-shaped face with high cheekbones, a firm chin, a pretty pair of rosy lips, and the daintiest nose he'd ever seen.

He blinked at her.

A dainty nose . . .

Hadn't he seen the tip of that nose before? And those curls . . .

They were such a particular shade of red, those curls, like . . .

like . . . someone. He couldn't remember who, but he'd seen that shade of red before, hadn't he?

Yes, he was certain he had. He groped for the memory, but it eluded him, shying away every time he got close—

Wait.

Catriona MacLeod. Yes, that was right. He'd been chasing her, hadn't he?

Her hood had fallen back, and the unruly mass of curls she'd been hiding underneath were loose now and floating around her face in the breeze.

And what an exquisite face it was, with creamy skin, a stubborn chin, and winged eyebrows over a pair of eyes the same dark shade of green as the darkest leaves in the woods.

"What . . . ?" He began, but his tongue felt thick and clumsy in his mouth, and it was too hard to make it form words, so he merely stared up at her, into those remarkable green eyes.

And all at once, a memory drifted through his mind, one from long ago.

When he'd grabbed her, right before they tumbled to the ground . . .

She'd gone still. Strangely, unnaturally still.

He'd seen that same sort of stillness only once before when he was a boy and he'd gone hunting with his father. They'd been after a stag and had spent hours trailing it through the woods. When they'd cornered it at last, and it had realized there was no way out, the stag had stilled in just the same sudden, unnerving way Catriona MacLeod did just before she hit the ground, its ears pricked, and tension in its long, graceful legs.

It had remained there just for an instant, as if suspended in time.

Right before it attacked.

It had charged directly at him and would certainly have killed him if his father hadn't gotten a shot off just in time to save him. As it was, he still had a scar on his arm from where the stag had caught him with the tip of his antlers.

In that single, frozen instant, he knew.

It had been a mistake to chase Catriona MacLeod. A colossal mistake, one of enormous—perhaps deadly—proportions.

For all her delicate appearance, there was nothing helpless about her.

"I don't . . ." What was he trying to say? He couldn't remember.

Her lips were moving. She was saying something, but he couldn't make sense of her words. "Wha . . . ?" He tried again, but it was no use. It was as if his mouth was full of gravel.

His tongue wouldn't cooperate.

The pretty lips opened again, and a few words fell out. They sounded like, "You're not Bryce Fraser."

Bryce Fraser? Who in the world was . . . oh, the apothecary, in the village.

No, he wasn't Bryce Fraser. Why would he be?

That couldn't be what she'd said, could it? Why would she think Bryce Fraser had followed her into the woods? It didn't make any sense, unless . . .

Unless . . . something.

Something disturbing, but his head was too dizzy to work out what, and his heart was pounding, and there was no time for puzzling over it, because her face was fading, black creeping in at the edges until the only part of her he could still see were her eyes, such an unusual dark green.

Had he ever seen eyes as green as hers?

The black tunnel at the edges of his vision swallowed her up before he could find the answer.

Chapter 6

Dear God. Oh, dear *God*, what had she done?

Cat dropped to her knees beside the man sprawled on the ground and snatched the limp stalk of monkshood from between his slack fingers.

But what if it was already too late for that?

Please don't let it be too late for that . . .

She stared down at him, the cold rain dripping from the end of her nose into her open mouth, then at the heather and monkshood scattered on the ground near her overturned basket.

He must have touched one of the monkshood stalks when he'd fallen!

Quickly, she gathered up the monkshood, taking care to make certain the stalks only touched her gloves, then wrapped them in her handkerchief and stuffed them into the bottom of her basket before piling the heather on top of them.

But again, it was rather too late now, wasn't it?

She'd already *poisoned* someone. Someone who was *not* Bryce Fraser.

He was as far from being Bryce Fraser as a man possibly could be.

The shock of silky dark hair hanging over his forehead was as unlike the pale strands that covered Bryce's skull as nighttime was from daylight, and his face—goodness, she'd never seen a man with such noble cheekbones or so perfectly angular a jaw.

As for the rest of him, well . . . at first glance, Bryce gave the impression of being a commanding figure of a man on account of his barrel chest, but one couldn't help but notice the thin shoulders and spindly legs upon a second glance.

Not this man. There wasn't anything spindly about him.

He was big *everywhere*.

His shoulders, and his chest, and his hands . . . goodness, she'd never seen hands as large as his before, with long fingers and palms the width of dinner plates, and that was to say nothing of his long, muscular legs, his thighs—

Never mind his thighs.

The point was, if she'd ever laid eyes on *him* before, she'd remember it.

Where had he come from? He wasn't from Dunvegan, that was certain. Possibly not even from Scotland at all, with his elegant dark green coat and silk hat, and his fine leather boots.

No, he was a stranger. She'd poisoned a stranger.

A stranger who'd *chased* her. A stranger who'd stalked her through the woods, caught her around the waist, and hurled them both to the ground. He'd followed her and accosted her, for pity's sake! God only knew what he might have done next if she hadn't happened to be carrying those stalks of monkshood.

Poisonous monkshood, and she'd been skipping through the forest with it as if it were as harmless as a handful of daisies and she intended to make daisy chains, or daisy crowns, or a bouquet.

A bouquet of poisonous monkshood? If this incident should come to light, there wouldn't be a soul in Dunvegan who'd believe *that*. Yet it had all been perfectly innocent. She'd only wanted a chance to study the plant. It wasn't as if she'd *meant* to poison him.

It had been an accident, nothing more. Why, it might have happened to anyone.

But she wasn't anyone. She was Catriona MacLeod, one of

the wicked MacLeod sisters, and if tales of this debacle should reach the magistrate, her fate was as good as sealed. No one would believe this elegantly dressed stranger had chased her through the woods. They wouldn't believe he'd followed her, grabbed her . . .

They wouldn't listen to a single word out of her mouth.

If he died, she'd end up swinging from a noose for murder.

She stared down at him, her heart lodged like a stone in her throat. "Sir? Wake up!" She grabbed his shoulders, shaking him hard, or as hard as she could, given the size of his shoulders and the body they were attached to. "Please wake up!"

Nothing. He was as limp as a large, brawny rag doll, his skin pale and clammy, and his eyes slits of bright blue jumping under his eyelids.

Oh, dear. He didn't look well at all.

Right, then. Think. She had to *think*.

Monkshood poisoning caused nausea, vomiting, seizures—dear God, please don't let him have a seizure.

Dizziness, heart arrhythmias—

She squeezed her eyes closed, muttered a quick prayer, and pressed her hand over the center of his chest. Underneath her palm, his heart was thrashing about like a wild thing, and his breathing was labored.

No, no, no. How could this be happening?

"Dear God, *please*." She gave his shoulders another desperate shake, but it was no use. There wasn't a thing she could do for him. There was no antidote for monkshood poisoning, no way to counteract it.

All she could do was remain by his side, wait, and pray he'd wake up again.

Except . . . well, there was one other thing she could do.

She could sneak off and leave him where he'd fallen. It wasn't as if anyone had seen what had happened. There was no one about, and aside from Glynnis, no one even knew she'd gone to the woods today. Not even her sisters knew.

Surely, she didn't owe the man who'd accosted her any courtesies.

She glanced down into his pale face and for an instant—for one shameful, cowardly instant, she began to rise to her feet.

She didn't get far.

This man was undoubtedly a scoundrel and a villain, but even so, she couldn't quite make herself leave him here to die alone.

Not die! He wasn't going to *die*, for pity's sake.

He'd wake up soon enough. Of course, he would.

Wouldn't he?

Oh, she didn't know! She'd found the stalk of monkshood in his hand, but there was no telling if it had touched any other part of him. If it had been anywhere near his mouth . . .

No! She couldn't bear to think about it.

There was just as much chance he'd only touched the stalk with his hand. Why, it might have been just the merest brush against his skin, hardly more than a graze, barely a touch at all. And he was a giant of a man, tall and broad-shouldered and muscular. Such a tiny amount of poison swimming about in such a large body wouldn't do any harm.

Would it?

She bit her lip as she peered down into his pale, sweat-sheened face.

Any *more* harm, that is. Because if the truth were told, he didn't look to be in the pink of health.

What was to be done? She couldn't simply leave him here to die, but the only other option . . . she glanced over her shoulder at the thick wooden door that led into the castle cellars.

Her only other option was to take him into the castle.

Into her *home*, amongst her *sisters*.

She dropped onto her backside next to him and wrapped her arms around her raised knees. It would be fully dark soon, within the next hour, and the temperature would plummet, and that was to say nothing of the storm that was quickly descending on them.

A bad one, Freya had said.

If the monkshood didn't finish him, exposure to the elements might do so.

But to bring this dangerous stranger into the sanctuary of her home, the home they'd gone to such extreme lengths to protect! Was she meant to let it all come crashing down now, after everything they'd done, everything they'd sacrificed to remain safe and keep their home intact?

This, all because some man she'd never laid eyes on had taken it into his head to chase her through the woods. If he *did* die, it was no less than he deserved!

Except . . . well, there was no denying she'd been preoccupied with poisonous plants recently. Why, only last night she'd been thinking about monkshood. Wasn't there a chance she'd subconsciously intended to do him harm? The chase through the woods had been so much like her dream! Mightn't she have lost her wits when the dream turned frighteningly real and done the unthinkable?

Wasn't there just the tiniest possibility that she wasn't entirely innocent in this debacle?

Oh, she didn't know! All she knew was that no matter how she looked at this situation, she lost. Either she left him here to suffer the consequences of his own actions, or she had to allow a potentially dangerous man into her home, amongst the sisters she loved more than anything else in the world.

How could she even be considering it? No, she couldn't permit him to get a single step closer to the castle than he was right now.

It was all over for them if he did.

But how could she leave him out here to die?

Dear God, what abominable choices!

Unless . . .

She could give him her cloak. It was a voluminous garment, with a full skirt and a deep, wide hood, and it was a warm one, made of thick, sturdy wool. It would keep him warm enough.

Of course, he might still die of monkshood poisoning, but at least she could reassure herself she hadn't left him out here to freeze.

It was something, anyway.

She struggled out of her cloak and laid it over the top of him.

There. That would do quite nicely—

No, dash it! It only covered his torso and a part of his chest! He looked like he was wearing a child's apron.

She shot him a resentful glance. How had she gotten herself into such a tangle?

Who *was* he? They didn't get many visitors in Dunvegan, but this man was certainly a stranger.

It was all so odd. She hadn't any idea who he was, and even less why he'd followed her into the woods. What did he want from her? What was he doing in Dunvegan, and what did he mean, chasing her as he'd done? Really, if a man didn't fancy a poisoning, he should know better than to chase a young lady through the woods.

But he had followed her, and she'd inadvertently, er . . . poisoned him, and there was no going back from it now.

The only question was, what was she to do about it?

A minute passed, then another as she sat there in an agony of indecision.

By now the cold had seeped into her bones. Her lips were trembling with it, and she was shaking violently. She pressed her knees against her chest and tucked her frozen fingers under them, but her thin wool day dress was no match for such a dousing, and it didn't help that her wet hair was dripping down her back.

Why, she had half a mind to take her cloak back. Not that it would do much to warm her in its soaked, bedraggled state.

Meanwhile, her victim . . . er, that is, her patient, showed no signs of reviving.

She scooted closer to him and pressed her ear to his lips. He was breathing, thank goodness, and a trifle easier than he had been before, but his skin was still deathly pale, and his eyes remained closed.

She brushed his coat aside and pressed her palm to his chest.

Still beating. Was it steadier, or was that wishful thinking on her part?

For that matter, did she even wish for him to recover? It would be a great deal easier for her if he died, although it would leave her with rather a large body to dispose of.

There'd be no hiding *that* from her sisters.

She held her breath, listening, her hand still pressed to his chest. One beat, two, and another . . . no, she wasn't imagining it. The irregular, frantic beats seemed to have evened out a bit, but he didn't show any signs of waking, and meanwhile, the rain went on.

At this rate, she'd expire from the cold before her neck got anywhere near a noose.

He was as soaked as she was, with a mass of dark, wet curls plastered to his forehead. He was quite a young man, certainly no older than his twenties.

Young for a murderer, at any rate. Because he must be a murderer, or something equally as unsavory, mustn't he? Proper gentlemen didn't chase young ladies through the woods and knock them to the ground.

If he did die of monkshood poisoning, it wouldn't be anyone's fault but his own. She'd only done what she must—what anyone else would have done in such a situation. He'd grabbed her, for pity's sake! He hadn't left her any other choice but to defend herself.

Her righteous anger carried her through the next half hour, but as the sky continued to darken and the rain became a downpour, her courage deserted her.

In the end, it came down to one simple, essential truth.

She couldn't simply leave him here. It would be as good as condemning him to death, and she was no murderer.

Which was a very great pity, really. It would have been much easier if she had been.

But here they were.

She turned her face up to the sky, blinking against the raindrops falling into her eyes. There were dozens—no hundreds—of ways in which this could all go wrong, but whether he deserved her help or not, she couldn't bring herself to leave him out here to die.

She stumbled to her feet and made her way through the castle door and into the dusty cellars, the skirts of her wet day dress clinging to her legs.

How in the world was she going to explain herself to Freya and Sorcha?

No doubt they were already going mad, wondering where she was. She'd sworn she'd return within a few hours. Another broken promise. It was becoming quite a habit of hers, making promises that in the end turned out to be lies.

Although, in her defense, she hadn't anticipated she'd accidentally poison someone.

As for him . . . well, if he'd meant her harm before—and he must have done, as there was no innocent reason for a man to chase a lady through the woods—wasn't he likely to be even more determined to harm her, now that she'd poisoned him?

If he did wake, perhaps he wouldn't remember any of this.

Those unlucky enough to experience monkshood poisoning tended to wake up foggy-headed and confused. With any luck, he'd suffer no lasting ill effects from the poison but would have convenient gaps in his memory.

It was the best she could hope for.

Until then, she'd simply have to pray that when the sun rose tomorrow morning, he was still breathing, and not a large, handsome corpse.

* * *

Hamish swam back to consciousness slowly, like rising from the murky depths of a pond to the surface, then wished at once that he hadn't.

Something was very, very wrong.

Everything, from the pounding ache in his skull to the knots in his stomach to the bitter taste at the back of his throat, was *wrong*.

What the devil had happened to him, and where the devil was he?

The questions chased each other through his mind, but he didn't open his eyes. No, he'd been in enough tight spots to know that when you woke without having the least recollection of the hours before you lost consciousness, the best course of action was no action at all.

But as he gradually regained his senses, a few things permeated the haze. Candlelight flickered against his eyelids, and the edge of a soft cotton sheet was tucked under his chin.

He was indoors, in a bed, and it was nighttime.

That was all well enough, but why did he feel as if a spike had been embedded in his skull? And who'd pulled his stomach from his body, turned it inside out, then stuffed it back inside him again?

Had someone attacked him? Or had he drunk too much whisky and was suffering the consequences of his foolishness? It wouldn't be the first time either had happened, but this felt different somehow, like he'd been bludgeoned half to death, and with the way his head was spinning, he could fall back into senselessness at any moment.

Given that he felt closer to death than life, it couldn't have been the vigorousness of perfect health that had woken him from his stupor.

But something had. Some sound. A voice speaking?

He listened, but at first, all he heard was silence. Gradually, however, he became aware of the faint hiss of a dying fire, the soft patter of rain against a window, and, so quiet he almost believed he'd imagined it, the rustle of a lady's skirts—

Wait. Skirts? Whose bloody skirts?

"He's rather a young man, isn't he?"

The voice was soft, and the hand that smoothed the sheet more firmly under his chin was gentle. He remained as still as possible, taking care to keep his chest moving up and down in the slow, steady breaths of sleep as he listened for any useful tidbits of information.

"My dearest girl, he's not a gentleman at all," a second voice said, an unmistakable thread of brittleness underlying the smooth cadence of it, like a skeletal hand inside a velvet glove.

The fog shrouding his brain was near impenetrable, but he groped about in the shadowy darkness of his mind until slowly it all started to come back to him in fragmented bits and pieces.

The Merry Maiden Inn, which was neither merry nor maidenly. The High Street, which was neither high nor much of a street. Ah, yes. He was in Dunvegan, a remote little village on the outside edge of nowhere.

But how had he ended up here? More to the point, where *was* here?

There'd certainly been a bottle of whisky somewhere along the way. Baird's Pub? Yes, that was it. He'd shared a dusty bottle of whisky with his new friend. Munro was the last person he remembered speaking to, but that didn't explain the rustle of skirts.

Munro was more of a shirt, breeches, and leather waistcoat sort of man.

Something must have happened after that.

There'd been something about a castle, and a cauldron, and hordes of attack birds, hadn't there? The closed door of the apothecary's shop, and a lady wearing a deep hood that hid her face, and a lock of red—

"Handsome, though," the first voice said. "You can't deny he's handsome."

"He's *unconscious*," said the second voice. "All men are more handsome when they're unconscious," she added with a dismissive snort.

"Really, Sorcha, you might show a bit more compassion. The poor man's been poisoned."

Poisoned! What the devil? Who would have poisoned him?

He went back over what he could remember of the past day and a half. It was all a bit muddled, but he didn't recall a poisoning.

Surely, if someone had poisoned him, he'd remember.

"Hush, Freya! He may be able to hear you," the second woman hissed. "And I'll save my compassion for men who *don't* chase Cat through the woods, thank you very much."

Cat, Freya, and Sorcha . . .

He'd heard the names before some—

God above, he was at Castle Cairncross! Cat, Freya, and Sorcha couldn't be anyone other than Catriona, Freya, and Sorcha MacLeod. Somehow, he'd landed right where he wanted to be, although how he'd ended up here was still shrouded in mystery.

No, wait. The woods. He'd been chasing a redheaded witch through the woods, and—

No, not a witch. He'd been chasing Catriona MacLeod.

Catriona MacLeod, who'd turned out to be every bit as wily as Munro had warned she was, otherwise he wouldn't be sprawled on his back with his head threatening to explode and his tongue too big for his mouth.

But why had he been chasing the MacLeod girl through the woods? He might not be as proper a gentleman as one might expect of a marquess, but he wasn't in the habit of chasing young ladies.

That is, not unless they asked him to.

Except, no . . . no, he remembered the thump of his footsteps over the soft ground, the curses he'd uttered as the heels of his boots sank into the mud with every step he took, his ragged breaths echoing in his ears as he ran, and in front of him, a slender figure, the hems of her dark brown cloak flying out behind her, his hand reaching out—

He *had* chased her! But it was worse than that, wasn't it?

He'd grabbed her, too.

What had come over him? It wasn't like him to behave in such a savage manner, yet he distinctly recalled chasing Catriona MacLeod through the woods, snatching a fold of her cloak, and jerking her backward into his chest.

Dear God. Of all the times he'd behaved with a touch less decorum than a gentleman should—and there had been more than one—this had to be the worst of them.

The least gentlemanliest.

Or something like that.

But what happened after that? Because none of this explained why he was now in a bed with the sour taste of vomit burning the back of his throat and his entire body aching as if he'd been in a brawl with a dozen footpads.

A dozen footpads, or one very small, very cunning young woman.

No, surely not. It was impossible that Catriona MacLeod, a young lady the size of a hummingbird, could have reduced him to *this*.

But she'd bloody well done something to him. He wouldn't be lying here otherwise.

A perfectly healthy man—some might even say a virile man—didn't fall into a swoon for no reason, and it wasn't as if roving bands of footpads frequented the remote Scottish woods.

The answer was right there, hovering just out of reach, but his brain was too sluggish to grasp it.

Think, man!

He'd been chasing after her, and he'd grabbed ahold of her cloak. Bloody foolish thing to do, except . . . hadn't she fallen? Yes! He'd caught her just as she'd pitched forward, but they'd both gone down hard anyway.

Had he fallen on top of her?

No. He'd caught her, hadn't he? Yes, he'd caught her, and turned her just in time to keep her from smacking face-first into the ground, and then . . .

Then he'd toppled over like a felled tree.

All he could remember after that was a pale, heart-shaped face looking down at him, a crown of wild red curls, and eyes the same dark green as the deepest depths of the forest.

Deceptively innocent, those eyes.

What a fool he'd been not to pay closer attention to Munro's warning! The man had tried to tell him the MacLeod sisters weren't as harmless as they appeared.

Sorceresses, he'd said.

Nonsense, of course. Sorceresses, mystics, conjurers—it was all nonsense—yet Munro had been right about one thing. The MacLeod sisters were a great deal more dangerous than they looked.

A trio of clever, wily vixens, and now they had him trapped in their lair.

Except one-third of the trio seemed to be missing. The most worrying one of all.

Where was Catriona MacLeod?

"I still don't understand how he ended up in this state." It was the first voice. Freya. "None of this makes any sense. I think you'd better explain it all from the start again."

Someone should bloody well explain it, as he'd quite like to know what had—

"Later, Freya." There was a long sigh, and someone shifted near the bed. "I'm exhausted, and it's all muddled in my head."

It was *her*. He knew it at once, although he'd never heard her speak before.

"Go on off to bed, both of you. It's late. I'll keep an eye on him for the rest of the night."

There was another rustle of skirts and the light sound of footsteps, then silence.

"You ruined my basket, you know." Her voice was a whisper, close to his ear. "The handle is crushed."

They were hardly words of seduction, but dear God, that voice. Just those few murmured words in that velvety whisper sent a rush of heat over every inch of his body.

Not the bad kind of heat, either, but the *good* kind.

The rhythm of it was like music, and the texture warm and rich, like a sweet melting on his tongue. Yes, that was it. Hers was the only voice he'd ever heard that had a *taste*. Honey, thick and sweet, dripping from the end of a silver teaspoon.

How could a vixen like Catriona MacLeod have a voice like that? The woman was as close to being a murderess as he'd ever come across, but somehow, she'd been gifted with a voice that made every nerve in his body jerk to sudden, aching attention.

But perhaps it wasn't so surprising, really.

The animals with the deadliest venom were always the most beautiful.

And she wasn't finished with him yet.

If she had been, she'd have left him where he fell and made her escape. She'd attacked a *marquess*, for God's sake. What sort of murderess lingered at the scene of a crime that could see her hanged?

An incredibly foolish one, or a madwoman.

Possibly both.

Unless . . . had she brought him here to finish him off in the privacy of her castle?

Because God knew she was up to something. Something nefarious.

She shifted again, and he watched her through slitted eyes as she rose to her feet and fetched his coat from the chair next to the bed. She began rifling through it, those small, busy hands poking into his pockets.

A thief as well as a murderess, then. How delightful.

It was rather a wasted effort on her part, however, as there wasn't anything much for her to steal. The only things he had of any value were his pocket watch and fob and a small gold ring, which he kept with him always.

The watch had belonged to his grandfather, and the ring to his father. The ring bore a crest—a recognizable crest, even here up in the northern wilds of Scotland, so he'd slid the ring off his finger and into an inside pocket of his coat this morning.

No sense in drawing unwanted attention to himself.

But that didn't stop Catriona MacLeod. The lady, it seemed, didn't miss a thing, because no sooner had he recalled the ring than she found it, and with a practiced flick of her fingers, liberated it from its hiding place.

He remained as he was and waited to see what she'd do now that she had a bit of gold in her hand.

Stuff it into her own pocket, no doubt.

But that wasn't what she did. Instead, she turned the ring over, studying it from every angle, and paying particular attention to the crest. Did she recognize it? Their fathers had been friends, once upon a time. She might have seen it in correspondence between them.

God, he hoped not. The last thing he needed was for her to figure out who he was before he had a chance to explain what he—

"Ballantyne."

It was just one word, uttered so softly he might have thought he'd imagined it if it hadn't been followed by a sigh.

Damn it. She did seem to know who he was, and now that she did, it didn't take particularly sharp powers of deduction to figure out what he'd come for.

This wasn't good. Not at all.

She'd already tried to kill him once, even before she discovered his identity. What was to stop her from smothering him with a pillow right now?

He could feel her gaze on his face, those green eyes, watchful and wary, awaiting the slightest twitch that would give him away, but he lay still, fighting the instinct to snatch the ring from her hand.

In the end, it wasn't necessary.

Catriona MacLeod didn't steal his ring. Instead, as stealthy as any thief, she slid the ring back into his coat pocket with one quick move, then she came back toward the bed.

Ah. Not a thief, after all. Small mercies.

Still a murderess, though. Or at least an attempted murderess, and here he was, not at all in a forgiving sort of mood.

She lingered beside the bed, gazing down at him. Did she regret nearly killing him? Or was she merely reconsidering the wisdom of leaving him alive?

Either way, she wouldn't get what she wanted.

He was done playing games with Catriona MacLeod, and he wasn't likely to get a second chance as good as this one.

Quickly, before he could reconsider it, he reached out and snatched her wrist. It was a rather impressive move, really, considering he was half-dead from poisoning.

"Oh! Let go!" She struck out at him, that tiny fist aiming for his nose, but he held her back, his fingers tightening around her wrist.

"I'm afraid I can't do that, Miss MacLeod. You see, you and I have some unfinished business between us. Let's begin with the attempted murder, shall we?"

CHAPTER 7

"Attempted murder? You're mad! I never tried to murder you!"

"No? How curious." He gave her wrist a quick tug, unbalancing her, and she stumbled against the side of the bed. "I could have sworn I just heard you admit to poisoning me."

Oh, no. No, no, no.

"I . . . you . . . I demand you release me this instant!"

"Demand it, do you?" He snorted. "You're not in a position to demand anything at all, madam."

Cat squirmed and flailed, but the man had a grip like an iron trap. How in the world could he have so much strength when he'd been poisoned with monkshood?

Accidentally poisoned with monkshood, that is, but alas, the facts were the facts.

She'd spent the past eight weeks moldering away inside the castle, and no sooner did she venture a toe outside the door than she poisoned someone! She hadn't expected her foray into the village would be a pleasant one, but she'd never imagined it could go so terribly, so fatally wrong. No matter how awful things seemed to be, they could always get worse, and here was the proof of it.

"Release me this instant! Or are you in the habit of manhandling young ladies?"

"Young ladies? No. Murderesses? Yes. Now stop squirming, if you please, madam. You're trying my patience."

She kicked and thrashed, but it was hopeless. Even weakened with the poison as he was, he was simply too strong for her. So, she did as he ordered, and forced herself to still, going limp against him.

He let out a satisfied grunt, his fingers loosening. "Ah, now there's a good lass."

Good lass, indeed. She put all the strength she had into the blow, and miraculously, her fist connected. There was a sickening crunch, and blood spurted like a dark red fountain from his nose, but the vile curses that should have followed never came.

Instead, his lips split in a bloodthirsty grin. "Why, you cunning little hellion."

Was he *amused*? Good Lord, the man truly was mad.

She tried once again to scramble away, but even poisoned and bleeding, he had disappointingly quick reflexes. She didn't even have a chance to get one foot underneath her before his hand snaked out, and he caught a fold of the cloak she still wore over her damp dress.

"I could have told you this cloak would be your undoing. Ridiculous garment. It's far too large for you. Rather handy for me, though." His grin widened as slowly, inexorably, he tugged her closer, then closer still.

She dug her heels in, her fingers scrabbling at the coverlet, but it was no use. With one mighty tug, he jerked her onto the bed and clamped an arm the size of a tree trunk around her waist, trapping her in place. "I admit this is a bit untoward, but it will have to do. You see, ever since you poisoned me, I feel I can't trust you. Pity, but you understand, of course."

If he imagined he could trick her into some kind of confession, he was sadly mistaken. He may have some vague idea of poisoning, but there was no way he could know it was the monkshood, and she wasn't going to enlighten him. "Understand? No, indeed. I haven't the faintest idea what you're talking about. I must insist, sir, that you release me at once."

He let out a short laugh. "I do hate to disappoint a lady, but you're not going anywhere. I'm well within my rights to detain you, given the circumstances. Poisoning is a nasty business. Don't you agree?"

Oh, why hadn't she left him to his fate and fled while she still had the chance? She should never have brought him here. It was the worst thing she could have done, aside from picking the monkshood in the first place. Why could she never leave well enough alone?

This was no trifling error, but a serious misstep, the sort that was certain to have, er . . . unfortunate repercussions.

Prison, for one. Hanging, for another.

Let it be a lesson to her: the next time she accidentally poisoned an enormous marquess, she should flee at once rather than fetching her sisters and dragging him back to her home.

Especially not one who'd sneaked into the woods behind her, then spent all afternoon creeping after her like a large, aristocratic spider waiting for a hapless fly to fall into his trap.

Because he must have followed her, mustn't he? There was no way he'd simply stumbled upon her, not as deep in the woods as she'd been.

Ballantyne, Ballantyne . . . no, the name didn't mean anything to her.

But that elegant coat and those glossy boots? He hadn't meant to end up in the woods today. He'd seen her in the village, recognized her, and followed her.

None of this was accidental.

She stared at him, her heart beginning to pound, beads of sweat gathering at the back of her neck as the puzzle pieces connected in her head.

The outside world didn't trouble itself much about tiny, remote, little villages like Dunvegan. This corner of Skye was like a world unto itself, but then out of nowhere a strange gentleman appears, and takes it into his head to follow her into the woods, chase her, and accost her?

This was no chance encounter. It was impossible.

He'd come here for *her*.

No, not *her*, specifically, but for all of them.

She, her sisters, and her father.

Of course! How could she have been so dull-witted as not to see it at once? They'd known all along that someone else would come, and here he was. "Who are you? What do you want with me?"

"I already told you. We have unfinished business between us, Miss MacLeod."

Miss MacLeod.

There it was. He knew exactly who she was, and exactly what he was doing. "Your business was with my father, not me."

"Your father is dead, madam."

Dead, yes. Dead, and buried, yet there was no escaping the repercussions of being Rory MacLeod's daughter. He continued to haunt them even now. "I'm aware of that, sir."

"Sir? Come now, Miss MacLeod, there's no need to pretend. You know very well who I am. You recognized the crest on the ring you liberated from my pocket."

He'd been awake when she'd been rifling his pockets.

Dear God, could she have made any more of a mess of this? "Ballantyne. Some lord or other, judging by your clothing." He'd likely never once ventured past the manicured paths of Hyde Park in those shiny boots of his.

"The Marquess of Ballantyne, yes. Very good. I imagine you also know why I'm here?"

Of course she knew. He'd come for the same reason they all did. He might be a marquess, but he was a thief, just like the rest of them.

The only difference was, he'd been cleverer about it than the others had. Why, anyone with their wits about them could see there was no way to approach Castle Cairncross via Loch Dunvegan without being seen well before they could reach the shore.

It left plenty of time for the wicked sirens to cast their spells.

Yet none of the others had thought to come to the village first and waylay one of them. How long had Lord Ballantyne been waiting in Dunvegan for either her or her sisters to venture into the village? Days? Weeks?

He was a wily one, yes, but in the end, he was no different from any of the others.

They all came here for one reason. They all wanted the same thing.

And now he was inside the castle with her, Freya, and Sorcha, and all of them utterly unprepared for this new danger that had just landed on their doorstep.

"Miss MacLeod? I asked you a question."

"Yes, my lord. I know why you're here." Why he was here, and why he might just as well have remained where he was. Edinburgh, or London, or wherever gentlemen wore shiny boots. "You're after my father's treasure."

He stiffened. "I hate to disillusion you, Miss MacLeod, but that treasure doesn't belong to your father. It never did."

No, it didn't. It didn't belong to anybody.

She didn't say so, however. The Marquess of Ballantyne wasn't her friend, and she didn't owe him any explanation. Instead, she let out a short laugh. "Well, no. Of course not. My father was a smuggler, Lord Ballantyne. None of the treasures he procured over the past twenty years belonged to him. I'm afraid I can't tell you anything more than that, as I didn't involve myself in my father's business affairs."

"It seems not. Allow me to elucidate the matter for you, then. It's quite simple, really. Your father didn't undertake this last venture of his alone. My father and two other gentlemen were his, ah . . . shall we say partners, for lack of a better word? Three-quarters of the bounty is ours to do with as we see fit."

Three-quarters of the bounty? My, he *was* going to be disappointed, wasn't he?

This was just like Rory. It wasn't bad enough he'd set off on some ridiculous hunt for buried treasure without a single word of explanation to any of them. He had to involve others in his mad schemes, as well. Not that she'd waste much sympathy on the Marquess of Ballantyne, or his partners.

They should have known better than to trust her father.

The only thing Rory had succeeded in doing was painting a target on her and her sisters' backs. Every smuggler, pirate, and scoundrel had the castle in their sights now, thanks to this fabled treasure, and none of them was the sort to rest until they got their hands on it. They'd rip the stones from the floors to find it, batter down the walls of the castle in search of jewels and gold coins.

They'd reduce her home to rubble to get what they wanted, without a second thought.

And she and her sisters? They had no money, no protection, and no place else to go. The only thing they did have was rumors of black sorcery, conjuring, and wicked deeds of magic that would follow them wherever they went now.

"You look puzzled, Miss MacLeod. Do you mean to make me believe you weren't aware your father had business partners?"

He sounded so skeptical, so outraged at that idea that another hysterical laugh swelled in her throat. "As I said before, my lord, my father wasn't in the habit of discussing his business dealings with me."

"No? A mistake on his part, I think. You and your sisters are, er . . . quite creative, if the rumors about you are true."

"Rumors are never true, Lord Ballantyne. Now, if you'd be so good as to unhand me, perhaps we might discuss this like rational adults."

"No, I don't think so, Miss MacLeod. Not until I have a few concessions from you. You did try to poison me, after all."

She hadn't *tried* to do a thing. In hindsight, that was a mistake. If she had poisoned him, she'd have done a proper job of it, and he'd be unconscious or dead, and she wouldn't be trapped on this bed with a haughty marquess on top of her.

Mercy, in the end, was nothing more than a wasted opportunity. It was something to keep in mind for next time. "Very well, my lord. What is it you want?"

"I already told you, Miss MacLeod. I want three-quarters of the treasure you have hidden in your castle."

Cat almost laughed. Three-quarters of nothing, then. "And if I refuse?"

"Then I'm afraid we'll have to make our way to the magistrate. Tedious business, dealing with magistrates, but I imagine he'll be interested to hear all about how you attempted to poison me."

"You followed me into the woods, Lord Ballantyne. You chased me and grabbed me. Whatever may have happened after that is your own fault."

"Do you suppose the magistrate will see it that way, Miss MacLeod? There's no proof that I followed you. Gentlemen are known to take a stroll through the woods on occasion."

"Not in those boots, they don't."

"As for my grabbing you, it's your word against—"

"My word happens to be the *truth*." Her hands curled into fists, her fingernails digging into her palms. "You're a liar, my lord, and a scoundrel, a cheat—"

"What did you poison me with, by the way? Was it whatever was inside the package Glynnis Fraser gave to you in the mews behind the apothecary's shop?"

The apothecary's shop? What did that have to do with . . .

Oh. Oh, *no*.

He'd seen her in the mews with Glynnis! She stared at him, her chest tightening with panic. He hadn't just followed her into the woods, then. He'd been following her since she first arrived in the village this morning!

This was much worse than she'd imagined, a nightmare.

"I daresay I'm not the only one who saw that exchange. What did she give you, Miss MacLeod? Cantarella? No, that can't be it. I'd be dead if it was. Well, no matter. I daresay Bryce Fraser will be happy to explain to the magistrate that you visited his shop today and spoke privately with his sister."

Oh, he would be. Bryce would be more than happy to cause her trouble.

"One need only look into your basket for proof that you had the means to poison me, Miss MacLeod."

He wasn't as clever as he imagined he was. He didn't know about the monkshood, and he wouldn't get anywhere with her basket. "Look all you like, my lord. You won't find any—"

She broke off, horrified. He *would* find poison in her basket.

The pennyroyal oil.

It had been a perfectly harmless purchase, but it went without saying that her protestations of innocence would fall on deaf ears. She could get rid of the pennyroyal oil—toss it into Loch Dunvegan—but even that wouldn't save her.

She'd been seen entering the apothecary shop by dozens of people. Not just Lord Ballantyne and Bryce Fraser, but Mrs. MacDonald, and every gentleman who happened to look out the window as she'd passed Baird's Pub.

Then, mere hours later, a marquess had been poisoned.

Those facts alone were more than enough to arouse suspicion against her.

Lord Ballantyne and Bryce Fraser could say whatever they liked about her, claim whatever madness they could dream up, and the magistrate, Mr. Alexander, could choose to believe them and do whatever he wished with her. Any words she uttered in her defense would count for nothing.

As for the truth, it would dissolve in the face of all the lies, disappear like a sandcastle swept away by the tide. No one would listen to her. No one would believe her. No one would stand up for her. She'd be locked up until the next assizes, and what would become of her sisters then?

She had no power at all.

Useless tears of rage and frustration sprang to her eyes, but she held them back, sucking in silent, desperate breaths until the pressure eased and she regained control over herself.

She'd be damned if she let *him* see her cry.

She had to get to Freya and Sorcha, and tell them . . . tell them . . . God, she didn't know! If there was a way out of this, she couldn't see it.

But one thing was certain. The mighty Marquess of Ballantyne wasn't likely to be pleased when he discovered he'd come all the way to Dunvegan because of a wild rumor. And who would suffer the brunt of his displeasure when he realized he'd be leaving here as empty-handed as he'd come?

She and her sisters, of course.

She had to get free of him, *now*. There was no time to waste.

Without warning, she surged upright, wrenched her arm free of his hold, delivered a stinging slap to his cheek, and tried to scramble off the bed.

His head snapped back from the blow, but it didn't startle him into releasing her. Instead, he caught her by the shoulders and flipped her onto her front, so she was splayed across his lap, his thick thighs under her belly.

Oh, dear God, she was on his *lap*. Had anything ever been more humiliating than this?

"That was a mistake, Miss MacLeod." He threw one heavy arm across her back. "You only delay the inevitable and annoy me in the process."

She twisted and arched and wriggled like a fish on a hook, kicking and thrashing to escape, but it was no use. He was simply too big.

"Have I mentioned, Miss MacLeod, that I can be quite unpleasant when I'm annoyed?"

"Do you imagine you've been charming up to this point, Lord Ballantyne?"

"It gives me no pleasure to manhandle you, Miss MacLeod. Come now, we both know you're not going anywhere, and I'm growing weary of these antics."

God above, the man had the nerve to sound bored!

This was all merely a game to him, but for her, Freya, and Sorcha?

It was their lives.

She slammed her fist into the mattress, an impotent howl of frustrated rage on her lips.

"I can't think why you're so angry, Miss MacLeod. I'm the injured party here. If I'm willing to overlook your attempt to murder me, surely you can see your way to—"

"Murder you! I never—"

"I beg your pardon, but you certainly did. I confess I do feel a bit guilty having to involve poor Glynnis Fraser in this sad business. I daresay she didn't know you'd poison a marquess once you left her shop, but she *did* hand you the weapon, nonetheless."

Lord Ballantyne didn't say so aloud—no doubt he fancied himself too much of a gentleman to threaten a lady outright—but he didn't need to.

His meaning was perfectly clear. He'd see Glynnis sent to the gaol right along with her, and God help them both, then.

It was over. The Marquess of Ballantyne had her right where he wanted her. There wasn't a thing she could do, not without implicating Glynnis, and that . . .

No. That she would never do.

She closed her eyes and rested her cheek on the coverlet, all the fight draining out of her.

"Nothing to say, Miss MacLeod? How curious. You were so chatty before."

Why, oh *why* had she ventured into the village today? Freya had been right all along. Nothing good ever came of it. Their luck just kept getting worse, and it was bound to get uglier before it was finished. Lord Ballantyne could do whatever he pleased with her, and there wasn't anything she could do to stop him.

"I'm waiting, Miss MacLeod."

Waiting for what? He already knew he'd won. Men like him always won. "Very well, my lord. It seems you're determined to have your way."

No matter if he had to lie and cheat to get it.

"Well, I can't deny that I do like to have my way."

Of course, he did. All aristocrats did. Why should he be the exception?

"But just so there are no further misunderstandings between us, Miss MacLeod, is this a surrender? From now on, do I have your word that you'll do as I say?"

"Yes, my lord. I'll do as you say." Until she could find a way to gain the upper hand again, that is.

"How generous of you. But then you're a reasonable young lady." There was a brief pause, then he shifted, and the weight of his arm disappeared. "I knew all along you'd come to your senses."

CHAPTER 8

Hamish had half expected to wake in the night with a pillow over his face—or worse, not to wake at all—but he was still breathing the following morning.

Catriona MacLeod had given him her word that she'd do as he bid her, and she was as good as her promise. So far, that is. He wasn't such a fool as to believe she wouldn't try and turn the tables on him the instant she saw an opportunity.

Strangely enough, he was almost looking forward to it.

He glanced at where she was slumped at the edge of the bed, dozing with her head pillowed on top of her crossed arms. She'd been sitting upright in the chair beside him when he finally succumbed to sleep, but sometime in the night, she must have shifted.

She had such an angelic face, for such a diabolical lady!

She was far from being the withered crone Dougal and Clyde had made her out to be. But perhaps that wasn't so surprising. They both fancied themselves dangerous smugglers. They were hardly going to admit they'd been frightened away by a tiny chit who was about as terrifying as a newborn foal.

He stared at her, lingering on her red, rosebud lips, her elegant cheekbones, and small, upturned nose. She couldn't be more than nineteen or twenty years old, but she looked even younger in her sleep, with that smooth, pale skin and the hint of vulnerability in her full lower lip. Some of her hair had come unbound from the twist at the back of her neck, and long curls straggled over her shoulders and spread across the coverlet in a tangled auburn wave.

Even in sleep, there was a most unsettling crease between her brows.

That anxious little crease was almost enough to cause him an uncomfortable twinge of regret. Or it might have been if he ever bothered with such useless emotions as regret.

What's done was done. What was the use in sniveling about it?

This was an unfortunate business, but as fate would have it, he'd made a promise to his father—a deathbed promise, no less—that he'd see it through to the end, and that was what he intended to do.

Still, he might have been a bit more gentlemanly about it.

"Cat?" Quick footsteps pattered down the corridor, and a young lady rushed into the bedchamber, a flurry of words bursting from her lips. "I hardly slept a wink last night for worrying! We never should have left you alone with . . . oh!"

She broke off with a gasp when she saw him, and he stared back at her, nearly as surprised as she was.

It wasn't that he'd *forgotten* there were two more MacLeod sisters, but it had, er . . . slipped his mind? Self-preservation, no doubt. The first sister had nearly killed him, and now he had two more vixens to contend with. It would be a bloody miracle if he didn't end up at the bottom of Loch Dunvegan.

This new one had the same curly hair and strange, dark green eyes as her sister, but this new MacLeod chit didn't have Catriona's, er . . . well, a gentleman didn't like to call a lady *menacing*, but there was no denying the eldest MacLeod sister was a ferocious little thing, for all that she was as sturdy as a bit of dandelion fluff.

This sister's eyes were softer, her face rounder, her chin a gentle curve instead of a stubborn angle. They were both petite, dainty even, but this girl, with her long, slender neck and pale, fluttering hands had a fragility her sister was lacking. Even her hair was a softer color, a muted reddish gold version of her sister's vibrant auburn.

She didn't look like the sort of young lady who'd attempt to poison a man. What a pity *she* wasn't the sister who'd come to the village yesterday. If she had been, he wouldn't be struggling not to cast up his accounts all over the crisp white coverlet.

He'd taken command of the situation last night, yes—and he'd done a masterful job of it, too—but he hadn't yet recovered from the poisoning. His mouth was as dry as dust, and his head felt as if it had come untethered from his neck and was floating into the beamed ceiling above them.

"Cat?" The girl nudged her sister, her throat moving in a rough swallow. "H-he's awake."

"Freya?" Catriona stirred and let out a groan. "Who's awake?"

Ah, so this was Freya MacLeod, the middle sister. The one who could conjure a violent storm from a clear blue sky, according to Munro. He stifled a snort. A violent storm, indeed. She looked as if she'd struggle to coax a kitten into her lap.

"The man." Freya backed away from him, her eyes wide. "Your, ah . . . the man you brought here last night. Why is he awake?"

Cat bolted upright, shoving the tangle of hair out of her eyes, and leapt to her feet. "It's all right, Freya." She held out her hands, as if she were attempting to calm a cornered animal. "I promise you it's going to be all right."

"All right? How can it be all right?" A strangled sound tore from Freya's throat. "And he's *bleeding*! Why is he bleeding?"

Bleeding? He glanced down at himself, blinking at the blood decorating his shirt. Oh, right, he *was* bleeding, wasn't he? It wasn't just a little blood, either, but great, rusty streaks of it, a startlingly dark red against his white linen shirt.

Good Lord, it looked as if he'd been beheaded.

Cat glanced at him, biting her lip. "Er, well, there was a bit of a mishap last night—"

"A *mishap*? Is that what you'd call it, Miss MacLeod?" Hamish raised an eyebrow. "You struck me in the face. It was hardly a mishap."

Freya sucked in a breath, her gaze darting to her sister. "Struck him!"

"He wouldn't let go of my wrist. If he'd simply released me when I demanded it, I wouldn't have struck him."

Catriona's voice was calm, but if the green sparks shooting from her eyes had been daggers, he would have been a dead man. She was quite magnificent, really, in a demonic sort of way. "I would have gladly released you, Miss MacLeod, if you hadn't tried to poison me."

"Poison!" Freya MacLeod repeated, her voice faint. "He knows about the poison?"

"I know plenty, Miss Freya. More than enough to drag your sister to the magistrate. The Crown doesn't look upon murderesses with a friendly eye."

"Murderess!" Freya paled, staggering against the bed post.

Despite being hardly able to keep himself upright, he lurched for her, fearing a swoon, but Catriona MacLeod darted between them, her eyes flashing fire, and caught her sister around the waist. "Don't touch her. Not a single finger, Lord Ballantyne."

He stilled, the strangest feeling sweeping through him as he stared into her glittering green eyes, something that was both anger and grudging admiration at once.

The girl was a termagant. She was a thief, just as her father had been, and quite possibly a murderess, as well, but there wasn't a bit of cowardice in her. Looking at her now, with her snapping green eyes and those red curls in a wild riot around her face, he could almost believe she was . . . not a sorceress, no, but there was something different about her, something he could feel, but couldn't explain.

Long moments passed, but neither of them moved, each staring silently at the other.

God only knew how long they might have remained that way if the bedchamber door hadn't burst open, slamming against the wall behind it with a mighty crash. "Is something amiss? I heard shouting."

"No, it's fine." Catriona broke their stare and turned toward the door. "Good morning, Sorcha."

"Do you think so, Cat? I beg to differ."

Sorcha MacLeod was tiny, smaller even than her sisters, but he recognized at one glance that she wasn't the sort of lady a man should underestimate.

What had Munro said of her? That she was the wickedest of the three sisters.

Now *that* he could believe.

She looked him up and down, her penetrating green eyes seeming to see everything in a single glance, then she just as quickly dismissed him, as if she found a large, bloodied stranger lounging in one of her bedchambers every day. "He's still alive? Pity."

"Sorcha!" Freya gasped.

"What? You can't deny it would be a great deal easier for us if he'd had the decency to die. It's what a proper gentleman would have done." She plopped down on the chair beside the bed. "Why does Freya look as if she's about to fall into a swoon?"

Cat let out a sigh and took Freya's hand. "Her nerves are a bit frayed. Last night was . . . rather trying."

"This morning, as well. I've been to the village."

"The village!" Cat and Freya said at once, identical expressions of horror on their faces.

"Why in the world would you do such a thing?" Cat demanded. "Did we not agree it's best if you stay away from—"

"Oh, for pity's sake, calm down, will you? It's not as if I attacked anyone."

"Not this time," Freya muttered under her breath.

"I merely went to see if anyone had missed him." She jerked

her chin toward Hamish. "No one has, thankfully. Do we know who he is yet?"

Hamish, who'd had quite enough of being discussed as if he were invisible, struggled upright. "I'm Hamish Muir, the Marquess of Ballantyne."

"A marquess?" Sorcha MacLeod huffed. "Useless creatures, marquesses. Whatever does a marquess want with us?"

"He wants Rory's treasure." Catriona's voice was grim. "Just like the rest of them."

Sorcha had remained expressionless throughout this discussion, but at mention of the treasure, her lips curled upward. "Is that so? You haven't told him, then?"

Told him? He looked from one sister to the next. "Told me what?"

Sorcha's smile widened. "Ah, now this should be entertaining. Shall we go to the library? I've lit the fire, and Freya can lie down. She looks as if she's about to topple over."

Catriona shook her head. "No. Take Freya upstairs, Sorcha. I'll explain everything to his lordship."

"Where's the fun in that? But very well. If you prefer it. Come on then, Freya." Sorcha rose to her feet and marched to the door, but turned at the last minute, her cool gaze moving over his bloody shirt. "Is that your handiwork, Cat?"

A faint flush rush in Catriona's cheeks. "I, ah . . . I may have struck him in the face."

"Drew his cork, did you?" Sorcha's lips curled in a bloodthirsty grin. "Nicely done."

With that, she marched out the door with Freya on her heels, leaving him staring after them.

The truth, in all its messiness, all its inconvenient ugliness, had caught up with her at last.

No, not just her, but all three of them.

Cat had known it would. The truth always did find its way out, one way or another.

She'd just never imagined it would happen *here*, in the sanctuary of her beloved library, at the hands of the odious Marquess of Ballantyne.

But why not now and why not him? If her father's death had taught her anything, it was that a world could turn itself upside down without any warning, and with no guarantee it would ever right itself again.

Smugglers, sorcery, poison, and now this, caught like a rabbit in a snare by a nobleman who could, if he chose, see her taken up for attempted murder.

Goodness only knew what Lord Ballantyne thought he had to gain from staring down at her with those glittering blue eyes. Did he think he'd be able to read all her secrets on her face?

Well, good luck to him.

Over the past few months, she'd become so adept at keeping secrets and telling lies that the truth no longer showed on the surface, like a canvas without paint, or a book without any words.

She perched on the edge of a settee, waiting, her hands folded in her lap while he paced. It was a miracle he could pace at all, or even stand, come to that. The effects of monkshood poisoning could linger for days, but poison, it seemed, was no match for the Marquess of Ballantyne.

No doubt his size helped.

She eyed him from under cover of her lashes. His shoulders were absurdly broad, and his legs so long that fewer than half a dozen strides took him from one end of the room to the other.

And his chest was . . . exceedingly firm.

A solid wall of muscle, really, much like his thighs were. If she hadn't felt them for herself, she never would have believed such thighs could exist, but when she'd been thrown over his lap with the heavy weight of his arm across her back and his body shifting beneath her with each of his labored breaths—

A strange little shiver tripped up her spine.

Revulsion, no doubt. It hadn't been a pleasant experience, being draped across his lap like a butterfly pinned to a board.

Not pleasant at all—

"I beg your pardon, Miss MacLeod." He paused in front of the fireplace, his gaze finding hers in the dim room. "I believe I must have misheard you because it sounded as if you just said there's *no treasure*."

His tone was cordial enough, and his expression was one of polite inquiry, but there was an unmistakable tension in his long body, and the sensuous lips she'd guiltily admired while he'd been unconscious had tightened into a stern line.

One could hardly blame him for being displeased. God only knew what Rory had promised him, and he'd come a long way only to find disappointment at the end of his journey.

There wasn't anything she could do about that, however. If she'd truly been the sorceress most of Dunvegan believed her to be, she could produce a treasure from thin air.

But she wasn't, and she couldn't. She couldn't even keep a simple promise to her sisters anymore. With every day that passed, control seemed to slip further from her grasp. But there was no sense in becoming maudlin. The sooner she made Lord Ballantyne understand he wouldn't find what he sought here, the sooner he could be on his way.

"You didn't misunderstand me, my lord. There is no treasure." She raised her chin. "I'm afraid that *you*, much like every other gentleman foolish enough to believe in hidden treasure, have fallen victim to the most fantastical rumors."

"Rumors," he repeated. "Explain yourself, madam."

"I believe I just did, my lord." It wasn't terribly complicated. "There *is no treasure*. Rory—that is, my father—returned to Dunvegan as empty-handed as when he left it. Alas, I'm afraid the rumors of a fortune in jewels and gold coins are precisely that. Nothing more than rumors."

Silence.

She waited, breath held, but against every expectation, Lord Ballantyne *didn't* fall into a murderous rage. He didn't shout or grab her again. He didn't say a single word, but stood quite still, his hands folded behind his back, his face expressionless.

Good Lord. Why didn't he say something? Had he fallen into a fit?

They gazed at each other warily, until slowly—so slowly she might almost have believed she was imagining it—one corner of his lips quirked up in . . .

A smile? He was *smiling* at her? "Does something amuse you, Lord Ballantyne?"

Incredibly, his smile widened. "Rather, yes."

Had the man lost his wits? "Er, you did hear what I said, did you not? There is no—"

"Treasure. Yes, I heard you."

"Well, then?"

He abandoned his post by the fireplace and approached the settee where she sat, moving so close to her she could smell the scent of woodsmoke on him.

For an instant, their eyes met. A jolt went through her, and for a strange, suspended moment, she couldn't look away. His eyes were blue. Not Bryce Fraser's pale, watery blue, but a bright, brilliant blue, like sunlight sparkling on water.

Goodness, she could feel those eyes all the way down to her toes.

He gazed at her with those disconcerting blue eyes. "I heard you perfectly well. What amuses me, Miss MacLeod, is that you seem to be under the impression I'd believe you."

Ah. Well, this was hardly surprising, was it? Given the proliferation of rumors about Rory's alleged treasure, and the fact that people generally didn't like to believe what was inconvenient for them to find true, she'd anticipated this.

But his disbelief didn't change anything for either of them.

"That is as you prefer, Lord Ballantyne, but the facts are

what they are. You might believe me a liar, but alas, that won't make a casket of treasure appear at our feet, will it?"

"You misunderstand me. I don't *think* you're a liar. I *know* you're a liar."

"I'm not lying."

"Yes, Miss MacLeod, you are, and just when I thought we were becoming such good friends, too."

His lips were still quirked in that strange half grin, and his blue eyes seemed, inexplicably, to be twinkling at her. Indeed, she might have been fooled into thinking he was enjoying himself.

But no. That wasn't the case at all.

That twist of his lips wasn't a smile, and that wasn't a twinkle of humor in his eyes.

Despite every appearance to the contrary, Lord Ballantyne was furious. The hand resting at his side was white at the knuckles, and his lean body was tensed, like a coiled spring on the verge of bursting into motion.

Underneath his easy gallantry, his polite manners, and charming smiles, Lord Ballantyne was much like every other aristocrat—that is, unaccustomed to being denied whatever bauble he had his eye on.

How often did anyone ever dare to defy a marquess, on any matter whatsoever?

Never. He wasn't the sort of man who'd gracefully accept disappointment.

"I know you're lying, Miss MacLeod."

His low, cold tone made her shrink back against the settee, even as her cheeks heated with shame. How she despised cowards! How she despised herself, for not being able to find a way out of the mess her father had plunged them into.

He took another step toward her until he was so close he was towering over her, and she was forced to crane her neck to look up at him. "Shall I tell you how I know?"

How was she to answer such a question? Either a yes or a no implicated her in some way.

Which, of course, was precisely what he intended.

So, she said nothing.

"Not a word, Miss MacLeod? Pity. I've grown rather fond of our chats. But no matter. We'll do this your way."

Her way? Did he imagine anything about the past twenty-four hours had gone according to her wishes? A large, outraged marquess with a grudge against her father—a marquess she'd poisoned with monkshood, no less—was looming over her like an impeccably dressed, albeit blood-splattered ogre, demanding she produce a fortune in gold coins and jewels out of thin air.

If it hadn't all been so dreadful, she might have laughed.

"Do you see this, Miss MacLeod?" He reached into his breeches pocket, withdrew something, and tossed it into the air. He caught it on his palm, then held out his hand to her.

It was a coin, a gold guinea, or—

No, not a guinea. She took it from him and held it up to the gray light coming through the window. It wasn't King George III's face carved on the coin. She turned it over, and instead of the shield of arms of England and Scotland, there was a cross. She traced a fingertip over four double interlocking *L*s, each one topped with a crown, and the four fleur-de-lis in each corner.

It wasn't an English guinea at all. It was a French Louis d'Or gold ten-piece with a profile of King Louis XIII on the front, a collar draped loosely around his neck, and a crown of laurel balanced on his sumptuous curls.

She squinted down at it, turning it in the light so she could make out the date.

Sixteen hundred forty.

"My father, Archibald Muir had three coins identical to that one, Miss MacLeod. I often admired them as a child, but he never let me play with them. He told me they were a reminder of a promise he'd made long ago, one he intended to keep when the time came."

"I don't see what that has to do with me."

That much was true. She didn't know anything about any promise, but it did have something to do with her father.

It *must* because she'd seen a coin exactly like this one before in Rory's—

"It's the strangest thing, but after his death, I couldn't find the coins among his personal effects. It was as if they'd disappeared."

"Surely, you don't expect me to explain how—"

"You can imagine how perplexed I was when a coin identical to the three my father had kept for so many years—a Louis XIII ten-piece coin dated sixteen hundred forty—arrived at my townhouse in London a few weeks after my father's death. There was no letter with the coin, nothing to explain its sudden appearance, but the seal on the envelope was a bull's head with two flags on either side and the word *Tenete* above it."

"Hold fast," she murmured.

"That's right. It's Clan MacLeod's motto, I believe, and the bull and flags Clan MacLeod's crest?"

"Yes, but—"

"The initials *RM* were underneath the crest." He nodded down at the piece of gold clutched in her palm. "Roderick MacLeod. That coin came to me from Castle Cairncross."

She closed her fingers around the coin in her palm. Her head was spinning, but she kept her face carefully blank. "It's an unusual coin, my lord, but I didn't send this coin to you, and its existence doesn't prove a thing about any treasure."

"I believe the pact my father mentioned was one he made with *your* father, and that it had to do with these coins. Meanwhile, your father, a notorious smuggler, is rumored to have claimed a treasure right before he died and brought it back here to Castle Cairncross." He leaned closer, his face mere inches from hers. "Do you believe in coincidences, Miss MacLeod? Because I do not."

She *didn't* believe in them, but she wasn't about to admit it to Lord Ballantyne. "I own it's curious, my lord, but—"

"Are you aware, Miss MacLeod, that the lost Jacobean gold was said to be made up in part of Louis d'Or coins? That treasure belongs to the clans, as restitution for the misfortunes they suffered during the Jacobite Rebellion."

"What treasure? There's no proof that a treasure even exists. Even if my father *did* find a treasure in Louis d'Or coins, how can you know for sure that he ever made it back to Castle Cairncross with it? For that matter, why should I believe my father sent you this coin at all? You might have gotten it anywhere."

"I give you my word as a gentleman, Miss MacLeod."

"Your *word*?" She laughed, but it was a bitter, ugly sound. "You've done nothing but lie since I laid eyes on you, Lord Ballantyne."

"You're full of excuses, I see. Forgive me, but I think your father *did* return here with the treasure. Do you know what else I think, Miss MacLeod?"

"N-no, my lord."

"I think you're hiding it here, somewhere inside this castle. I imagine there are any number of hidden nooks and alcoves in which to hide a treasure."

"I'm not. I'm telling you the truth, my lord. My father returned to the castle with a pistol ball embedded in his thigh and a raging fever, but he did not return with any treasure."

But she knew already it was hopeless.

Why would Lord Ballantyne believe her, when every smuggler in Scotland was talking about Rory MacLeod's treasure? Why would he believe her when she had every reason to lie?

Of course he thought she was hiding the treasure from him, so she and her sisters might keep it for themselves. A choked laugh tore from her throat as she glanced around the library at the threadbare rugs, the weak fire, and the empty decanters arranged across the sideboard.

It hardly looked like a household rich with treasure.

He reached for the coin and plucked it from her hand, his fingers grazing her palm. "We've reached an impasse, I'm afraid, Miss MacLeod."

She glanced up at him, her breath catching as the light fell on his face. He was half-lost in shadows, but in the flickering firelight, with his sharp cheekbones, angular jaw, and that rough prickle of dark beard, he looked . . .

Savage. Just like every other smuggler who'd come here.

Aristocrat or not, Lord Ballantyne was a dangerous man, and he was *here*, inside her home, and she and her sisters were at his mercy.

She straightened her shoulders and met his gaze. "What is it that you want, Lord Ballantyne?"

"Why, only to fulfill my promise to my father, Miss MacLeod. I want what belongs to the clans." The half grin that had quirked his lips earlier was back again, but this time there was nothing playful about it, nothing humorous.

"I will have it, Miss MacLeod." He tossed the Louis d'Or ten-piece in the air, caught it between his fingers, and slipped it back inside his pocket. "Even if I have to tear your castle apart to get it."

Chapter 9

The castle was never silent, not even during the darkest hours of the night, but it had never been as quiet or as dark as it was tonight.

The air was still, and the waters of Loch Dunvegan were calm when Cat rose from her bed, crept to her bedchamber door, and eased it open. She paused on the threshold, listening, but aside from the rhythmic wash of the waves against the rocks below, there was nothing to hear.

Yet it wasn't an easy quiet, for all that the murmur of the water was as soothing as a lullaby. It was a wary, suspicious hush that did nothing to calm her ragged breaths or still her shaking hands.

She'd had the dream again tonight, but this time, her pursuer hadn't been nameless or faceless. He'd been an enormous marquess with blue eyes who'd chased her through the woods before succumbing to a poisoning—an *accidental* poisoning—and was now inside the castle walls, in the heart of her home, like a snake lying coiled and silent in a nest of baby birds.

It was her nightmare, come true.

Weren't nightmares meant to lose their power once they came true? It seemed not, because here she was, tiptoeing about and peeking around doors in the middle of the night like a thief in her own castle while Lord Ballantyne slept peacefully two floors below where she stood.

It was so awful, so resoundingly dreadful it might almost have been laughable, but there was nothing amusing about finding herself under the thumb of a powerful marquess who could ruin her with a single word to the magistrate.

How had things come to such a sad pass, so quickly? Why, she couldn't even leave her bedchamber without looking over her shoulder, waiting for the moment an arrogant marquess would leap out at her from the shadows.

Lord Ballantyne had retired to his bedchamber after their argument in the library this afternoon. She hadn't heard a single word from him since, but it was too much to hope he'd remain quiet for long. No doubt he was plotting his next move, biding his time, and waiting for the best moment to strike.

There was no sign of him lurking in the hallways tonight, however. The corridor outside her bedchamber was deserted, and aside from the usual creaks and groans of the castle bracing itself against the wind, silent.

No whispered voices, no muted patter of creeping footsteps.

It was only a temporary reprieve, a stay of execution until he returned to full vigor. He'd cause her no end of trouble then. Her day of reckoning was coming at the hands of the Marquess of Ballantyne, and like most reckonings, it was certain to arrive sooner than she'd hoped, and at the worst possible moment.

But it wouldn't be tonight, it seemed.

A small mercy, that, but she'd seize it, all the same. She had a few matters to attend to—matters she'd just as soon keep to herself—and this would likely be the last chance she'd get to see to her business without Lord Ballantyne peering over her shoulder.

Yet she lingered inside her bedchamber still, one eye pressed to the crack in the door. It seemed too much to hope—a miracle, even—that Freya and Sorcha had gone quietly to their beds after dinner. After the dramatic events of the day, she'd been waiting for them to storm her bedchamber tonight, but there wasn't so much as a shadow to be seen or a footstep to be heard in the darkened hallway beyond her bedchamber door.

She slipped through it, pulling it closed behind her, and made a mad dash up the staircase to the third floor, phantom footsteps chasing her the entire way. By the time she reached the alcove that led to the turret, she was nearly panting with dread, but there was no one there.

She was alone.

She darted into the alcove and ran up the narrow stairs inside the wall of the turret to the top floor of the castle.

Her workroom was just as she'd left it yesterday morning before she'd embarked on her ill-fated trip to the village. Her flasks and bottles were scattered about her worktable. Stray bits of maidenhair fern littered the floor beneath it, and a trace of the heavy, earthy scent of black licorice lingered in the air.

It seemed impossible that only a little more than a day had passed since she'd left here, their dwindling finances her greatest concern! It was incredible how much havoc a single day could cause. One small misstep had upended everything, leaving the bits and pieces of the life they'd cobbled together after her father's death scattered at their feet, like a puzzle carelessly dropped on the floor.

She paused beside her worktable to light the lantern, but after turning the wick down low, she left it where it was, the muted glow leaving the corners of the room in shadows.

Instead, she let the pale moonlight through the window light her way to the other side of her workroom, her bare feet silent against the cold floors as she made her way to a set of double doors set into the stonework.

Despite being massive arched affairs made of thick slabs of heavily carved wood, one wasn't likely to notice the doors unless they knew to look for them. She'd locked those doors on the day of her father's death, then she, Sorcha, and Freya had dragged a large cabinet in front of the door on the left.

Since then, none of them had set foot in the room on the other side of the doors. They'd closed them and walked away. If she'd had any other choice, she may never have darkened the threshold of the room again, but as it was . . .

Choice was rather in short supply these days.

She slid her hand into the pocket of her cloak and withdrew the heavy iron key she'd taken from a wooden box hidden on the bottom shelf of her dressing closet. She fitted it to the lock in the door on the right, and it opened with a rusty groan of protest, leaving her just enough room to squeeze through the gap.

As soon as she stepped inside, a blast of stale air hit her in the face.

It was frigid on the other side, and musty, as well, as if the doors had been closed years ago and never opened since. The iron hinges were coated with dust, and the thin silk filaments of abandoned spiderwebs lingered in the cracks the passing of centuries had wrought in the wood.

She stood for a moment, inhaling the familiar scents of dust and old paper, but as she stepped over the threshold and into the room, she caught a hint of the sweet, powdery scent of the pipe her father used to smoke, and her chest tightened.

It was everything Rory, that scent, every memory of a childhood condensed into a single breath. Memories of sitting on his knee as he shuffled papers about his desk, of hours spent tramping through the woods at his side, her small hand tucked into his much larger one. The scratch of his bristled cheek against hers, his woodsy scent a part of him as surely as his arms around her had once been.

That scent was a part of her now, too.

Dear God, how angry she was at him!

And how terribly she missed him. It was as if an abyss had opened right in the center of her chest, and no matter what she did, or how hard she tried, there was no way to close it, and no way to fill it.

It was a throbbing emptiness, just beneath her breastbone.

Tears sprang to her eyes, but she dashed them away with an

impatient swipe of her hand. There was no time for that nonsense, not with Lord Ballantyne breathing down their necks.

The room was just as she'd left it months ago.

Rory's coat was draped over the back of his chair, and the usual mountain of papers was spread across his desk, a letter opener tossed carelessly on top of them. A glass with a few drops of whisky stood on one corner, and on the other was the dirk he'd carried everywhere with him, its brass handle gleaming in the thin ray of moonlight peeking through the high, narrow window cut into the stone wall behind the desk.

She approached, took up the dirk, and slid it from its leather sheath.

It had belonged to Rory's father, her grandfather, and Rory had cherished it. She'd never met her grandfather, as he'd died before she was born, but Rory had always spoken of him with hushed reverence. He used to spend hours cleaning and sharpening the dirk and oiling the leather sheath.

She ran her thumb over the blade. It was dull now, and the steel was discolored.

But she hadn't come here for this. The time for indulging in fond memories had long since passed. She tossed the dirk and sheath onto the desk, swallowing the lump in her throat, and seated herself behind it in her father's chair, taking in the chaotic mess of paper spread over the surface.

There were letters, bills of lading, rough drawings, and old maps, some of them worn nearly through at the seams, and others only fragments, bits of paper with torn edges. To the untrained eye, it all appeared random and unconnected, but in his own slapdash fashion, Rory had kept meticulous records.

The trouble was, none of it made any sense to anyone but him. She'd have to go through all of it at some point and read every scrap of paper, one at a time.

Soon, but not tonight. Tonight, she'd come for something else.

That coin that Lord Ballantyne had produced with such fanfare from his pocket this afternoon, the Louis d'Or ten-piece . . . she'd seen that coin before, or one identical to it.

Had he noticed the shock on her face when he'd shown it to her? Dear God, she hoped not. She'd done her best to remain expressionless, but she'd recognized that coin the instant she laid eyes on it, and she'd never been a convincing liar.

There was nothing ordinary about that coin.

The Louis d'Or ten-piece had never been put into common circulation. It was a pleasure coin, a royal gambling piece made to be used only in court games.

It was rare. Exceedingly rare.

Lord Ballantyne had told her he didn't believe in coincidences.

Neither did she.

He'd said something about a pact between their fathers, about the coin in his possession having come from Castle Cairncross. Lord Ballantyne was almost certainly a liar, but it was difficult to believe he was lying about this.

It was simply too unusual an occurrence to be brushed off as a coincidence. It was impossible that her father and Archibald Muir, Lord Ballantyne's father, should both be in possession of such an unusual coin without there being some connection between them.

As to what the connection might be, well . . . that was anyone's guess.

A lost treasure, perhaps? If it had been anyone other than her father, she would have dismissed the idea as pure fantasy, but lost treasures had been Rory's stock in trade.

Or *stolen* treasure, rather.

He'd been a smuggler, after all. Wine, brandy, tea, an occasional bolt of silk or lace, and yes, jewels and gold coins. In his lifetime, Rory had gained and lost several fortunes, and none of it by honest means.

But he was dead now, and it didn't matter anymore.

What *did* matter was the coin.

She unlocked the desk, slid the lower drawer on the left side open, and removed the false bottom, as she'd seen her father do a hundred times before.

A tiny key lay nestled in the shallow alcove underneath.

It was slippery in her hands as she slid it into the lock in the top middle drawer. It rolled smoothly open, and tucked inside, just where it had always been, was a small, green velvet pouch, a gold tasseled drawstring tying it closed.

She scooped it up but stilled at the soft clink of coins, the weight of it in her hand.

There was more than one coin inside.

Slowly, her fingers clumsy, she plucked at the drawstring and upended the contents of the pouch into her palm.

Then she sat there, frozen, staring at them.

There were three coins. Three, where before there'd only been one.

She took each coin up, one by one, and held them up to the moonlight to see the dates.

Sixteen hundred forty, sixteen hundred forty, and sixteen hundred forty. All three coins were identical to the one Lord Ballantyne had shown her in the library today.

But where had the other two coins come from? And *when* had they come?

She sat with them clutched in her hand and tried to recall the last time she'd opened the pouch. It had been some months ago, weeks before Rory had gone off on his last ill-fated adventure.

The one that had ended in his death.

She'd come into this room to leave some letters for him, found the pouch lying on top of the desk, and paused to peek inside. It was a beautiful coin, exquisitely carved, with finely milled edges. She rarely let a chance to admire it pass her by.

There'd only been one coin in the pouch that day. She was certain of it.

She fell back against the chair, her head spinning.

Something was amiss with this entire business, and it had been from the start. Rory had given up smuggling after her mother's death, but then out of the blue one day, he'd announced he intended to embark on an adventure, one final quest for treasure.

By the following morning, he was gone, without another word of explanation to any of them.

She closed her eyes, her fingers curling tightly around the coins.

Did she dare to share this information with Lord Ballantyne? She didn't trust him. In truth, she didn't trust much of anyone these days, but especially not *him*. Nothing would change that. Not after he'd shown himself so willing to lie to suit his purposes, then threatened to tear her castle apart.

She'd taken one risk already when she'd told him the truth about her father's missing treasure. Rory had returned from his mysterious quest a few weeks after his departure without any treasure and maddened with a raging fever from a pistol ball embedded in his leg.

What she hadn't confessed to Lord Ballantyne, however—or indeed, to anyone, not even her sisters—was the nature of his ravings as she'd nursed him in those last weeks before he died.

He'd gone on and on about a promise he'd sworn to keep and a fortune in gold coins buried where no one would ever find them. He'd babbled names at her, names she hadn't recognized at the time—Archie, Malcolm, and Angus—and clutched at her hand, his skin burning hot to the touch, and begged her to help him keep his word.

None of it had made any sense, and she'd dismissed it all as fevered delusions.

Now, however . . . well, perhaps she'd been too hasty, because here was Hamish Muir, the son of a gentleman named Archibald Muir, or Archie, presumably, insisting there was a treasure and a pact between their fathers, and essentially repeating everything her father had tried to tell her.

Was it possible there actually *was* a treasure? That Rory had gone in search of it, that it had somehow eluded him and remained buried somewhere, waiting to be discovered?

A fortune in Louis d'Or gold coins . . .

The money was of no consequence to her. It didn't belong to her, and she didn't want as much as a single gold coin of it. But if the treasure could be found and turned over to Lord Ballantyne as he demanded, then there'd be no need for the smugglers to continue their assault on Castle Cairncross.

Mightn't there be some way she and Lord Ballantyne could help each other? He wanted the treasure, and she had both Rory's deathbed confessions and his maps and notes right in front of her. If there truly was a treasure, she might be able to help him find it.

Until the rumors of the hidden treasure were put to rest, she and her sisters were trapped between the villagers on one side, who grew more suspicious of them with every day that passed, and Loch Dunvegan on the other, where it was only a matter of time before another band of smugglers would attempt to storm the castle.

If there was some truth to this rumor about Rory's treasure, and the treasure could be found, it would put an end to this business for good. They'd be rid of Lord Ballantyne, and rid of the smugglers, and they might go back to things as they'd been before the villagers began to turn on them.

There was only one problem. She'd sooner trust Bryce Fraser or Mrs. MacDonald than she would Lord Ballantyne.

He'd followed her. He'd *chased* her, for pity's sake. Her encounter in the woods with him was the closest she'd ever come to having one of her nightmares come true.

Since then, every time he opened his mouth, either a lie, a threat, or an accusation had come tumbling out. He'd accused her of lying to him, of poisoning him, and he'd threatened to take her to the magistrate. He'd threatened to take *Glynnis* to the magistrate.

He'd said he was going to tear her castle apart.

How could she ever bring herself to trust such a man?

The answer was as plain as day. She *couldn't*.

She'd already told him too much, and he'd wasted no time making her regret it. She wouldn't make that mistake again. No, it was out of the—

Thump!

She jumped, and the coins slipped from her fingers and fell onto Rory's desk with a heavy clunk.

Oh, no. That thump had sounded like the thud of a boot heel on the stone floors.

She crept to the door and peeked through the gap, and yes, she could see shadows dancing against the walls as someone passed through the lantern light.

Someone large. Far larger than Freya or Sorcha.

That left Lord Ballantyne. He was snooping about inside her workroom!

Quickly, she snatched up the tiny key she'd left on the desk, and after a bit of fumbling, managed to slide it into its hiding place before fitting the false bottom back into the drawer. Then she shoved the coins into the pouch, tucked the pouch back into the middle drawer of the desk, and locked the desk again before hurrying into her workroom.

"Good evening, Miss MacLeod."

He was standing in the dim pool of light cast by the lantern, casually turning over the leaves of a large book he'd spread out on her worktable.

"Following me, again?" Had there ever been a more arrogant, infuriating man than he? "Tell me, Lord Ballantyne. Do you make a habit of following young ladies when your presence is not welcome?"

"That depends entirely upon the young lady, Miss MacLeod."

"Are you reading my books? Why, how dare you?"

He didn't look up but continued turning over the pages,

pausing every now and again to read. "What are Strangeway Drops?"

"What?"

"Strangeway Drops." He tapped the page in front of him. "Myrrh, sweet almond, roots of Angelica, half a pint of wine—"

"Is that my mother's remedy book?" By God, it was! She could make out the familiar worn dark green binding in the light cast by the lantern.

"You didn't answer my question." He let out a sigh as if she were excessively tiresome. "What are Strangeway Drops?"

"If you must know, it's a cure for inflammation, but you have no business—"

"Snakeroot! Good Lord. Any self-respecting chemist should know a patient doesn't want snakeroot in their wine." His gaze swept over her, his expression unreadable.

Oh, dear. Her ankles and toes were bare. She couldn't be alone in a dimly lit room with Lord Ballantyne while her ankles were bare. It wasn't proper.

"Having trouble sleeping, Miss MacLeod?"

"No. Why should I be?" She shuffled awkwardly from foot to foot as she tried to hide her bare feet from him, but her heels got caught up in the voluminous hems of her night rail. She grabbed the corner of her worktable as she stumbled forward, and the iron key slipped from her fingers and landed with a ringing thud on the floor by her feet.

His bright blue eyes roved over her face before darting to the key on the floor between them. "Perhaps a guilty conscience is keeping you awake."

"Nonsense. I haven't a thing to be guilty about." She leaned down to snatch up the key and stuffed it back into the pocket of her cloak, cursing it as a troublemaker.

But it was too late. By then, he'd seen everything she wished to hide from him—the key, the doors behind her half-hidden by the cabinet, and the guilty flush staining her cheeks.

Lord Ballantyne might be a liar, a thief, and a villain who chased young ladies through the woods until they had no choice but to accidentally poison him with monkshood, but he was no fool.

He held her gaze, pinning her where she stood, the shadows surrounding them turning his eyes a darker shade of blue. "You wouldn't be keeping secrets from me, would you, Miss MacLeod?"

Dear God, he looked as if he were about to leap upon her, and she could do nothing but stare back at him, her heart fluttering like a bird's wings behind her ribs. "You, ah . . ." She licked her lips. "You're not well, Lord Ballantyne. You should be in bed."

For an instant, it looked as if his gaze darted to her mouth, but his eyes were on hers again in the next instant, holding her captive.

She must have imagined it. "I advise you to return to your bedchamber, my lord."

"How conscientious you are about my health, Miss MacLeod. I'd be flattered if I wasn't certain your concern had less to do with my well-being and more to do with your wish to avoid the noose."

She let out a quiet sigh. Really, she wished he'd stop saying the word "noose."

"But there's no need for you to worry," he added. "I feel a great deal better. Fortunately for both of us, I'm nearly myself again."

Was it a good thing he didn't appear likely to succumb to monkshood poisoning or a bad thing? She hardly knew anymore, but there was no denying he seemed vigorous enough.

She'd given him one of her father's plain white linen shirts to replace his blood-splattered one, and he wore only that and his breeches. The loose neck of the shirt revealed the burnished skin of his chest, and his tight breeches clung to the muscles of his legs.

Ahem. Far *too* vigorous, by half.

It was an utter scandal for her to see him in such a state of undress, but what was more scandalous still was that no matter how desperately she wanted to, she couldn't seem to tear her gaze away from him.

"It seems I've come just in time. Lucky, isn't it?" He straightened and came toward her, the shadows surrounding him giving way to a shaft of moonlight pouring through the window, emphasizing the elegant bones of his face, and gilding his hair with silver.

"I shudder to think what I would have missed, otherwise." He leaned one hip on the edge of her worktable, his long legs stretched out before him, his knee brushing the skirts of her night rail, and the warmth from his body heating the sliver of space between them.

Somehow, she couldn't catch her breath. "I'm sorry to disappoint you, my lord, but despite the rumors about us, my sisters and I lead rather dull lives here at Castle Cairncross."

"Dull?" He waved a hand around her workroom. "It looks as if you manage to keep yourself well occupied, Miss MacLeod." He plucked up the flask of licorice extract she'd made yesterday. "What's this?"

Her fingers itched to snatch it away from him. "Black licorice extract."

He brought the flask to his nose and took a sniff. "What do you use it for?"

She huffed out a breath. "Do you truly want to know, Lord Ballantyne, or is this some ploy to trick me into revealing something about the treasure?"

He smiled. "I thought there wasn't any treasure."

"I never said that. I only said it wasn't here at Castle Cairncross." She took the flask from him and set it aside on her worktable. "As for the extract, if you must know, I use it to sweeten my maidenhair cough syrup. Glynn—er, I mean Mr. Fraser, the apothecary, sells it in his shop."

"I see. How do you make it?"

She eyed him. Was he making fun of her? Aside from Glynnis and her mother, she hadn't met a single person who was interested in her "potions," as Freya called them.

He raised an eyebrow at her, waiting.

"It's simple, really. I strip the plant down to the root, cut it into long strips, pound it with a mallet, then mix the pulp with water and simmer it for half a day or so. Once it thickens, I add a bit of sugar, boil it again, and store it in glass jars."

She peeked up at him. Plants and potions and medicines were endlessly fascinating to her, but whenever she spoke of them, people's eyes tended to glaze over.

But he was still listening, and it didn't *look* like he was secretly laughing at her. "How fascinating. What other kinds of medicines can you make?"

"All sorts of things." Despite herself, she was warming to her subject. "Did you know that the dried leaves of Wood Betony ward off headaches?"

"Indeed? I did not know that, Miss MacLeod."

"Oh, yes. Lemon Balm steeped in Canary wine can be used to treat venomous spider bites, and *Alchemilla vulgaris*—commonly known as Bear's Foot—makes an admirable wound treatment."

His lips quirked. "Is that so?"

"Yes, indeed. Certain evergreen ferns native to Britain—*Asplenium scolopendrium*, or Hart's Tongue—is a wonderful treatment for burns, and I make a heather oil liniment for those who suffer from inflamed joints, and—oh!" Without thinking, she seized his arm. "Gout!"

"Gout?"

"Yes. Eating fresh cherries can help alleviate gout. Now, I can't claim to have made that discovery myself—not through scientific methods, at least, as we found it out quite by accident when my Aunt Isobel visited some years ago—but nature is the most fascinating thing imaginable. Don't you think so, Lord Ballantyne?"

He didn't reply, but stood quite still, staring at her with a curious expression on his face.

"Lord Ballantyne?"

"Fascinating, yes." He cleared his throat. "Far more fascinating than I ever could have anticipated."

Chapter 10

This wasn't going at all the way Hamish had imagined it would.

It had begun so promisingly, too. For all her cleverness, Catriona MacLeod was as predictable as the eastern sunrise, and the western sunset.

He'd suspected it would only be a matter of time before she crept from her bedchamber tonight and went scampering about the castle like a busy little mouse with bits of cheese hidden in every corner.

She'd proved him right.

The grandfather clock on the first-floor landing had just struck midnight when her bedchamber door had cracked open, and the tip of a curious little nose emerged. Soon enough the rest of the lady followed, tiptoeing like a thief through the hushed castle corridors after the rest of the household had fallen asleep.

It was hardly surprising. He'd only been inside the castle walls for little more than a day, and mostly unconscious for half of that, but he'd already concluded there was no end to the number of secrets she was hiding.

And here was the proof of it.

She was accomplished at sneaking. He'd give her that. She'd been as stealthy as a Covent Garden pickpocket when she'd slipped from her bedchamber and darted up the stairs.

But not stealthy enough to evade *him*.

After the two younger MacLeod sisters had gone to their

beds and the castle had fallen silent, he'd done some creeping of his own. It had been the easiest thing in the world to tiptoe up the stairs after her when she'd retired to her bedchamber tonight and hide himself in an adjacent corridor.

Then, it had simply been a matter of waiting.

Sure enough, she'd come sneaking out of her bedchamber like a proper thief and darted up the stairs. He'd been after her in an instant. That was the trouble with sneaking. All it took to set the whole business awry was one person waiting in the shadows to follow in your footsteps.

From there, she'd led him up to the third floor, then into the alcove to the winding staircase clinging to the walls of the turret to the uppermost floor of the castle, and into a room with a heavy, sweet scent lingering in the air.

There was a long, scarred table in the center of the cavernous space, and deep bookshelves lining the walls. It looked like a laboratory of some sort, which was curious enough, but Miss MacLeod scurried past without a glance and hurried instead to a large cabinet at the back of the room.

At least, he thought it was a cabinet until he heard the squeal of a door opening.

A secret door leading to a secret chamber? Well, of course, what else? From what he knew of Catriona MacLeod, she likely had secret chambers tucked into every corner of this godforsaken castle.

Clever of her, really. Secret chambers were excellent places to hide stolen treasure.

He'd had half a mind to follow her into her hidden lair, but she'd see him as soon as he appeared on the threshold. No, it was far better to leave her to whatever clandestine business had lured her from her bed, then catch her by surprise when she came back out.

So, he'd settled in to wait, ready for whatever came next.

Ready for *her*. Or so he'd thought.

But nothing could have prepared him for the sight of her when she'd emerged from her hiding place in her filmy night rail, like a vision in white floating across the floor as if she were one of the moonbeams streaming through the windows above them.

Moonbeams, for God's sake.

A man only starting waxing poetic about moonbeams when every other sensible thought had fled his head. But there she was, a dainty wraith haunting the top floor of the castle, her bare pink toes peeking out from under her hems and the thick locks of her hair bound in a long, loose plait that hung down to the vulnerable curve of her lower back.

He'd nearly swallowed his tongue.

It was a small mercy she hadn't left her hair entirely unbound and spilling over her shoulders in a riotous tangle of red curls, or there was no telling how ridiculous a fool he might have made of himself, staring at her like a half-wit.

But even constrained as it was, her hair was close enough to unbound that a gentleman with a vivid imagination—a gentleman like himself, for example—had no difficulty at all mentally unraveling that plait until those silky locks flowed freely into his hands.

He'd said . . . something. Good evening, perhaps? Something of that sort.

He couldn't quite recall it now, because his cock, troublesome organ that it was, had chosen this moment to make a nuisance of itself, and it was diverting all the blood from his brain to between his legs.

They'd exchanged a few words—something about her mother's remedy book, and black licorice, or . . . wait, that couldn't be right, could it? Why the devil would they have been discussing black licorice?

It was all a bit fuzzy, really.

Perhaps he hadn't quite recovered from the poisoning, because somehow, instead of demanding answers about her father's treasure or quizzing her about the mystery surrounding the Louis d'Or gold pieces, they'd ended up talking about gout.

Not why she'd sneaked from her bedchamber tonight, and not whatever it was she'd been doing in that secret chamber of hers, but *gout*, for God's sake.

She didn't seem to find anything amiss in it, however.

Indeed, the more she talked, the more animated she became, her face lighting up like a sunrise. Soon enough she was telling him all about milk thistle, ginger root, and alfalfa, and lamenting the lack of sunshine in western Scotland that prevented her from growing proper hibiscus root, which she claimed was meant to work wonders on gout.

And here they were, back to the gout again.

She was delivering a treatise on the various cures for gout, and he . . . well, damned if he wasn't hanging on her every word. Somehow, with every syllable that fell from her lips, it became more difficult for him to tear his gaze away from her.

This wasn't supposed to happen. He'd only asked about her plants and medicines in the hope she'd become distracted enough that a secret or two would find its way from her clever, witchy brain to her lips.

He wasn't supposed to find her conversation interesting. He didn't even know what Wood Betony *was*, for God's sake.

He was meant to be charming *her*, not the other way around.

What good was it being a charming marquess, if he couldn't flirt her secrets out of her? But alas, somewhere between the black licorice extract and the venomous spider bites, he'd forgotten all about the treasure and fallen under her spell.

How could this have happened?

He'd never had any interest in wound treatment or inflamed joints before, but her rapt expression as she spoke, the bright light in her green eyes as she went on about Hart's Tongue and Lemon Balm, and the graceful movement of her slender arms and dainty hands as she elaborated on some point or another . . .

He couldn't look away from her.

". . . Devil's Claw is an effective treatment as well, but alas, *Harpagophytum procumbens* only grows in dry, desert-like conditions and can't be grown in Scotland. It's part of the sesame family, you know, my lord, and . . ."

He watched her, his throat as dry as the South African desert where—apparently—*Harpagophytum procumbens* thrived in the heat.

The chit was downright enchanting, damn her.

He mustn't let her make him forget that for all her sparkling green eyes and the fetching locks of hair curling around her face, Catriona MacLeod was a liar.

She might deny it all she liked, but her father's treasure was here, locked up somewhere inside this castle, maybe even in the very next room, on the other side of the double doors she'd just crept through.

Right, then. It was time to take control of the situation. He was a marquess, for pity's sake, a sophisticated gentleman with a wealth of worldly knowledge at his fingertips, and she was a wee scrap of a girl hardly out of pinafores, who'd likely never set foot outside of Dunvegan.

She was no match for him, no matter how fetching she was.

It wasn't as if he'd never encountered a distracting lady before. Catriona MacLeod would hardly be the first he'd charmed into revealing her secrets. It was a simple enough matter, after all. A few smiles, a subtle compliment here and there, and an occasional admiring glance should be enough to loosen Miss MacLeod's tongue.

That is, her tongue was loose already. She was currently expounding on the merits of *Salix alba*, or White Willow, but it was past time to ease her back to the matter at hand.

The treasure. The bloody *treasure*.

He hadn't traveled all the way from London to Dunvegan to learn about gout, or White Willow, or the various remedies for spider bites. He wasn't opening an apothecary's shop, for God's sake. He was stealing a treasure back from the thief who'd stolen it from him.

How hard could it be to coax Miss MacLeod into giving away a few tidbits of information? He was bloody delightful, damn it. The trick was not to come at the thing too abruptly, or to say anything unpleasant that would startle her into awareness.

He opened his mouth, an elegant bit of flattery about the depth of her knowledge regarding the intricacies of gout at the edge of his lips.

"Which of your potions did you poison me with, Miss MacLeod?"

What the devil? How had *that* slipped out? Poison wasn't *pleasant*.

She'd been chattering happily about tree bark and Burdock root, but as soon as the word *poison* fell from his lips, she went silent, her shoulders hunching as if she were trying to disappear into herself.

The strangest thing happened then.

Inexplicably, without warning, his heart sank right down to his toes.

It was like watching a candle being snuffed out, the bright, warm glow vanishing with a careless pinch of his fingers.

Why had he brought up the poison? Yes, he wanted to know the truth about what had happened in the woods, but there was no place for the truth in a flirtation.

They sat there, each of them eyeing the other in silence.

She'd treat him to the sharp edge of that clever tongue of hers now, then she'd gather that cloak around her shoulders and march off in a cloud of offended dignity.

All at once, the thought of her leaving was unbearable. It was startling how badly he wanted to keep her there. "I beg your pardon. Perhaps I shouldn't have—"

She interrupted him with a long sigh. "I suppose there's no

use in explaining once again that I didn't try to poison you, is there, Lord Ballantyne?"

Was there any use in it? Less than half an hour ago, he would have said no.

But now . . . he toyed with the tarnished brass scales on her worktable, setting them bouncing with a touch of his finger as he considered it. If she hadn't poisoned him, how had he ended up flat on his back in the woods?

She must have done *something* to him, but he couldn't recall what, nor could he imagine what a lady as threatening as a butterfly could have done during their brief tussle that had knocked a man of his size off his feet.

He let out a sigh of his own, his gaze meeting hers. "Shall we see? Give me your explanation of the events in the woods yesterday, Miss MacLeod. You may yet be able to persuade me you did not, in fact, attempt to murder me."

Strangely enough, it was the truth. For all her secrets, he'd never come across a lady who seemed less like a criminal than Catriona MacLeod.

Of course, she could just be an accomplished actress.

She was certainly lying about the treasure—a few mesmerizing words about gout and festering wounds wasn't going to change his mind about *that*—yet somehow, he couldn't quite make himself believe that a lady who took such tender care of her sisters was a vicious murderess.

If she truly had poisoned him, why hadn't she left him in the woods to die? Why would she go to the trouble of poisoning him only to draw the line at dumping his lifeless corpse into Loch Dunvegan, never to be heard from again?

Instead, she'd brought him back here and tucked him into bed. It didn't make any sense. Neither Catriona MacLeod nor her sisters wanted him anywhere near their castle—that much was obvious—yet here he was.

"Miss MacLeod?"

She dropped onto one of the stools, and sat for some minutes without replying, staring down at her folded hands in her lap, but then she rose and took up a basket that was sitting at the other end of her worktable.

A basket with a broken handle.

It was the same one she'd carried to the village yesterday. She reached in, took out a small, dark glass bottle, and held it up. "This is what Glynnis gave me in the mews yesterday."

She uncorked the bottle, took up a clear glass flask sitting on her worktable, and tipped a small pool of pale yellow oil into it. A strong herbal scent redolent with mint rose between them. "Do you know what this is, Lord Ballantyne?"

He joined her at the other end of the worktable. "Cantarella?"

"Goodness, no. Cantarella is a white powder, and one can't simply wander into an apothecary's in Dunvegan and purchase Cantarella. This isn't Versailles, my lord. This is pennyroyal oil."

"Pennyroyal?" That was all? Pennyroyal was harmless enough. "What, like the tea? It smells like mint."

"It does, yes, and pennyroyal leaves do make rather a nice tea. It's perfectly safe in small doses, even beneficial, but concentrated pennyroyal oil, like what you see in this bottle, is a dangerous poison if ingested."

"Are you telling me, Miss MacLeod, that you poisoned me with pennyroyal oil?" It didn't seem likely. He'd remember it if she'd poured that stuff down his throat.

"No, my lord. As I said before, I didn't poison you at all. I'm explaining to you that the presence of this pennyroyal oil in my basket is the reason your threat to see Glynnis Fraser taken up by the magistrate was an effective one."

"I don't understand. If they sell this oil at the apothecary, then why—"

"Because she sold it to *me*, Lord Ballantyne. Anyone else in Dunvegan can wander into the apothecary's, purchase a bottle of pennyroyal oil, and march right back out again without anyone thinking twice about it, but if one of the wicked MacLeod witches attempts it—"

"It raises suspicions."

She gave a short laugh. "To say the least, yes."

"The villagers are not as trusting as you might like?" In fact, they were downright hostile. He'd seen the way the men at Baird's Pub had looked at her as she'd passed by the window.

"I'm afraid not."

"But you ventured into the village anyway."

"Yes. I had a half dozen bottles of maidenhair syrup to sell to Glynnis." She replaced the stopper in the glass bottle and set it aside. "I buy pennyroyal oil for the same reason everyone else in Dunvegan does—to rid the castle of rats. But as you said yourself, I doubt the magistrate would see it that way."

Good God, what had he brought down upon the MacLeod sisters' heads when he'd sent Clyde and Dougal here to retrieve the treasure? He couldn't have predicted they'd turn sorceresses to defend themselves, but was it any wonder they'd resorted to extremes?

It was a bloody miracle neither Dougal nor Clyde had been shot. It should have been him who'd come to Dunvegan that first time and approached the sisters directly, no matter what he thought of Rory MacLeod.

Instead, he hadn't spared a single thought for what might happen to the MacLeod sisters. Not a single thought for three young women who'd lost their father only months earlier, who were now left alone in this old castle without even a servant for protection.

If Catriona MacLeod ever discovered he'd been the one who sent that first lugger, that *he'd* been the one responsible for destroying all their peace . . . well, she never could find out. It was as simple as that. It would cause all manner of trouble, and he didn't have time for delays.

He glanced from the bottle of oil on the table back to her face. "If it wasn't the pennyroyal oil that made me ill, what did?"

"This." She reached into the basket again, withdrew a pair of gloves, and slipped them over her hands.

He'd seen those gloves before, hadn't he? Yes. She'd donned a pair of cotton gloves before she picked the purple flowers. He remembered it because they'd appeared unnaturally white in the gloom of the woods.

Those purple flowers—

"Monkshood, Lord Ballantyne." She rummaged in the basket and withdrew a small clutch of flowers wrapped in a handkerchief. She laid the bundle on the worktable, peeled the handkerchief aside, and carefully took up one of the stalks, holding it up to show him. "Every part of the plant is poisonous, and you don't need to ingest it to suffer from its effects. Just a brush against the skin is enough to cause monkshood poisoning."

Just a brush against the skin . . .

After the chase, when they'd both tumbled to the ground, hadn't one of those purple flowers gotten stuck to his lip? Yes! There'd been a half dozen or so of them scattered over the ground near him, as well.

He'd peeled the stalk off his lip, and it had been only an instant afterward that he'd become too dizzy to remain on his feet. Within seconds, he'd lost consciousness entirely.

Good God. Catriona MacLeod had been telling the truth all along.

She *hadn't* poisoned him. It had been an accident. A strange accident to be sure—it wasn't every day a marquess tumbled into a pile of poisonous monkshood—but an accident, nonetheless.

She was no murderess. On the contrary, she'd *saved* him.

And he'd repaid her by accusing her of being a murderess and threatening her with the magistrate. Hadn't he also said something about seeing her neck fitted for a noose?

He *had*, damn it. Twice.

If she was telling the truth about this, wasn't it possible she was telling the truth about the treasure, too? It would change everything if she was, but how far could he trust Catriona MacLeod? If the treasure really was here inside the castle walls, she had every reason in the world to lie to him about it.

But be that as it may, she *hadn't* been lying about the poison. "It seems I owe you an apology, Miss MacLeod. I beg your pardon for, ah . . ."

"Calling me a thief and a murderess? Accusing me of lying and threatening to see me hung?"

"Er, yes. All those things." His cheeks were hot—an unusual occurrence, to say the least—but he was a gentleman, and a gentleman apologized when he'd done something wrong.

No matter how painful it was.

"I beg your pardon most sincerely, Miss MacLeod. I should not have accused you when I couldn't remember what happened. Indeed, it seems as if you went to rather exceptional efforts to help me. I'm most appreciative."

She didn't reply at once, only regarded him with narrowed eyes, as if he were one of her curious plants. Devil's Claw, perhaps. Yes, that would be fitting.

"Are you saying, Lord Ballantyne, that you no longer intend to drag me before the magistrate?"

He hesitated. The magistrate was his bargaining chip, the one bit of leverage he had over her. As soon as he admitted he had no intention of seeing her taken up, she'd toss him out of her castle and bar the door behind him.

Yet he couldn't bring himself to carry on with the threat, all the same. Not now that he knew the truth. "You didn't commit a crime, Miss MacLeod. I have no reason to bring you before the magistrate."

She raised an eyebrow. "That's not quite the resounding affirmative I'd hoped to hear, my lord, but I suppose it will have to do." She wrapped the handkerchief around the monkshood, returned it to the basket, then drew her gloves off. "I daresay you'll be on your way back to London first thing tomorrow."

She turned away from him, but he caught her wrist before she could flee back to her bedchamber. "Not so fast, if you please, Miss MacLeod. There's still the matter of the missing treasure to resolve."

"There is no treasure, Lord Ballantyne, and thus, nothing to resolve."

She tugged at her arm, but he didn't release her. "Alas, it's not as simple as that. You see, despite my no longer believing you're a murderess, I haven't yet decided you're not a liar."

"Then we've reached an impasse, my lord." She lifted one shoulder in a shrug, but he could see her uncertainty, the shadows of hopelessness in her dark green eyes.

Catriona MacLeod was no fool. She must know it was only a matter of time before another lugger came, its body painted black, its dark sails billowing as it skimmed across Loch Dunvegan to the shores below Castle Cairncross.

She must know she and her sisters couldn't keep on as they had been. "I'm afraid an impasse isn't good enough, Miss MacLeod. I came to Dunvegan for my father's sake, to fulfill a promise to him, and that's exactly what I mean to do."

"Well, I suppose you could tear apart my castle, as you threatened to do earlier."

He hid a wince. He *had* threatened that, hadn't he? Perhaps it was time to cease making threats and extend an olive branch. "There's no reason for us to be at odds, Miss MacLeod. We could help each other, instead."

"Ah, but I'm afraid that's out of the question. You see, I don't trust you, Lord Ballantyne, and I don't see that changing anytime soon."

"What of it? I don't trust you either, Miss MacLeod, but deep suspicion and distrust is no reason there shouldn't be a fruitful partnership between us." He gave her a winning smile. "We want the same thing, after all."

She didn't return the smile. "What do you think I want, Lord Ballantyne?"

"To be free of the burden of the treasure, of course."

"I told you, there isn't—"

"Yes, I know you claim there is no treasure, but whether that's true or not, it won't keep the smugglers from attacking your castle. As long as they believe it's here, the luggers will keep coming. Stealthy things, luggers, with their black-painted bodies and dark sails. Difficult to detect, you know."

She didn't reply, merely regarded him in silence, her expression unreadable.

Surely, she must see how impossible her situation was. "You and your sisters will have no peace, Miss MacLeod, until the rumors are put to rest for good."

"Just what is it that you want from me, my lord?"

What did he want? It was a damned good question. It had been clear enough yesterday, before he'd seen her outside Baird's Pub, with that one rebellious lock of auburn hair fluttering in the breeze, but since then, nothing seemed to make sense anymore.

It must be the monkshood poisoning. Yes, it was certainly that, and *not* because the glow from the lantern behind her turned the loose wisps of her hair into a red-gold halo.

"I want to fulfill my promise to my father. I want the fortune back in the hands of the clans, where it belongs. And I want to help you and your sisters."

It was the truth. It hadn't been at first, but somehow, it was now.

"That's generous of you, my lord, but there's still one thing I don't understand."

"Yes? I'm listening, Miss MacLeod."

"I never said a single word to you about the luggers. How then, Lord Ballantyne, do you happen to know so much about the smugglers who attacked the castle?"

He gazed down into her dark green eyes, gleaming in the lantern light.

Such a clever little witch, but not as clever as she supposed.

"You sound suspicious, but you must know everyone in Dunvegan talks of little else. I hadn't been in the village a day before I'd heard dozens of wild stories about the MacLeod sisters and Castle Cairncross."

"Stories, yes. That's an apt word for them." She gave him a thin smile that didn't reach her eyes. "I wouldn't have taken you for a gossip, my lord."

"There's a grain of truth to every rumor, Miss MacLeod."

"A grain of truth is like a drop in the ocean, Lord Ballantyne. In the end, a single drop matters very little. Now, if you'd be so good as to unhand me. I'm weary and wish to return to my bedchamber."

CHAPTER II

Cat tugged at her arm again, and this time, Lord Ballantyne released her.

She marched across the floor of her workroom to the corridor beyond, her back straight, but underneath her night rail, her legs were wobbling. She hurried toward the stairs without daring to look back to see if he was following her.

But as she passed the arched window just outside her workroom, a sudden uneasiness made her pause and glance out into the darkness.

A shiver darted down her spine, as menacing as it was inexplicable.

She almost felt as if she were being watched, but everything appeared much as it always did on the other side of the glass, the sky a dark canopy over the waters of the loch, and below it, the ceaseless waves nipping at the rocks.

It was just her imagination, running wild with her again. She turned her back to the window and began to make her way downstairs to her bedchamber, but just as she reached the top step of the turret, something made her go back.

This time, when she peered out the window, she saw it. A movement, just at the edge of the horizon, where the sky met the water.

Something was there. Something that shouldn't be there.

It was nearly invisible, the black hull swallowed by the rolling swathe of gray water surrounding it, but she knew what to look for now. The flutter of a sail, dark but unmistakable on a moonlit night like tonight, and the subtle line of white foam where the hull broke against the waves. The blades of the oars, the water dripping from them catching the moonlight.

It was quite a way offshore still, but the wind was brisk, and it was advancing quickly, its destination unmistakable.

Another lugger, and it was coming directly toward Castle Cairncross.

She pressed closer to the glass, her knuckles going white, the rough edge of the casement scraping her fingers. Had she truly thought the last time would be the end of this?

What a fool she was.

There would *never* be an end to it. Lord Ballantyne was right. The boats would keep coming, again and again, until they got what they wanted.

As long as the rumors about the treasure persisted, the smugglers would haunt the shores of Castle Cairncross, and soon enough, the day would arrive when she and her sisters couldn't hold them off any longer.

God help them, then.

She squeezed her eyes closed, and after a few shaky breaths, she managed to push back the dark wave of panic crashing down on her. That day would come, yes, but it wouldn't be today. She, Freya, and Sorcha had done this before, and they could do it again.

They had to.

"Miss MacLeod?" Lord Ballantyne came up behind her, joining her at the window. As soon as he saw it, his entire body stiffened. "That's not a—"

"It is. Smugglers, judging by the dark color of the sails, and they're headed this way. I beg your pardon, my lord, but I must wake my sisters."

She went to hurry past him, but he caught her arm. "Wait, Miss MacLeod. What can I do?"

She hesitated, her gaze finding his. He'd offered to help them tonight, but it hadn't come from the goodness of his heart. She wasn't so naïve as to think his sudden selflessness had arisen from anything other than pure self-interest, but try as she might, she could find nothing but concern in those bright blue depths.

With one slow, indrawn breath, she made up her mind. For better or worse—*please let it not be worse*—she was going to have to trust him.

At least, for now.

There would be time enough for questioning Lord Ballantyne's motives, but that time wasn't tonight. Her every misgiving about him had vanished like a sandcastle swept away by the tide as soon as she caught sight of that dark sail flapping in the wind.

She no longer had the luxury of not trusting him.

"There's a jar of white powder on the shelf beneath the one where you found my mother's receipt book." She rummaged in her cloak pocket, found the iron key, and pressed it into his hand. "Bring it to my worktable, then go into my father's study and fetch the hat on the hook behind the door."

"His *hat*?" He stared down at her as if she'd lost her wits. "What in the world do you intend to do with—"

But she was already halfway down the turret stairs, her night rail clutched in her hand and the taste of blood on her tongue from biting down hard on her cheek. Down, down . . . dear God, had there ever been a more tedious staircase than this one, or a more treacherous one? The steps were narrow and uneven, worn in the center from the treads of countless feet over the past two hundred years.

"It's all right, just take care," she muttered to herself, forcing her feet to slow and take each step carefully. If she tumbled down the stairs, tonight's battle would be over before it began.

There was no time for her to break a limb. Not now.

Finally, after an endless eternity of stairs, she alighted on the third floor and ran down the hallway toward Sorcha's room. It would take some time to ready Athena and Artemis, so she'd wake Sorcha first and send her straight to the roof—

"What is it, Cat? What's happened?"

Cat stumbled to a halt in front of Sorcha's bedchamber. Her sister, with the strange sixth sense shared by all the Murdoch daughters, was already waiting on the threshold. "Is it another boat?"

"Yes, I'm afraid so. We'll need Athena and Artemis. Quickly, dearest."

Sorcha didn't waste any time. She merely nodded, turned, and darted back into her bedchamber.

"Cat?" The bedchamber door beside Sorcha's burst open, and Freya hurried into the hallway, rubbing the sleep from her eyes. "How much time do we have?"

"Not enough." There was never enough time for this. "I don't suppose there's another squall headed our way?"

"Not that I'm aware of, no." Freya had gone as white as her night rail, but she straightened her shoulders, and her gaze was steady as she met Cat's eyes. "I'll fetch Father's pistols."

"Another lantern, too, if you would, Freya." Sorcha emerged from her bedchamber, her cloak thrown over her shoulders and a lantern in her hand. "It's certain to be as dark as Hades up there."

Cat ran past Freya, who was hurrying toward the main staircase, but just as she'd ducked into the alcove that led to the turret stairs, she remembered something. "Wait!"

Freya froze at the top of the staircase, and Sorcha poked her head around the corner of the alcove. "What is it, Cat?"

"Lord Ballantyne is on the roof." The last thing she wished to explain at this moment was why she should have been up on the roof with him, alone, but if she didn't warn Sorcha, her sister might set the birds on him as soon as she caught sight of him.

"Lord Ballantyne!" Freya exchanged an incredulous look with Sorcha. "For pity's sake, Cat, what in the world is Lord Ballantyne doing on our roof in the middle of the night?"

"More to the point, what were you doing up there with him?" Sorcha asked, her eyebrow raised.

"He . . . I . . . there's no time for me to explain that now, but I assure you, it was perfectly innocent. I'll tell you about it later."

Or *never* if she had her way. She couldn't even explain it to herself.

She brushed past Sorcha, calling over her shoulder as she darted up the stairs with Sorcha on her heels. "Hurry with the pistols, Freya!"

Lord Ballantyne was standing at the perimeter wall when they came through the door, staring out at the loch. Sorcha didn't spare him a word or a glance but hurried around the corner toward the flat space on the roof where she kept the birds' box perches.

"How close have they come?" Cat joined him at the wall and peered out over the water, sending up a quick prayer of thanks that the moonlight had made it possible for them to see the approaching lugger at all.

They'd been lucky again, but their luck was bound to run dry. Sooner or later a day would come when they got no warning at all.

"Close enough to see the men's hands on the oars. I can't quite tell, but from here it looks like there are half a dozen of them. Perhaps more."

Half a dozen? Dear God.

"You and your sisters need to leave the castle at once, Miss MacLeod. It's not safe for you here. I'll escort you into Dunvegan myself. No one will dare question your presence."

"No." If they left now, they'd never return. She knew it down to the marrow of her bones. "We're not leaving, my lord. If you'd prefer to go—"

"Don't be ridiculous, Miss MacLeod." He drew himself up with all the offended dignity of a gentleman whose honor had just been impugned. "Despite what you may think of me, I am *not* the sort of gentleman who abandons three helpless young ladies in need."

"Helpless, Lord Ballantyne?" She raised an eyebrow.

Incredibly, a small smile rose to his lips. "Perhaps not. Very well, then. What do you intend to do?"

"The only thing we haven't yet tried, my lord." She met his gaze, the words hovering on her lips. As soon as she said them, he'd think she'd gone mad.

Perhaps she had. "We're going to haunt the castle."

"Haunt the . . ." he broke off, shaking his head. "Never mind. I haven't the faintest idea what you mean by that, but whatever you intend to do, it must be done quickly. The wind is brisk, and it's blowing west. Those villains will be on your shores before you know it."

"I'm aware. Sorcha is readying the birds. Freya's gone to fetch my father's pistols, but I hope it won't come to that." It hadn't, yet. They'd managed to frighten off their attackers before the boats could reach the shoreline.

But half a dozen men! What would it take to frighten half a dozen smugglers away?

She was about to find out. They all were.

"I told you I'd help you, Miss MacLeod, and I meant it, so perhaps you'd be so good as to explain how you mean to haunt your castle."

"I've something in mind." She turned and hurried back into her workroom, where she found the jar of powder she'd asked for and her father's hat waiting for her on her worktable.

"That doesn't surprise me in the least," Lord Ballantyne muttered, following her into her workroom. "I confess I'm rather eager to see what you'll do with your father's hat." He plucked it up from the table and turned it this way and that, frowning. "It's not the usual sort of thing the smugglers wear, is it?"

"No, but my father wasn't the usual sort of smuggler." Rory hadn't been the usual sort of anything. His hat was proof of that.

Many of the smugglers wore simple woolen caps, but some had adopted the blue coats and navy blue or black tricorn hats the American naval officers wore.

Not her father, however. Rory had never been one to follow in another's footsteps. No, nothing would suit her father but a French military cavalier hat. The left side of the brim was rakishly cocked, with an extravagant white plume tucked into a silver corded hatband on one side and adorned with a square silver buckle. For the most part, these sorts of hats were made of felt, but Rory's was made of supple black leather.

It was a distinctive hat, one recognized everywhere by villagers, harbor masters, and excise men alike as the hat that graced the head of the legendary smuggler, Rory MacLeod.

Which was lucky for them, as it happened.

It was a bit crazed, what she had in mind for the hat. There was every chance that it would fail spectacularly, but they couldn't count on the weather to assist them, and rumors already abounded about Sorcha's sparrowhawks. Artemis and Athena were still frightening enough, but they no longer offered the advantage of surprise.

Hence, the haunting.

It had taken her ages to prepare this. She'd spent long weeks digging in the woods, then she'd undertaken the backbreaking work of dampening, turning, and grinding until at last she'd amassed a large pile of shredded, rotting plant matter.

Then, she'd painstakingly processed it, until at last, she'd produced the jar of white powder sitting on her workroom table.

All her efforts had come down to a single jar of powdered phosphorus. There was nothing left to do now but pray it would work.

"If you'd be so good as to fetch me that large bin, Lord Ballantyne?" She nodded toward a copper tub in one corner of her workroom.

"Delighted, of course, Miss MacLeod."

He fetched the tub and placed it in front of her on her worktable while she darted over to another shelf and took down a large glass jar filled with honey, muttering under her breath. "How much is the proper amount? Perhaps I should have used the egg yolk, instead—"

"Er, Miss MacLeod?"

"Yes?" Cat twisted the top off the jar of honey and dumped half of it into the tub. "Oh, dear. That looks like too much, doesn't it?"

"That depends. Just what is it you're doing with it? Making scones?"

"Scones? Why would I be making scones at a time like this, my lord? I'm making paint. Phosphorus paint, to be specific."

His eyebrows shot up, and he moved closer, leaning over the worktable. "Are you, indeed? I've read about this. That German fellow—the alchemist. What was his name? Damned if I can recall."

"Hennig Brand, and he's a chemist, not an alchemist. Alchemy isn't a true science, much to Herr Brand's disappointment." She eyed the jar of powder. How much should she use? She didn't like to waste it, but if she used too little, it wouldn't glow properly.

"Yes, that's the fellow. A bit of a strange one, Brand. He

thought he could turn base metals into gold by boiling—" he broke off, staring at her, aghast.

"Boiling urine, Lord Ballantyne? I believe that's what you were going to say, but you may rest easy, my lord. This phosphorus is made from plants."

"Plants," he repeated, shaking his head. "I might have known."

"Rotted plant matter, rather. It took me weeks and a mountain of detritus to make this small jar of phosphorus powder. I've dragged half the woods up here to my workroom. I only hope it will be enough."

He was staring at her, his mouth agape. "How the devil did you work out that you could make phosphorus powder from plants?"

"I don't know for certain that I can, yet." She opened the jar of phosphorus powder and carefully added it to her honey, one teaspoon at a time. "Have you ever wandered through the woods at night, my lord?"

"No. There are no woods in London." None to speak of, anyway.

"That's a great pity." She gave her concoction a stir, then paused to assess it. "It needs more powder, I think. If you had ventured into the woods at night, my lord, you would have noticed that some plants glow."

"*Glow*? What plants?"

"All manner of plants. Bishop's weed, night phlox, white campion. *Ipomoea alba* is a particularly beautiful one, although I confess, I've only seen pictures of it."

"Ipomo—"

"*Ipomoea alba*. Moonflower, my lord. It's too cold for them to grow here, which is rather tragic. I'd dearly love to see one. If I ever have a conservatory of my own, I'll grow dozens of them. There!" She finished stirring. "What do you think, Lord Ballantyne? Is it glowing?"

He leaned closer and peered into the tub. "By God, it is.

Nicely done, Miss MacLeod! But what do you intend to do with it?"

"Cat!" Sorcha hurried into the workroom. Freya was behind her, carrying two pistols. "Come quickly. They're altogether too close for comfort now."

"Yes, I'm nearly done!" She yanked open one of the drawers in her workbench and snatched up the wide paintbrush she'd stolen from Freya's art supplies. Working quickly, she smeared the phosphorus paint over the leather hat from the top to the brim, sending globs of glowing honey flying everywhere.

Then she hurried to the door with the hat balanced on her fingertips, pausing only to snatch up a walking stick she'd left in the corner.

"Please let this work, please let this work." She repeated the words like a prayer as she ran around to the other side of the roof, where Sorcha and Freya were waiting for her.

"Is that . . . oh, Cat!" Freya covered her mouth with her hand, her eyes wide. "How in the world did you do it? It's magnificent!"

And it was. She'd been worried it wouldn't glow brightly enough, but once the moonlight caught it, it was as if it had come to life, casting an eerie, faintly green glow.

"Thank God. Athena and Artemis are doing a good job of it, but the boat is still coming our way." Sorcha took the hat from Cat and plopped it on top of the walking stick. "Do you suppose they're close enough to see it yet?"

"I don't think you want them any closer." Lord Ballantyne held out his hand. "Here, give it to me, Miss Sorcha. I'm the tallest. Douse those lanterns, if you would, Miss Freya. It will spoil the effect if they see us, and the glow will be brighter without the light interfering with it."

Sorcha handed over the walking stick with the hat perched on top of it, then she, Cat, and Freya stepped back into the shadows, nearer to the wall of the castle, and watched as Lord

Ballantyne marched back and forth in front of the perimeter wall, waving the hat about.

"Does it look like a haunting?"

"It certainly looks strange." Freya was staring at the hat with wide eyes. "Perhaps it looks haunted from a distance?"

Sorcha crept forward and peered over the edge of the wall just as a shout came from the loch below them. "I think it's . . . oh, no. No! They're still coming!"

No! Surely not. Cat rushed toward the wall, her heart racing.

But it was true. The men aboard the lugger were calling out to each other, and clearly uneasy, but they weren't frightened enough to turn back.

They kept coming, closer and closer—

"Here, take this, Miss Sorcha." Lord Ballantyne thrust the walking stick into Sorcha's hands and disappeared into the workroom without another word.

Cat watched his broad back retreating, and a wave of despair washed over her.

Was he abandoning them?

She peered into the darkness, hoping with everything inside her that the lugger had turned back, but it was there still, close enough she could see it plainly, coming toward them more quickly now.

How had they ever imagined they could do this? They should have left the castle an hour ago when she'd first spotted the boat, just as Lord Ballantyne had advised, and now it was too late.

Before she could wholly succumb to her despair and sink to her knees in exhaustion and defeat, Lord Ballantyne came dashing back out. He was wearing her father's coat and carrying the copper tub in his hands. "Paint the coat, Miss MacLeod. Quickly!"

"Paint the . . ." Why, it was brilliant! She snatched the paintbrush. "There's not much paint left."

"It's all right. Start with the neck, then paint across my

shoulders and down my arms. That will give the outline of a man. If there's any left, paint my chest with it."

Cat was already painting, her hands shaking, while Lord Ballantyne turned this way and that, crouching down so she could reach him.

"There! That's the best I can do."

"It's perfect." Sorcha stood back to survey the effect and gave a quick nod. "Go on, then, Lord Ballantyne, and do your best to be terrifying, won't you?"

He didn't answer, but there was no doubt he'd taken Sorcha's words to heart, because he plopped the hat on top of his head, and then, in the next instant he'd leaped up onto the ledge of the wall.

Freya darted forward with a gasp. "What are you doing? If you should fall, you'll smash your skull to bits on the rocks below! Lord Ballantyne, I must insist you come down from there at once!"

"Not to fear, Miss Freya. I have excellent balance."

And he *did*. He strode back and forth across the narrow ledge as if he were strolling through a park, waving his arms about, and stamping his feet.

"Good God." Sorcha cast an admiring glance at him. "If that doesn't frighten them away, nothing will."

Cat stared up at him, her mouth agape. He looked positively enormous with his broad shoulders and long legs, and her father's hat atop his dark hair, the white plume waving wildly in the wind.

Another series of shouts rose up from the loch below, louder this time. Lord Ballantyne continued to prance about on top of the ledge like some sort of crazed ghost, and Cat didn't know whether to fall into a swoon or burst out laughing.

Why, the man was mad! The mad marquess.

"They're turning back!" Sorcha jumped up and down, breathless with triumph. "My God, it worked! They're turning back!"

And so, they were. A haunted hat might not be enough to frighten off half a dozen hard-bitten smugglers, but it seemed that an actual ghost was.

The ghost of Rory MacLeod.

Once he was certain they weren't coming back, Lord Ballantyne jumped down from the ledge in one graceful leap, as cool as you please.

"Congratulations, Miss MacLeod." He swept the hat from his head and offered her an extravagant bow. "Castle Cairncross is now haunted."

CHAPTER 12

"Much to my surprise, Lord Ballantyne, it seems you aren't utterly useless, after all."

Sorcha MacLeod was lounging comfortably in a window seat as if terrorizing smugglers with the pretend ghost of her dead father was an everyday occurrence like brushing her hair or lacing her boots.

At Castle Cairncross, perhaps it *was*.

Hamish shed Rory's hat and coat and wiped the beads of perspiration from his forehead. What was he meant to do after masquerading as a dead smuggler? Haunting a castle wasn't an everyday occurrence for him, and with the way his legs were wobbling, it was a miracle he hadn't tumbled off that ledge and . . .

How had Freya MacLeod put it? Oh, yes. Smashed his skull to bits.

Grisly chit.

"Those birds." He dropped down onto one of the stools by Catriona's workbench. "Where did they come from? I've never seen anything like that before."

"Artemis and Athena? They're wonderful, aren't they?" Sorcha swung the leg dangling from the edge of the window seat back and forth. "I trained them that attack maneuver myself."

"Of course you did." What else was there to say to such a declaration? "Er, well done?"

She gave him a toothy smile. "*I* think so."

He knew about the birds—Dougal and Clyde had babbled incessantly about them, in fact, although in their telling, there'd been dozens of them, and they'd been monstrous things, with a call so deafening it scrambled a man's brains in his head and razor-like claws that could tear flesh from his body. Even now, the hideous attack birds were a feature of the story they told down at the Lamb and Fig every night.

He might have known the horde of birds would turn out to be two small sparrowhawks.

Still, the wild stories did have a grain of truth to them. A single grain of truth, a drop in the ocean amidst the dozens of lies that had been told about the MacLeod sisters since their father died and the first lugger appeared on the shores of Castle Cairncross.

The lugger *he'd* sent.

There was no sorcery at work here. Just falconry.

It was the nature of rumors to exaggerate the truth, of course, but he'd never seen quite so egregious an example of it as what had befallen the MacLeod sisters.

There were no witches at Castle Cairncross. Just three young ladies defending their home. Three *clever* young ladies, with remarkable, but not mythical abilities.

Although none of this explained the sudden storm Dougal and Clyde had described on the night they'd approached the castle. "What about the storm, the night the first lugger came?"

"You mean the storm with the torrential rains and thunder so powerful it nearly tore a gash in the sky? The one with the unholy lightning strikes that could only be the work of the devil himself?" Sorcha snorted. "I suppose someone in the village told you about that. They do love their stories."

He glanced at Catriona, who'd taken the place beside Sorcha on the window seat. She hadn't said a word since they'd all returned to the workroom, and she didn't say a word now, but kept her face turned toward the window, the moonlight caressing the curve of her cheek and the stubborn edge of her jaw.

She looked terribly small, huddled in the corner of the window seat. Small and lonely, her slender shoulders sagging under her burdens. Everything about her, from those white cheeks to her slumped posture, spoke of exhaustion and defeat.

An odd sensation rippled through him as he gazed at her—not fear, precisely, but something akin to it.

How little she weighed, and how small she'd felt that day in the woods, when he'd caught her in his arms as she was falling, how thin and delicate the bones in her back. If those scoundrels who'd tried to attack the castle tonight had gotten inside, they would have broken her, snapped those fragile bones in their brutal grip.

He gazed at her face, at the long, dark lashes brushing her cheekbones, the tender curve of her lower lip, and the strange feeling intensified, his thoughts bouncing from one side of his skull to the other, as if they were puppets dangling from a string.

Damn it, what were she and her sisters doing in this castle still, without so much as a servant to protect them? They should have left months ago after the first boat came.

Before he could voice that thought into words, another arrived on its heels.

Why hadn't he noticed before how pale and fine her skin was? And why couldn't he stop wondering what it would be like to take her into his arms and bury his face in the tempting curve between her shoulder and neck?

Without thinking, he began to rise to his feet, to go to her, but Sorcha's voice broke the silence and brought him to his senses.

"Didn't you know, my lord? Freya here can conjure storms from a clear blue sky! It's remarkable, isn't it?" Sorcha gave a short bark of laughter, but there was no amusement in it. It was a cold, hard sound, like a fist slamming onto a table. "So remarkable as to be impossible, but that hasn't stopped the waggling tongues. Why let common sense get in the way of a good rumor?"

"It was a coincidence, nothing more." Freya was gazing out the window, her legs drawn up underneath her and her arms hugging her knees, her cheeks as pale as the moonlight shining on the waters of Loch Dunvegan below.

"Coincidence? My dearest girl, why explain it as a coincidence, when sorcery is so much more titillating?"

Freya, who seemed to lack her younger sister's sangfroid, said nothing in reply to this but went on in a dull, flat tone. "The lugger happened to come into the loch just as a squall was breaking over Skye. Such squalls are not at all unusual, particularly in the summer months. I've seen dozens of storms just like the one that night. There's nothing magical or mythical about them."

That was it then. A sudden storm and a few trained sparrowhawks had spawned dozens of rumors that would likely follow the MacLeod sisters for years.

If they didn't see them sent to jail first. Not for being witches, as the Crown no longer credited accounts of wicked men and women consorting with the devil. Indeed, it was a crime for a British citizen to accuse another of having magical powers or practicing witchcraft.

It was not, however, a crime to accuse another citizen of *pretending* to be a witch.

A fine distinction, yes, but it applied here. The sisters couldn't legally be hunted and executed for practicing witchcraft, since the Crown's official position was that witches didn't exist, but it remained a crime to claim to have such powers.

The MacLeod sisters could be taken up as charlatans. It was no small matter, either. Such a crime could see them locked up in Bridewell for up to a year.

"You see, Lord Ballantyne, the damage a few gossiping tongues have caused."

Hamish had been staring at Rory's hat, which was sitting on the table in front of him, but his head jerked up at the sound of

Catriona's soft voice. She'd turned away from the window and seemed to be trying to rouse herself.

"I can't regret that storm. It was exceedingly fortunate for us that it came up right when it did. If it hadn't . . ." she trailed off with a shudder, but there was no need for her to say another word.

They could all finish the thought in their own heads.

If that storm hadn't come up right when it did, the boat would have landed on the shoreline just beneath the castle. From there, it would have been only a matter of moments before the smugglers were inside.

The MacLeod sisters would have been obliged to shoot them then, or else find themselves at the smugglers' mercy. Of course, the smugglers in question had been Dougal and Clyde who, for all their boasting about their piratical adventures, would never have laid as much as a finger on any of the sisters.

But Catriona, Sorcha, and Freya couldn't have known that. Smugglers weren't upon the whole, celebrated for their compassionate nature, and for all that Dougal and Clyde weren't murderers, there was no question whatsoever that they would have taken Castle Cairncross apart stone by stone in search of the treasure.

He'd threatened to do the same thing, just this morning. Was it any wonder she hadn't wanted him in her castle? To her and her sisters, there was no difference between him and the smugglers. Given the circumstances, it was a bloody miracle Catriona hadn't left him in the woods to die.

"We can't keep going on like this." Freya didn't turn to face them but continued to stare out the window. "I didn't think we'd succeed in frightening them away this time. It took ages for them to go."

"But they did go, Freya," Sorcha said. "That's the thing to remember."

"This time, yes, but what about next time, Sorcha?" Catriona shook her head. "Freya is right. It will only become more difficult as the rumors continue to spread. We owe our escape this time to Lord Ballantyne, but it's mere chance he happened to be here, and that he fit into Rory's coat."

"Smugglers are an arrogant lot." Sorcha leapt down from the window seat and began pacing from one end of the workroom to the other. "Soon enough it will become a competition to see which of them is man enough to capture Rory MacLeod's treasure. It won't be long before every smuggler in Britain is floating about in Loch Dunvegan, waiting for the chance to storm the castle."

"But where are we meant to go from here?" Freya's stricken glance moved from Sorcha to Catriona. "We've just orchestrated a haunting, for pity's sake! What is there left for us to do? Explode something? Set the castle on fire?"

Sorcha stopped pacing. "Not a fire, but an explosion could be rather amusing."

"Stop it, Sorcha!" Freya rose to her feet, her hands clenched into fists. "There's nothing amusing about any of this. Stop behaving as if none of it matters."

Hamish stared at her. Freya was a shy, quiet little thing, much more so than either of her sisters. He would have said the chit didn't have a bit of fight in her, but she did have a few barbs on her tongue, after all.

She was a MacLeod, all right.

"We can't remain here, Cat." Freya reached for Cat's hand and pressed it between hers. "It's only a matter of time before someone gets hurt. I don't like it any more than either of you do, but . . ." She glanced between her two sisters, swallowing. "We need to leave Castle Cairncross."

Sorcha snorted. "Why, what a wonderful idea, Freya. There's just the tiniest problem. We haven't a penny to our names, and we don't have anywhere else to go."

"The Duffys will take us—"

"No." Cat's voice was quiet, but final. "We can't ask that of them, Freya. It's gone too far with the villagers for us to drag the Duffys into this mess. They'd never refuse us if we did ask, but they'd pay a price for helping us."

"But there's no other way, Cat."

"Yes, there is." Slowly, Catriona rose to her feet. "There is one other way."

For a long moment, no one spoke. Sorcha and Freya looked at each other, their eyebrows raised, but Catriona wasn't looking at either of them.

She was looking at him.

And he . . . God, he couldn't take his eyes off her. Had it only been yesterday he'd dismissed her as a tiny, insignificant thing when he'd seen her outside the window of Baird's Pub?

She doesn't look like she's up to summoning so much as a butterfly . . .

Now, he couldn't imagine how he'd ever been so blind.

The way she'd fought for her sisters tonight, and for her home, her cleverness and bravery, and that ingenious bit of trickery with the phosphorus paint. He'd known many ladies in his time, many of them beautiful, and many of them brilliant, but he'd never seen anything like Catriona MacLeod.

"Lord Ballantyne? You said earlier you believed we might be able to help each other."

"I did, yes." Was she considering it? Although he couldn't say why, he found himself rising to his feet. "And I meant it, Miss MacLeod."

"You said you think we want the same thing, my lord, and perhaps we do, or nearly so." She eyed him, her lips pursed. "But given our earlier encounter, I'm hesitant to trust you."

Well, he could hardly argue with that reasoning. He'd done nothing since he'd regained consciousness but make accusations and threats, and that was after he'd chased her through the woods.

He hadn't precisely covered himself with glory, but perhaps it wasn't too late to acquit himself as a gentleman ought to do. "Our fathers were friends at one time, Miss MacLeod. This business with the treasure involves them both. I'm convinced the only way we'll unravel this mystery is to confide in each other."

"I don't relish the idea of confiding anything to you, my lord, but I don't see any way out of this mess without your help. I'd like to propose a partnership of sorts, but—"

"A partnership, with *him*?" Sorcha glared at him as if he were something unspeakable that she'd just scraped from the bottom of her boot. "For pity's sake, Cat, he's part of the problem!"

"He is, indeed, and I daresay a partnership between us will prove uncomfortable, but I have reason to think he's right about our fathers. I think there was some sort of pact between them."

"Oh? What made you change your mind, Miss MacLeod?" He drew closer to her and studied her face in the dim light.

"I, ah . . ." She hesitated for an instant, but then said in a rush, "I found something. Something unexpected."

"Is that so?" He drew closer still, his heart beginning to hammer with anticipation in his chest. "Something like a treasure, here inside the castle? In the secret chamber behind those closed doors, perhaps?"

"Secret chamber? My, you do have a fanciful imagination. Or perhaps you've just been listening to village gossip. I'm sorry to disappoint you, my lord, but I already told you my father didn't bring any treasure back to Castle Cairncross."

She held his gaze steadily, not a hint of a lie hiding in those green depths, but even so, he wasn't sure if he believed her. Her father had been a liar and a thief, after all, and she was a MacLeod, just as he'd been.

And, of course, she had every reason to lie.

But it no longer mattered. This was an ancient castle, and a large one, with endless nooks and crannies where three wily chits could tuck away a fortune in gold coins. Even if the treasure was hidden here inside the castle—and he was no longer convinced it was—he might look forever, and never find it.

As for taking the castle apart piece by piece, the idea no longer appealed. He needed Catriona MacLeod, whether he liked it or not. "Then you know where the treasure is?"

"No. Not exactly. I didn't believe there was a treasure at all, until . . ." She hesitated, biting her lip.

"Until?"

She let out a breath. "Until our conversation in the library this afternoon."

Ah, now this was getting interesting. "Oh? And why is that, Miss MacLeod?"

Again, she hesitated, but then she gave a decisive little nod, as if making up her mind about something. She reached into the pocket of her cloak and withdrew the iron key. "Wait here, please. I'll return in a moment."

She marched to the doors set into the back wall of her work-room and fitted the key to the lock. The door opened with a groan, and she disappeared into the other room.

He glanced at Sorcha and Freya, but Freya avoided his eyes, and Sorcha only shrugged. "Don't ask us. We haven't the least idea what she's up to. Cat has more secrets than a bawd in a Covent Garden brothel."

A *bawd*? God above.

"For pity's sake, Sorcha!" Freya put her hand on her sister's arm. "Hush, will you?"

Sorcha MacLeod was grinning like a madwoman, and there was no telling what she might have said next if Catriona hadn't squeezed through the narrow opening of the door, then closed it with a thud, and locked it behind her.

When she stepped into the circle of light cast by the lantern, she had a small, green velvet pouch in her hand. She pulled the drawstring and turned the pouch over.

Three gold coins spilled out and landed on the worktable with a soft clink.

"Are those . . ." He raised his gaze to hers.

"Yes."

He drew closer, his breath held, but he already knew what he was going to find.

And there they were, atop the scarred worktable, gleaming dull gold in the moonlight. He stared down at them, his heart suddenly pounding in his chest.

"Louis d'Or ten-pieces."

"Louis d'Or ten-pieces, yes." Catriona reached for the lantern on the worktable and turned up the wick. It flared to life, bathing the worktable in a bright glow. "Check the dates, my lord."

He picked up one of the coins and held it up to the lamplight, and just as he'd suspected, it was identical to his father's coin, with the year sixteen hundred forty proudly displayed in the bottom center of it, right under the carving of Louis XIII.

"Is that Father's gold ten-piece?" Freya had abandoned her perch on the window seat, and now crowded closer to the worktable. "I don't understand. He only has one coin, doesn't he?"

Sorcha was staring down at the coins with a frown, as if she thought her father's single coin had somehow spawned a second and third when she hadn't been watching them. "Where did the other two come from?"

Catriona shook her head. "I'm not sure. I just discovered them tonight. I came upstairs to check the date on Father's coin after Lord Ballantyne showed me his father's Louis d'Or gold ten-piece in the library this afternoon."

Freya gasped. "You mean there's a fourth one?"

"Yes. Curious, isn't it? Perhaps you'd be so good as to show your coin to my sisters, my lord."

It was only fair. She'd shown him hers, after all. Hamish reached into his breeches pocket, withdrew his own coin, tossed it onto the table with the other three, then turned to Catriona and gestured to the coins on the table. "May I have a closer look, Miss MacLeod?"

She nodded. He picked them up one at a time and studied each one carefully. All four of the coins were identical, just as she'd said. "You do realize this can't be a coincidence, do you not, Miss MacLeod?"

"I don't believe in coincidences, my lord."

"But what does this mean?" Freya was staring down at the coin in her palm. "Someone must have brought the other two coins into the castle."

"Yes. I'm not sure who, but I know where we can find out."

Freya laid the coin on the worktable, and they stood there for some time in silence, looking at the four coins. They might have remained that way until the sun rose if the distant chiming of the grandfather clock hadn't reached them in the workroom.

It was two o'clock in the morning.

Freya stirred. "We'd better rest now, while we can. Goodness only knows what challenges tomorrow will bring." She took Sorcha's elbow and led her to the door, but paused on the threshold, and glanced over her shoulder. She had the most curious expression on her face. "Goodnight, Cat. My lord."

Then she and Sorcha were gone, leaving him alone with Catriona.

He opened his mouth to say . . . something. That they should retire to their beds, perhaps, or something similarly unnecessary, but he was strangely tongue-tied. So, he said nothing, but neither could he make himself look away from her.

There was a daub of phosphorescent paint on her face. Just a small one, a tiny glowing circle of white. If she'd been smiling, it would have been right at the place where the corner of her mouth met her cheek.

He'd never seen her smile. To be fair, she had little to smile about, but if a smile were to find its way to her lips, what would it look like? And how ridiculous was it that he was certain he'd dream of her smile tonight without having ever seen it before?

"I intend to pay a call on the Duffys tomorrow, my lord."

He dragged his gaze away from her mouth, clearing his throat. "The, ah . . . the Duffys, Miss MacLeod?"

"Yes. Our former butler and housekeeper." She didn't look at him but busied herself picking up the coins still scattered across the table. "I assume you wish to accompany me?"

"Indeed, I do. If we're to be partners, there can be no secrets between us."

He expected her to argue, but she only nodded. "I'll meet you in the entryway at nine o'clock tomorrow morning then, Lord Ballantyne."

With that, she slid three of the coins into the green velvet pouch and held out the fourth one to him.

He took it, trapping it in his palm. The gold was still warm from her fingers.

She tucked the pouch into the palm of her hand and made her way to the door.

"Wait!" he called, just as she was about to disappear into the corridor.

She turned. "Yes?"

"Why did you decide on a truce between us? What made you change your mind?"

It was a foolish question. He already knew she'd say a truce with him was the last thing she wanted, and she'd only agreed because she had no other choice.

But he wanted to hear her say it, all the same, if for no other reason than it might shake him loose from this perplexing spell that had fallen over him.

But Catriona MacLeod was nothing if not surprising, and this was no exception.

She didn't say that. She didn't say anything at all, but just when he'd reconciled himself to yet another unanswered question, she murmured, "You helped us tonight, Lord Ballantyne."

"Yes?" Had she imagined he'd stand by and let them be overrun by smugglers? What sort of monster did she take him—

"You didn't have to."

For an instant, he bristled, but the ill-tempered retort on his lips died when she met his eyes. What he read in those green depths . . . well, he understood her, then.

She wasn't saying they hadn't needed or wanted his help. She was pointing out that he'd had no obligation at all to help them, yet he'd done it anyway.

In her own oblique way, she was thanking him. It should have gratified him, but instead, it only emphasized once again how few people had lifted a finger to help the MacLeod sisters since this mess began.

"Nine o'clock, Lord Ballantyne." She turned once again to the door. "Don't keep me waiting."

Chapter 13

"Here you are, at last, Miss MacLeod. I'd begun to fear you'd forgotten me."

Cat paused on the third-floor landing. Lord Ballantyne was standing at the bottom of the stairs, his face upturned, and one imperious eyebrow raised.

Goodness, he did take up a great deal of space, didn't he? Castle Cairncross boasted soaring ceilings, a massive carved mahogany staircase, and a sweeping stone floor, yet somehow, he managed to dwarf it all.

The moment he spoke, he was all she could see.

Forget him? No, there was no forgetting *him*. A lady didn't forget to brush her hair, or lace her boots, or don a proper pair of gloves before leaving the house, and she didn't forget that a tall, broad-shouldered, blue-eyed marquess would be waiting for her when she emerged from her bedchamber of a morning.

Especially not *this* marquess. Not after what had happened last night.

His dark hair was mussed this morning, and the bottle-green coat she'd once thought so elegant was now rumpled and shapeless. His boots were muddy, and what had once been a flawless cravat was now in sad disarray. He was wrinkled and besmirched, and he was frowning as well, his brow furrowed as he glared down at the pocket watch in his hand.

He looked more like a cantankerous schoolmaster than a fashionable aristocrat. There was absolutely no reason, then, that her heart should be fluttering like a panicked bird behind her breastbone at the sight of him.

It was ridiculous, and she wouldn't allow it.

He'd done them a good turn last night, yes. There was no denying it. No doubt, some would even claim he'd behaved heroically, leaping up onto the ledge as he'd done, and risking his own neck to frighten away their intruders.

Not *her*, of course, but other, more impressionable people.

He did seem to have won over Freya with his ghostly antics last night. Even Sorcha, who wasn't the sort of lady to be impressed by anyone or anything, had grudgingly admitted he wasn't entirely useless. It was high praise, coming from Sorcha.

She was grateful to him, of course. Fetching her father's coat just when they'd been on the verge of ruin had been a stroke of genius, and the way he'd leapt onto the ledge without the slightest hesitation had been impressive.

Stirring, even. The man had exceptional, ah . . . balance. She wasn't going to deny credit where it was due.

But gratitude wasn't trust, and she *didn't* trust Lord Ballantyne.

No matter how adorably boyish he looked this morning, with the locks of his silky dark hair standing upright at the back of his head, and—

"I believe we agreed to meet at nine o'clock." He peered down at the face of his pocket watch. "You're late."

"Late? Nonsense." She swept down the staircase with as much dignity as she could command. Just as she reached the bottom step and joined him in the entryway, the grandfather clock struck the nine o'clock hour. "It's just nine now."

"It's a minute past nine, according to my pocket watch."

"Your watch is wrong, my lord."

"Don't be absurd." He tapped the watch face, frowning down at it. "It's a Thomas Mudge."

"Is that a spot of blood on your coat?" She squinted at the dark red speck.

Oh, dear, it did look very much like blood.

"It is, indeed, Miss MacLeod. Noses bleed rather copiously when they're struck, I'm afraid. I considered leaving my coat behind, but a gentleman does not make a call on their neighbor without a proper coat."

Her lips gave a traitorous twitch. My, he was every inch the fashionable London lord, wasn't he? "I daresay Duffy and Mrs. Duffy will appreciate your, ah, sartorial efforts, my lord, but if you're at all uncomfortable, I'm perfectly able to make this call on my own."

"That didn't take long, did it?" He snapped his watch closed, tucked it into his pocket, and turned to her, that haughty eyebrow ticking up another notch. "You've only just come down the stairs, and already you're trying to wriggle out of our agreement. Shame on you, madam. You disappoint me excessively."

"I'm not trying to wriggle out of anything, Lord Ballantyne." Not entirely, that is. "I only thought you might prefer to—"

"I prefer we get on our way, Miss MacLeod." He offered her an extravagant bow and opened the front door for her. "Shall we?"

She stepped outside, stifling her sigh.

They had reached a truce of sorts last night, but it was a truce of necessity, not inclination. Those were the most uneasy sorts of truces, and perhaps it would be best if it remained that way.

It wouldn't do to become too comfortable with him. It would only muddy the waters.

She and Lord Ballantyne weren't friends, and they wouldn't be friends once this was over, either. This was a business arrangement, nothing more, and she'd do well to remember that whenever he turned that charming grin on her.

But she had agreed to the truce and given her suspicions about the Louis d'Or ten-pieces, it was only fair for him to accompany her on her visit to Duffy this morning.

Although his presence would be difficult to explain—

"Have you decided which lie to tell yet?" he asked, as if he'd read her mind. "Distant cousin, or a hopeful suitor, perhaps?"

Suitor? She held back a snort.

Duffy was getting on in years, but he would have had to have lost his wits entirely to believe any of the wicked MacLeod witches had a suitor. "We'll tell them you're a friend of my father who happened to be in Dunvegan."

"Does anyone ever *happen* to be in Dunvegan, Miss MacLeod?" He shot her a grin. "It's not the sort of place one stumbles upon, is it?"

She didn't *want* to smile back at him, but her lips insisted upon curving upward. "Not often, no."

"May I carry your basket for you, Miss MacLeod?" He nodded at her marketing basket. She'd removed the broken handle and replaced it with a bit of thick leather cording.

"That's not necessary, Lord—"

"I insist." He grasped the piece of cording and slid the basket gently from her arm. "Good Lord, it's heavy. What have you got in here? Not monkshood, I hope."

" 'Eye of newt, and toe of frog, wool of bat, and tongue of dog,' of course." She gave him a sly smile. Perhaps it was the fresh air or the watery sunshine that had broken through the clouds, but as soon as they'd stepped outside the castle, her spirits had lifted.

"Good God." He stopped on the pathway and held the basket out to her with another one of those irrepressible grins. "Perhaps you should carry it after all."

She laughed. "You've nothing to fear, my lord. It's just a few jars of Freya's orange marmalade for Mrs. Duffy, some Dundee cake, a wee dram of whisky for Duffy's achy joints, and the last of the bay leaf from my mother's kitchen garden."

He lifted the cloth and peered into the basket. "So it is. How kind of you, Miss MacLeod."

"One doesn't pay a call on a friend in Dunvegan without bringing a gift, Lord Ballantyne." Skye wasn't London, but it wasn't as if they were utter savages.

"How civilized of Dunvegan." He tucked the cloth back in place with an amiable nod. "I approve wholeheartedly."

They made their way down the castle's drive in an easy silence, skirting the woods in favor of the pathway that led toward the west side of Dunvegan.

Away from the village, thank goodness.

She'd promised Glynnis she'd bring that liniment in today, but she couldn't bear another trip into town just yet. She hadn't made up the liniment, in any case. She'd have to do it tonight. No doubt she'd be awake by midnight, wandering the castle just as she always did.

Then again, last night she'd slept as soundly as an infant cradled in its mother's arms.

It made no sense that last night, of all nights, should be the first in months she'd slipped easily into a dreamless slumber. She'd reconciled herself to a sleepless night after that harrowing scene with the smugglers.

At the very least, she'd expected to be tossing and turning with nightmares about an enormous, glowing marquess, his mouth frothing from monkshood poisoning, chasing her back and forth across a narrow ledge with nothing but empty darkness on the other side of it.

But she'd fallen asleep the moment her head found her pillow and hadn't so much as twitched for the rest of the night. There'd been no terrifying dash through the woods, no pitchfork-wielding villagers, and no heavy hand on her shoulder dragging her down to the ground.

It had been months since some part of her night—and on occasion, the entire night—hadn't been given over to nightmares.

She didn't care to speculate on why that should have changed last night, but maybe . . . well, she and her sisters had lost so much these past few years. First her mother, then her father, then Duffy and Mrs. Duffy, and now the castle itself was threatening to slip through their fingers.

There'd been a part of her that had feared they'd keep losing things until there was nothing left. And while Lord Ballantyne's presence in the castle was hardly reassuring, it *was* a presence.

A warm body, where before there'd been none.

Not that her restful night had anything to do with *him*, of course. Not a thing—

"You and your sisters are close to the Duffys, I think?"

"As close as people can be, yes. Duffy served as our butler, but he's always been much more than that to us. He was a dear friend of my father's, and my grandfather before him, and Mrs. Duffy was nursemaid to me and my sisters when we were younger. They're like grandparents to us."

"But I believe you told me you recently dismissed them?"

Had she told him that? No, she didn't think so, but someone had.

She cast him a sidelong glance. Lord Ballantyne had been gossiping about her family when he was staying in Dunvegan. It wasn't surprising, but it was a timely reminder.

They weren't friends, and she must be careful what she said to him.

If he had been gossiping, no doubt he'd gotten an earful. "Duffy is nearly sixty years old, my lord, and Mrs. Duffy scarcely less than that. We didn't dismiss them, we pensioned them."

"I see." His teasing grin had vanished, and he was frowning again.

Had one of the less friendly villagers told him they'd tossed the Duffys aside, as if their years of faithful friendship meant nothing to them?

Or perhaps he thought Duffy and Mrs. Duffy had left them after the accusations began. He might think the Duffys believed the worst of the rumors and had relinquished their places to get away from the MacLeod witches.

The Duffys would never have done such a thing, not in a thousand years, but why should the gossips care about the truth?

Yet it didn't sit right with her, that Lord Ballantyne should think so ill of them as that. She opened her mouth to say so, but then snapped it closed again.

What did it matter? It wasn't the last or the worst that would be said of them, and she and her sisters had long since stopped trying to defend themselves against gossip. They may as well try and pick the leaves off every tree in the woods than attempt to silence the wagging tongues.

She kept quiet as they wound their way down the path and through the edge of the woods, close enough to the coastline that they could see the gray waters of Loch Dunvegan peeking through the trees.

Soon enough, they rounded a bend in the pathway, and she pointed to a small, stone cottage with the steep, thatched roof that was so common in the Highlands. It was nestled above a shallow notch in the land, some distance above the loch. "That's their cottage."

It was such a dear, familiar sight, that tiny little cottage! She had a great many happy memories of playing there as a child with her sisters, picking the blackberries in the brambles behind Mrs. Duffy's tiny garden until their hands and mouths were stained purple with juice.

A wistful sigh must have slipped out of her because Lord Ballantyne wrapped a warm hand around her elbow and urged her forward. "Come, Miss MacLeod. I daresay they'll be delighted to see you."

Delighted turned out to be an understatement.

An older gentleman with gray hair and stooped shoulders answered the door, and as soon as he caught sight of Miss MacLeod, his entire demeanor changed. He straightened to his full height, and his mouth curved in a beaming smile that took years off his face. He didn't appear to notice Hamish, he was so thrilled to see her.

"Well, well, well, here she is! It's past time you came to pay a call, Miss Catriona. Where are your sisters, eh?"

"They both send their love and promise to come as soon as they can." Miss MacLeod held out the basket to him. "Freya's sent some of her jam, and Sorcha made Dundee cake."

Mr. Duffy took the basket and peeked underneath the cloth she'd folded neatly over the top. "A wee bit of something for my joints, too." He gave her a wink and ushered them inside. "Come in, come in. Mrs. Duffy will be beside herself."

"Is that my dearest girl?" Quick footsteps sounded in the hallway, and the next moment, a tiny, white-haired lady appeared. She flew across the room as fast as her legs would carry her and clasped Miss MacLeod's face in her hands. "Oh, my precious girl!"

"I've missed you, *seanmhair*." Miss MacLeod's voice was thick, and the hand that reached up to clasp Mrs. Duffy's was shaking.

"And I missed you, *ogha*." The old woman's faded blue eyes swam with tears as she kissed Miss MacLeod's cheeks, one after the other. "You look worn out, love. Are you getting enough sleep?"

"I'm very well, indeed." Miss MacLeod gave the old lady an affectionate smile. "You're not going to fuss, are you?"

"Why, what a silly question, Catriona. Of course I am." Mrs. Duffy patted her cheek. "And your sisters? How do they do? Is Freya still spending all her time up on the roof?"

"Yes, I'm afraid so. I'm obliged to regularly scold her for it. I worry she'll catch her death up there with the wind coming off the loch, but I can't deny she's made great strides forward with her studies over the past few months."

"Ach, well, she's a clever girl, is Freya." Mr. Duffy gave an indulgent nod. "What of Sorcha? Is she still running about the woods like a wild thing with those birds of hers?"

"Oh, yes. More so than ever. I think she's searching for another pair of abandoned baby sparrowhawks to add to her falconry."

"I daresay she'll find them, too." Mrs. Duffy waved an airy hand in the air. "That one knows those woods as if she were born to it, but that's your mother's blood flowing in her veins, isn't it? The Murdoch daughters are all remarkable in some way." Mrs. Duffy caught both of Catriona's hands in hers. "She would have been proud of all three of you, *ogha*."

"Who's this you have with you, lass?" Duffy had spotted Hamish at last and was scowling at him in a decidedly unfriendly manner. "I've never seen his face before."

Mrs. Duffy was staring at him over Miss MacLeod's shoulders, her eyes wide. "*Ogha?*"

"Forgive me." Miss MacLeod turned to him just in time for him to see her throat move in a nervous swallow. "This gentleman is Hamish Muir."

"Muir?" Duffy repeated. "Did you say Muir?"

Ah, he recognized the name. It was obvious from the old man's suddenly wary expression.

"Yes, *seanair*." Miss MacLeod glanced from Duffy to Hamish, biting her lip. "He's the Marquess of Ballantyne."

"Is he, now? What does a marquess want with you, lass?" The question was directed to Miss MacLeod, but the old man's gaze remained pinned on Hamish.

"It's a bit complicated, I'm afraid. Lord Ballantyne and I have something to ask you, *seanair*. Perhaps we might come in and sit down?"

"Aye, of course, of course. We'll have some Dundee cake and tea. Duffy, take Catriona and Lord Ballantyne inside, and I'll be along in a moment with the tea."

Mrs. Duffy took the basket from her husband, then bustled off toward the kitchen while Duffy led them to what passed for a drawing room in a Highland cottage. It wasn't elegant or grand, but it was cozy and warm from the fire in the stone fireplace.

"What's this all about, lass?" Duffy asked, as soon as they were seated, and Mrs. Duffy had joined them with a tray laden with the tea things and four generous slices of Dundee cake.

"It's, ah . . . well, I'm not quite sure how to put this, but I was sorting through my father's papers the other night, and I came across something odd."

"Odd?" Duffy exchanged a glance with his wife. "Eh, well, your father had all sorts of doings, and all of them odd in one way or another. What did you find, lass?"

Hamish was watching Duffy carefully. The old man was a cagey one, but the sudden pinch between his brows and the way his fingers tightened around his teacup gave him away.

He knew something. A great many somethings, in fact, including what Catriona was going to ask him, even before she mentioned the coins.

"I came across the green velvet pouch where my father kept his Louis d'Or gold ten-piece, *seanair*, only when I opened it, I found *three* gold pieces, instead of just the one he's always had. All three of them are identical to his—all Louis XIII ten-pieces, dated sixteen hundred forty."

Duffy froze with his teacup halfway to his lips, his gaze meeting Mrs. Duffy's over the top edge. Some silent communication passed between them, then she gave him a brief nod.

"I wondered how long it would take you to find those coins. Not long, eh? You're a clever lass, Catriona." Duffy set the teacup on the table beside him with a sigh. "Aye, there's three coins now, right enough."

Catriona let out a breath. "Then you do know something about it. I felt certain you would. It's, ah . . . it's rather important, *seanair*, that you tell me and Lord Ballantyne whatever it is you know."

"Aye, I know something about it, but little enough you're bound to be disappointed, lass." He gave Hamish a measuring look. "You're Archie Muir's son, then? You've my condolences on his recent passing, my lord. He was a good man."

Hamish set his own teacup aside, his hands suddenly unsteady. He hadn't expected this. The shock of hearing his father's name on Duffy's lips ripped open the raw wound in his chest. The grief threatened to pour through the ragged edges, and he swallowed to ease the tightness in his throat. "You knew my father, Mr. Duffy?"

Duffy shook his head. "Nay, my lord. I never laid eyes on the man myself, but Catriona's father had naught but good to say about him."

"They did know each other, then?" He'd known it, of course. How his father had crossed paths with Rory MacLeod remained a mystery, but they'd fallen into each other's way at some point. Nothing else made sense, but there was a relief in hearing it confirmed.

"Oh, aye, these past twenty-nine years and more."

Hamish exchanged a look with Catri—er, that is, Miss MacLeod, before turning back to Duffy. "Where did the coins come from?"

"Eh, well, I can't tell you as much about that as I'd like, my lord, but I know this. Rory had that one coin for years, ever since he returned from some mad adventure up north, near Eilean nan Ron. I asked him about it, once. It's an odd old coin, ye ken, and not the sort of thing a man stumbles upon, but he never did tell me how he came by it."

Hamish leaned forward, bracing his hands on his knees to hide their shaking. "Did he ever tell you anything about it?"

"Nay, not much. Only that it had something to do with a promise he'd made."

A promise he'd made. Those were nearly the same words his own father had used when he'd spoken to him about the coins. "Was it you who sent Mr. MacLeod's coin to me at my London townhouse?"

Duffy hesitated for a moment, but then he nodded. "Aye, that was me. Some years ago, Rory told me that his coin was to go to a gentleman in London once he passed—one Archibald

Muir. He made me promise I'd see to it after he died, and so, I did."

"How strange," Miss MacLeod murmured. "He never said a word to me about that coin, or to Freya or Sorcha, as far as I know."

"He didn't like you girls involved in the smuggling, lass. A dangerous business, that. He never wanted you too close to it."

"The coins have something to do with the smuggling, then?" It would make sense. There were a few vague rumors still floating about London that his own father had dabbled in smuggling as a young man. Whether it was true or not was anyone's guess, but if his father had been a smuggler, he'd given it up after he married Hamish's mother, as her father, the English Marquess of Ballantyne hadn't looked upon Scottish smugglers with a friendly eye.

"As to that, I can't rightly say, my lord, but if it did, Mr. MacLeod never said so to me."

Hamish's heart sank at that discouraging reply, but he did his best to hide his disappointment. "I see. Thank you, Mr. Duffy. You've been quite helpful."

Not as helpful as he'd hoped, but at least they now knew there had in fact been some sort of promise between his father and Rory MacLeod. As to the nature of that promise, well . . . they'd likely never know.

"Not so hasty, my lord. There is one more thing ye may find interesting."

"What's that, *seanair*?" Miss MacLeod asked, reaching for the teapot to refill Hamish's cup.

"After Mr. MacLeod's passing, I went to his study to fetch the coin, so as to send it off to Archibald Muir in London and fulfill my promise to him, and what do you think I found, but four gold coins, instead of just the one."

"Four coins." Catriona had gone still with the teapot poised over Hamish's teacup. "And you'd never seen the other three coins before that?"

"Nay, lass. Someone sent them to your father, right enough, but I don't know who." Mr. Duffy shook his head. "I didn't know what to make of it at the time, and I still don't."

"Do you have any idea when the coins arrived at Castle Cairncross, *seanair*?" Catriona asked. "Oh, thank you, *seanmhair*," she added, as Mrs. Duffy relieved her of the teapot. "I have a feeling the timing is rather important."

Hamish had the same feeling, and he waited with some impatience for Mr. Duffy to gather his thoughts.

"I can't say for sure, lass. I never saw the coins until after your father passed, but I've a feeling they came right before your father made up his mind to go off on that last adventure of his."

Hamish's heart began to pound. "What makes you say that, Mr. Duffy?"

"Just a feeling, my lord. Something happened, and I can't think of what it could have been except those coins coming when they did. He wasn't acting like himself, right before he left that last time. I wish he'd have just stayed put." Mr. Duffy's voice had gone thick. "He was a good man, your father, Catriona. Not an easy man, but a good one."

Catriona didn't speak, but she nodded, her eyes bright.

"Ach, well, we all meet our end one way or another." Mr. Duffy passed his hand over his eyes. "I wish I could tell you more, but that's all I know."

"You've helped us tremendously, *seanair.*" Catriona reached out to squeeze Mr. Duffy's hand. "But perhaps that's enough about my father for now." She turned to Mrs. Duffy with a bright smile. "Won't you show me your garden, *seanmhair*? How is your *Astrantia* faring? Is it blooming still?"

Mrs. Duffy beamed at her. "Oh, aye. It's as pretty a pink as you'll ever see."

They all set their teacups aside and rose to their feet, but Hamish hung back, stopping Catriona with a hand on her arm.

"*Astrantia*?" he murmured in her ear. "What in the world is *Astrantia*?"

"The name comes from the Latin word for star, my lord," she whispered back. "But it's commonly known as masterwort."

"Masterwort? Good Lord. It sounds poisonous."

"Only a little bit, my lord. Nothing like monkshood. It's quite effective at curing headaches, and handy, as well, as the flowers can be dried and stored for later use."

His lips twitched. "How wonderful, Miss MacLeod, but if it's all the same to you, I'll keep my distance."

Chapter 14

"Tell me, Miss MacLeod. Is there blood spurting from my eyes?"

"Blood?" Cat glanced up from the papers piled in her lap. It had been hours since they'd spoken, and Lord Ballantyne's voice was loud in the silent room. "No. Should there be?"

"One would hope not, but after hours of trying to decipher your father's notes, I fancied I felt blood trickling down the side of my face. Perhaps it's just my brains leaking out of my ears."

My goodness, such dramatics. "If you have a headache, my lord, I'd be happy to mix up a batch of *Astrantia* tea for you."

He cast her a withering look. "Is that a joke, Miss MacLeod? Because it's not amusing in the least, and thus, an utter failure."

Well, then. Someone was out of temper.

Although to be fair, she could hardly blame him. After they'd returned from their visit to the Duffys, they'd gone straight upstairs to her father's study, and they hadn't stirred one inch since, the soft shuffle of papers as they turned them over one by one the only sound in the room.

She'd been hopeful at first, certain they'd find something in the mountain of papers her father had accumulated that might help them determine where he'd gone on his final adventure, or at least what direction he'd taken.

But it wasn't going well.

Lord Ballantyne snatched up a torn bit of paper from the pile on Rory's desk, glanced at it, then tossed it aside in disgust. "I can't make sense of any of this."

Cat peered down at the paper in her hand. It was a drawing of . . . well, something. The wall of a cave, perhaps? She'd been turning it this way and that for the better part of the past ten minutes, and she still couldn't decide what it was.

No, not a cave. It looked more like a sheet of rock, or a ledge, but what was the dark blob to one side of it? Was it a mountain, or an unusually large bird?

Her father's papers were, generously speaking, a trifle disorganized.

Ungenerously speaking, they were a chaotic mess of half-finished letters, unintelligible drawings, smudged maps worn at the seams, and endless bits of paper with incomprehensible notes in her father's untidy scrawl.

One of these notes only had one word written on it.

Cairn.

It had been underlined three times with dark, thick slashes of ink, and thus was presumably important to her father, but she couldn't make any sense of the cursed thing. One could hardly stir a step in Scotland without stumbling over a cairn. How was she to know which cairn he was referring to?

"Did your father ever have a single comprehensive thought, Miss MacLeod? Was he capable of speaking in complete sentences? If so, one can't tell it from his papers."

She abandoned the drawing of the rock wall and took up the next paper in her pile. "I'm sure it all made sense to him."

"Well, it's bloody hieroglyphics to us. What do you suppose this is? A dagger, perhaps? I've seen this drawing a dozen times on a dozen different crumpled bits of paper, none of them with a single word of explanation."

She took the small, grubby bit of paper he held out to her and smoothed it against her knee. "It looks like it, yes. A hand holding an upright dagger, with some sort of circle around it."

He rubbed a weary hand over his eyes. "Does it mean anything to you?"

She bit her lip as she carefully considered her answer. The drawing didn't mean a thing to her, but Lord Ballantyne's patience was already wearing thin, and she didn't want to push him over the edge. "Let me see if I can find a similar drawing in my pile."

He snorted. "Neatly done, Miss MacLeod, but don't think for one moment I didn't notice how you sidestepped that question."

"There's no need to . . ." She trailed off, her eyes going wide.

The thin sliver of the sky visible in the window behind Lord Ballantyne's head had gone the deep, dark purple of twilight.

When had the sun gone down?

"Goodness, how long have we been up here?" She rose to her feet, catching the messy pile of papers before they could slide off her lap. "Why, it must be eight hours or more."

Lord Ballantyne unearthed his pocket watch from his coat pocket and flipped open the case. "It's been nearly ten hours, and we're no closer to finding anything useful than we were when we began. We've accomplished nothing."

"Not *nothing*, my lord. All told, it's been rather a revealing day. We now know for certain there was a promise made between our fathers, and that it had something to do with a treasure."

It must. Where else could they have found four identical Louis d'Or gold coins, if they weren't part of a larger treasure? It would be a small miracle to find even one such rare coin, never mind four of them.

"Very well, Miss MacLeod—next to nothing, then. Where do you suggest we go from here? It will take us months to get through your father's papers. By then, someone else will have made off with the treasure."

"I own it's rather daunting." She'd hardly made a dent in the pile of papers in front of her, and Lord Ballantyne's own pile was discouragingly tall, as well. "Perhaps we should go over what we know once again. We may have missed something that could prove useful."

"Go right ahead, Miss MacLeod." He propped his feet on the desk in front of him, rested his head on the back of the chair, and closed his eyes before waving an imperious hand at her. "I'm listening."

"I can see that, my lord." Still, it might help her to go over it again. "There are four coins."

"Yes. That fact has been well established, Miss MacLeod, since all four coins are here on top of the desk."

"Hush, will you? I'm thinking." Four coins, one of which had initially belonged to her father, and one to Lord Ballantyne's father. "If Rory made Duffy promise to send the coin to your father once he'd died, then it's reasonable to assume your father had a similar arrangement on his end."

Hamish opened one eye. "I suppose that makes sense. I daresay Williams, his man of business, would know."

"It stands to reason, then, that the same is true of the other two coins, as well. That would mean there were four gentlemen involved, each with their own coin . . . wait, that's it! Of course. How did we not see it sooner?"

Hamish opened the other eye. "See what?"

"You told me, Lord Ballantyne, that your father had three coins at one time, but then after his death you searched for them, and only found one."

"Yes. You don't think—"

"That your father received the two other coins once the gentlemen who had them passed away? Yes, I do think so. It wasn't a promise between two men, but a *pact* between four of them. Each of them had a coin that was to go to one of the others after he passed."

"Malcolm Ross passed away first. He died at Culloden, and then Angus Dunn was next, some eight years later, of a fever.

My father was the third one to pass away, and so he never had more than three of the coins."

"Yes, and my father was the last." Cat leapt to her feet, too excited to sit still. At last, they were getting somewhere. "Your father's coin and the two others in his possession came to Castle Cairncross after your father's death. That's how my father came to have four coins."

"But if that's the case, why did Duffy send your father's coin to London? Wouldn't he have known my father was dead already, since he'd received his coin?"

"My father would have known of it, yes, but there's no reason Duffy would have. He merely sent the one coin to your father after Rory passed, as my father had instructed him to do. If he hadn't done so—"

"Then I never would have known to come to Castle Cairncross."

"Yes, just so. Duffy said he thought the coins arrived here only just before my father's sudden decision to embark on another treasure hunt. The coins were the signal to the last man still alive to retrieve the treasure. That man was my father."

"But where did he go? And who were the two other men?"

"Malcolm and Angus," she said at once.

His boots hit the floor with a thud, making her jump. "Am I correct in assuming you didn't just come up with those names out of the blue?"

"Of course I didn't, my lord. You recall I told you my father died of an infection from a wound in his leg. During his feverish ravings, he repeated three names—"

"Archie, Malcolm, and Angus," he murmured. "My father, Archibald Muir, Malcolm Ross, and Angus Dunn."

Cat ceased her pacing, her heart leaping into her throat. "You *know* them?"

"I do, yes. Or I did. Both gentlemen have been dead for some years, but their sons, Callum Ross and Keir Dunn, are among my closest friends."

Cat dropped down into a chair, her head spinning. "That's some of the puzzle solved, isn't it?"

"Yes, but there are still a few large pieces missing. Why did they make the pact in the first place, first of all? If the four of them stumbled over some treasure, why not just take it at once? Why was there a need for a pact at all? And, perhaps more importantly, where is the treasure now?"

Yes, they'd have to answer those questions, wouldn't they?

But how? Rory's papers were no help. There wasn't anything to be done, was there?

Unless . . . there *was* one way they might get more information, but it was a bit risky. If they pursued it, there was a chance they'd learn what they needed to know, but there was also a chance they'd end up . . . well, there was no sense in mincing words, was there?

There was a chance they'd end up *dead*.

"Why do you look like that, Miss MacLeod? What are you thinking?"

She looked up and found Lord Ballantyne watching her with bright blue eyes that seemed to see right through her. "I do have one idea, but—"

"Let's have it then, Miss MacLeod." He gestured at the pile of papers on the desk. "It can't get much worse than this."

Yes, it could. It could always get worse, and anyone who thought otherwise was either foolish or lucky.

But they'd gotten this far, hadn't they?

"There's an Irish gentleman in Carrick, South Ayrshire, near Girvan. For many years my father was the head of a smuggling crew, and this gentleman, Cormac Donigan, was his partner."

"Yes? Go on, Miss MacLeod."

"Mr. Donigan is still running that crew, smuggling claret, rum, and tea through a series of caves in the area." They were a raw, rough crew, too, one made up of liars, thieves, and various other blackguards.

But it wasn't true what they said, about there being no honor among thieves. The men in her father's former crew were fiercely loyal to each other, and to Rory.

In life, and in death.

Especially Donigan. She'd met him once, quite a few years ago, when she was around eleven years old or so. She didn't remember much about him, other than that he had lovely gray eyes, and he'd given her a beautiful silver hairbrush.

Stolen, no doubt, but she'd treasured it. She still used it every day.

Lord Ballantyne's blue eyes gleamed in the lantern light. "You think this Donigan may know where the treasure is?"

"I can't be certain of that, but I'd be surprised if he didn't know *something* about it." Whether he'd agree to reveal it was another question. He was a smuggler, after all, and could decide instead that he'd rather separate their heads from their necks.

But she didn't think so. The loyalty Rory's old crew felt for her father would extend to his daughter. At least, she hoped it would. It would be rather a grievous miscalculation if she was wrong.

"Girvan is a good distance from Dunvegan," Lord Ballantyne muttered, more to himself than to her. "A six-day's ride, but I could make it in five."

"*You* could make it in five?"

He glanced at her, as if he'd only just recalled she was there. "Perhaps four, if I have good luck with changing horses."

He could make it in five days if *he* had good luck with the horses?

She stared at him, anger uncoiling in her chest. Why, he was speaking as if he were going by himself!

But no, she must have misunderstood him. "You mean, of course, that *we* could make it in five days. Isn't that right, Lord Ballantyne?"

His eyebrows shot up. "No, I didn't, Miss MacLeod."

He had the nerve to look surprised! Did he imagine she'd stay here, lazing about the castle while he went off to play the hero? If he did find the treasure, what was to stop him from running off back to London with it?

"Have you forgotten our truce already, my lord?"

"Of course not, but our truce doesn't include my taking a young lady three hundred or more miles to South Ayrshire to meet with cutthroats and brigands. The ghost of your father truly would haunt me if I did that."

Slowly, she rose to her feet. "You misunderstand me, Lord Ballantyne. I'm not asking for your permission. I'm informing you that I *am* going, whether you approve of it or not."

"The devil you are." He rose as well, mimicking her, until they stood face to face.

Or rather, face to chin. "What do you intend to do, my lord? Stroll up to Cormac Donigan, announce that you're a marquess, and demand he answer your questions?"

He shrugged. "I daresay I'll think of something. I always do."

"Another man with more bravery than sense!" She threw her arms up in the air, thoroughly disgusted. "You, Lord Ballantyne, are just like my father."

"Is that a compliment, Miss MacLeod, or an insult?"

God help her, she hardly knew anymore. "If you arrive in Ballantrae without me, you can be sure Donigan's men will carve you up and toss your bloody bits into Solway Firth."

"What a charming description, Miss MacLeod. One can't fault your imagination."

"The point, my lord, is that you *need* me. There's a chance Donigan will speak to Rory MacLeod's daughter, but he doesn't owe you any loyalty. Besides, Scottish smugglers despise the English." It was part of the reason they were smugglers in the first place, for pity's sake!

"I'm only half English. The other half of me is pure Scot."

"That's neither here nor there."

"Perhaps not, but you must see that I can't permit you to come with me. You can't go running all over Scotland alone, with a gentleman who isn't your spouse. Your reputation—"

"Half of Scotland thinks I'm a *witch*, Lord Ballantyne. My reputation is already tarnished beyond repair. If there is one positive outcome of this mess, it's the freedom that comes with having no reputation left to lose."

He opened his mouth, but then he turned abruptly toward the window without a word, leaving her staring at his broad back.

He didn't speak for some time, and when he did, his voice was quiet. "Have you forgotten, Miss MacLeod, that your sisters also need you? Or do you mean to leave them here alone for several weeks while you scurry off to South Ayrshire?"

The righteous anger swelling in her chest drained away, leaving her as limp and flat as a sail abandoned by the wind, and she fell heavily back into her chair.

Of all the things he might have said, he'd hit upon the only one that could dissuade her.

Of course, she couldn't leave Freya and Sorcha here alone. What had she been thinking? Even if she was here, they may not be able to withstand another attack, but without her, Sorcha and Freya didn't stand a chance.

The papers on her father's desk blurred in front of her eyes. What was the use? No matter which way she turned, she was trapped.

"Miss MacLeod." Lord Ballantyne came away from the window and crouched beside her chair. "Catriona. Look at me."

"No." If she looked at him now, she'd burst into tears.

Warm fingers touched her chin, turning her face up to his. "Look at me."

He was so close she could see the dark prickles of hair on the curve of his jaw. Not just the shadow of his beard she'd seen a dozen times since he'd invaded her home, but each tiny, defiant pinprick emerging from his otherwise smooth skin.

Oh, dear. They were far too close to one another.

A wiser lady would have pushed him away, but she remained where she was, her back pressed against the chair.

"I'm sorry, Catriona. It's not fair, but I don't know what else to do."

"I know." She let out a breath, and the tightness in her chest eased a little. "Me, neither. Perhaps it's for the best. After days trapped in a carriage with you, I'd almost certainly bloody your nose again."

He chuckled. "It wouldn't be the worst thing. No worse than monkshood poisoning, for instance."

"There's no need for gallantry, Lord Ballantyne." A reluctant smile crossed her lips. "It's perfectly acceptable for you to admit you don't like me."

"Is that what you think? That I don't like you? You're quite wrong, you know. I like you very much. This despite never, in my twenty-eight years of life, having had the misfortune to come across such a trying creature as you."

Ah, no sweet murmurs would fall from those hard lips, then. It was just as well. They weren't friends. How many times must she keep reminding herself of that?

But they were no longer enemies, either.

The truce between them remained an uneasy one, and yet . . .

There was something else there, as well, a strange heat that only seemed to burn hotter with every word, every glance they shared.

Passion, it seemed, cared nothing for the state of one's heart.

Her wariness of him, her distrust and suspicion were no match for the quiver of desire in her belly, the shivers of awareness dancing down her spine.

"I assure you, Lord Ballantyne, I feel no fondness for you, either. You're arrogant, overbearing, and presumptuous, and quite the most unpleasant man I've ever encountered. I can hardly bear the sight of you."

"Then we're in agreement." He eased closer and caught one of her curls between his fingers. "Each of us despises the other?"

"Yes. With the heat of a thousand suns." But her eyes felt

heavy, too heavy to hold the weight of her lids, and her arms, traitorous limbs that they were, were stealing around his neck, her fingers sinking into the hair there.

It was so silky, so unexpectedly soft.

Despite everything that had passed between them, she wanted him. She shouldn't, but she did. Deep down, a secret part of her had been aching for him since he'd woken in the bedchamber that first morning.

It was inevitable, this kiss. It had been gathering like a storm between them from the start. She'd known it would come to this from the first moment she looked into his eyes.

And now it was too late. Much too late, because he was closer now, his lips parting. "This is madness," he murmured against the tender skin behind her ear. "Pure madness," he said again, even as he nuzzled his face into the curve between her shoulder and neck.

A soft gasp fell from her lips, and she rested her hands on the hard, warm plane of his chest to steady herself, her eyes closing at the sensation of his heart beating steadily against her palm.

She'd known him for only a matter of days, yet somehow it felt as if she waited weeks for his kiss, a lifetime.

When it came, it was the lightest touch, the merest brush of his lips, more a trail of warm breath against her throat than a kiss.

Yet it was enough. Enough to set her entire body atremble, her doubts and misgivings falling away as she pressed closer to him, enough to tear a shaky moan from her lips.

He nipped her neck, then raised his head, his breath coming in shallow pants as he gazed down at her with hot blue eyes. "You've bewitched me, Catriona."

Was that what he thought? Was he just like all the others who told tales about her, with their endless whispers about her spells and potions?

Did he imagine she'd cursed him?

Her fingers curled against his chest, either to push him away, or drag him closer. She didn't know which, but in the end, it didn't matter.

Because he lowered his head, and there was no time to question it, no time to do anything at all before his mouth settled on hers, his tongue sweeping against the seam of her lips.

A demand, not a request.

She couldn't think after that. She could do nothing but give way to the seductive teasing of his tongue, to welcome him, her breath catching as he surged inside, hot and damp and slick, his hands falling to her waist to urge her closer as he ravaged her mouth.

She'd been kissed once before, but not like this. It was as if her world had just tilted on its axis, and everything that had once been right side up was now upside down. It put her in mind of the time Sorcha's birds had somehow gotten into her workroom and flown about in a panic, leaving smashed glass and overturned books in their wake.

Perfect order, reduced to utter chaos in a matter of seconds.

No, she'd never been kissed like *this*, so she could feel it everywhere, the tips of her breasts tingling and her belly pulsing.

She gasped again, softly, more a breath than a sound, but he must have heard something in it, because his lips gentled against hers, his kiss turning from an exploration to a seduction, the tip of his tongue tracing her mouth, toying with her lower lip.

"Open for me, Catriona." His breath was hot, his mouth trailing lower to brush the hollow of her throat, then pausing to drop a kiss on her collarbone before he was once again hovering over her parted lips, their ragged breath mingling. "Let me inside."

She did. Oh, she did, because she could do nothing less, her head dizzy with desire for him, this man she hardly knew and didn't trust, her body a traitor to her better judgment.

"Yes," he hissed on a ragged breath when she opened her mouth to him once more. "So good for me, Catriona."

It was just a kiss. It didn't mean anything, nor did it change anything, but for this single moment, this fleeting, dizzying moment, she'd let herself have this.

Have *him*.

Everything inside her was clamoring for him, a spray of goosebumps puckering her skin as he slid one hand into the back of her hair and rested the other palm against her throat, stilling her for his touch.

"Kiss me, Catriona." His eyes were blazing, two deep pools of glittering blue fire, his cheeks flushed, and his dark hair disheveled from her seeking fingers. "Kiss me back."

Her tongue darted out eagerly to meet his, tangling in a slick, hot duel, the tenderest of battles, because it had gone too far between them for her to pretend any longer.

"Your heart is pounding." He abandoned her lips to drop a tiny kiss onto her throat, right over her fluttering pulse. "Do you want me, Catriona?"

He didn't wait for a reply. There was no need. He already knew the answer.

"God knows I want you." He ran his nose up the side of her neck, inhaling deeply. "The last woman in the world I should want. Treacherous thing, desire."

Treacherous. Yes, that was the right word for it, because even as you knew you were making a grievous mistake, you never wanted to stop.

She might not have stopped. She might have gone on until there was nowhere left to go and the word *stop* lost all its meaning, if he hadn't drawn back, panting, and set her gently away from him.

"This isn't . . . I shouldn't have . . . you're an innocent." He dragged a hand through his hair. "Go to bed, Catriona, before I forget I'm a gentleman."

An innocent? A laugh threatened, but she held it back.

Yes, she supposed she was innocent, and likely to remain so into her dotage, but she'd never felt less innocent in her life than she did right now.

But even as the rejection stung, a part of her was grateful to him.

His kiss hadn't only made her forget herself, it had made her forget her anger over the unfairness of what had befallen them, and she couldn't let that happen. Once it did, she may never find her way back to it, and what would become of them then?

She could never allow herself to forget what she owed to her sisters, and to her father.

Gently, she pushed him back, away from her, and rose to her feet. "You're right, of course, Lord Ballantyne. I beg your pardon."

"Catriona."

She'd reached the door by the time he said her name. She turned back to find him standing beside the desk, tension radiating from him, and his hands clenched into fists. "Wait. I—"

But there was nothing to wait for. "Goodnight, Lord Ballantyne."

She didn't pause, but turned and made her way into the corridor, and from there down the winding turret steps.

What, after all, was the point in waiting? Whatever this madness was between them, it ended here, like a flower torn from the garden before it could bloom.

Finished, before it even had a chance to begin.

Chapter 15

Six days later.

"No, Miss MacLeod. It's out of the question. I'm appalled you'd even contemplate such a thing, after what happened last time."

"*Last* time? Last time you chased me through the woods, Lord Ballantyne!" Catriona tried to march past him and out the front door of the castle, but once again, he moved to block her way. "I demand you let me pass!"

"As I said, after what happened last time, it's imperative that you—"

"If anyone is to blame for what happened last time, my lord, it's *you*!" She punctuated this tirade with an infuriated stamp of her foot.

Good God. Had there ever been a more ill-tempered woman? "That's one way of looking at it, I suppose, but it's rather an oversimplification of what—"

"Step away from the door *this instant*," she hissed through clenched teeth.

"I'd like to accommodate you, Miss MacLeod, I truly would, but if you won't attend to your own safety, then I have no choice but to do it for you." He crossed his arms over his chest and peered down his nose at her. "I can't permit you to—"

"*Permit* me! *You* permit *me*!"

There went her foot again. The heel of her boot struck the stone floor with a sharp clunk, and her cheeks were turning an alarming shade of red.

At least, he thought they were. It was difficult to tell with the hood of that blasted cloak pulled over her face. She looked like a turtle that had lost its way inside its shell.

He despised that hood. He despised that *cloak*. Most of all, he despised the basket she carried looped over her arm. That damned basket was a harbinger of bad things to come. The very sight of the wretched thing made the vein in his forehead pulse.

The vein he hadn't even realized was there until the first time he'd encountered Catriona MacLeod. Now it was his constant companion.

"I have eight jars of liniment in this basket, and I *will* be taking them to Fraser's Apothecary in Dunvegan, my lord, whether you approve of it or not." She held out her arm and shook the basket at him.

It was like waving a scarlet cloth in front of an enraged bull, and like an enraged bull, he reacted without thinking, snatching the basket away from her and holding it behind his back. "If you insist upon going into the village, Miss MacLeod, then I'm coming with you."

"Did it ever occur to you that I don't wish for your company?"

"Don't be absurd. Of course, you do. Everyone wants my company. In case you haven't noticed, Miss MacLeod, I'm excessively charming."

"I assure you, I *don't*." She glared at him, her hands on her hips. "And you're not nearly as charming as you think you are, Lord Ballantyne."

That was another thing he'd come to despise—the sound of his title falling from her lips. She'd called him Hamish the night she'd kissed him, and it had been like the most delicious secret whispered in his ear.

That is, she'd kissed him *back*. He'd been the one to initiate the kiss, but she'd returned it. Once a lady returned a man's kiss, shouldn't she be required to call him by his Christian name?

There should be a rule about that.

But he could hardly blame her for being out of temper with him, after what had happened in her father's study three days ago. God knew he hadn't wanted to pull away from her, but he wasn't a despoiler of virgins.

And there was that other small matter, as well, of him having been the one who'd sent the first lugger to Castle Cairncross. He wasn't going to confess to it—he was enough of a blackguard to hide a truth that would prove inconvenient to him—but he *wasn't* enough of one to kiss her when he was lying to her.

Or to kiss her *again*, as it were. Not that he'd had the opportunity.

Ever since that first kiss, she'd been avoiding him as if he had an infectious disease. No matter where she was—the breakfast room, her father's study, her workroom—if he dared to even linger in the doorway, she'd leave at once, marching past him with her pert little nose in the air.

If he'd known that kissing her would change everything between them, he would have exerted a bit more self-control. Instead, he'd given in to a moment of passion, then he'd ended it before it even had a chance to begin. Since then, Catriona had retreated behind an icy propriety that was, he was certain, designed to prevent another kiss from happening.

He'd made a mess of the entire business, and he deserved her ire, but after six days of chasing her through every room in this blasted castle, he'd had enough. "Is this about our kiss, Miss MacLeod? If it is, perhaps we should discuss it."

It was the wrong thing to say.

He knew it as soon as the words were out of his mouth, but alas, by then it was too late.

"Arrggh! You are the most arrogant, infuriating man! It has nothing to do with that! I made a commitment to Glynnis Fraser, and I have a rather urgent need for the money she promised me. That's all. Not everything is about *you*, Lord Ballantyne."

"If that's all it is, then you can have no objection to my accompanying you." She couldn't truly think he'd let her stroll off to the village by herself. He'd seen the way the men at Baird's Pub had looked at her as she'd passed by the window the other day.

Like starving men with drool trickling down their chins, moments away from falling on a delectable feast.

However they might feel about the MacLeod sisters, there hadn't been a single man in that pub who'd failed to notice how attractive Catriona MacLeod was.

Then, of course, there was the matter of Bryce Fraser, and that strange comment she'd made about the man when Hamish had followed her into the wood.

You're not Bryce Fraser . . .

He didn't remember much from that day, most of his memories having disintegrated in a haze of monkshood poisoning, but even with his head wobbling on his neck as it had been, he remembered *that*.

Why would she think Bryce Fraser was chasing her through the wood?

There were dozens of answers to that question that would lead to his fist landing in Bryce Fraser's face, but none that would end with Catriona marching off to the village without his escort.

"You may as well reconcile yourself to the inevitable, Miss MacLeod. Either we both go to the village, or neither of us does. Which will it be?"

She glared at him, a dark scowl gathering like a thundercloud on her face. How the lady managed to make even a scowl look fetching was a mystery, but he had the most overwhelming urge to drop a kiss between those puckered brows.

Meanwhile, she looked as if she'd happily box his ears.

After a great deal of huffing and muttering, a great many heavy sighs, and one last dramatic roll of her eyes, she gave in at last. "Very well, Lord Ballantyne. We'll both go."

"I knew you'd come to your senses, Miss MacLeod."

"Would you be so good as to return my basket to me, my lord? I'd rather carry it myself."

"Of course." He reluctantly handed it back to her with a bright smile. "It looks like the sun may break through the clouds. I daresay we'll have a lovely walk."

They didn't, in fact, have a lovely walk, because Catriona refused to speak a word to him the entire way. Even worse, Mrs. MacDonald was the first person they saw when they reached the High Street.

Of course she was, because wicked old harridans like Mrs. MacDonald had a talent for always being in the very last place one wished to find them.

Catriona offered Mrs. MacDonald a brief nod, but he saw her cast a nervous glance over her shoulder at the old woman once they'd passed. As for Mrs. MacDonald, she'd stopped in her tracks as soon as she caught sight of them and hadn't ceased glowering since.

But Mrs. MacDonald wasn't the only culprit. He and Cat had hardly ventured two steps before the staring began.

He didn't give a damn if they stared at him, but Catriona had tensed as soon as the first head had turned in her direction, and she hadn't relaxed since.

"Come, Miss MacLeod, this errand can wait. Let's turn back and come another day." They weren't likely to receive a warmer reception then, but he couldn't bear to see Cat so straight-backed and stiff, as if she were hiding a fireplace poker under that damned cloak of hers.

"No, I won't be so silly as that when we've already come this far, and I did promise Glynnis that heather liniment."

"She can get along without the liniment for another few days. Glynnis Fraser will understand if you don't bring it to her today."

"No, it can't wait. If another boat should come while you're off searching for the treasure . . ." She trailed off into silence, glancing away from him, but it didn't matter.

He already knew what she was going to say. If another boat should come, she and her sisters might be obliged to flee the castle, and if it came to that, she'd rather not have empty pockets.

Although if all went as he hoped it would, none of them would be obliged to flee Castle Cairncross in the middle of the night with a band of angry smugglers on their heels.

He'd, ah . . . well, he'd done something. In secret, without consulting Cat. It was either a brilliant idea, or a horrendous one. He couldn't decide which, but they'd find out soon enough.

Even today, perhaps.

He let out a heavy sigh. "I already told you, Miss MacLeod, that I'd be more than happy to provide you with the funds to—"

"No. We don't want your money, Lord Ballantyne." Her chin hitched up. "I'm perfectly capable of taking care of my sisters myself."

He couldn't argue with that. She *had* taken care of her sisters—they'd taken care of each other—and under exceptionally difficult circumstances. There weren't many young ladies clever enough to fend off multiple smugglers' attacks by populating their castle with ghosts and witches.

But Catriona MacLeod wasn't just any young lady. He hadn't known her for even a day before he'd drawn that conclusion.

By this point, they'd reached Fraser's Apothecary at the end of the High Street, but he stopped Cat when she reached for the doorknob. "Give me your basket, if you please, and wait here. I'll go inside and see to the business with Glynnis."

She raised an eyebrow at him. "Is there some reason, Lord Ballantyne, why I shouldn't go into Fraser's Apothecary?"

There were a dozen reasons, but he was no longer certain whether they were *her* reasons, or his. "I was under the impression you're not fond of Bryce Fraser."

She frowned. "I don't recall saying anything to you about Bryce Fraser, one way or another, Lord Ballantyne."

"But you did. Right before I slipped into a poison-induced delirium that day in the woods, you said, " 'You're not Bryce Fraser.' "

"I—I did?"

"Yes." He took a step toward her, his hand brushing hers as he took hold of the leather strap of the basket. "Why would Bryce Fraser have been chasing you through the woods, Cat?"

"Well, as it happened, he *wasn't*, my lord. *You* were."

"But you thought he was. That was why you ran, wasn't it? Because you were desperate to get away from him. So, answer the question. Do you have some reason to be afraid of Bryce Fraser?"

She bit her lip, avoiding his eyes. "I have reason to be wary of everyone in Dunvegan, my lord."

"But *more* reason to be wary of him, isn't that right, Catriona?"

She huffed out a breath. "Very well, if you must know. After my father died, Mr. Fraser decided he wished to court me. He was quite insistent, and not at all pleased when I, er . . . declined to encourage him."

Not at all pleased? What the devil did that mean? Was she intentionally being vague, so he wouldn't know whether he should kill Bryce Fraser or not? "I see. And is he *still* insistent, Catriona?"

"Goodness, no. He gave up after the first of the boats came, and people started whispering rumors about me and my sisters."

Ah. Well, that told him everything he needed to know about

Bryce Fraser. A man who waited until a lady was vulnerable before initiating a courtship, then abandoned her at the first whiff of scandal was no gentleman.

At least one good thing had come of his sending Clyde and Dougal to Castle Cairncross, but it was only a tiny speck of brightness in a sea of impenetrable black, like the pinprick of a star in an overcast sky.

"I can only imagine Mr. Fraser was grateful to put an end to his courtship. No man wants to marry a witch, after all." She gave a nervous laugh. "But he still bears me a grudge over it, I'm afraid."

A grudge. Enough of a grudge she had reason to fear he'd chase her through the woods?

Good Lord, what would become of her once this business with Rory's treasure was concluded? He'd leave Dunvegan and return to London, his promise to his father fulfilled, but Catriona would be left behind with the likes of Mrs. MacDonald and Bryce Fraser.

Just the thought of her having to tiptoe around that villain for the rest of her days made a surge of hot blood roar through him, angering his forehead vein and sending it into a frenzy.

None of this was fair. Not to Cat, and not to her sisters. She'd made it clear she wouldn't accept his money, but there must be something he could do for her, some way to repair the damage he'd—

"Hamish—er, I mean, Lord Ballantyne? Are you all right? You look a bit strange."

"I'm perfectly well. Let's just get this errand finished, shall we?" They'd go inside, she'd transact her business with Glynnis Fraser, and he'd do his best not to leap over the counter and seize Bryce Fraser by the neck.

As it happened, Bryce Fraser's neck was destined to survive for another day.

Not because Hamish's temper had cooled by the time he and

Catriona were standing at the polished wooden counter in front of a wall of tiny drawers and bottles, the sharp scent of camphor hanging in the air.

But because Bryce wasn't there. They found Glynnis Fraser alone.

"Cat! Here you are, thank goodness. I expected you last week, and I've been wondering what became of you." Glynnis's gaze drifted over Cat's shoulder, her eyes widening when she caught sight of Hamish. "Is, ah . . . is everything all right?"

"Yes. It just took me more time than I expected to make up the liniment. I do beg your pardon. I have it here." Cat turned and took the basket from him, clearing her throat. "Glynnis, this gentleman is Hamish Muir, the Marquess of Ballantyne. He's . . . er, our fathers were dear friends, and he's come to Dunvegan to pay his respects. My lord, this is Glynnis Fraser."

Miss Fraser's gaze darted from his face back to Catriona's, and some silent communication passed between the two of them. Whatever Glynnis gleaned from this exchange must have reassured her, because she offered him a tentative smile. "It's a pleasure to meet you, Lord Ballantyne."

Hamish bowed. "Miss Fraser."

The ladies embarked on their business then, neither of them paying him much attention as they discussed the merits of *Allium sativum*—otherwise known as garlic—as a remedy against bacterial infections.

It should have been the dullest half an hour of his life.

Instead, he caught himself memorizing the Latin names for the various species of the plants and, as always seemed to be the case now, watching Catriona.

She made the most fetching moue with her lips whenever she was expounding on some interesting point, and she moved her hands as she spoke as if she were coaxing music from an invisible orchestra.

Kissing her had been a mistake.

Not because she was naïve, or innocent, or because less than two weeks had elapsed since he'd first laid eyes on her. It wasn't because he was a liar, or she was vulnerable, or because he was a marquess whose kiss was ungentlemanly at best, and at worst ruinous. It wasn't because they didn't trust each other, or because he still believed her father to be a scoundrel and thief.

That is, those were all perfectly splendid reasons why he would have done well to keep his hands and his lips to himself, but none of them were the reason that made all the other reasons he should never have kissed her pale in comparison.

No, that reason was—

"May I offer you a bit of cordial, my lord?"

Hamish wrenched his gaze from Catriona's face and turned to Glynnis Fraser. She was holding out a glass with a thimbleful of orange liquid in it. "What is it? It looks like Godfrey's Cordial."

"It has some of the same ingredients as Godfrey's but without the laudanum."

Hamish swirled the orange liquid in the glass. "Isn't Godfrey's intended for infants? It's been some time since I suffered from colic, Miss Fraser."

Glynnis laughed. "It is intended for infants, yes, but I can assure you it won't do you any harm, my lord. This has a bit of ginger in it, which does wonders for treating the headache. Cat and I often test our cordials this way."

He glanced at Cat. She offered him a demure smile, and then—God help him—she parted those sweet pink lips around the edge of her glass and took a dainty sip.

And that, right there, was the reason he shouldn't have kissed Catriona MacLeod.

Now that he'd kissed those lips once, he could think of nothing but kissing them again. Somehow, Catriona MacLeod had managed to do what dozens of fashionable young ladies in London had tried and failed to accomplish.

She'd turned him into a besotted schoolboy.

Him, the Marquess of Ballantyne, one of the *ton's* most sought-after gentlemen, admired by everyone for his charm and sparkling wit had been reduced to a pathetic, lovesick fool by a stubborn, maddening, Scottish lassie who had a preoccupation with poison.

Perhaps she was a witch, after all, and she'd cast a spell on him. A brilliant, beautiful witch with the sweetest lips he'd ever kissed.

There must be some reason why he was behaving as if he'd never kissed a lady before. Because he *had*, and more times than a proper gentleman should have done. He'd kissed too many pairs of lips to count, and many of them plumper, pinker, and more experienced than Catriona MacLeod's.

Amorous widows, seductive courtesans, eager mistresses . . .

But never—*never*—had he obsessed over a lady's kiss the way he was hers.

All he could think about was tracing the tip of his tongue over the slight bow in her upper lip, then nipping her plump lower lip until it was as red as ripe cherries, then lingering over the slight upward curve at each corner. Every morning, he woke with the remembered taste of her on his lips, so sweet he'd be shaking with need before he even opened his eyes.

Meanwhile, while he was consumed with the taste, texture, warmth, and plumpness of her lips, she was putting as much distance between them as she could possibly manage.

It was driving him mad. *She* was driving him mad.

When he was a child, treacle tarts were his favorite sweet. Their cook at the time, Mrs. Babington, had made an exceptional treacle tart. To this day, he'd never tasted a better one, but she'd been a stern, hard-hearted sort of woman, and she'd taken great pleasure in denying him even the tiniest bite of the treat until it was served at the dining table after dinner.

There'd been nothing he could do but stand there, gaze at it, and *want* it.

Catriona MacLeod was just like that treacle tart.

Since that kiss, she'd been cool, proper, and scrupulously polite. She'd erected a frigid wall of reserve between them and banished him to the other side, and it felt just like being a child again, his mouth watering over that perfect treacle tart. It was torture of the most exquisite kind, so frustrating and titillating at once he couldn't say whether he wanted it to stop or go on forever.

"There you go, Lord Ballantyne." Glynnis Fraser gave him a cheerful smile before taking his empty cordial glass from his hand and returning it to the tray on the counter. "I daresay that will take care of any future headaches you may have had today."

"That's a great relief, Miss Fraser."

But it wasn't his *head* that was the problem. Certain, er . . . other parts of his body were swollen and aching, but it wasn't the organ between his legs that worried him.

It was the one inside his chest.

"It looks as if we'll arrive home just in time for tea," Catriona said to him as they reached the bottom of the long drive that led to the front entrance of the castle.

Dear God, not another tea.

This was another new edict Catriona had invented after their kiss in the workroom. The following day, she'd announced that henceforth, they would all sit down together for a proper tea.

This stilted affair took place in the drawing room—a shabby room none of the MacLeod sisters had set foot in before Cat decided they must all take their tea there.

It was another ploy to keep distance between them, another way to fill the day with the sort of formal nonsense that prevented any real intimacy. Their afternoon tea was an orchestrated affair with pale blue porcelain teacups, silver teaspoons, and tiny frosted cakes, but with little conversation.

He despised teatime nearly as much as he did Catriona's basket.

It was unbearable, sitting on the disastrously uncomfortable settee in that drawing room with his teacup balanced on his knee and exchanging inane remarks about the weather with Catriona, Freya, and Sorcha MacLeod.

"I don't want tea."

"I beg your pardon, my lord?" She turned to him with a smile that looked as if it had been painted on her lips.

"I said, I don't want tea. I can't think of a single thing more tedious than afternoon tea."

"What on earth is wrong with—"

"Stop it, Catriona." He caught her arm, bringing them to a halt in the middle of the drive. "Why are you doing this?"

"I don't know what you mean, my lord. Doing what?"

But she did know. He could see it in the way her throat worked, and the hot flush of color that swept from her neck into her cheeks. "I beg your pardon for the, ah, incident in your father's study the other night. I shouldn't have . . ."

Kissed you. The words were on the tip of his tongue, but he didn't say them, because they were a lie. He didn't regret kissing her. If he had the chance, he'd do it again in a heartbeat, despite all the reasons he shouldn't.

"I don't wish to discuss this with you, my lord." She turned away from him and continued her way up the drive, leaving him to follow her or not, as he chose.

He chose to follow her, of course. He was beginning to think he'd choose to follow her anywhere. "Wait, Cat. There's something I need to tell you. I've arranged for us to go to—"

"*Nooooo!*"

"Dear God, what was that?" Catriona's cheeks went white, and she began racing up the drive. "It sounded like Sorcha!"

Another shriek followed the first, this one higher pitched and edged with panic. "What do you think you're doing? Release her at once!"

The cries were coming from the direction of the castle.

He didn't pause to hear any more but went tearing up the drive with Catriona on his heels. But what he found when he reached the entryway brought him to such a sudden halt that she slammed right into his back.

"Ouch! What in the world?"

What, indeed? If he'd had every word in the English vocabulary right at the tip of his tongue, he couldn't have described the scene that was unfolding in the drive.

Callum and Keir had arrived, but they'd been, er . . . waylaid on their way into the castle by Sorcha, who was . . . well, she seemed to have leapt onto Callum's back and was preventing him from going any further by holding a blade to his throat.

Callum had Freya trapped against his chest. Keir stood on the other side of the drive, his face a mask of horror.

When Keir caught sight of Hamish, his brows lowered in a dark scowl. "Ah, there you are, Ballantyne. What a lovely welcome you've arranged for us."

Hamish gaped at him for a full minute before he gathered his scattered wits enough to speak. "Callum! What in God's name do you think you're doing?"

"*Me*, Ballantyne? What am *I* doing? Why, nothing much, just attempting to get this hellion off me before she slits my throat." He reached behind him and tried to snatch a fold of Sorcha's coat, but she only scrambled higher, climbing up Callum's back as if she were scaling a tree. "Perhaps you'd better ask her what *she's* doing?"

"I should think it's obvious." Sorcha tightened her legs around Callum's hips, grasped a handful of his hair, and jerked his head back, pressing her blade more firmly against his throat. "Sending you back to wherever you came from, or else to the devil. Your choice."

"Some help, if you'd be so kind, Ballantyne?" Callum cast an accusing glower at Keir. "He's bloody useless enough."

"I beg your pardon, Callum, but the lady leapt onto your back before I could stop her. Rather an exciting welcome to Castle Cairncross, all told."

Cat stood beside Hamish with her hand over her mouth, her green eyes so wide they looked as if they might desert her head at any moment. "What's happening? Who are these men, and why are they manhandling my sisters?"

Callum grunted. "I beg your pardon, madam, but your sister is manhandling *me*!"

"This is how we treat smugglers!" Sorcha was clinging to Callum like a burr while he spun around in circles, trying to dislodge her. "If you didn't wish to be manhandled, then you should have found another castle to attack!"

"They're, ah . . . they're not smugglers, Miss Sorcha." Hamish cleared his throat. "They're my friends. Er, Callum Ross and Keir Dunn, these young ladies are Freya and Catriona MacLeod. The one on your back, Callum, is Sorcha MacLeod."

"Delightful to meet you, Miss Sorcha." Callum had caught one of Sorcha's ankles and was tugging on it as if it were a stubborn corset lace. "Now we're friends, perhaps you'd be so good as to *get off me*."

"Lord Ballantyne?" Cat edged closer to him, one eye on Sorcha, and lowered her voice. "Is there a reason your friends are standing in my drive right now?"

Here it was. Either she'd be pleased, or he was destined for more stilted teatimes. "Yes. I wrote to them and asked them to come to Castle Cairncross to watch over Sorcha and Freya, so you could come with me to Ballantrae to see Donigan."

"You did?" Slowly, her lips began to curve . . . up, up, up, and then there it was.

A smile, like a flower opening.

"Yes." He could have said more—that she deserved to go, that he wanted her with him, that he hadn't liked seeing the life drain out of her when she thought she'd be left behind—but what emerged from his lips instead was an awkward, "It didn't seem fair otherwise."

She gazed at him for a moment, the smile still on her lips, then she turned and strode across the drive, waving her hands at her youngest sister.

"Sorcha! Get off that man at once!"

Chapter 16

Ballantrae, South Ayrshire
Six days later.

"That's the smuggler's den?" Hamish squinted at the neat fisherman's cottage on the crest of the hill above them. "What sort of smuggler keeps a flower garden? It looks like some wee grandmother's cottage."

"Well, it wouldn't be much use to the smugglers if it *did* look like a smuggler's cottage, would it?" But despite her bravado, Cat's spine prickled with uneasiness. Of all the places one might imagine a thieving villain would live, this sweet little cottage with its whitewashed walls and cheerful garden seemed the least likely.

Had she mistaken the location? Or had Donigan abandoned the cottage for one of the many hidden caves tucked along the shore of Ballantrae Bay? For all she knew, he might have returned to Ireland by now.

If he had, they'd never find him, and their quest would end here.

But after six long days of bumping along the endless roads from Skye to Girvan, her bones rattling with every mile and the dirt from the road insinuating itself into every wrinkle and fold of her skirts, was she really going to scurry off back home without even daring to knock on the cottage's door?

Cowardice begets cowardice . . .

"Perhaps the garden is filled with poisonous plants?" Hamish nodded toward the tiny bit of land on one side of the cottage door. "Monkshood, Hemlock, and Deadly Nightshade? Such a garden as that might prove useful to a smuggler."

"There's one way to find out, I suppose." She clambered down from her perch next to him on the box seat, stumbling a little as her boot heels sank into the ruts the carriage wheels had made in the soft dirt.

Hamish had brought the carriage to a stop on the road well below the hill, out of sight of anyone who happened to be peering out the windows. One didn't like to reveal themselves to a band of hardened smugglers before they were ready.

Such a thing could prove dangerous. Or deadly.

There was a dozen different ways this could go wrong. She may have mistaken the cottage. Even if she had found the right one, who was to say Donigan was even here?

The only way they were getting inside that cottage was if Donigan recognized her as Rory MacLeod's daughter.

Otherwise . . . well, perhaps it was wiser not to dwell on what might happen otherwise, but smugglers weren't known for their hospitality toward unexpected visitors. If they walked into that cottage, there was a chance they might never walk out of it again.

But they were here now, and she wouldn't give in to her fears. Not this time, even if her hands *had* gone clammy and she was shaking in her boots. "We'd better walk up the hill. They'll hear the carriage coming."

The deep violet purple of twilight had taken over the sky. In this dim light, they should be able to sneak up the side of the hill without anyone noticing them.

"Another bloody hill," Hamish muttered, but he jumped down from the box readily enough. "I'll go alone, first. If all is well, I'll come back for you."

"No, indeed. You've forgotten, my lord, that you need me. I

don't imagine Mr. Donigan will be pleased to find an English marquess on his doorstep."

"I don't like this, Cat. We're far too exposed. Anyone could snatch you up and drag you inside before I can stop them."

"There's no other way. We already agreed on this, my lord."

He opened his mouth to argue but then snapped it closed and dragged his hands through his hair. "Yes, all right, but you'll stay behind me. Do you understand?"

She did, and she would—right up until they reached the cottage door, that is. If Donigan was here, it was important that he saw her first.

"Very well." She was filthy and exhausted from days of driving, and her backside would likely never recover from the abuse the carriage seat had inflicted on it, but somehow, she managed a grin for him. "After you, Lord Ballantyne."

They began to climb. It wasn't a steep hill, but it was difficult to navigate the loose rocks and tree roots. They skidded along, making more noise than they should have, but no one leapt out from the shadows at them, and the front windows of the cottage remained dark.

They paused again below the crest of the hill and peeked over the top.

Now they were this close, she could see the muted glow of one lamp burning in a back room, but otherwise, there wasn't any sign that any human, smuggler or otherwise, had ever inhabited the place. The cottage sat in the middle of the small, deserted garden, still and silent.

On the one hand, the calm was reassuring, but on the other, well . . . if they were set upon by a gang of smugglers on their way to the door, there was no one about to help them. "I don't suppose there's anything for it but to go knock on the door, is there?"

"By all means, let's knock on the smugglers' door." Hamish clambered over the last rise, then held his hand out to assist her. "What could possibly go wrong?"

A dozen grisly answers to that question flitted through her mind, but she pushed them aside. They'd gotten this far, hadn't they? This wasn't the time to let her courage fail her.

She took his hand, and they made their way toward the door. One step, another, a dozen more, her heart pounding heavily as if each one took them another step closer to their doom, but there were no footsteps behind them, no blood-curdling screams, no pistol shots shattering the silence around them.

Perhaps it was some wee grandmother's house, after all?

"You don't suppose I made a mistake with the direction, do you?" There were dozens of cottages nearly identical to this one scattered around the bay. It would be the easiest thing in the world to mistake one for another. "Perhaps we should have waited until tomorrow and come when it's light out."

He didn't answer.

"Hamish?" She turned, a whispered question on her lips, but it died on her tongue before she could utter it.

A man dressed all in black had one meaty arm wrapped around Hamish's neck. He'd come upon them so quickly, so silently, that for a moment, she thought she must be imagining him.

Until she saw the blade.

It was long and curved, glinting in the moonlight, and the wicked edge of it was pressed to the vulnerable skin of Hamish's neck.

"No!" She leapt toward him instinctively, her heart vaulting into her throat, but she didn't make it even one step before another man caught her around the waist, and without a single hesitation, wrenched both her arms behind her back.

That was when she heard the voice.

It was deep and rough, with just a touch of amusement, the man's fetid breath hot on her neck as he leaned closer. "Where do ye think you're going, lass?"

"Don't. Bloody. Touch. Her."

Hamish was deadly calm, his voice as cool as the winter wind when it blew off Loch Dunvegan, but the thread of dark menace and the way he bit off each word sent a chill down Cat's spine. She'd never heard him speak that way before, not even when he'd accused her of poisoning him. For all his charming smiles and that alluring twinkle in his bright blue eyes, Hamish Muir wasn't a man to be trifled with.

"Yer not in any position to be making demands, mate." His captor angled the blade slightly, and a thin stream of blood trickled down Hamish's neck.

"Don't!" Her voice was trembling with such fear she hardly recognized it.

But Hamish only laughed. *Laughed*, even as the man increased the pressure on the blade, and the drops of blood turned into a thick rivulet and a scarlet bloom appeared in the folds of his white cravat. "Is that so? Very well, then you can explain to Mr. Donigan why you've attacked the daughter of his dear old friend, Rory MacLeod."

The moment he uttered her father's name, everything—from the grip the man had on her arms to the very air around them—shifted, turning heavy and tense.

Finally, the man who held Cat's arms found his voice. "Rory's dead."

"He is, indeed. Well done. But a man can be dead, and his daughters still be very much alive. It's not terribly difficult. Surely, you can see how that works?"

Cat stared at him. Was he *mocking* the man? Mocking the man with the six-inch glittering blade even now embedded in his flesh! She was shaking with fear, but a hysterical laugh bubbled up in her throat.

Dear God, he was as mad as a Bedlamite.

But for all the riskiness of it, it was working, because Hamish's captor cast an uncertain glance at the man holding Cat, and his hands loosened around her arms.

"How do we know she's Rory's girl?" the first one said. "I never seen her before."

Hamish shot the man a disdainful glance. "Miss MacLeod, would you be so good as to remove your hat?"

Her hair. Of course! Why hadn't she thought of that? The MacLeod red was distinctive, even amongst so many redheaded Scots. Anyone who'd known Rory might recognize her hair to be the same shade as her father's.

"Let go." She tried to squirm free, but the man who held her didn't yield. Instead, he reached up and without a single word, tore Cat's hat from her head. Half her hairpins went with it, and a few locks of her hair tumbled over her shoulders.

A low, harsh noise that sounded distinctly like a growl rumbled from Hamish's chest. "You'll pay for that, *mate*."

But neither man seemed to hear him. They were both staring at her hair. "That's Rory's red, right enough," Hamish's captor said, his throat moving in a rough swallow. "Bring the lass in. I'll take care of this one."

"No!" Panic rushed over her, and she began to struggle in earnest, squirming and twisting and flailing like a wildcat. "He's my . . . my husband! He's Rory's son-in-law, and a much beloved one!"

The man behind her uttered a curse and began dragging her toward the door. "Bring him in. We'll let Donigan decide."

The two men hustled them through a narrow hallway to a back room, where the lantern she'd noticed through the window sat in the center of a long, narrow table.

A tall, dark-haired man was seated in one of the chairs on the opposite side, studying a map spread out on the table in front of him. He glanced up when they entered the room.

It had been at least a dozen years since she'd seen him, but she knew him at once. He had a touch of gray at his temples that hadn't been there before, and time had worn a few lines into his face, but she'd know his eyes anywhere. They were a cool, light gray with an unusually dark ring around the irises.

It was Donigan. Those eyes were as distinctive as the MacLeod red hair.

If he was surprised to see two strangers dragged into his presence, one of them with blood running down his neck, she couldn't see it on his face. His expression didn't alter in any way, not even so much as a twitch of his eyebrow.

He merely sat back in his chair, and drawled, "Well, what have we here?"

"Found these two creeping about outside." The man shoved Hamish forward. "This one's got a mouth on him."

"That explains the blood." Donigan considered Hamish for a long moment, then turned his gaze to her. "And this one?"

Her captor grunted. "She says she's Rory MacLeod's daughter."

"Oh? I can't think what one of Rory's girls would be doing out here." Once again, Donigan's expression didn't change—the man was a cipher—but the energy around him shifted, and his gaze sharpened. "Which daughter would you be, lass?"

Cat raised her chin. "Catriona. The eldest."

Slowly, Donigan rose from his chair and took up the lantern sitting on the table. Hamish tensed when he approached her, but Donigan merely held the lantern up to her face.

He gazed down at her for a long time, studying her features one by one, until at last, he lowered the lantern. "Aye, she's a MacLeod, all right. I'll be damned. You're a long way from Dunvegan, girl."

Cat sucked in a deep breath, her eyes closing, a relief so profound rushing through her that she nearly dropped to her knees.

Thank God.

But then Donigan turned to Hamish, and she tensed once again.

"Who's this gentleman you've brought with you, Catriona?" Donigan studied Hamish with the same careful attention he had her. "He looks like an Englishman. We don't care much for Englishmen around here."

"He—he's my husband, Mr. Donigan. Rory's son-in-law," she added, in case it wasn't obvious.

"Your husband, is he?" A small smile drifted over Donigan's

lips. "How odd. I don't remember Rory mentioning one of his daughters had married."

She hadn't any idea what to say to that, so she said nothing.

"Ah. That's wise of you, Catriona. If you've got nothing to say to help yourself, best to say nothing at all." Donigan chuckled. "You're your father's daughter, I see."

Was she, indeed? She'd always thought of herself as her mother's daughter, but perhaps Mr. Donigan was right. Perhaps there was more of Rory in her than she'd ever realized.

After all, she was here, wasn't she? "Yes, I suppose I am."

"It's nearly three hundred miles from Dunvegan to South Ayrshire." Donigan leaned back against the table behind him. "Unless you and your sisters are no longer at Castle Cairncross?"

"We're still there." As far as she knew, at least. There was no telling what may have happened at the castle in the week she and Hamish had been gone. It was a blessing that Callum and Keir were there—although Sorcha hadn't seen it that way—but after everything that had happened, she couldn't rest easy.

"Three hundred miles, then," Donigan repeated. "Did you come all this way just to see me? I'm flattered, Catriona, but this can't be merely a social call."

"Er, no." She glanced at Hamish, but he tipped his head toward Donigan, as if urging her to go on. "We . . . that is, my husband and I . . . need your help."

Donigan took his time replying, and the silent moments ticked by until Cat thought she'd scream. But then he straightened and pulled two more chairs away from the table. "Rory was a good friend to me. I'm indebted to him, and I'm a man who pays my debts."

Cat sucked in a deep breath. It was all right. It was going to be all right.

"Sit down." Donigan waved them toward the chairs. "Tell me what I can do."

* * *

Cormac Donigan didn't look like any smuggler Hamish had ever seen.

If it hadn't been for the man's two henchmen—one of whom had come close to opening one of his veins—he would have mistaken Donigan for a gentleman.

"You mean to say, Catriona, that your father returned to Castle Cairncross without any treasure?" Donigan ran a hand over the scruff on his chin. "Rumor had it otherwise. Every smuggler in Carrick was talking about the fortune he made away with."

"I'm aware of the rumors." Cat let out a bitter laugh. "Some of the smugglers you mention have decided to secure that treasure for themselves. More than one lugger has approached the castle by Loch Dunvegan and attempted to land on the shore."

"Boatloads of smugglers and no treasure?" Donigan shook his head. "I see how that might prove to be a problem. No doubt they all think it's there. Your father never left a treasure behind. In all the years we worked together, I never knew him to fail to secure his bounty."

"Do you know where he went this last time? He refused to speak much about it, and he left without a word to my sisters and me about the treasure or about where he was going."

Donigan raised an eyebrow. "You're going after the treasure?"

Hamish tensed. If Donigan had a mind to beat them to it—and really, what was to stop him from seeing his henchmen finish what they'd started—they may not yet be out of danger.

"Yes, but not for the reasons you might suppose. We don't care about the money, but we'll never have any peace at Castle Cairncross until that treasure is found. Can you tell us anything about it?"

"I'm afraid not, lass. If I knew, I'd tell you. Rory's always had his secrets, but not like this time. He never breathed a word about it, not to any of us."

"Oh." Cat slumped in her chair.

"There was something different about that treasure," Donigan went on. "I can't say what, though. Like I said, he didn't confide in me this time. But I'll tell you this. He never came this way. Not to Ballantrae, or to South Ayrshire. If he had, I'd have known of it."

Wonderful. That only left the rest of Scotland, then.

"Does this coin mean anything to you, Mr. Donigan?" Hamish reached into his coat pocket and handed one of the Louis d'Or ten-pieces to Donigan.

Donigan studied it, turning it this way and that. "No. I've never seen one like it before, but there's those that say there were coins like that in the monies Louis XV of France sent to Bonnie Prince Charlie, back in seventeen forty-six."

"There are those that say that, yes." Hamish braced his hands on the table and leaned closer, looking Donigan in the eyes. "What do *you* say?"

"I say that money was never found. It was lost up Lochaber way, near the Sound of Arisaig. It might be that it's still there, hidden in a cave somewhere. But I'll tell you this. If there was ever a man who could find the lost Jacobean gold, it was Rory MacLeod."

"But you never heard of any rumors to that effect?"

"No, but Rory was a sly one, and patient, too. It could be he found something up there years ago and hid it in one of the caves thereabouts." Donigan slid the coin back across the table toward Hamish. "There's nothing a smuggler likes more than a cave."

Hamish had had the same thought when he'd first seen the coin, but it was pure speculation.

But then all of this was pure speculation. No matter which way they went, they could be heading in the wrong direction. Lochaber was a two-days' ride east from Girvan, while Dunvegan was directly west from here.

It would add four days to their journey. That was quite a way to go on a wild goose chase. If there'd been something in Rory's papers indicating he'd gone toward Lochaber, it would have been worth the extra time, but there'd been nothing at all that pointed in that direction.

But that was the trouble. There'd been nothing that had pointed in *any* direction. Or if there had been, they hadn't been able to decipher it.

"What of this drawing, Mr. Donigan? Does this look at all familiar to you?" Catriona offered Donigan a wrinkled slip of paper with a rough drawing on it.

Hamish glanced at it. It was the dagger, the one that had appeared multiple times in Rory's papers. He'd drawn it over and over, sometimes with the ring around it, and other times without.

It meant nothing to him or to Cat, but he could see at once that Donigan recognized it by the way he suddenly straightened in his chair.

"That's Clan Mackay's crest. Bad enough drawing of it—Rory was no artist—but that's it, all right." Donigan traced the drawing with one finger, then handed the paper back to Cat. "An upraised arm, with the hand holding the dagger aloft, with a clansman's belt surrounding it."

"Yes, of course! I see it now. It is a remarkably bad drawing, but there's no mistaking it." She peered down at the paper, then handed it to Hamish. "Do you recall Clan Mackay's motto, Mr. Donigan?"

"*Manu Forti*. With a strong hand. A warlike clan, Clan Mackay. Your father didn't have any love for the Mackays. He said they betrayed the Scots by taking George II's side against the Jacobites."

"I remember." Cat smiled, but there was sadness in it. "Where is Clan Mackay's seat?"

"Castle Varrich, in Strathnaver, up north in Tongue, but it's a ruin now. The clan chief removed to Tongue House some years ago." Donigan glanced from Hamish to Cat. "If you mean to go up there, you take care, lass. You don't want to make an enemy of Clan Mackay."

"Of course not," Cat murmured.

Hamish smothered a snort. He knew her too well to accept that meek reply. He could already see the wheels turning in her head.

"I've had my housekeeper prepare a bedchamber for you. You don't want to be wandering around out there this late at night." Donigan gave Hamish a bloodthirsty grin. "You never know what kind of blackguard you might run into."

"A bedchamber?" Cat's head jerked up. "You're very kind, Mr. Donigan, but we don't need—"

"Yes, you do, lass. There's a ship loaded with tea and rum foundering in Ballantrae Bay as we speak. She's going to wreck, and every blackguard hereabouts is down on the shore now, waiting for it to happen. You don't want to be anywhere near there tonight."

"Oh. Well, in that case . . ."

She glanced at Hamish, and he grinned back at her. "Is something wrong, *mo ghaol*?" He shouldn't tease her, but it was her own fault for blushing so charmingly. "Your cheeks are as red as *Papaver rhoeas*."

Red poppies.

"No. Of course not. Why would there be?" She turned back to Donigan, swallowing. "We're, ah, happy to accept your hospitality, Mr. Donigan."

She didn't add, *because we have no other choice*, but she may as well have.

"Come along then, *leannan*." Hamish rose to his feet and held his hand out to her. "Let's go to bed."

CHAPTER 17

The bedchamber was the size of a pocket handkerchief.

"It's not much, but you'll be comfortable enough. I'm off to see about that foundering ship. Can't let all that tea and rum end up in the wrong hands, can I?" Donigan winked at Cat. "I won't return by morning. I wish you both a pleasant journey back to Dunvegan."

Cat was staring at the bed, but she turned and offered him a weak smile. "Thank you for your assistance, Mr. Donigan. We're grateful to you."

"Anything for one of Rory's girls." With that, Donigan stepped out into the hallway and closed the door behind him, leaving her alone with Hamish.

Alone, in a deserted cottage, in a bedchamber so diminutive one couldn't get from one side of the room to the other without crawling over the bed. Everything, from the braided rug on the floor to the chair tucked into one corner to the dressing table with the wee pitcher and basin atop it, was so tiny it was like stepping into a doll's house.

Everything, that is, except the bed. It was a massive, sprawling thing with four wooden posts, a pretty carved headboard, and a thick blue coverlet.

The only thing in the room more intimidating than that monstrosity of a bed was Hamish himself. How had she forgotten how *potent* he was? She'd grown so accustomed to riding beside him in the tight confines of the carriage it had quite slipped her mind.

But as soon as he stepped into the tiny room he seemed to swell in size, the width of his shoulders expanding, his muscular legs in his tight breeches doubling in length, and the top of his head nearly touching the ceiling.

All at once, he was the mighty Marquess of Ballantyne again, and she was meant to spend the night with him in a bedchamber no larger than a teacup. Why, they'd be right on top of each other, so close if she dared to draw a breath, *his* lungs would expand with it.

"You needn't look so dismayed, Catriona. I'm not going to leap upon you. I am a gentleman, you know."

Leap upon her? My goodness. "Don't be absurd, my lord. I'm not dismayed. Why should I be dismayed? I assure you I've never in my life been less dismayed than I am right now."

Except, of course, she *was* dismayed. Disturbed, even, and not only because he dominated every inch of the tiny space. That alone was bad enough, but to make matters worse, he was in, er . . . a shocking state of undress.

He'd removed his blood-stained cravat as soon as they'd sat down with Donigan, and as their conversation had worn on into the wee hours, he'd abandoned his coat, as well.

She was alone in a bedchamber with a half-dressed marquess. A vigorous, half-dressed marquess in tight breeches that accentuated his long, muscular legs and a loose, white linen shirt, the open neck of which revealed a patch of sun-bronzed skin and a handful of fascinating, crisp dark hairs.

Any young lady in her place would be dismayed to find herself in such a predicament, only . . . well, perhaps she wasn't quite as dismayed as she should be.

"It's, ah, cozy, is it not? All but the . . ." He cleared his throat and gestured awkwardly toward the bed. "All but the bed."

"The bed, yes." There was no ignoring that bed, was there?

They both stood there staring at it, neither one of them daring to look at the other, until at last, Hamish cleared his throat. "Are we returning to Dunvegan tomorrow?"

"Dunvegan?" she repeated stupidly, as if she'd never heard the name before.

"Yes, Catriona. Dunvegan. On the Isle of Skye? Surely, you've heard of it?" He gave her a teasing grin. "I hear there's a trio of redheaded witches living in an ancient castle there."

"My, you are amusing this evening, my lord. As far as returning to Dunvegan tomorrow, I think we should put off our return for another week, and go to Tongue, instead."

"Not Lochaber?"

"No." She couldn't explain why, but everything inside her—every telltale flutter and twitch, was urging her to go to Tongue. "You recall what Mr. Duffy said about Rory's gold coin? He was in Eilean nan Ron right before he returned to Dunvegan with the coin. Eilean nan Ron is only eight miles from Tongue. Besides, I have a feeling about Tongue."

She eyed Hamish, biting her lip. It was one thing for her to trust her flutters and twitches, but it was quite another to ask *him* to trust them. Tongue was a long way to go only to find out she'd made a mistake.

"Very well, then." He retreated to the chair in the corner and began removing his boots. "We'll leave for Tongue tomorrow morning."

He was . . . that was all? Tongue was another six days' journey from here, and he'd agreed to undertake it on top of the six days it had taken them to get to Ballantrae, all because she had a *feeling*?

Had anyone outside of her own family ever had such faith in her before?

No. That was the sort of thing she'd remember.

He noticed her staring at him and froze with one boot still hanging off the end of his foot. "If you'd rather I didn't . . . if you'd rather I not remove my boots, Miss MacLeod, then I will, of course, yield to your preference."

His boots? Why would she object to . . . oh.

Oh.

He thought she'd object to him removing his clothing. But these were his boots, for pity's sake. Surely, no harm could come from her catching a glimpse of his feet. "I have no objection whatsoever, my lord."

"Thank you."

Was he blushing? Lord Ballantyne, *blushing*! She never imagined she'd see such a thing. Still, a man with nefarious designs on a lady's virtue didn't *blush* when he accompanied her into a bedchamber.

She was perfectly safe with him.

Perfectly, unquestionably, undeniably safe.

She stifled a sigh, retreated to the other end of the bedchamber, and began unbuttoning her cloak, her own cheeks heating.

His head jerked up. "What, ah . . . what are you doing?"

Her hands went still on the buttons. "Removing my cloak? It's a bit damp."

"Right. Yes, of course. Please do carry on, Miss MacLeod."

Dear God, neither of them would get a wink of sleep at this rate, and they had a long drive ahead of them tomorrow. Perhaps it would be best to just acknowledge the awkwardness of it outright, so they might get past it.

As the lady, it fell to her to do it. Hamish had a bit of the fashionable rogue in him—this was undoubtedly not his first time alone in a bedchamber with a lady—but he was still far too much of a gentleman to suggest there was any tension or, ah . . . physical awareness between them at all.

She opened her mouth, but before she could say a word he rose to his feet and nodded down at the chair he'd just vacated. "I'll sleep here."

"What, in the chair?" She looked at him, then looked at the chair.

"Certainly." He glanced at the chair and couldn't quite hide his grimace. "I'll be, er . . . perfectly comfortable, I assure you."

"You will not sleep in that chair, my lord. It's far too small for you."

"The floor, then."

The floor? With his long legs? He'd have to tuck them under the bed or brace them upright against the wall.

For pity's sake, this was absurd. He couldn't sleep in that minuscule chair or on the floor when there was a bed perfectly able to accommodate them both. Why, it was so large there was no need for their limbs to touch.

"Nonsense. You'll sleep in the bed, my lord."

"No, Miss MacLeod, I will not."

He glared at her, such a picture of scandalized outrage that she was obliged to stifle a laugh. Goodness, men were ridiculous creatures.

She marched briskly to the bed and arranged the pillows down the center of it. "There we are. This side, Lord Ballantyne, is yours." She gestured to the left of the bed. "And this side is mine, and never the twain shall meet."

"A few pillows? That's your solution?" He rubbed the back of his neck. "You can't really believe that makes any difference."

"Very well, my lord." She plucked up one of the blankets and tossed it to him. "Here. You can wrap this around yourself, and I'll slip under the coverlet. There's no chance of impropriety that way."

He muttered something under his breath—something about the flimsiness of pillows and something else about . . . amorous gentlemen?

No. She must have misheard him.

In any case, she was done arguing with him. "Do as you will, my lord, but we've a long drive ahead of us, and it will be especially tiresome for a gentleman who hasn't slept."

He said nothing, and after a moment of uncomfortable silence, she returned to her corner of the bedchamber and slid her cloak from her shoulders. Then she made quick use of the basin, marched to the bed, seated herself on the edge, and removed her boots.

Hamish didn't stir, but she could feel his eyes on her the entire time, that deep blue gaze burning into her until she was certain her clothing was going to burst into flames. Only when she'd slipped beneath the coverlet at last did she meet his gaze. "Goodnight, Lord Ballantyne."

He didn't reply, nor did he move from his place in the middle of the room.

Well then, he might stand there all night, if he liked. She turned resolutely onto her side, and squeezed her eyes closed, but despite her exhaustion, sleep had never been further away.

She lay there, her muscles tense, listening.

It took far longer than she'd anticipated for him to give up, although perhaps it shouldn't surprise her that he'd held out as long as he did. Over the past few weeks, she'd discovered that he was almost as stubborn as she was.

But at last—*at last*—he stirred, and a moment later, the chair squeaked.

Did he really intend to sleep in that blasted chair? He was the most infuriating man she'd ever—

The chair squeaked again, there was a soft pad of footsteps, and then . . .

She stilled, her breath held.

The opposite side of the bed sank under his weight. There was a soft rustling sound, and she felt him stretch out beside her.

For a long time, neither of them said a word.

But she didn't fall asleep, either.

He blew out the lamp, leaving the room as dark as one of the smugglers' caves. "I intend to remain on my side of the pillows, Miss MacLeod," he said at last, his voice hushed, yet oddly formal. "I trust that you will stay on yours."

Despite herself, a smile rose to her lips. Did he fear for his virtue? "Of course, my lord."

Soon afterward, Hamish fell asleep, but she lay awake for a

long time, listening to the soothing sound of his deep, even breaths.

It was surprisingly nice, lying next to him this way.

Of course, she was exhausted, even more so than she'd been after the first lugger had come to the castle, and the dream had started. The bed was a comfortable one, too, and the coverlet over her soft and warm.

Yet it was more than that.

It was him, too. Hamish. Not Lord Ballantyne anymore.

Not in her head, at least. No, she'd long since started thinking of him as Hamish, though she took care not to say it aloud.

But whether she spoke his name or not, he was simply Hamish to her now, the man with the fetching lock of silky dark hair that insisted upon falling over his forehead and the unexpectedly boyish grin.

The man who'd made it possible for her to accompany him on this journey because he saw how much it mattered to her to have a hand in her own fate.

The man she'd been so certain would prove to be her own, and her sisters', ruination.

But somehow, he hadn't. Between the monkshood poisoning, the smugglers, and the ghost of Rory MacLeod, she'd grown to trust him.

Him, of all people. The last man in the world she ever thought she'd trust.

Since her father had died, and her world had been torn asunder, she'd begun to believe she'd never trust anyone ever again.

It was such a lonely way to live, to look at people and feel only suspicion.

Perhaps nothing would come of this journey. They might go all the way to Tongue and find nothing. The treasure might be destined to remain lost forever, and Hamish to return to London empty-handed.

But he'd leave her with something, something she'd thought she'd lost forever.

Her faith in people, and in herself. He'd given her that.

It was the last thought she had before she drifted off to sleep.

When she woke again later it was to a darkened room, but the first fingers of dawn were just beginning to light the eastern sky.

It was the cold that had woken her. She was so cold she was shivering, her bones aching with it. She lifted her head from the pillow and peered into the darkness, blinking.

Perhaps she should fetch her cloak? But it was likely still damp, and the idea of leaving her cocoon made her shudder. Instead, she turned onto her other side and tucked the coverlet tightly under her chin.

Hamish was still beside her, an indistinct shape lost in the folds of the blanket, but as her eyes adjusted to the darkness, his features began to emerge, one by one.

His straight nose, and angled jaw, the prickles of his beard shadowing his chin.

He was lying on his back, his dark hair, which was much too long now to be fashionable, a tousled mess of waves against the pillow beneath his head. His mouth was slightly open, his chest rising with his slow, deep breaths, those sensuous lips parted—

Sensuous? Goodness, where had that word come from?

She edged closer, propping her head on her hand and gazing down at him. He looked younger in his sleep, his face more vulnerable, the lordy aristocratic arrogance of the Marquess of Ballantyne swept away, leaving only Hamish in its place.

He didn't appear to be cold.

What would those crisp dark hairs on his chest feel like? Would they be springy under her fingertips? Prickly, like the ones on his chin, or soft, like his hair?

Well, she wasn't going to *touch* him, that was certain. Goodness, no. That would be . . . untoward.

Although it was unlikely he'd notice, as deeply asleep as he was.

He did look remarkably warm. Really, it was hardly fair that he should be so warm, while she was left to shiver.

She lifted her hand, hesitating as it hovered close to his face. Did she dare?

Slowly, she reached for him, pressed her cold fingertips to his cheek, then snatched her hand back as if she'd been burned.

He *was* warm, even as the fire waned, reducing the log to ashes in the grate, while outside the cold rain poured down, beating relentlessly against the window.

How did the man contrive to be warm under such circumstances? That large, solid body of his must do a wonderful job of retaining heat.

What would it be like to sleep next to such a man every night? To know if she awoke in the darkness with the cold pressing in on her, all she needed to do was move closer and press her body against his.

Not that she'd ever do such a thing, of course.

Why, she'd freeze before she allowed herself to do something so brazen, particularly after she'd promised to stay on her side of the pillows.

What if he woke, and found her nestling against him? Dear God, how humiliating that would be.

But all it would take was a moment pressed against that warm body. Perhaps if she just lay a little closer to him, she could, er . . . borrow some of his body heat? He seemed to have plenty of it.

More than enough to share.

Just for a moment, and then she'd return to her side of the bed. Once she was warm, she'd be able to drift back to sleep again.

No. It was out of the question. Why, it was scandalous to even consider such a thing.

But she was already easing closer to him, narrowing the space between them until it was no wider than a sewing needle, and . . . she took a deep breath, her eyes dropping closed as the thin sliver of space between them thawed with their combined body heat.

Stealthily, she eased a bit closer, her gaze on his face, searching for any telltale twitch of wakefulness, but there was nothing. His breathing was deep, his chest moving steadily up and down.

So, she wriggled closer, then closer still, easing the pillow between them out of the way so she might rest her arm against his.

Oh, that was much better, even though she was barely touching him.

Surely, no harm would come from moving a little closer.

My, he did have warm legs, didn't he? And his chest was . . . well, it was an impressively solid sort of chest and no doubt as toasty as the rest of him. If she just laid her head there upon his chest, just for a little while, the shivers racking her body would cease.

She mustn't fall asleep like this. No, it wouldn't do to fall asleep, when she'd promised to remain on her side of the pillow barrier. Very well, then. There would be no sleeping. She'd even keep her blinking down to a minimum, just in case.

She pressed closer, so the entire lengths of their bodies were touching, rested her head against his chest, and wrapped one arm around his torso to keep herself balanced.

There! Yes, that would do very well.

He even smelled nice, like the woods, pine and cedar, and a hint of the whisky he and Donigan had been drinking tonight.

It was an unexpectedly pleasant scent. Comforting, even.

But not so much so that she'd fall asleep.

As long as she didn't fall asleep, he'd never have to know.

Hamish had been lying still for such a long time both of his legs had fallen asleep.

When he'd felt her edging closer to him, he'd thought he was imagining it, but then her arm brushed against his, and then the side of one sweet, curved thigh, and then . . . he'd held his breath as one small hand had crept closer, and closer . . .

His patience had paid off, because her hand was now tucked

against his chest, and her head was resting on his shoulder, the wisps of hair that had come loose from her bun tickling his chin.

It shouldn't have been as titillating as it was. She was covered from head to toe in the carriage dress she'd donned when they'd left Kilmarnock this morning. It was a thick, sturdy garment, and between that, his blanket, and the coverlet, it wasn't as if he could feel her curves against him.

But it didn't matter. He'd known it wouldn't, just as he knew a dozen blankets and a bedful of pillows wouldn't matter.

It was *her*.

She might have been wrapped from head to toe in endless layers of cotton wool, and lying next to her in bed would still be the most arousing experience of his life.

It was a privilege to lie next to her. To tuck her small body against his and keep her warm throughout the night. There wasn't a man alive who could share a bed with a lady like Catriona MacLeod and not wish to take her in his arms.

Even so, he never would have initiated such intimacy with her. He had no right to hold her. He'd already stolen her first kiss—a kiss he shouldn't have taken and hadn't deserved.

But she'd come to him tonight, and he simply couldn't refuse her.

Whether she realized it or not, Cat had come to trust him. A lady didn't rest her head on the chest of a man she didn't trust.

But she shouldn't trust him, because of all the people who'd hurt her, he'd been the one who'd hurt her the most.

He stared into the darkness, and listened to the rain falling outside, the ping of the raindrops against the window keeping time with the beating of his heart.

He'd sent the first lugger to Castle Cairncross. Everything that had come after that—the second and third boats, the rumors about Cat and her sisters, the villagers' hostility toward them, and their dire financial situation—all of that was *his* fault.

Cat's life, and her sisters' lives had become a torment, because of him.

And she had no idea.

It hadn't bothered him, at first, to keep it from her. He'd always been a selfish man, one who made choices according to what was easiest for him, but now . . .

Now, he wanted to be a better man, for *her*.

Yet all his good intentions meant nothing, if he kept lying to her.

Being the better man meant telling her the truth about Dougal and Clyde and the first lugger that had sent every smuggler in Scotland to Castle Cairncross.

No matter what it cost him and no matter the consequences.

But not tonight. For just this one night he'd hold her in his arms.

Tomorrow would come soon enough.

So, he lay still, his breathing deep and even, and just held her, his senses overwhelmed by her—the slight weight of her against him, the soft locks of her hair brushing his chin, and the sweet, earthy scent of her, like green growing things, and the breeze from Loch Dunvegan that drifted through the woods at night.

She let out a soft sigh in her sleep and nestled against him, her fingers curling around a loose fold of his shirt. Only then did he allow himself to ease her closer, wrap an arm around her shoulders, and press his face into her hair.

Chapter 18

Hamish woke the next morning to a sleepy body sprawled on top of him, warm morning light caressing his eyelids, and his cock pulsing insistently against his belly.

Sunlight and a tempting, sleep-tousled lady in his arms?

He opened his eyes, expecting to find his familiar, dark blue silk bed hangings surrounding him and the naked body of his latest paramour draped over him, her dark hair spread across his bare chest.

But there were no blue silk bed hangings. There were no bed hangings at all, and his chest wasn't bare. Had he fallen asleep in his shirt? Why was he still wearing his breeches? And why weren't the heavy locks of hair spread over his chest the sleek, dark tresses he'd expected, but instead a glorious tangle of russet curls?

His eyes popped open so suddenly then, it was a wonder they didn't roll out of his head.

He wasn't in London at all. He was in Ballantrae, with the brightest sunlight he'd seen since he'd crossed the border into Scotland streaming through the window, and a warm, drowsy Catriona MacLeod nestled in his arms with one of her slender thighs resting between his legs.

And his cock—dear God, his cock was pressed against her lower belly, and damned if the greedy organ wasn't pleased to be there, if the twitching and throbbing and general fuss it was making was any indication.

There was nothing unusual in that, of course. He was a man, after all, and cocks weren't the most gentlemanly of organs. They did tend to make a nuisance of themselves in the mornings.

Which was all very well, until a man woke with an innocent lady in his arms. Not just any lady, either, but one he lov—

Er, respected. An innocent lady he admired and respected, who deserved far better than to find herself on the receiving end of his crass bodily functions.

God above, this was a disaster.

What was he to do? Perhaps he could slip out from underneath her before she woke, and became aware of the embarrassing reality of a man's nether regions.

Yes, that made sense. It was the only proper action to take in such a situation.

That was what he'd do, then, and very soon, too. In just a moment, he'd release her and retreat to the farthest corner of the room until some of the blood returned to his brain, and he remembered he was meant to be a gentleman.

But first, he'd breathe her in one more time. Just one more breath of her, like sea salt and a dew-drenched forest on a summer morning. He'd inhale that scent so deeply into his lungs he'd taste it on the back of his tongue for hours to come.

And surely, it wouldn't do any harm if he held her just a little longer, and let his cheek rest against her hair? And if he let his fingertips trail across her jaw . . . not enough to wake her, of course, but just enough that he could feel that silky skin gliding against his finger—

"I don't think I've ever slept so soundly in my life."

He stiffened, his fingers going still against her cheek.

"What time is it? Goodness, the sun is so bright, it must be past nine." She shifted against him and stretched her arms over her head, her cheeks still flushed with sleep and a drowsy smile on her lips. "I can't recall the last time I slept so late."

She was so close, close enough he could see the faint spattering of freckles across the bridge of her nose, and all his good intentions threatened to explode in a surge of desire.

All at once, it was all he could do not to wrap his arms around her, pull her closer, wind his fingers in her hair, and drop a dozen tiny kisses onto her eyelids and the tip of her nose.

But he wouldn't. If he did—if he gave in to . . . well, whatever it was he felt for her, there was no telling where it would end.

Or if it would end at all.

And that . . . no, that was out of the question.

It might not have been, if he'd only felt passion for her, but the tangled chaos of feelings that had been uncoiling in his chest since he'd first caught a glimpse under the hood of her cloak was far more complicated than desire.

That is, there *was* desire. A burning, dizzying, consuming desire that made him careless, reckless, but there was respect there, too, and admiration, and an affection so profound it bordered on . . .

Tenderness? Was that what one called the unfamiliar feeling lodged under his breastbone? Was it tenderness, when the need to protect a lady overcame a passion so fierce that the briefest glance into her green eyes was enough to send him to his knees?

God, he didn't know. He didn't know anything anymore, except that desire was a simple, straightforward emotion, one he'd experienced dozens of times before. He knew what to do with desire, and how to act on it, but what he felt for Cat was anything but simple.

Especially now, when she looked so lovely, all warm and tousled, with her cheeks as pink as peonies.

"Hamish?" She sat up a little, and propped her head on her hand, her brow creasing as she gazed down at him. "You're quiet. Are you concerned about our late start this morning? It's a full day's journey to Barrhead."

"Our late . . . oh. No, it's all right. We both needed the sleep." He hadn't given their journey today a single thought.

She was all he could think about, all he could see.

Looking at her now, with the sunlight caressing the pale skin of her throat and limning her auburn curls with a halo of gold, the emotion pressing down on his chest wasn't worry, or weariness, or even lust.

Not *only* lust.

Was it love? How was he meant to *know*? He'd enjoyed the favors of many women in his time—women he'd admired and for whom he'd had great affection. He'd wanted them, yes, but never—*never*—had he felt about any woman the way he felt about her.

As if he'd die if he couldn't touch her. As if he couldn't breathe without her there.

A swell of feelings rushed over him then, each struggling for supremacy. He couldn't make sense of any of them, he couldn't think or reason at all. He could only feel them, like a tidal wave crashing over him.

He cupped her cheek in his palm. "Catriona MacLeod, may I kiss you?"

Long, silent moments passed as she gazed at him. Did she want him as much as he wanted her, or was she an instant away from leaving him alone in this bed, haunted with dreams of her? He waited, breathless with desire and tenderness, and fear, waiting for the moment she'd pull away from him.

But that wasn't what she did.

Instead, she gave him a shy nod. "Yes."

The breathless word hardly had a chance to leave her lips before he was kissing her. "Kiss me back, Cat." He slid his palm up the long, slender line of her back and into her hair, urging her head closer to his. "Kiss me as a woman kisses the man she's taken to her bed."

A teasing grin rose to her lips. "This isn't my bed, my lord."

"Very well, Donigan's bed." He caught her hand and brought

it to his mouth, kissing her fingertips one by one, her warm skin like silk beneath his lips. "But for right now, it's *our* bed."

"So it is." Her long curls brushed his face as she leaned over him, and then . . . then she was kissing him back, just as he'd demanded, her lips needy and gentle at once, the tip of her tongue teasing the seam of his lips, a delicate dance of need and desire.

What could he do but open them? Open, and welcome her inside.

God, she was sweet, the sweetest thing he'd ever tasted, so innocent and sensuous at once, but not at all afraid, either of him, or of her own desire.

He kissed her until they were both breathless. When she drew away, her lips were a deep red color and swollen like summer cherries bursting with juice.

He traced the sensuous curve of that plump lower lip before his hand slid lower, down her neck and between her breasts, his palm resting over her wildly beating heart for an instant before he brushed his thumb over the peak of her nipple. "So beautiful, Cat. So perfect."

"Oh." She sucked in a sharp breath. "Oh, that's . . ."

"Yes? Does that feel good, love?" He did it again, the gentlest brush of his fingers, his breath catching as her nipple pebbled under his caresses.

"Yes." She threw her head back, letting out a soft moan as he continued to toy with her, stroking the pads of his fingers over her nipples again and again in a lazy caress.

He could have watched her forever, spent a lifetime savoring the small gasps and sighs that tore from her lips, but she was no shy, retiring maiden, either in bed or out of it, nor was she afraid to take what she needed.

Not from him, and not from anybody. It was one of the things he most loved—

One of the things he most loved about her.

"You're a tease, my lord." Cat caught his wrist and brought

his hand to her breast. "Touch me properly or don't touch me at all."

He let out a strained laugh. "How could I refuse such a gracious request?"

"You can't. A gentleman never refuses a lady's request in the bedchamber."

"Oh?" He grinned back at her. "What do you know about what happens between a gentleman and a lady in the bedchamber, Miss MacLeod?"

"Very little, admittedly, but . . ." Another of those adorably shy smiles drifted across her lips. "But a lady does wonder about such things, on occasion."

"Then no one has ever touched you like this before?" As soon as the words left his lips, he wished them back. Why had he asked her that? He hadn't meant to. He had no right to question her about any previous lovers, no right to the dark possessiveness swelling in his heart.

And yet, and yet . . . he couldn't take the words back.

He gazed at her, awaiting her answer.

"No." For a moment her face clouded, and she looked away. "Half the people in Dunvegan think I'm a witch, Hamish. What would become of me and my sisters if they believed me a wanton, as well?"

In some ways, it was just the answer he'd hoped for, as he couldn't bear the thought of another man touching her, but at the same time, it was the last answer in the world she should have been compelled to give him.

What else had she and her sisters endured since Rory died? What small slights and indignities and veiled threats did they face every time they ventured into the village?

But now wasn't the time to ask. He didn't want the villagers, or Dunvegan, or Castle Cairncross and all its cares and worries here in this bedchamber with them.

He only wanted her.

They were here now, together, and they may never have this moment again, so he let it go, and caught her hips and shifted her atop him. "May I loosen the buttons of your dress?"

She nodded, and he reached behind her, tracing his fingers up and down the delicate line of her spine as he loosened the first six or seven buttons and eased the dress from her shoulders, so only her shift covered her.

All he wanted in the world right now was to touch her, to coax more sighs and soft moans from those lovely lips. He cupped her breast in his palm, a groan tearing loose from his throat at the heat of her, her warm silky skin, her generous curves overflowing his palm.

"You're beautiful here." He brushed his thumb over one of her nipples, his mouth going dry when it peaked under his touch. "So sensitive."

"That's . . ." She caught her lower lip in her teeth. "More of that, please."

"Yes." But first, he reached up and began to pluck the hairpins from her hair. Half of it had come loose from its pins already, but he wanted to see all of it.

She helped him, removing the ones hidden amongst the thick tresses until at last it tumbled over her shoulders in a cascade of curls, like an auburn waterfall, a few errant locks teasing at her pale pink nipples, just visible under the thin white cotton of her shift.

Dear God, what a sight that was, like an erotic game of hide and seek.

He caught one of the curls between his fingers, watching her face closely as he dragged it over the stiff peak, and her lips parted on a soft moan.

"Yes. Just like that, Catriona." He teased her with the lock of her hair and his fingers, caressing her until her nipples were flushed and swollen, and she was whimpering with need and squirming above him.

He urged her closer with a gentle tug. "Come here."

She came to him willingly, eagerly, this woman who had no reason to trust anyone, least of all him.

"Very well, then, Lord Ballantyne. I'm here. What do you intend to do with me, now that you have me?"

Do? The better question was, what *didn't* he intend to do?

He eased her closer, until she was hovering over him, her long curls tickling his chest and scattering in waves of red across his pillow. "Taste you."

"Taste me? What do you . . . oh. Oh, my goodness."

Her soft exclamation, the surprise in her voice, that soft, breathy gasp when his mouth closed around her nipple . . . dear God, had there ever been anything as erotic as that? As *her*, with her flushed cheeks, her nipple hard against his tongue?

He licked and circled and teased her through the thin cotton of her shift, darting his tongue at the turgid peak until she was trembling in his arms, breathy cries and gasps falling from her lips.

He couldn't get enough of her. Her taste, her curves pressed tightly against him, and her hair falling over him in disheveled waves.

She threw her head back, a rush of words spilling from her lips, one overflowing the next until there was no making sense of them, other than that they were words of desire.

"Hamish. I—I need you. Please."

Triumph swelled inside his chest, stealing his breath.

She wanted him. Needed *him*.

For now, yes—only for now—but at this moment, in this bed, with their bodies tangled together, she was his.

And she was driving him mad.

The breathless pleas on her lips, her fingers tangled in his hair, the way she trembled against him . . . he'd dreamed about her this way, hadn't he? Dreamed it, yes, but the dream of her was nothing at all compared to how it felt to have her in his arms.

"Look at me, Cat." He buried his hands in her hair, and tilted her head down to his, so he could see her face when he touched her. "Look at me."

He was gazing up at her—no, gazing *into* her, as if he could see every thought turning in her head, his blue eyes hot and gleaming.

Those eyes . . . dear God, had she ever encountered a man with more expressive eyes than his? Such a perfect, bright blue, like a summer sky lit by the sun.

Her mother's words came back to her in a rush then, about a lady reading everything she ever needed to know about a man, the worst and the best of him, with one look into his eyes.

What she saw in Hamish's eyes . . . oh, she could hardly bear to look for fear that she was imagining it.

He didn't tell her he wanted her. He didn't say anything at all. He didn't need to. The brush of his fingers under her chin, his parted lips, and those *eyes* . . . there could be no mistaking the desire burning in those midnight depths.

Were her eyes telling him the same thing? When he looked into her eyes, could he see that she'd dreamed about him last night? Strange, heated dreams of his mouth taking hers, his fingertips tracing her skin. Dreams from which she woke damp and aching, a fire burning in her lower belly and her legs twisted in the coverlet.

She knew little about desire, but she knew she wanted him. Even when she hadn't liked him, even when she hadn't trusted him, she'd wanted him.

And now . . . now she knew him, she wanted him even more.

Perhaps it had been a mistake, that first kiss between them in her father's study, with the moonlight pouring through the window and the rhythmic wash of the waters of Loch Dunvegan against the shore.

Would she have allowed it, if she'd known his kiss would stay with her and haunt her every dream?

"You should send me away, Catriona." His voice was deeper than she'd ever heard it, a seductive murmur close to her ear, his warm breath stirring the wisps of hair there. "If you order me out of this bedchamber, I'll go at once. You need only say the word."

So simple. Just a single word.

She opened her mouth, gathered her breath, but she couldn't utter the word that would send him away any more than she could pluck the stars from the sky or cup the moon in her hand.

She didn't want him to leave her. He'd be gone soon enough, once they'd found the treasure. He'd return to London, and she'd go back to pacing her lonely castle at night, pausing at the arched window and gazing at the moonlit water surrounding her.

But it wouldn't ever be the same again. His absence would haunt her, just as his kiss did. Every time she turned around, she'd see his ghost hovering in the shadows.

This madness between them—and it was madness, this sweet rush of dizzying blood through her veins—she'd been struggling against it since that first night when he'd lain unconscious in a bedchamber, and she'd watched him, her fingers itching to trace the sensuous curves of his lips.

Even then, she'd known. Even when she'd feared and resented him, she'd wanted him. Why it should be him who stole her breath, *him* who made her heart stutter in her chest, was a question without an answer.

It just *was*.

"Tell me to stop, Catriona." There was a strange desperation in his voice as he traced her lower lip with his thumb. He trailed his fingers over the curve of her jaw and skimmed them down her throat, the warm brush of his skin against her like a promise, or a hint of madness. "Tell me to stop."

"I don't want you to stop." She let her eyes close as his fingers moved lower, the rough pad of his thumb brushing against the hollow of her throat. "I want you to touch me."

A hoarse groan fell from his lips at her words. His hand was shaking when he reached for her, his palm warm as he rested it against the curve of her neck. Behind her, the sun rose higher in the sky, the clear light curling around them as he closed the space between them.

"Madness," he murmured, his lips brushing the sensitive skin under her ear. His lips were hot, open, and she had to hold her breath to keep from crying out when his warm breath rushed over her ear, his tongue darting out to lick her earlobe.

Madness, yes. It was mad and reckless to set loose the passion that burned between them, yet at the same time it was so *right* it was inevitable, in the way of the sun cresting the horizon, or the rolling gray waves of Loch Dunvegan crashing against the rocks underneath Castle Cairncross.

As old as time itself.

But she didn't say so. She said nothing at all, only waited, the silence swelling around them, her body tensed for the moment his next touch would come. Would it be his hands around her waist? His lips against hers? Every inch of her quivered, but she didn't move, only gazed down at him, into eyes no longer blue, but dark with desire.

In the end, it was his hands, sinking into her hair, his long, rough fingers cradling her head, holding her still for his touch. Her own hands fluttered for an instant, but then of their own accord they settled on his broad shoulders, and her eyelids fell closed once again.

His kiss, when it came, was as gentle as a spring breeze rustling the leaves in the woods just beyond the castle. It was the kind of kiss lovers shared between them, so sweet and tender tears sprang to her eyes.

This would end in misery for her. She knew it, even as she parted her lips for him and welcomed him inside. She'd been lonely before he came, but once he left . . .

There was no loneliness that cut more deeply than the loneliness of lost love.

But this was not the time to think of it. She'd made her decision, and she didn't regret it. She couldn't regret it, with his hands in her hair, and his lips on hers.

Soon enough, the sparks that seemed always on the verge of bursting into flames between them ignited in an explosion of heat, desire, and a frantic desperation she had no defenses against.

There was nothing for her to do then but kiss him, her fingers sinking into his shoulders as she met his passion with a burning desire of her own. She parted her lips underneath his and he surged inside, the groan that tore from his chest in response exploding in her belly and setting all her nerve endings alight at once.

"So soft, Cat. So perfect." Hamish gathered handfuls of her hair into his fists and eased her head back, exposing her neck to his mouth. "How can your skin be this soft?" He teased her with the lightest brush of his lips against her neck, then pressed a trail of tiny kisses down to the hollow of her throat.

"Oh." She twisted her hands in the dark strands of his hair, holding him against her, a long, shuddering sigh leaving her lips.

"Yes, that's it." He tore his mouth away, his eyes wild as he toyed with her lower lip, pinching the sensitive flesh gently between his fingers. "Open for me, Cat. I need to taste you."

She did—dear God, she did—because she wanted to taste him as badly as he did her, and because in that moment, with his hands buried in her hair and his hot breath on her neck, she could refuse him nothing.

It was a mistake to give him a part of herself, because once she did, she'd never get it back again. No part of her would ever be the same after him. But the distant future, the threat of heartbreak was no match for the desire sweeping through her, stealing her sanity, her reason.

It was already too late for her.

He cradled her face in his hands and gazed down at her for an instant, his expression unreadable, but he left her no time to wonder what he was thinking, or what he saw when he looked at her. "Do you want me, Cat?"

"Yes." She clutched his shirt with her fists. "I want you. I—I trust you, Hamish."

After months of looking upon everyone with suspicion, they were difficult words for her to say, but no less true, for all that she stumbled over them.

She *trusted* him.

What happened next was . . . well, it was so quick she couldn't make sense of it at first. One moment she was perched on top of him, her hands on his shoulders and his arms around her waist, and the next . . .

The next, she was on her back on the bed, and he was halfway across the room.

"Hamish?" She scrambled to her knees, her head spinning.

What had happened? Had she done something wrong, said something—

"This is . . . we can't do this, Cat." He was standing at the window with his back to her, his rib cage jerking with his panting breaths.

No. She must have misheard him.

But when he turned from the window his eyes were shuttered, and his lips, so soft and open only moments before when he'd kissed her, had gone so tight his mouth was white at the edges.

She hadn't misunderstood him.

She groped for her bodice with shaking hands and held it up against her chest, suddenly ashamed of herself. "I don't—" she began, but then she stopped.

What was there to say? She'd come as close to throwing herself into his arms as a lady could—*twice*, in fact—and this was the second time he'd rejected her.

Finished, before it even had a chance to begin . . .

"I have no right," he murmured, without meeting her eyes. "Forgive me, Miss MacLeod."

Miss MacLeod. Not Catriona, or Cat, but Miss MacLeod.

And then he was gone, the door of the tiny bedchamber where she'd spent the night in his arms closing behind him.

Chapter 19

It was sixty-two miles from Ballantrae to Barrhead. Sixty-two long, dusty—and, as it turned out—*silent* miles.

Hamish had made arduous journeys before—he, Callum, and Keir had once ridden from Edinburgh to London in three days—but the eight hours he spent in the carriage with Cat were the longest he'd ever endured.

Eight interminable hours, yet when he brought the carriage to a stop in the innyard of the Thistle and Crown in Barrhead, he still hadn't confessed the truth about the first lugger to her. Love, for all that it was meant to be the most enchanting emotion in existence, had made an utter coward of him.

He'd tried to tell her. He'd opened his mouth countless times over the course of the day, but just as the truth had been on the verge of tumbling from his lips, he'd closed it again. As it happened, it was no small matter confessing to the woman you loved that you'd betrayed her, even when that betrayal had happened months before you'd met her.

And given he'd spent a good part of the morning debauching her before abruptly abandoning her in bed, unsatisfied and without an explanation, such a confession was likely to be less than welcome.

The worst of it was, she didn't even seem to be angry with him. It might have been easier if she'd raged at him as he deserved, but when she'd emerged from the bedchamber after his disgraceful performance that morning, she'd been perfectly civil to him.

Pale, but civil. Aloof, but civil. Subdued, but civil.

Civil, and *silent*, or nearly so. Between the time they departed from Ballantrae to the time of their arrival in Barrhead, she spoke a grand total of a dozen words to him.

That was one and a half words per hour. He'd counted each one, and before they'd even made it past Maybole, he'd been ready to tear his hair out with frustration.

They'd gotten a late start, and it was dark when they arrived at Barrhead, the sun having long since sunk beneath the horizon. Cat had been flagging since Kilmarnock, and by the time he tossed the ribbons to the boy that emerged from the Thistle and Crown, she'd fallen into a fitful sleep, her long auburn eyelashes resting against her pale cheeks.

"Catriona?" He gave her a gentle nudge but resisted the urge to brush the loose locks of hair away from her face.

"Mmmm?" Her eyes fluttered open, and she took in the white stone building with the smart, painted black trim. "Where are we?"

"In Barrhead, at the Thistle and Crown."

"Oh." She struggled upright, blinking. "Did I fall asleep?"

"About an hour ago, yes." He leapt down from the box and rounded the front of the carriage to assist her down, hoping his smile didn't look as besotted as it felt.

She was still groggy and wobbly on her feet, so instead of offering her his hand, he caught her around her slender waist.

It was a mistake.

He should have realized she'd be averse to being touched by a gentleman who'd insulted her so grievously only that morning, but for all his vaunted charm, gallantry, and ease with the ladies, he was not especially good at being in love.

The moment he touched her was the moment everything went terribly wrong.

She gripped his shoulders, but instead of letting him help her down, she pushed him away, and the polite mask she'd been wearing all day slipped. "No!"

Her tone was so sharp even the stable boy paused, his eyes going wide.

Catriona cleared her throat, her face flushing. "I, that is, thank you, my lord, but I can manage it myself."

She looked almost panicked. He released her at once and stepped back, mortified. "I beg your pardon. I was . . . I didn't want you to fall."

"I've been ascending and descending carriages without your assistance for twenty-three years, Lord Ballantyne." She gave him a withering look. "I daresay I can do so again without your help."

She didn't say she didn't want him to touch her, but that was what she meant, and he couldn't blame her.

This was what came of kissing young ladies he had no business kissing.

It was what came of telling lies.

Good Lord, could he have made any more of a mess of this? He had to tell her the truth about Dougal and Clyde and the first lugger—now, tonight—but it would have to wait until he secured a room.

The innyard of the Thistle and Crown wasn't the place for that discussion.

"Of course." He took another step backward to give her room. "I beg your pardon."

"Thank you, my lord." She leapt lightly to the ground. She didn't look at him, but instead devoted all her attention to brushing the dust from her skirts.

"Er, may I take you into the dining room while I secure us a bedchamber, Miss MacLeod?" He took a cautious step toward her, his hand extended. It was the most basic of courtesy to escort her inside, but it was best not to assume anything when dealing with young ladies whose feelings had been hurt.

She froze, one hand still fisting a fold of her skirts and eyed his hand as if it were a venomous serpent. "You mean two bed-chambers, Lord Ballantyne."

Two bedchambers? "No, Miss MacLeod, I don't. You can't stay in a bedchamber alone."

"I don't see why not, my lord. We'll both be much more comfortable that way."

He and the stable boy stared at her.

She couldn't truly believe he'd agree to such a thing. "Young ladies don't travel alone, Catriona, and they don't spend the night by themselves at a public inn."

"Is that so, my lord?" She eyed him, one eyebrow raised and her lips pursed.

"Yes, it's so, and you know it as well as I do, Cat. You don't even have a servant with you, for God's sake!"

She huffed, her pert little chin lifting. "I'm accustomed to managing without a lady's maid, Lord Ballantyne."

Damn it. He'd seen that stubborn expression on her face before, and knew it meant they *were* going to have this discussion in the innyard of the Thistle and Crown, after all. "It's out of the question, Miss MacLeod. You're mad if you think I'll allow such a thing."

"Allow it?" She stepped closer, braced her hands on her hips, her green eyes snapping. "I don't recall asking your permission, Lord Ballantyne."

"Lawks," the stable boy breathed, glancing between the two of them.

Lawks, indeed, but he'd been waiting all day for her anger to burst forth, and now it had, his blood heated, rushing through his veins like wildfire. He closed the distance between them, so close the tips of his boots touched hers, and he could see the tiny flecks of gold in her eyes.

"As far as anyone beyond that door knows . . ." He pointed toward the entrance to the Thistle and Crown. "You're my *wife*. Anything less than that will expose you to scorn and ridicule, and I won't have it."

"Scorn and ridicule." She let out a short laugh. "That would be dreadful, wouldn't it? Yes, by all means, let's avoid *that*, my lord."

Well, that was plain enough. He hid his wince. "Allow me to make myself abundantly clear, Miss MacLeod. For the remainder of this journey, you are the Marchioness of Ballantyne, and we *will* be sharing a bedchamber."

He stood there, waiting for the argument, the huffing, the inevitable stamping of feet, but the lady was nothing if not unpredictable. She'd never been one to do as he expected, and she didn't do so now.

Not a single word fell from those sweet pink lips. Instead, she gathered her icy cloak of dignity around her, turned on her heel, marched toward the entryway of the Thistle and Crown, and disappeared inside without a backward glance, leaving him in the innyard, gaping after her.

"She's a fiery one, eh, my lord?" The stable boy gave him a sly wink.

There was nothing for Hamish to do but follow her. He strode across the innyard, muttering to the boy under his breath as he passed. "You have no idea, lad."

Once inside, he quickly secured the largest bedchamber the innkeeper had on offer, despite her objections. He ordered dinner brought up, then marched into the dining room, collected his *wife*, and hurried her upstairs with a firm hand on her arm before she had a chance to bloody his nose again.

He led her into the bedchamber and closed the door behind them. "We have some unfinished business between us, Miss MacLeod."

"It's a large bedchamber, at least." She strode to the window, the sharp click of her boot heels against the wooden floorboards grating in the quiet room. "Thankfully, there's plenty of space for you on the floor, Lord Ballantyne."

Ah. There'd be no solicitousness for his comfort tonight, then. No sweet insistence that he enjoy a proper night's sleep, and no careful arrangement of pillows down the center of the bed. No nestling close against him, her head on his chest and her curls tickling his chin.

It was no less than he deserved, yet for all that he'd earned her wrath, anger stirred in his chest. "Perhaps you didn't hear me, Catriona. I said, we have unfinished business between us."

"Plenty of blankets, as well," she went on, as if he hadn't spoken. "Here you go, Lord Ballantyne." She stripped the blanket from the bed with one sweep of her arm, snatched up a pillow, and tossed them both at him. "I wish you a pleasant night."

Oh, but she was furious with him. At last, after hours of cool civility, she was abruptly, utterly furious with him, that stubborn chin thrust high, with sparks of anger snapping in her green eyes and a deep pink flush rushing up her neck and surging into her cheeks.

She was glorious, magnificent, burning as she was with justified fury, her wild red curls crackling with it. Never in his life had he wanted a woman the way he wanted her. But he wouldn't make the same mistake he'd made this morning, or the first time he'd kissed her in her father's study.

Never again.

He and Catriona MacLeod were going to have it out right here, and right now, until there were no more secrets and no more lies between them.

He glanced at the pile of bedding at his feet, then stepped over it and stalked toward her, closing the space between them one slow, measured pace at a time.

Her hands shot up to stop him. "Not another step, my lord. You're not welcome on this side of the room."

He paused, raising his eyebrow. "My, we are in a temper, aren't we?"

"Why, I have no idea what you mean, my lord." Her voice was as sweet as a treacle tart, but her green eyes had narrowed to slits. "I think only of your comfort."

"*My* comfort!" He edged closer to her, his heart pounding in his chest. "That's kind of you, Miss MacLeod, but what makes you think I'd rather sleep on the floor than beside you in the bed?"

She didn't back away, but thrust her chin higher, as if she were daring him to keep coming. "Please, my lord. Let's be frank with each other, shall we? You've made it perfectly clear you don't want me." She jerked her chin toward the bedding on the floor. "I should think you'd be relieved."

"*Don't want you?*" He took another step toward her, then another, until he was close enough to reach out and touch her. "Is that what you think, Cat?"

Of course, it was. What else was she meant to think, when this morning he'd been as skittish as a maiden on her wedding night? Yet, it surprised him still that she could believe he didn't desire her, when he wanted nothing more than to sink to his knees for her.

How could she not know it?

"I don't wish to discuss it!" She snatched another pillow from the bed, hurled it to the floor, and pointed one dramatic finger at it. "There's your bed. Go to sleep, Lord Ballantyne."

Lord Ballantyne didn't go to sleep.

No, he kept coming, slowly, stealthily, and dear God, he'd never looked quite so resolved as he did now in the dim light, his body tensed to spring, his breeches accentuating his long, muscular legs.

Some emotion rushed through her, sudden and warm, like an unexpected burst of sunshine escaping the clouds, but she couldn't define it. It felt a little like panic, but the sort of panic inextricably tied to anticipation, excitement, her belly quivering with it, her teeth sinking into her lower lip.

He caught his breath, his gaze on her mouth. "Nibble all you like, Cat. It won't stop me."

"S-stop you from what?"

But she knew. Of course, she knew. She wasn't fooling anyone.

Not him, and not even herself.

Not any longer.

The corners of his lips twitched. "I think you know, Cat, but I'd be pleased to show you."

He edged closer—one step, another, the firelight behind him casting him in shadow until he was standing before her, far closer than was wise, so close his breeches brushed against her skirts, his heady scent of vetiver and woodsmoke dizzying her.

This was the moment to turn away from him, to retreat to the other side of the bedchamber—or better yet, to escape the room entirely—but instead of diving for the door, she merely stood there watching him, as if her feet were rooted to the floor.

"Shall I show you, Cat?" he murmured as he eased closer, the hard plane of his chest like a wall bearing down on her.

She parted her lips with a soft gasp, and then he was there, his arms around her waist, stilling her as his lips found hers, and he surged inside with a breathless groan, his mouth hard and hot and wild.

Then suddenly, the floor beneath her feet was gone.

"Oh!" Had she swooned from a kiss? Was that a thing that could happen?

"There," he whispered against her ear. "That's much better."

She hadn't swooned. He'd scooped her into his arms as if she weighed no more than a bird and sat her down on the edge of the bed. Her lips were still tingling from his kiss, the familiar melting warmth gathering in her belly.

Now he would kiss her again, and again, and she'd find herself in just the same humiliating position as she'd been in this morning. No, she wouldn't allow it to happen a third time.

She had her pride, dash it.

So, when he took a step toward the bed, her hand flew up to stop him. "Not another step, if you please, my lord."

He didn't listen to her. He kept coming, but just as she was about to scramble over the bed to the other side, he dropped down onto his knees in front of her.

She froze. "W-what are you doing?"

"I told you, Cat. We have unfinished business between us, but first." He took her hand, his touch gentle, as if he feared he'd frighten her away. "Would a man who didn't want you, didn't desire you, kiss you that way?"

She lifted her hand to her mouth and pressed her fingers to her trembling lips. "I—I don't know."

But she did know, despite having only ever kissed two gentlemen. Bryce Fraser—although that was more a case of him forcing an unwanted kiss upon her—and Hamish Muir.

The first one she'd rather forget, but the second . . .

Nothing in her life had ever made her feel the way kissing Hamish Muir did. He was like the slow curl of a flame around a log in the fireplace, one that smolders with a bright red glow before it catches alight and explodes into a roaring blaze.

And she . . . well, she was the log. It was hardly a flattering comparison, but his touch made her feel as if she were bursting into flames.

She was no expert on kisses, but a lady should be able to tell instinctively when a man wanted her. She'd felt Hamish's tightly leashed desire when he held her, his body straining to get closer, the wild thump of his heart under her palm.

He'd kissed her two times now, and both times he'd wanted her. Or she'd thought he did, right up until the moment he'd pulled away.

She didn't require a third rejection to conclude she'd made a mistake.

"Catriona." He tipped her face up to his with a finger under her chin. "I *do* want you. I've never wanted any woman the way I want you. Don't you understand? You drive me mad."

A part of her—the absurd, credulous, dim-witted part—wanted to believe him, but the other part of her—the part that knew better, the part that lived deep inside of her that questioned everyone and doubted everything—cursed herself for a fool. "For a gentleman as consumed by passion as you claim to be, my lord, you've had remarkable success resisting me."

"Do you think so? I would have said it's just the opposite. If I have resisted you, it isn't because I don't want you. I can't stop thinking about you." He caught her hands gently in his and drew her toward him, his forehead meeting hers. "You've bewitched me, Catriona."

"Bewitched you? What an interesting choice of words. You sound just like the villagers in Dunvegan. Do you think me as wicked as they do, Lord Ballantyne?" He wouldn't be the first to accuse her of casting an evil spell upon him.

"I don't think you're wicked at all, Catriona." He reached for a lock of her hair, caressing it with his fingertips. "I think you're lovely, and brilliant, and brave."

Brave. She had been brave, once, but it had been a long time since she'd thought of herself that way. Of all the words he might have chosen, why had he settled on that one?

It made sudden tears well in her eyes, but she didn't let them spill onto her cheeks. Over these past few months, she'd cried enough tears to last her lifetime.

"Why, then?" She raised her chin and met his eyes. "This morning, I thought—"

"I know what you thought, Cat, and you may believe me when I say it took all my restraint to leave you alone in that bed, but there's something I haven't told you yet, and it may change the way you feel about me."

Oh, no. Yet another secret.

"I want you, Cat, but I don't make a habit of taking innocent young ladies to my bed, and I certainly don't tell lies to them to get them there."

More secrets and more lies. She had a childish urge to slap her hands over her ears, but she was no longer a child. "The unfinished business you mentioned, I suppose?"

"The unfinished business, yes." He drew in a breath, then let it out again in a long, slow sigh. "The lugger that came to Castle Cairncross, that first time—"

"No." She shot up from the bed, nearly knocking him backward, and hurried to the other side of the room. Suddenly, she didn't want to hear what he had to say. It was going to change everything—she knew it as surely as if he'd already confessed. "I'm not brave, Hamish. I've been terrified every moment since my father's death. I'm a coward."

"No. There is no bravery without fear, Cat." He rose to his feet. Behind him, the fire climbed higher in the grate, the flames curling around the log, devouring it. Their shadows flickered against the wall, his becoming one with hers. "Being afraid and being a coward aren't the same thing."

Then she was both—afraid and a coward, because everything inside her was screaming at her to stop him from speaking another word and shattering the fragile trust she'd found in him when she'd thought she'd never trust anyone again.

Even if it was the truth.

"The lugger, Cat. The first one that came to Castle Cairncross in July." He swallowed. "I . . . I sent it."

He'd sent it? No, she must have misunderstood him. "You? But . . . but why?"

Dear God, had there ever been a more foolish question than that? There'd only ever been one reason, and his reason would be the same as all the others.

He was the same as all the others.

"I sent two of my cousins to Castle Cairncross to fetch the treasure. Dougal and Clyde wouldn't have hurt you and your sisters. They were only there to secure the treasure."

Cold enveloped her, heavy and sluggish, seeping into her veins until her entire body went numb with it. "And when they didn't find it, my lord? What then? You can't possibly know whether they would have hurt us or not, once they learned of their disappointment."

But it was more than that, wasn't it? Worse than that.

She dropped down into a chair near the window, her strength draining out of her.

Everything that came after that first lugger—the accusations of sorcery, the villagers' scorn, the loss of Mr. and Mrs. Duffy, and the two other luggers that had followed the first to the shores of Castle Cairncross—all of it had started with that first lugger.

And *he* . . . he'd been the one to send it? He'd been the cause of all this misery. He'd brought it all down upon their heads! Hers, Freya's, and Sorcha's lives would never be the same again, because of him.

She'd trusted him. She, who never trusted anyone, had trusted *him*.

Why? Because he was a dashing marquess, with an elegant bottle-green coat and glossy leather boots? Because of a few kisses and a few pretty words whispered in her ear.

Dear God, what a fool she was!

He'd made no secret of the reason he'd come to Castle Cairncross. He'd told her what he wanted from the very start. He'd shown her who he was, yet against her better judgment—no, against reason itself—she'd *trusted* him.

Because of a handsome face and a pair of bright blue eyes.

It wasn't even his lie that was the worst of it. After months of suspicion, months of scrutinizing every face she saw, she'd at last let her guard down enough to trust someone again, and he'd betrayed her.

Her, and her sisters.

She could no longer trust herself.

"Cat, listen to me." He knelt by her chair and took one of her hands in his. "If I'd known what would happen—"

"It's all right, my lord," she said dully, drawing her hand away. "I don't blame you. I blame myself."

"No! Cat, please listen to me—"

"No, I think . . . if you'd be so good as to excuse me, I think I'd like to go to bed now." She rose unsteadily from the chair and crawled into the bed without bothering to remove her cloak or even her boots.

Instead, she turned her back to him, drew the coverlet over her head, and squeezed her eyes closed.

Chapter 20

Tongue, Scotland
Five days later.

If a man didn't enjoy any peace of mind after admitting to an unpleasant truth, did it mean he might just as well have kept his sordid secrets to himself?

As it turned out, confession wasn't as good for the soul as he'd been led to believe, and the truth *didn't* always set one free. If either of those things had been true, he would have been covered in the glory of a deed well done and staggering under the weight of his own virtuousness.

But of course, these things never went the way they were meant to go. Instead, his soul was as blemished as it had ever been, and as for the truth, that whole business about it setting a liar free had been greatly exaggerated.

Five days had passed since he'd confessed the truth to Cat about the first lugger, and he was more miserable now than he'd ever been when he was a liar.

It was a just punishment, and he was reconciled to it, but for one thing.

Cat was miserable, as well. She never said so, but he'd learned to read her, as if her heart had been laid bare in the pages of a book and he'd memorized every syllable.

Not a single reproach fell from her lips, but the hurt was there in every blink of her eyes, every sigh on her lips, her hunched shoulders, and the way her gaze darted away from his when he tried to catch her eye. Her strained civility and her excruciating politeness were far more painful than a reproach could ever be.

Unlike most ladies, Cat's tongue hadn't grown sharper after he'd confessed his betrayal, it had grown sweeter. Sweeter and colder, every word she spoke like a shower of ice crystals.

"That's curious."

He'd been staring at the carriage ribbons wound between his fingers, but at Cat's voice, he roused himself from his morbid reflections. "What is?"

"That inn, just there." She nodded toward an inn on one side of the road, a sprawling old place done in painted white stone, the arched front in the middle of a squat turret set into the façade of the building. "Do you suppose the name is merely a coincidence?"

To the left of the entrance, a painted black sign hung from two chains fixed to an iron pole, the chains creaking in the breeze coming off the Kyle of Tongue, the name of the establishment emblazoned on it in scrolling gold lettering.

The Golden Coin.

He turned to her. "I thought you didn't believe in coincidences."

Behind the inn, the sun was setting in vibrant streaks of pink and bright orange, the wash of colors staining the sky. She shaded her eyes from the light as she considered the sign for a moment. "I don't. Shall we go and speak to the proprietor?"

The fading glow caught at the loose wisps of her hair, plucking at the countless red-gold threads hidden among the darker auburn. It turned her curls into a symphony of color, and he looked away, swallowing.

"By all means." He jerked his attention away from her and back to the ribbons, stifling the roar of despair echoing in his chest. It was torture to be so close to her he could inhale her scent, and not be able to touch her, but he had no one to blame for it but himself.

"Well, now, what have we here?" A cheerful woman as round and squat as the turret out front was bustling about inside the dining room, slapping down frothing pints of ale on the long tables that stretched from one end of the room to the other, but she paused when Hamish and Cat entered.

She wasn't the only one. Every head seemed to turn in their direction, and the chatter in the room quieted.

"Why, you poor wee thing." The squat lady bustled over, frowning as she took Cat in from head to toe. "You look right peaked, you do. Now you just come on over here, lass, and sit down before you topple over, eh?"

Cat shot him a startled glance, but she made her way to the place the lady indicated and sat obediently enough. "You're too kind, madam."

"It's Mrs. Geddes, lass. You look done in, you do. Have you come a long way?"

"All the way from Ardross, yes." Hamish took the seat beside Cat. "I'm Mr. Muir, and this lady is my wife, Mrs. Muir." He'd shed his title after they'd left Barrhead, English marquesses not being a favorite with the Scots.

"Are you, now? He's a strapping one, isn't he?" Mrs. Geddes scrutinized him, then turned to Cat with a sly grin.

"He's, ah . . . well, I suppose he is rather . . ." Cat glanced at him, then trailed off, blushing up to the roots of her hair.

Mrs. Geddes let out a loud cackle. "Why, aren't you just the sweetest thing?" She patted Cat's hand. "I'm just teasing, Mrs. Muir. Don't you pay me any mind. What will you have? I've got some lovely Scotched scallops and gooseberry pie. Shall I fetch two plates?"

Hamish's stomach growled at the mention of gooseberry pie. "Yes, and please be so good as to bring me a pint of ale, Mrs. Geddes, and some wine for my wife."

"Of course, Mr. Muir. Right away."

As it turned out, Mrs. Geddes was the proprietress of The Golden Coin. Her white hair and lined face hinted at a lady well advanced in years, but she was as nimble as a cricket, and her gooseberry pie was one of the best he'd ever eaten.

"There now, that put some pink in your cheeks, Mrs. Muir." Mrs. Geddes beamed at their empty plates.

Cat smiled. "It was lovely, Mrs. Geddes."

"Thank you, lass." Mrs. Geddes plucked up their plates with one hand and ran a clean cloth over the table with her other. "Now, will you be wanting a room tonight, Mr. Muir?"

Hamish drained the last of his pint, the bitter ale making quick work of the last of the dust coating his mouth and throat, then set his empty glass on the table. "Yes, please, if you have one."

"Oh, aye, I've a lovely large room at the back. It's nice and quiet, and the window looks out onto the Kyle of Tongue. Right pretty it is at night, and the bed's a good one," she added, with a wink for Cat.

"Er, that sounds perfect, Mrs. Geddes. If you could send a bath up as well, I'd be most appreciative, but before we retire for the evening, I'm curious about something."

"Oh? What's that, lass?"

"I wondered how you came to name your establishment The Golden Coin. It's rather an unusual name, isn't it?"

"Eh, not so much around these parts, on account of the lost treasure, you know." Mrs. Geddes leaned closer, lowering her voice. "That was twenty-nine years ago now, you ken, but Scots don't forget such things."

Cat exchanged a glance with Hamish. "Lost treasure, Mrs. Geddes? What lost treasure?"

"Why, don't say you've never heard of the Skirmish of Tongue, lass?"

"Oh, of course, Mrs. Geddes. Every Scot knows about the Skirmish of Tongue, and the fate of the ship *Le Prince Charles Stuart*."

"Why, it happened right in front of our noses, right out there in the Kyle of Tongue. That ship ran aground just offshore, ye ken, and there was naught to be done about it, once it did."

Mrs. Geddes shook her head. "Those poor Scottish lads didn't have a chance."

No, and neither had the Jacobean cause. *Le Prince Charles Stuart* had been carrying a fortune in gold from King Louis XV of France to help fund the Jacobite Rebellion. It had been a staggering blow for the Jacobites when the English recovered the gold.

"It's a tragic story, but I never heard of there being any lost treasure in connection with it." Cat toyed with her empty wine glass, turning it between her fingers, but she kept her gaze on Mrs. Geddes. "But perhaps there's more to the story than I realized."

"Ach, well, there always is, isn't there, lass? Not many skirmishes take place in British waters that don't involve money in one way or another, Mrs. Muir." Mrs. Geddes leaned closer. "Thirteen thousand pounds of it in the case of *Le Prince Charles Stuart*, if the rumors are true."

"But that skirmish was a rout, wasn't it? By the time Clan Mackay and the English forces aboard the *Sheerness* finished with the Jacobean crew of *Le Prince Charles Stuart*, all that money was gone. What Clan Mackay didn't take was meant to have been returned to George II's coffers."

"Well, now, lass, that depends on who you ask, doesn't it?" Mrs. Geddes's blue eyes were twinkling. "If you'd asked George II at the time, I'm sure he'd have told you his men recovered every penny. That was the official story, ye ken, but a story's only as good as the person telling it."

Cat's slumped shoulders straightened, the weariness from a long day of travel seeming to fall away from her like water shaken from a dog's coat. "And if I didn't ask George II, Mrs. Geddes?" she asked. "If, for instance, I asked one of the villagers in Tongue? One who was living here at the time the Skirmish took place?"

"Well, then I daresay you'd get another answer." Mrs. Geddes gave Cat a wise nod. "The truth's a complicated thing, Mrs. Muir. It tends to vary, depending on who tells it."

"Indeed, it does." Cat was quiet for a moment, considering her words carefully, then, "Did you happen to live here in Tongue when the Skirmish took place, Mrs. Geddes?"

"Aye, Mrs. Muir, I did. I was not but a wee young girl at the time, of course, but it may be that I remember a thing or two." Mrs. Geddes gave them a coy smile. It was clear she'd told this story dozens of times and took great pleasure in it.

Cat, who now seemed to be enjoying the game as much as her hostess, was grinning back at her. "Oh? What sort of things would those be?"

"Ach, well, mostly just rumors, you know, and not the sort of thing you'd put much stock in, but there are those who say the lads aboard the *Le Prince Charles Stuart* stuffed their pockets with gold and left it scattered on the ground when they knew they were being overtaken by their enemies."

Hamish had heard that rumor before. It was said that the crew of *Le Prince Charles Stuart* made away with some of the gold when they'd been forced to flee their foundering ship. They'd escaped on foot under cover of night, taking as much of the gold as they could carry with them. They'd set off on a march toward Inverness, nearly a hundred miles south, where supplies were being amassed for the triumphant return of Bonnie Prince Charlie.

"Thousands of pounds in gold coins scattered across the ground! My goodness." Cat patted her chest. "If that's the case, it must have been a great stroke of luck for the villagers, as I daresay they made off with it."

"Well, if they did, you can be sure they didn't say so!" Mrs. Geddes cackled. "Others claim the crew dumped all the gold into Lochan Hakel, the little freshwater loch at the southern end of the Kyle. To hear them tell it, villagers were plucking gold coins from that loch for years to come. Why, there's one farmer as tells a tale about finding a gold coin wedged in the hoof of one of his cows after the animal had been wading in the loch."

Lochan Hakel? Now that was interesting. The fleeing crew of *Le Prince Charles Stuart* hadn't made it to Inverness. They'd never even made it out of Tongue. A contingent of men led by Captain George Mackay, the son of Lord Reay, the chief of Clan Mackay had intercepted them at the head of the Kyle, not far from Lochan Hakel. A battle had ensued. Five or six of the Jacobite men had been killed, and others wounded, and the rest were forced to surrender to Clan Mackay.

Whatever gold the clan didn't take for themselves was allegedly returned to George II's government, but if that wasn't the case—if the crew of *Le Prince Charles Stuart* had dumped the gold—Lochan Hakel was a logical place to have done it.

"This is all quite fascinating, Mrs. Geddes. I've never heard any of this." Cat turned to Hamish. "Have you, Mr. Muir?"

"Not a word of it, Mrs. Muir. What other stories do you have for us, Mrs. Geddes?"

Mrs. Geddes hesitated, then leaned closer, lowering her voice. "Well, there was one other tale that's been bandied about, but I can't testify to the truth of it. I didn't see it myself."

Hamish tensed. Mrs. Geddes had been having a wonderful time teasing them, drawing out her story bit by bit as if she were tossing out breadcrumbs, but suddenly she'd gone as somber as a church sermon.

"See what, Mrs. Geddes?"

Mrs. Geddes glanced around them, but no one was paying them any attention. "It may be that a few members of *Le Prince's* crew escaped the *Sheerness's* soldiers and Clan Mackay and they didn't go away empty-handed, neither."

"Oh? Who were they, Mrs. Geddes?"

"No one knows, but old Mr. Leith swears he saw three lads—young lads, no more than sixteen or seventeen years by the looks of them go aboard a small fishing boat that came out of nowhere, manned by a rough-looking gentleman with red hair."

Red hair! Cat glanced at him, and he knew she was thinking the same as he was.

Could the three young men have been Archie Muir, Malcolm Ross, and Angus Dunn? And the man in the boat . . . could he have been Rory MacLeod?

For weeks now, Hamish had racked his brain trying to figure out how his father had crossed paths with Rory MacLeod all those years ago. It must have been a rather extraordinary occurrence, as the two men had lived quite different lives.

They knew from Mr. Duffy that Rory had been in Eilean nan Ron near the time the Skirmish at Tongue had taken place. Eilean nan Ron was less than eight miles from Tongue, and Duffy had said when Rory returned to Castle Cairncross from Eilean nan Ron, he'd had the Louis d'Or ten-piece with him.

But his father had never mentioned the Skirmish of Tongue to him, nor had he said a word about having served on the *Le Prince Charles Stuart*. But then his father never spoke much about his past, particularly those parts of it that might have irritated the sensibilities of his aristocratic father-in-law.

The Skirmish of Tongue took place in March of seventeen forty-six, and his father hadn't married his mother until September of seventeen forty-seven . . .

Was it possible his father, along with Malcolm Ross and Angus Dunn had been aboard the doomed *Le Prince Charles Stuart*, but that by some strange stroke of luck or providence, they'd escaped with a portion of the gold?

Of course, it was. Anything was possible, and if there'd been a battle afoot between the Jacobean soldiers, Clan Mackay, and the English Crown, God knew Rory MacLeod would have found his way into it. He'd had no love for Clan Mackay and would have delighted in foiling them.

But if this was true, then what had happened to the treasure?

"You know, this is all quite fascinating, Mrs. Geddes. I'd love to hear more about it. I'd like to pay a call on Mr. Leith. Where would I find him?"

Mrs. Geddes blinked. "You don't find him at all, Mr. Muir. He's been six feet under these past five years or more."

Oh. Well, that was unfortunate.

"But there's others who may be able to tell you something about it." Mrs. Geddes nodded at an old man who was sitting at an adjacent table, nursing a pint of ale. "That's Mr. Laing, just there. He was a good friend of Mr. Leith's, God rest his soul. Mayhap he can tell you more."

"I daresay Mr. Muir would love to share a pint with Mr. Laing." Cat gave him a significant glance before she rose to her feet. "I believe I'll retire to our bedchamber, however. Mrs. Geddes is right. I'm quite done in."

"Are you sure?" Hamish rose as well, and leaned closer to speak directly into her ear. "This looks promising."

"Yes, it does, but there are, ah, too many curious eyes in here." She nodded toward the other end of the table, where a man with dark hair half-hidden under a woolen cap was staring intently at her.

"You just go right on, lass, and I'll see to it that bath is sent up to you." Mrs. Geddes gave her a kind smile. "That and a good night's sleep will set you to rights quick enough."

"Thank you, Mrs. Geddes."

Hamish jumped to his feet. "If you'd be so good as to send Mr. Laing another ale, or perhaps a dram of your finest whisky, with my compliments, Mrs. Geddes? I'm going to see my wife to our bedchamber, but I'll come back down."

Mrs. Geddes nodded, smiling. "Aye, I'll do just that. Mary? Come here, lass, and show Mr. and Mrs. Muir to the blue room, will you? There's a good girl."

Hamish ushered Cat out of the dining room, his hand resting on the arch of her back, and they followed Mary up the staircase to a spacious, comfortable chamber in a quiet part of the inn.

"Oh, how pretty." Cat strode across the room to a large window that offered a sweeping view of the Kyle of Tongue. "It reminds me a little of Castle Cairncross, though the coastline is not as rugged."

"The room will do, then?" It was by far the best room they'd been given since leaving Ballantrae. There was plenty of space on the floor for him to spread out, unlike that hovel of a bedchamber in Aviemore. His back still hadn't recovered.

Cat turned from the window and gave him a smile that didn't quite reach her eyes. "Yes, it will do nicely."

"You're certain you don't wish to hear for yourself what Mr. Laing has to say?" From the start, she'd insisted on being a part of this, and it wasn't like her to beg off.

"No. I can't abide being stared at, and I think it's best this way. Gentlemen of Mr. Laing's age tend to be more comfortable with other gentlemen. You'll get more from him without me there." She turned back to the window. "I'll want to hear everything he tells you, of course."

"Of course," he murmured. "Well, then. Goodnight, Cat."

"Goodnight, Lord Ballantyne," she said, without turning around.

It was plain enough that she wished to get rid of him, so he left her staring out the window and made his way down the stairs, his heart like an anvil in his chest.

Baths were glorious things. It had been so long since she'd soaked in one, she'd quite forgotten it.

She let her head rest against the back of the tub and gazed out the window. It was dark now, but moonlight offered just enough of a glow to illuminate the waters of the Kyle of Tongue rippling in the gentle breeze.

It didn't really look much like Castle Cairncross. She'd only said it did because it had been so dreadfully awkward standing here with Hamish, she'd been desperate to fill the silence, and couldn't think of anything else to say.

Awkward still, even after so many days of spending every moment in each other's company. If she could judge by how quickly he'd taken to his heels, he must feel the same way.

His efforts not to inflict his presence on her should have gratified her, but instead, it made her unbearably sad. If she'd only been able to hold onto her righteous anger against him, this all would be a great deal easier, but not even a day after his confession, her anger had already slipped through her fingers.

No one was more surprised at it than she was, but nothing—not her anger, her confusion, or her hurt feelings—was a match for the desire that burned like a conflagration between them.

Now she hardly knew what she felt anymore. Her emotions shifted by the minute. No sooner did one settle on her than another took its place, like a butterfly landing on an outstretched hand, only to fly away again in a blur of bright color.

If she'd had her wits about her, she'd do the wise thing and leap through the window and scurry right back to Castle Cairncross, where it was safe. Anything, but permit her desire for a man like this to overcome her reason.

Hamish had *lied* to her. A lie of omission, yes, but a lie was still a lie.

Wasn't it? She didn't know anymore.

The only thing she did know beyond any doubt was that the Hamish Muir who'd lied to her was the same Hamish Muir who followed her through the woods, accused her of poisoning him, and threatened to take her to the magistrate.

That Hamish Muir had said he'd rip her castle apart, one stone at a time.

If he'd still been the same Hamish Muir she'd so heartily despised in those first few days, she'd be enjoying her bath instead of thinking about the forlorn look on his handsome face when he'd left the bedchamber earlier.

But that haughty, arrogant marquess wasn't the same man who'd helped save her and her sisters from the last lugger, or the man who'd walked with her to the Duffys the following day, a grin on his face and her basket over his arm. He wasn't the man who'd kissed her with such tender passion in her father's study, or the man who'd fiercely defended her against Donigan's henchmen, despite the blade pressed to his neck.

He wasn't the man who'd confessed the truth about that first lugger.

He could have lied about it. She never would have found out the truth if he hadn't confessed it. He might have finished what they'd begun in Donigan's bedchamber in Ballantrae without ever experiencing so much as a twinge of conscience over it.

But he hadn't, because he *wasn't* that man.

He wasn't like any man she'd ever known before. To be fair, aside from Bryce Fraser, she hadn't known any men at all. Bryce was the only man who'd ever tried to court her. Goodness knew a lady could scarcely find a man worse than Bryce, but Hamish wasn't only a good man in comparison to the monster Bryce was.

He was a good man, period.

And she was . . . alas, she was who she was. She squeezed her eyes closed, shutting out the sight of the moon floating in the darkened sky.

Hamish had called her brave, but it wasn't true.

She had been brave once, but she wasn't the lady she'd once been. Since her father's death, and everything that had followed afterward, she was no longer able to look at people as she'd once done.

Now she regarded them all with suspicion. Fear, even.

She could forgive Hamish for sending the first lugger—she *had* forgiven him—but she couldn't ever trust him again. Not because what he'd done was unforgivable, or because he deserved her distrust, but because she didn't trust anyone anymore.

It was simply who she was now.

Hamish deserved better than that. Better than her.

She gripped the sides of the bathtub and rose to her feet, shivering as the cooling water streamed down her legs and back.

She fetched the towel the maidservant had left, wrapped it around herself, and dropped into the chair in front of the fire to dry her hair.

It was quiet in the room, the only sound the low crackle of the fire, and the distant chime of the tavern clock hanging on the wall of the dining room below.

She pulled the towel closer around her throat, watched the flames dancing in the grate, and did her best to think of nothing.

CHAPTER 21

Hamish woke the next morning to the splash of water in the basin.

It had been late when he'd returned to the room last night. Cat had been fast asleep in the bed, so he'd quietly pilfered a blanket and pillow, then stretched out in front of the fireplace so the warmth from the last smoldering embers might lull him to sleep.

He cracked one eye open, stifling a groan, and there in front of him was a pair of bare feet peeking out from underneath the hem of a dress the color of spring leaves. Cat was at the washbasin, her pink toes curled against the floorboards, and he stifled another groan, his mouth going dry.

Toes. They were *toes*, for God's sake. Toes were hardly the most titillating portion of a lady's anatomy, but that never seemed to matter when it came to Cat. He was enamored of every inch of her, from the tips of those adorable toes to the ends of each wild auburn curl atop her head.

"Good morning, Miss MacLeod." He struggled to his feet, his back protesting every minute he'd spent sleeping on hard floors for the past six nights. "You're up early."

"I beg your pardon, my lord. I didn't mean to wake you." Cat glanced at him over her shoulder, then turned back to the looking glass. "I never heard you come back last night. Were you up very late with Mr. Laing?"

He swallowed. Her face was scrubbed clean, her cheeks as pink as her toes from her vigorous wash with the cold water in the basin. Damp wisps of hair curled around her face, and the bright shade of her green dress turned her eyes the color of a tender spring plant just emerging from the ground after the last frost, its eager face turned toward the sun.

He'd never seen her wear that dress before. If he had, he'd remember it.

"Late enough, yes." He hadn't been in any hurry to spend another night on the floor, and as it happened, Mr. Laing was a fine old gentleman with a sharp memory. "Mr. Laing claims to recall your father being in Tongue around the time of the Skirmish."

She was paying meticulous attention to her ablutions, taking care not to look at him, but *that* made her whirl around, the washing cloth still clutched in her hand. "You mean to say he saw my father here?"

"He claims to, yes. I was surprised at it, too, but he was adamant. He said he didn't know it was your father at the time—Rory's face wasn't as famous then as it later became—but he recognized the redheaded man he'd seen in Tongue as the legendary Rory MacLeod after coming across a sketch of him in a broadside some years later. He said Rory had a memorable face, and there was no mistaking it."

All the MacLeods had memorable faces, it seemed. God knew he couldn't get Cat's face out of his head. Waking or dreaming, she was there, as if she'd been painted under his eyelids.

Cat abandoned her washing in the basin and sank down on the edge of the bed. He joined her, and they sat there together, their legs nearly but not quite touching, the only sounds the bustle of the inn waking up and the gentle murmur of the water outside the window.

He would have given anything to know what she was thinking during those silent moments, but when Cat roused herself at last, she said only, "If Mr. Laing is remembering correctly, and my father was here in Tongue at the time of the Skirmish, then—"

"Then we have every reason to believe the story Mrs. Geddes told us is true."

It was not, evidently, what she'd been about to say, because she turned to him in surprise. "What, you mean to say you believe Rory rescued three young Jacobean soldiers aboard *Le Prince Charles Stuart* from a disastrous fate?"

"Well, we don't know if it would have been disastrous, but—"

"That Rory emerged from the shadows in a fishing boat at just the right time and made away with three young men with a fortune in gold pieces stuffed in their pockets?" She shook her head. "I suppose anything is possible, but it sounds too fantastical to be true."

Yet it *was* true. He'd become convinced of it as Mr. Laing had told the curious tale of what he'd witnessed on the day of the Skirmish of Tongue. It was as unlikely as she claimed, yes, but there were too many details that corresponded with what they already knew about the lost treasure for it to be otherwise.

Rory's presence near Tongue at the time, the pact between the four men, the gold coins, and even Rory's animosity toward Clan Mackay. It was as if Mr. Laing had given him the puzzle's frame, and all the pieces were now falling into place.

"It might be too fantastical to be believed for another man, but your father's entire life was made up of fantastical tales, Cat. I daresay this is the least of them."

"But your father's *wasn't*, my lord. How can we be certain he was even on board the *Le Prince Charles Stuart*, or in Tongue at all? Even if he was here, it seems far-fetched to think he'd risk his life to steal a portion of the gold. I can believe it of *my* father, but yours was no smuggler."

Wasn't he? There must be a reason why the rumors of Archibald Muir's reckless youth had persisted for all these years, but he didn't know if the rumors about his father were true, and he likely never would.

"We can't be *certain* of anything, Cat, but I wouldn't be surprised to find my father was involved in the Skirmish and never told me. He was a Scot, remember, and a rather fierce Jacobite in his earlier years, but he became less forthcoming about his past after he married my mother. My grandfather was an English aristocrat and not an admirer of the Old Pretender."

"No, I imagine not." Her brow puckered. "If we're correct about the pact, then the other two men who escaped on the fishing boat that day must have been Malcolm Ross and Angus Dunn."

"They must have been, yes. It seems likely the lifelong friendship between Malcolm, Angus, and my father started on board the *Le Prince Charles Stuart* and was strengthened by their shared experience during the Skirmish of Tongue."

"Then you think the four of them hid the treasure here twenty-nine years ago, and Rory came back five months ago to retrieve it?"

"After my father died, yes. It fits with everything else we know to be true."

For the past week, as they'd made their way from Ballantrae to northern Scotland, his instincts had been telling him they'd find the answer to the mystery here in Tongue. Now he was more convinced of it than ever. There were simply too many coincidences to believe otherwise.

"Mr. Laing didn't happen to catch sight of my father here in Tongue five months ago, did he?" Cat asked, with a hopeful look.

"No. I think he would have mentioned it if he had."

"I suppose that would be too good to be true. Why do you think they went to all the trouble to make the pact, Hamish?" Cat tapped her lower lip, thinking. "If Mr. Laing's story is true, they had the gold right in their hands. Why hide it, when they could have just taken it with them then?"

"I daresay it was too risky. The crew from the *Sheerness* was chasing them, remember, and that's to say nothing of Captain George Mackay and his men combing every inch of dirt from the shore of the Kyle of Tongue to Lochen Hakel for them. If they did get away with a significant portion of the gold, it would have been heavy and difficult to carry."

"They must have decided it was safer to leave the treasure behind and escape with their skin while they had the chance. Twenty-nine years, Hamish! It's as enduring a promise as I've ever heard of."

"Indeed. We may never know the whole if it, but my guess is the pact was in part a promise that none of them would come back on their own to steal the treasure. The money was never theirs. It belongs to the clans."

"All this time I thought Rory had gone off on one of his usual quests after a ship laden with tea or rum when he'd only been trying to right a wrong done to the clans."

"Yes." It was fitting, really, that her father should have been the last to survive, and the one to go after the treasure. Rory MacLeod had been a smuggler, right until the very end, when he'd become a hero.

"Who's to say the treasure is still where they hid it, though? It's been twenty-nine years, Hamish. Surely someone else has found it by now."

"Perhaps, but just five months ago, your father believed it was still here." He hesitated, clearing his throat. "I, ah, I did your father a terrible injustice, Cat, and I beg your pardon for it."

She turned to him, startled. "What injustice?"

"From the moment the coin arrived at my townhouse in London, I was certain Rory had broken his promise and taken the gold for himself, but for such an infamous smuggler, your father was a man of conscience. He kept his word."

And in the end, keeping his word was what had led to his death.

Perhaps she was thinking the same thing, because she rose

from the bed and went to the window, her back to him as she gazed out at the water. "I did him an injustice, too. I believed the worst of him, and it's too late to beg his pardon for it."

Her voice broke on that last word, and a roar of despair echoed inside him. There was nothing he wanted more than to go to her, to cradle her head on his chest and help soothe her battered heart, but if there was ever a man who had no right to touch her, it was him.

He'd lied to her. He'd taken away everything that mattered the most to her, and now there seemed to be no way for them to get back to where they'd been that morning in Ballantrae, when he'd woken beside her. Had that only been six days ago?

Six days, since he'd held her in his arms.

It seemed as if he'd lived a dozen lifetimes since then, and with every hour that passed, she only slipped further away from him. What a terrible irony, that the man who could talk his way into the good graces of every debutante, matron, and grandmamma in London couldn't find a single word to say to earn him the forgiveness of the lady he'd fallen in love with.

"There's one question that remains unanswered." Cat was still at the window, her arms wrapped around herself, her elbows cupped in her palms.

"What question?"

She turned then, and for the first time since he'd told her the truth, her eyes met his. "Where did they hide the treasure?"

"You're his daughter, Catriona. No one knew him better than you and your sisters did." He rose and took a step toward her, unable to help himself. "You tell me where he hid the treasure."

"I wish I could." Her shoulders lifted in a helpless shrug. "Over these past few months, I've begun to wonder if I ever knew my father at all."

Her eyes were shiny, and he couldn't bear it any longer.

He held out his hand to her. "Mr. Laing told me the ruins of

Castle Varrich, the ancient seat of Clan Mackay, are less than a mile's walk from Tongue. Shall we go and see it?"

She glanced out the window. "It looks as if it's going to rain."

"Then we'll get wet. Come, Cat. We're not getting anywhere sitting in this room. Let's go downstairs, have breakfast, and take a walk. The fresh air will do us some good."

She stared down at his hand for some time, unmoving, but just when he was certain she'd refuse him, she rested her fingertips in his palm, as if it were the easiest thing in the world for him to offer his hand, and for her to take it.

As it turned out, Castle Varrich wasn't so much a castle as a tall, narrow tower of crumbling stone with nothing but open sky where the roof had once been, but it must have been an imposing place in its day.

It wasn't large. It had likely only been three stories, with the bottom floor reserved for livestock, but it was situated at the peak of an impressive hill, near the edge of a promontory, with sweeping views of the Kyle of Tongue in every direction, and the wide sky stretching out in an endless swathe above it.

"It's lovely up here, isn't it?" Cat had wandered a short distance from the castle, closer to the downward slope of the hill, and was gazing out at the Kyle of Tongue below them. "Lovely, but cold."

"That's because Scotland despises me." The sun had been struggling through the clouds when they'd left The Golden Coin, but by the time they'd reached the top of the hill where the remains of the castle stood, it had vanished and the wind had picked up, whipping at Cat's skirts and hair. "Every time I venture outside, the heavens threaten to release a fury upon my head."

"They haven't opened yet." She shivered, drawing her cloak tighter around her, and gave him a small smile. "But I daresay they will soon enough, now you've challenged them."

She was wearing the brown cloak again. Or rather, *still.* It was a threadbare, bedraggled-looking garment, and he didn't like to see her forced to make do with it. If he hadn't known she didn't have any other, he might have even been ungentlemanly enough to say so.

It was useless in today's sharp wind, however, and he'd be damned if he'd stand here and watch while she shivered beside him. "Here." He slid his coat off his shoulders and strode over to her. "Have mine."

But no sooner did he wrap his coat around her than she tried to slide it off again. "That's not necessary, my lord. I don't need—"

"Hush." He caught her hands in his, lowered them gently to her sides, then arranged the coat over her shoulders, and closed it more snugly around her neck. "Yes, it is necessary."

She gazed down at his hands for a moment, then tipped her head back and glanced shyly up at him. "It, ah, it's quite warm, isn't it?"

"Indeed, and especially so on you, as it's more of a blanket than a coat." He gazed down at her, his heart beginning to pound at the softness in her eyes. Had there ever been a woman with more beautiful eyes than hers?

She turned her head toward the collar of the coat and drew in a dainty breath. "It smells like you."

"Does it, indeed?" He laughed, startled. It was the last thing he'd expected her to say. "What, ah . . . what do I smell like, Miss MacLeod?"

Her cheeks turned scarlet, but to his surprise, she answered him. "A bit like the woods, but also a little like leather, although that's only since we embarked on our travels. I daresay it's from holding the ribbons. When we were at Castle Cairncross, I thought I detected a hint of port, as well—"

She broke off, biting her lip.

"You've, ah, given this some thought, I see." He reached for her and gently plucked her lip out from between her teeth.

"Oh, no. Not at all, my lord. I just . . ." She peeked up at him from underneath her lashes. "Well, perhaps a little. I'm quite sensitive to scents, you know, Lord Ballantyne, because of my plants."

"Yes, of course. That makes perfect sense, Miss MacLeod."

She was looking at him. Not past him, and not through him, but *at* him for the first time in six days, and for the first time in six days, his heart was soaring. Castle Varrich could have fallen to pieces right beside them, and he wouldn't have noticed it.

Was there hope for them yet? The question was on the edge of his tongue, but he didn't have a chance to speak it before she took a step backward, away from him, and the moment was lost.

"Thank you for your coat, my lord."

Anything. Anything for you.

He didn't say it aloud. He didn't want to frighten her away.

She'd looked at him, and that was enough. For today, that was enough.

"Have you spotted any interesting plants in Tongue, Miss MacLeod? I saw quite a bit of this one on our way up the hill." He strode over to a plant with dark green, pointed leaves with a rough, deeply veined surface. "This one looks as if it—"

"Oh no, Lord Ballantyne. Don't touch those!"

But her warning came too late. He bent down, seized one of the plants, and instantly regretted it as a streak of pain shot through his hand. "Ouch! The damn thing bit me!"

"It didn't bite you, my lord. It stung you. That's *Urtica dioica*."

"Urtica what? In English, if you please, Miss MacLeod."

"Stinging nettle." She was biting her lip again, but this time it was to hold back a laugh. "The stems and leaves have hollow hairs on them that break off when you touch them and inject an acid into the skin."

"Acid?" That wasn't encouraging. "Do you find this amusing, Miss MacLeod?"

"Oh, no. Of course not, my lord. It's just that . . ." she trailed off, pressing her lips together, her green eyes dancing.

"Just what?"

"Well, it's not as if there's a shortage of stinging nettles in Scotland. Haven't you ever seen it before? It's quite distinctive."

"Are you laughing at me, Miss MacLeod? Because it looks as if your lips are twitching."

"Certainly not. I wouldn't dream of it, my lord."

He frowned at the offensive plant. "I suppose it does look vaguely familiar."

"I imagine it does. It's a bit too late now, however."

"They're not poisonous, are they? I'm not going to wake up in a bed a week from now with no recollection of what happened to me, am I?"

"No, nothing like that, but it can cause a rash, and it's rather painful, I'm afraid." She strode over to him. "Here, let me see."

He held out his injured hand to her.

"Ah, yes. See here, my lord?" She pointed to his palm, where a spray of raised red bumps was forming. "Not to worry, you'll be as good as new in a day or two after the itching subsides."

"Itching? Wait, did you say a day or two?"

She made a noise that sounded suspiciously like a hastily smothered laugh. "Perhaps a little longer." She bent her head over his hand and traced a finger over the red bumps on his palm.

Ah. Perhaps there were some advantages to a nettle sting, after all. He stilled, his eyes nearly dropping closed at the sensuous drag of her fingertip over his heated skin.

"Is there an antidote?" His voice was much huskier than it had been a moment before. "Something to ease the sting?"

"Yes. The leaves of *Rumex obtusifolius* eases the sting."

"*Rumex*—"

"Dock plant, my lord. Jewelweed works as well." She glanced around them with a frown. "It's often found growing near stinging nettle, but I don't see any. I'll just go back down a little way and see if I can find some, shall I? It's a touch wetter down there."

"Yes, all right."

"I'll be back in a moment." She disappeared around the corner of the pathway, and he turned his attention to trying to extricate the thin nettle hairs still protruding from the side of his hand, which turned out to be a useless endeavor, much like a dog chasing its tail.

Soon enough, however, he became aware that she hadn't returned.

Surely, it shouldn't take that long to find jewelweed?

He hurried to the head of the winding pathway. He could see a good distance down the hill from here, but there was no sign of her.

Catriona had disappeared.

CHAPTER 22

The only plant that didn't seem to be growing on the pathway that wound around the side of the hill leading to Castle Varrich was jewelweed.

Cat meandered along, poking into the patches of green things lining the path and hidden among the outcroppings of rocks, searching for the familiar oval leaves of *Impatiens capensis*. She couldn't stir a step without stumbling over patches of mountain heath, and there was enough maidenhair fern to make dozens of bottles of cough syrup, but nothing for a nettle sting.

There wasn't even an obliging bit of dock plant to be found.

Poor Hamish. The nettles wouldn't do him any real harm. Indeed, stinging nettle tea did wonders for painful joints, but for such a humble plant, their sting was surprisingly painful. Those angry red bumps on his hand were likely to get worse before they got better.

She really shouldn't have laughed at him. It hadn't been kind of her, but there'd been something comical about his shocked expression when the stinging nettle had "bit" him. His eyes had popped so wide they'd nearly rolled out of his head. He had the most expressive eyes, and that blue . . . well, it wasn't every day a lady came across eyes as blue as his.

A man's eyes reveal the best and the worst of him . . .

She couldn't look into Hamish's eyes without her mother's words coming back to her. It would have been easier if she hadn't been able to see so much in those beautiful blue depths. If she hadn't been able to read him so well, perhaps she wouldn't have noticed how exhausted he was.

Exhausted, and dejected.

This morning, before he woke, she'd spent a humiliating amount of time gazing at him, guilt piercing her chest at the disheveled tangle of dark waves atop his head and the violet circles under his eyes. But then that was what came of her banishing him to the floor every night, wasn't it?

He'd been so refined when he'd first come to Dunvegan, too! It had taken her just over three weeks to ruin a perfectly good marquess. Yet for all his fashionable elegance, his glossy boots and costly coat, there was nothing false about Hamish—no shadows in those clear blue eyes. Everything he thought, everything he felt, everything he *was*, was right there in his eyes.

He didn't hide anything. Not like she did. Since her father had died, there'd been a small, secret chamber inside her heart no one could touch, and it had been growing closer and tighter with every day that passed.

Grief had made her smaller than she'd been before.

Smaller, and angrier, her shoulders hunched to keep her anger close, clutching it against her heart the way a miser hoarded gold.

It was no way to live a life.

If she'd noticed it, she may have been able to put a stop to it, but it had come on so slowly, she hadn't realized it was happening until she woke up one day with nothing but anger and grief in her heart. She'd been so furious with Rory for so long, she couldn't remember how to be anything else anymore.

He'd *left* them. He'd been there one day, then gone the next, all her pleas and protests falling on deaf ears, as if she and her sisters didn't exist. He'd abandoned them when they'd most needed him, and then he'd gone and *died*, leaving them at the mercy of every villain in Scotland.

At least, that was what she'd told herself these past few months.

But time was the ultimate truth-teller, wasn't it? As the days passed, the layers of anger had started to peel away, leaving only an aching, empty abyss inside her chest, with nothing to fill it but her memories of him.

And when those memories faded? What then?

Had he ever thought of that? Had he thought of them even once, when he'd been out on that last adventure? Had he ever wondered how they were faring without him, or worried about what would become of them if he never returned? How they'd struggle without him?

How terribly they'd miss him?

So many questions, yet she'd lied to Hamish when she'd told him she didn't think she'd ever truly understood her father. For all her helpless fury at him, nothing could ever change the fact that she'd known him, inside and out. She, Freya, and Sorcha knew Rory better than anyone aside from their mother.

You're his daughter, Catriona. You tell me where he hid the treasure.

Hamish was right. If anyone could guess where he'd hidden the treasure, it should have been her.

Should have been, but *wasn't*, because here she was, all these months later, as much in the dark as she'd ever been. She didn't have the faintest idea where to begin to search.

Where, of all the potential hiding places in Tongue, had Rory secreted away the treasure? If ever there was a question without an obvious answer, it was that one. She'd mulled it over until her head was spinning, but the threads refused to come untangled.

If Rory had been a simple man, perhaps it wouldn't have been so difficult, but the inside of her father's mind had been a complicated place. One only needed to attempt to read his papers to see that.

She'd do well to forget about it now and concentrate on finding the jewelweed. It was the least she could do for Hamish, after banishing him to the floor for the past six nights because she was too cowardly to sleep beside him.

She continued to follow the pathway as it wound down the side of the hill, prodding half-heartedly at the clumps of greenery as she passed. For pity's sake, how could there not be a single bit of jewelweed? There was a never-ending supply of it in the woods at home.

She wandered on, lost in her thoughts until at last she came to a stop and glanced back up the hill. Oh, dear. She hadn't meant to come so far. Hamish would be wondering where she'd gotten to by now.

She wrapped his coat more tightly around her as she turned and began to make her way back up the hill. It had grown much colder as she'd been wandering, and it was a miracle the dark clouds scudding across the white sky hadn't opened yet.

They'd simply have to do without the jewelweed for the moment. Perhaps Mrs. Geddes would know where they could find—

She came to an abrupt stop in the middle of the pathway, every thought of the dock plant and jewelweed forgotten. In front of her, half-hidden underneath a thick slab of moss-covered rock that hung over the edge of the downward slope of a hill was a collection of dark stones, one stacked atop the next in a neat pile.

How strange. How had she not noticed that when they'd climbed up the pathway earlier? Or perhaps the better question was, why had she noticed it now?

She drew closer, her heart quickening in her chest.

Yet there was no reason she should find herself so breathless. It was only a cairn, much like thousands of other cairns one could find in every corner of Scotland. It wasn't even a grand one. She'd seen cairns that were thrice her own height with enormous slabs of rock at their base.

This was a paltry little thing in comparison, no higher than her hip, and not remarkable in any way, aside from its being nearly obscured by the stone ledge hanging over it, and just far enough off the pathway one risked a tumble down the hill if they got too close to it.

Yet she drew closer anyway, oddly mesmerized by the sight of it.

There was a tangle of weeds and grasses creeping up the side of it, but here at the edge of the pathway she could see the stones were an unusual color, much darker than any of the others scattered nearby, but there were stones of every description to be found in Tongue.

Still, something about it tugged at her memory, as if she'd seen the stones somewhere before . . .

Well, how absurd. Of course, she hadn't seen it before. How could she have when this was her first visit to Castle Varrich?

She shook the foolish thought away. She'd kept Hamish waiting long enough, and the wind had picked up as the sun moved behind the dark bank of clouds to the east of the castle ruins.

She turned her back on the cairn and began once again to climb up the hill, but she hadn't gone more than half a dozen steps before she was turning around again and hurrying back down.

It wouldn't do any harm to take a closer look, just to satisfy her curiosity. Once she found there was nothing remarkable in it, she'd be on her way.

Yet as she got closer, the odd feeling of familiarity intensified. It was as if she'd been on this pathway before, approaching the castle ruins from this direction, with the Kyle of Tongue just beyond the next rise, and the misty outlines of Ben Loyal and Ben Hope in the distance.

With every step she took, the stacked dark stones loomed larger in her vision, until it was impossible *not* to see it, until it all became clear in a single flash, like a lightning strike over

Loch Dunvegan—a single streak of light that illuminated everything for miles around it.

Rory's papers. She sucked in a breath, her heart fluttering.

He'd made a drawing of that cairn. There was no mistaking the height and shape of it, or the outline of the mountains in the distance. He'd even shaded the stones with heavy strokes of a pencil to indicate their darker color.

And that ledge above the cairn. Hadn't she seen something like that in his drawings, as well? Or was she simply imagining it?

Rory's papers were as cryptic as they could be. There was no denying that. She'd gone back to look at his notes several times after she and Hamish had given it up that first time, and had even made some notes of her own, but so much had happened since then it was all a blur in her mind.

Dash it, she had to *think*!

There'd been piles of maps, of course. Rory had always loved maps. But they'd mostly been of various locations on the Scottish coastline. There hadn't been one of either Eilean nan Ron or Tongue.

As for the notes, those were indeed hopeless. There were some bits of paper with no more than one word on them. Rory had always been cagey about his secrets, and he'd written his notes as if he expected they'd be stolen one day.

He'd written them to confuse, not to elucidate.

The drawings, though. Those had been different. There'd been a great many of them, and all of them were meticulously executed, far more so than his scribbled notes. There'd been drawings of birds and roads, trees and caves, mountains and fishing cottages, and dozens upon dozens of cairns, as if he'd been drawing—

Landmarks.

She stilled, her gaze on the small cairn, lightning striking for the second time.

Why, of course! That was precisely what he'd been doing.

Drawing landmarks near where he'd buried his stolen contraband, so he might find it again when he returned. Even among all the smugglers stealing goods along the Scottish coast—and there were a great many of them—Rory had been renowned for his endless number of hiding places.

He'd had goods stashed everywhere from Drummore to Thurso, and he'd constantly moved them from place to place, so they were impossible to track.

It was one of the reasons he'd never been caught.

His notes might look like nothing but a collection of chaotic scrawls, but there was a method to his madness. The drawing of the hand holding the dagger had turned out to mean something.

Clan Mackay's crest.

None of the drawings had made any sense to her at first. Landmarks themselves weren't much good without any context. A tree in Drummore looked much like a tree in Thurso, and there were thousands of fishing cottages in Scotland. One couldn't distinguish one from another, especially in a drawing.

But she knew a great deal more about Rory's final quest now than she had when she'd first inspected his drawings. Could it be that he'd drawn the cairn to mark where he'd buried the treasure? He'd drawn it repeatedly, much as he had Clan Mackay's crest.

It couldn't be that easy, could it? It seemed impossible she'd just stumbled upon it, but there was no mistaking that cairn. It had to be significant in some way.

What had Hamish told her about Castle Varrich? That it was Clan Mackay's original country seat. The family had long since moved to Tongue House on the eastern shores of the Kyle of Tongue, but at some point, these ruins had been the home of the chief of Clan Mackay.

Would Rory and his three friends have been audacious enough to bury the gold they'd stolen from Clan Mackay in a cave right beneath the clan chief's former country seat?

How needlessly risky that would be, even with the family no longer on the premises! It would have been the height of foolishness to take such a chance. It would have been an act of pure arrogance, to thumb their noses at—

Arrogance, yes. Risky, dangerous, and arrogant, and yet wasn't that precisely the sort of thing Rory would have done? Buried the treasure he'd helped steal from Clan Mackay right underneath the ruins of their country seat?

It *was*. It was precisely what he would have done.

She glanced back up the hill, biting her lip. She should fetch Hamish, but the cairn wasn't all that far removed from the pathway. It was at a steep pitch, yes, so she'd have to take care, but she'd never let a climb stop her before.

She'd just have a peek, then she'd scurry back up and fetch Hamish. Carefully, she made her way from the pathway toward the cairn, clutching at the taller plants to keep her balance, her boot heels finding every rock and treacherous tangle of grass as she went, until at last she was near enough to the cairn to reach out and touch it.

What to do next? Was the treasure buried underneath the cairn?

Slowly, one stone at a time, she began to take the cairn apart. It was easy enough at first, as the stones at the top were small enough that she had no trouble lifting them, but the two stones on the bottom were heavier, and the one resting on the ground was partially submerged in the dirt underneath it with what looked like decades of earth holding it firmly in place.

Had Rory never made it as far as Tongue five months ago, then? If he had been here, wouldn't the stone be loose? She gave it another determined nudge, but it was no use.

It was too heavy.

Even if she'd brought something to dig with, it would still be nearly impossible to liberate it. There wasn't enough room. To one side of the cairn there was another small outcropping of rock, and directly behind it was the mossy stone ledge.

She squeezed into the space between them to see if she might overturn the stone from that angle, but the bit of ground behind the outcropping was soft, and the space narrow, no more than the length of her foot. She couldn't get any leverage.

"Dash it." She braced a hand on the ledge and began to tug on her leg to free it, but now she was closer, she noticed a draft of cool air was creeping down the back of her dress.

Cool air, coming from a ledge of solid stone? No, that didn't make sense.

She laid her hand flat against the top of the ledge, the layers of thick moss damp under her palm, and explored the contours of it, working her hand first from side to side before sliding it lower.

That was when she felt it. Or *didn't* feel it, more accurately. Under the top edge of the ledge, instead of finding a sheer rock face, her hand met nothing but air.

There was a hole carved into the rock face!

It was impossible to tell how deep a hole it was, but it was large enough that her entire hand fit easily inside it. She shifted, pressing the front of her body as hard against the ledge as she could, and reached into the hole until her entire arm was submerged, all the way to her shoulder.

Dear God. It was either a very large hole or a very small cave.

What had Donigan said about caves? That there was nothing a smuggler appreciated more than a cave, because they were the ideal place to hide stolen contraband. Goodness knew Rory was fond of them. There'd been hundreds of caves among his drawings.

The treasure was inside the hole. She knew it, in the same way she always seemed to know what Sorcha and Freya were going to say before words even left their mouths.

But if Rory had hidden the treasure in the cave, what were the odds it was still here? He'd returned to Castle Cairncross with nothing to show for his journey but a festering wound in his leg.

The wound that had led to his death.

He'd come here to retrieve the treasure, and someone had shot him for his trouble. Didn't it stand to reason that whoever had shot Rory had also taken the treasure?

It did, but what did reason matter in such a situation?

After all she and Hamish had been through, all this distance they'd come, was she really going to return to Dunvegan—to her sisters, who were depending on her—without searching inside this cave for the treasure?

The treasure her father had *died* for.

No. Whatever was hidden inside that hole was coming with her. If she could reach it, that is.

But that's what rocks were for, wasn't it?

She edged away from the face of the ledge, taking care not to unbalance herself, and topple down the hill.

The smaller rocks at the top of the cairn wouldn't do her much good, and even if she could have lifted the larger ones, they were too big to fit into the narrow gap between the ledge and the rock outcropping.

So, after a bit of deliberation, she chose one of the stones that had made up the middle part of the cairn. It wouldn't add much to her height—only another few inches at the most—but it was the largest one she could carry.

It would have to do.

Somehow, she was able to maneuver between the cairn and the ledge without dropping the stone, and managed to wedge it tightly between the bottom of the ledge and the outcropping of rock. She hopped on top of it and stuck her hand as deep into the hole as she could reach.

Nothing. She passed her hand from side to side, her fingers straining, but after a dozen tries with no success, her heart sank.

Perhaps she'd been mistaken, and Rory hadn't hidden the treasure here at all, or it might be underneath the rock at the bottom of the cairn. Either that, or it was in the hole, and she simply couldn't reach it.

She needed Hamish. She should have fetched him at once.

But first, just one more try.

This time, she jumped up and clung to the edge of the rock with one hand while searching with the other.

No. It was no use. There was nothing—

Wait. Just there. Her fingertips had brushed against something on the right.

Something slick and cool, like . . . leather? A leather bag?

The rock shifted under her feet as she crouched down low, and jumped once again, her fingers grasping, and . . . yes! She had it.

Now, if she could only bring it up without dropping it.

Slowly, carefully, like an angler with a reluctant fish dangling from the hook, she began to ease it upward, one tiny increment at a time. It was quite light—much lighter than a bag with hundreds of golden coins stuffed inside it should be, but it felt as if something were rolling around inside it.

A little more, a little more . . . no sudden movements, or jerking on the strap . . .

There! With one final tug, she freed it from its hiding place and had it in her hand. It was a worn leather bag, not very large, and for the most part limp. If there was any gold in it, it couldn't be more than one or two coins—

"Well done, lass." A thick arm wrapped around her neck, the muscled forearm pressing into her throat. "I thank ye kindly for finding that for me."

Cat let out a strangled gasp and instinctively jerked the bag down, hiding it in the folds of her cloak, but it was too late. The man—for indeed it was a man, who had seemingly appeared out of nowhere—had already seen it.

"Hand it over, girl. Now, ye hear?"

He had a tight grip on her, but out of the corner of her eye, she managed to catch a glimpse of a big, rough-looking fellow with a limp hank of greasy hair falling into his eyes and a mean twist to his mouth.

He looked strangely familiar—

"Ye can either hand it over to me, or I'll take it from you, and send you over the edge of the cliff for my trouble. Yer choice, but one way or another, I'm having that bag."

"No." Her fingers tightened around the bag's strap. "It doesn't belong to you." It was a ridiculous argument, of course, as he wasn't the sort of man who seemed troubled by thorny ethical questions.

Predictably, he sneered at that. "I been waiting months for one of ye MacLeods to come and finish what Rory started. Didn't expect *you*, though."

She went still, her head spinning. He knew Rory. Not only that, but he recognized her as a MacLeod. What did he mean, he'd been waiting for—

"It's not safe, ye ken, a wee little bit of a thing like you wandering around out here all alone." He spat on the ground by her feet. "But mayhap yer not as clever as your father was. I followed ye here from The Golden Coin, and damned if you didn't take me just where I hoped ye would. Straight to Rory's treasure."

Dear God. He must be one of the men who'd been sitting in the dining room at The Golden Coin when she and Hamish arrived yesterday evening . . . yes! He was the one who'd been staring at her so intently! He must have taken one look at her and known at once that she was a MacLeod.

It wasn't the first time her red hair had given her away.

"Rory may have slipped through my fingers, but you won't be so lucky. I'm not a crack shot, ye ken, but I'm handy enough with a blade." He held his other hand in front of her face and tested the blade of the dirk clutched in his meaty fist with the pad of his thumb. "Now then, lass, just hand over that bag, and you and I will get along just fine, ye hear?"

"No." Her tone was as haughty as she could make it. "If you want the bag, you can take it yourself."

"Do you think I won't?"

She shrank back as he shifted the dirk to the hand wrapped around her throat and reached around her for the bag with the other.

There was nowhere for her to go, no way to flee. The rock ledge was directly in front of her, the steep hill to her right, and behind her . . .

Behind her, his blade pressed to her throat was the man who had almost certainly murdered her father.

CHAPTER 23

The air around Hamish had gone unnaturally still.

Aside from the long grasses at the edges of the pathway rustling in the wind, there was no sound and no movement. Even the dark clouds hanging over the ruins of Castle Varrich had settled in place, as if they were holding their breath, waiting for something.

For Cat.

He'd made his way to the bottom of the hill and then back up again. He'd peered around every corner and behind every rock, searching for a bright flash of red hair or the skirts of a spring green dress tossing in the wind, but it was no use.

There wasn't any sign of a small lady in a navy-blue coat with a handful of dock plants clutched in her fist.

It was as if Cat had disappeared entirely.

"Impossible." Ladies didn't simply vanish into the air. "Impossible."

He repeated the word in his head a dozen times as he hurried to the pathway and began to make his way down the hill for the second time, but his heart refused to hear it.

Nearly half an hour had passed since she'd left him at the top of the hill. Since then, he'd asked himself a hundred times why he hadn't accompanied her.

Could she have stumbled on the pathway and tumbled down

the hill? Cat had the climbing instincts of a mountain goat, but anyone could slip. If she'd ventured off the pathway and lost her footing near one of the rocky outcroppings, she might have hit her head.

His mind darted from one nightmare scenario to the next, all of them ending with her broken and bleeding at the bottom of some out-of-the-way ravine, but perhaps she'd simply paused to take in the view and lost track of time.

Yes, that would make sense.

No doubt she was just around the next corner. "Cat? Catriona!"

There was no answer.

She wasn't around the next corner, or the next one, or the one after that. He kept on, his heart climbing deeper into his throat with every step, until it threatened to choke him.

Where *was* she? Had she returned to The Golden Coin, or—

"It's not safe, ye ken."

Hamish frowned. It was a man's voice, and he sounded damned pleased with himself, his every syllable dripping with smug satisfaction.

". . . a wee little bit of a thing like you wandering around out here all alone."

He froze, the hair on the nape of his neck rising. Wee little bit of a thing? There could be no doubt who *that* was.

He started forward but then paused at the crunch of footsteps over loose rocks and the man's voice, speaking again. Hamish couldn't catch what he said this time. Something about The Golden Coin, and—

Rory's treasure.

A deafening roar filled Hamish's ears. It was some moments before he realized it was the thud of his own heartbeat.

". . . may have slipped through my fingers, but you won't be so lucky."

His every muscle pulled taut, and his chest heaved as panic

and fury choked him. Some blackguard had cornered Cat, and he knew all about Rory and about the missing treasure.

"I'm not a crack shot, ye ken, but handy enough with a blade."

The threat and the menacing tone in which it was spoken made the blood thundering through Hamish's veins run cold. He had to get to Cat now, but where *was* she?

He waited, straining to hear anything—another word or another footstep—that would give it away. The man's voice was close, but he couldn't see—

"Now be a good lass and do as I say."

Below him. They were *below* him.

Slowly, he lowered himself to the ground, taking care not to make a sound. He dropped flat onto his stomach and shimmied forward, using the toes of his boots to push himself along, the dirt sinking into his fingernails until the ground disappeared underneath his hands, giving way to empty space.

He was on top of a rock ledge, above them, but not at the proper angle to see them.

He crawled toward the edge, one torturous inch at a time. Closer, then closer still, nearly there, just a little further, until . . . yes! The top of the man's black knitted cap appeared, a tangle of dark hair sticking out from underneath the flat brim.

He squirmed closer until the cap and the dark hair gave way to a slash of thick eyebrows, a pair of mean brown eyes, and a scraggle of dark beard, the mouth hidden among the untidy hair twisted in a snarl.

Those eyebrows and that filthy beard. He'd seen this villain somewhere before, but he couldn't recall where he'd—

Wait. It was the man from The Golden Coin, the night he and Cat arrived in Tongue! He'd been in the dining room when they entered and had stared at Cat until she'd grown so uncomfortable she'd retired to their bedchamber.

It hadn't been mere admiration, then, but something far more sinister. The man must have recognized her that night and had been keeping his eye on her since. There was no chance he just happened to be here at the castle ruins at the same time they were.

The blackguard must have followed them here from the inn.

He wasn't one of Clan Mackay's men, by the looks of him. He wore a filthy, ill-fitting brown coat and the dark pantaloons of a common smuggler. He was carrying a dirk in his right hand with a thick, wooden handle and a long, curved silver blade with a wicked point at the tip.

But it didn't matter who he was. All that mattered was that he had Cat at his mercy, with one massive arm wrapped around her neck, the blade of the dirk against her throat, and an ugly look in his eyes.

Hamish had seen that look before. The man wouldn't hesitate to use that dirk on her.

Every instinct screamed at him to leap off the ledge and tackle the man to the ground, but if he was a smuggler, then he knew how to use a dirk, and Hamish had no weapon.

He did have the element of surprise, but if he should miscalculate, or fail to take the man down with one blow, there was no telling the chaos that would erupt, and Cat would be right in the middle of it.

No. He couldn't let that happen.

He needed a weapon. A large, loose rock would do the job, but he'd have to go search for one, and all it would take was a scrape of his boot, or a pebble toppling over the edge of the ledge to give away his hiding place, and there was no way he was leaving Cat here alone at the mercy of that villain.

"Now then, lass, ye just hand over that bag, and you and I will get along fine, ye hear?"

Bag? Hamish shimmied a little closer to the edge of the ledge, taking care to keep his head down. Cat was standing directly beneath the ledge, almost entirely out of his sight, but he could see the edge of one of her arms and her hand with the strap of a leather bag hooked around her fingers.

The hems of the brown cloak pooled in the dirt and rocks at her feet. Beside her were a few large, dark-colored stones piled on top of each other.

It looked like the remains of a cairn.

A marker, then, but for what? Rory's hidden treasure?

No, it couldn't be. It didn't make any sense.

Why would Rory build a cairn to mark where he'd buried the treasure? Marking the place with a cairn would only draw attention to the hiding place. It was as good as inviting someone to come and take the treasure.

"No. I won't hand anything over to you."

At the sound of Cat's voice, he jerked his attention back to the scene unfolding below him. She hadn't made any attempt to free herself from the man's clutches, but her chin was raised, and her expression was haughty, even with that dirk to her throat.

Foolish, beautiful, brave, ridiculous lass!

She'd never been one to shrink away from a challenge, even when she should have. Like her father, Cat had more bravery in her than was good for her.

"If you want the bag, you can take it yourself," she added.

Dear God. Why, of all the things she could have said, had she chosen to say *that*? Nothing would give that blackguard more pleasure than to manhandle—

"Do you think I won't, lass?" The man threw back his head in a laugh and pressed the blade tighter against the tender skin of her throat.

Hamish tensed, one eye on the dirk in the blackguard's hand and the other on Cat.

Waiting was the hardest thing he'd ever done, but he'd only get one chance at this. So, he stayed where he was, his breath ragged, every second seeming to last a lifetime.

Damn it, he had to find a weapon, but where? If only he had some monkshood! But there was a disappointing dearth of poisonous plants around.

The best he could do was stinging nettle.

Stinging nettle. It wasn't the dangerous weapon monkshood was, but the man wouldn't be expecting a stinging nettle attack.

It was far from a perfect plan, but it was all he had.

He glanced around him, and yes, just there, a little to his right, there was a tangled patch of weeds and grass, and among them the pointed leaves of stinging nettle.

Slowly, he backed a few inches away from the edge of the ledge, then slid across the dirt to the patch of nettle. There wasn't as much as he would have liked—just a few plants, but they'd have to do.

He seized half a dozen stalks in his fist, ignoring the sting, then slid back to the edge of the ledge, the pebbles shifting underneath him, and peered over the side.

By this point, the man had snatched the bag away from Cat. He'd shoved her to her knees and clamped one meaty hand on the back of her neck and was looming over her as he struggled with the bag with his other hand, his face contorted with eager greed.

But greed never did pay off, did it?

The villain hadn't seemed to notice how light the bag was, or how limp.

So limp it looked as if it were empty.

Anyone could see there was no fortune in gold coins hidden inside that bag. It wasn't the treasure, and that blackguard was going to find that out soon enough.

A roar of rage tore through the silence and echoed around them.

Now, in fact.

"What the devil is this?" The man tossed the bag aside and held out his hand.

Cat and Hamish both leaned closer, then Cat let out a gasp.

There, in the center of the villain's palm was a small gold signet ring set with a red stone. Not ruby or garnet, but jasper, and there was something carved into the face of it.

He couldn't see it clearly from his hiding place, but he could guess what it was. That sort of ring generally boasted a heraldic coat of arms, and it didn't take a genius to deduce which clan the crest belonged to.

Clan MacLeod.

The man had loosened his grip, and Cat managed to jerk away from him and scramble to her feet. "My father's ring!"

"Where are the bloody gold coins?" The man caught Cat by the throat and wrenched her toward him, a snarl of rage on his lips. "I know ye know where it is! Tell me, or I'll snap your neck for you!"

As soon as the villain touched her, Hamish stopped thinking. He didn't remember rising to his feet, nor did he remember leaping over the ledge onto the villain's back.

He didn't feel the blow that landed on the side of his head, catching the corner of his eye, or the point of the dirk sinking into his shoulder.

Cat's scream was the only thing he heard—hoarse, panicked, and heavy with anguish, and even then, even while he was amid the struggle, he knew it would be a long time before he forgot that scream.

And, oddly enough, he remembered the nettles. The sting of them in his palm as he snatched a fistful of the blackguard's shirt in one hand, and with the other shoved them into his gaping mouth and pushed them as far down into his throat as he could reach.

The man's reaction was satisfyingly quick, and even more satisfyingly extreme.

He released Cat at once, letting out a howl that reverberated with such resonance in the open space around them they could have heard it in Tongue. He slapped both hands over his mouth, and the dirk and Rory's ring fell to the ground.

"Quickly, Cat! Fetch your father's ring."

She darted for it while he made quick work of the smuggler,

who was in no position to defend himself. With one blow to the face, he knocked the man to his knees, then hefted one of the heavier rocks scattered around them and brought it down on the man's head.

Not hard enough to kill him—he was no murderer—but certainly hard enough to knock him unconscious until the authorities could be summoned, and the man properly dealt with.

The man toppled over into the dirt with a soft whimper, and lay there, still.

"Cat." Hamish caught her in his arms and held her against him, his eyes closing as he cradled her head in his hands and buried his face in her hair. She was trembling, her chest heaving with her frantic breaths, but she was warm and alive, and she was in his arms.

He held her, their hearts pounding in rhythm together before he reluctantly released her and took her hand, scooping up the dirk with his other one. "Come on, love." He pressed a kiss to the top of her head. "I've seen enough of Castle Varrich for the day, haven't you?"

"I've seen enough of it for a lifetime." Cat whirled around and rushed toward the pathway, but she didn't let go of his hand.

She wrapped her fingers around his and kept them there all the way back to Tongue.

"Oh, dear. Does it hurt?" Cat glanced up in time to catch Hamish's wince.

"No. Not much."

She shook her head, a smile twitching at the corners of her lips. He was nearly as bad a liar as she was. He'd said the same thing about his eye, which was now swollen shut and turning a shade of dark purple that reminded her of twilight at Castle Cairncross.

"And your shoulder? How does it feel?"

"It's fine."

Oh, yes. He was perfectly fine, even though the blood was seeping through the bandage she'd fashioned from one of his cravats.

Another item from his elegant wardrobe, ruined.

He was likely cursing the day he'd met her.

They were sitting atop the bed in their bedchamber at The Golden Coin, one of his hands cradled in hers while she ran a wet, soapy cloth over the red rash the stinging nettles had left.

He'd been quiet since they'd returned from the castle ruins. If he hadn't been gazing at her as he was, she might have believed he was a million miles away, his thoughts anywhere but on what would soon unfold between them in this bedchamber.

It hadn't yet, but like a sharply indrawn breath on the verge of bursting free, it would.

All the unsaid words were swelling between them, waiting to be spoken.

"I—" she began, at the same time as he said, "That man—"

They both gave a nervous chuckle, then she waved her hand at him. "You go first."

"That man at the ruins. Do you know who he is?"

"No." She didn't know anything about the man, aside from what he'd let slip while he was threatening her, but she had her suspicions. "I can't be certain, but I think . . ." she hesitated, meeting his gaze. "I think he's the man who shot my father."

Hamish gave a slow nod. "Can you tell me why you think so?"

"He knew who I was, Hamish. I think he recognized me as Rory's daughter on the first night we arrived in Tongue, and he's been watching us ever since."

"Yes. I think so, too. I'm certain he followed us to the ruins today." He gave her a brief smile. "There are no coincidences."

"No, there aren't. He told me he's been waiting for months for one of the MacLeods to return to Tongue and finish what Rory started."

"Months," Hamish repeated.

"Yes. He must have seen my father here five months ago when he came to retrieve the treasure. I think he recognized him as the infamous smuggler Rory MacLeod and decided to see what might come of following him."

Hamish thought this over. "If you're right, and he did follow Rory to the castle ruins, he would have known the treasure was there already. Why not just take it five months ago? And why bother to follow us today?"

"I wondered the same thing, at first." It had puzzled her, but in the end, she knew Rory better than she ever dreamed she had. "I don't think he ever did follow Rory to the castle ruins. I think Rory removed the treasure from underneath the cairn days before that blackguard ever realized he was in Tongue and had already hidden it in another location."

"A second location?" A small smile rose to Hamish's lips. "That would have been a damned clever way to confuse anyone who happened to be following him."

She smiled. "Diabolically clever, yes. I think he moved the treasure as soon as he arrived in Tongue, finished whatever other business he had here, then when he was ready to return to Dunvegan, he went back to fetch it."

"That blackguard from today must have followed him *then*. He shot Rory, intending to steal the treasure from him, but Rory got away from him."

"Yes, and I daresay that man has been searching the second location these past five months for a treasure my father had long since absconded with. It would have been just like Rory to move the treasure from one place to another. He'd been doing the same thing with his stolen contraband for years."

"What else did the man say?" Hamish's fingers tightened around her hand. "Did he confess to shooting your father?"

"Not in so many words, but he said he . . ." Her voice was

shaking, and she paused to take a deep breath. "He said he wasn't a crack shot, but that he was handy with a blade. H-he shot my father, Hamish."

"Shhh. I know. I know, sweetheart." He brought her hand to his lips and pressed a gentle kiss on her palm. "He's a thief and a murderer, and the Crown will make quick work of him. You revenged your father today, Cat."

"We did. *We* revenged him together, Hamish."

He smiled. "So, we did."

They sat there for some time, their fingers entwined, and let the bedchamber darken around them. Finally, she stirred and fetched the signet ring from Hamish's coat pocket and held it out to him. "It belonged to my great-grandfather. My father treasured it."

He took it and studied the crest. "Why do you think he left it in place of the treasure?"

"Because he knew someone would eventually find the bag buried under the cairn, and he wanted everyone to know Rory MacLeod had been there, and he'd fooled them all."

He handed the ring back to her with a shake of his head. "Rory confounded them to the end, didn't he?"

"Yes. That was my father, a surprise to the very end."

Dear God, what a trial he'd been.

How dearly she'd loved him, and how dearly she loved him still.

"And the treasure remains lost," Hamish murmured, the smile once again on his lips. "God only knows what he did with it."

"It will turn up one of these days, at the least convenient time, and in the last place we ever would have thought to look for it."

"I would expect nothing less of the celebrated Rory MacLeod. But you never told me how you managed to find the bag."

"The cairn. There was a picture of it among his drawings. I

turned to come back up the hill to fetch you, and there it was, as plain as day. It's rather astonishing I stumbled over it as I did, but as soon as I saw it, I knew."

"His papers weren't as disorganized as we thought, then."

She laughed. "No, they were, but I think I . . . well, I knew my father, better than even I realized. That treasure was buried here in Tongue, just as we thought it was."

"A cairn, of all things." Hamish gazed down at their entwined fingers, then turned her palm up, placed the signet ring in the center of it, and closed her fingers around it. "This is yours now."

His voice was a bit rough. When she looked into his eyes, the expression in those deep blue depths made her breath catch, and all at once she didn't know what to say or do. So, she snatched up the damp cloth and ran it over his palm again. "I think I've got most of the nettles out."

"Yes, I think so. Thank you."

"It's the least I can do, my lord, after you saved my life." She cast a shy glance at him, but looked quickly away again, her cheeks heating.

He caught her chin between his fingers and raised her face to his. "I have no doubt you'd have found a way to save yourself, one way or another, Cat."

Yes, perhaps she would have, but this time, she hadn't had to do that.

Because he'd been there. Not just today, but almost from the moment he arrived at Castle Cairncross. Since the night the third lugger had come, he'd been by her side through all of it. She'd never had that before, and it was lovely, really, to have someone always by your side.

No. Not just someone, but *him*.

He'd lied about the first lugger, yes, but it was one misstep amongst the dozens of kindnesses he'd done for her. That should have been her first thought, the moment he'd told her the truth.

That it hadn't been, made her ashamed of herself.

She didn't want to go through the rest of her life nursing all the little injustices done to her and ignoring all the truth and goodness in her life, and all the gifts she'd been given.

Like Hamish.

She didn't want to bear him a grudge for the one mistake he'd made. She'd never wanted to become the sort of lady who had a small, hard, suspicious heart.

And she didn't have to be. It was never too late to become the person you'd always wanted to be. It was really that easy, wasn't it? How strange that it had taken her all this time to learn that the best way to forgive was to simply make up her mind to do it.

"I don't want your gratitude, Cat." He drew closer, his gaze holding hers. "You know that, don't you? I want . . ."

She waited, suddenly breathless. "Yes?"

He met her gaze, his eyes as soft as dark blue velvet, like a sky at midnight. He only looked at *her* that way, with that softness in his beautiful eyes.

Why had it taken her so long to notice that?

"I want your love, Cat. I want your heart for my own. I want *you*, more than I've ever wanted anything. I know I lied to you, and hurt you, but I'll do anything to earn your forgive—"

"Shh." She pressed her fingers to his lips. "There's nothing to forgive, Hamish. I love you, too, so much. I confess I didn't know it at first, but I should have. My mother used to say a lady could learn all she needed to know about a man by looking into his eyes."

He traced her lips with his fingertip. "What do you see when you look into my eyes, my love?"

When she looked into his eyes . . . oh, there was no single answer to that question.

She saw the man who'd donned her father's hat and coat and haunted her castle to save her and her sisters. The man who'd taken her on this journey with him, even after she'd lost any hope of going. The man who'd protected her from Donigan's henchmen, taking a blade to his throat, for *her*. The man who'd learned the Latin name for red poppies, just to please her.

The man who kissed her with everything he had, and everything he was, and held her as if she were the most precious thing he'd ever had in his arms.

She gazed at him, her heart stuttering in her chest. "Everything, Hamish. When I look into your eyes, I see everything."

CHAPTER 24

Duirnish, Scotland
Three days later.

Cat woke to sunshine dancing over her eyelids, a muscular arm resting in the curve of her waist, and a large, warm palm cradling her belly.

Before she even recalled where she was, her lips had curved in a smile. She gave a lazy stretch, her toes curling against the foot pressed between hers. It had only been three days, but already she couldn't imagine waking up without Hamish's arms around her.

Alas, there would be no lingering in bed this morning. After the long weeks of grueling travel, they would arrive at Castle Cairncross today.

She sat up and tossed the coverlet aside, but before her feet could touch the warm floor, gentle fingers closed around her wrist. "Just where do you think you're going, Miss MacLeod?"

She glanced over her shoulder at Hamish, her heart fluttering at the sight of his sleepy blue eyes, tousled hair, muscular chest, and . . . goodness, so much bare, golden skin. His chest alone was enough to send her pulse into dizzying flutters, but the rest of him . . . well, did a lady ever become accustomed to waking up beside such a man as Hamish Muir?

"Have you forgotten we're leaving for Dunvegan this

morning?" She dragged her fingertips across his jaw, smiling at the scrape of his rough beard against her skin. "I expected you'd want to leave early, as it's a full day's drive."

"Early? God, no. I'm not in a hurry to abandon any bed you're in, Catriona." He slid the palm of his hand down her naked spine. "You have the most beautiful skin. So pale and delicate, like the petals of a blush pink rose."

"But if we're to arrive at Castle Cairncross before dark—"

"Have I told you how enamored I am of your smile, Miss MacLeod?" His own lips curved in a drowsy grin as he gazed at her. "I've never in my life seen a lovelier smile than yours."

He *had* told her. Every morning since they'd left Tongue, in fact, but there wasn't a lady alive who didn't shiver with pleasure at such words falling from the lips of the man she loved. "Are you listening to me, Lord Ballantyne?"

"And your hair." He caught one of the curls hanging loose down her back and held it up to the light streaming through the window, his lips parting as the morning sun set the red and gold strands alight. "It's like a sunrise."

"My, how poetic you are this morning, my lord." Cat closed her eyes as his fingers brushed over the arch of her back. "But Cairncross Castle is waiting for us."

"I do feel quite . . . inspired." He dropped a soft kiss on the end of her nose. "As for Castle Cairncross, it's not going anywhere. It's been standing for centuries now. I think we can trust it to remain intact for a bit longer."

He gave her wrist a little tug, tumbling her onto her back into the soft tangle of sheets and downy pillows, and her resistance dissolved like the thinnest, silkiest filament of a spider's web. "I suppose the castle can wait another hour."

A groan rumbled in his chest as her arms slid around his neck. "Two hours. These things can't be rushed, you know." He nuzzled his face into the curve of her shoulder, then pressed a lingering kiss behind her ear before sliding lower and nibbling at the corner of her lip.

She sank her fingers into the silky hair at the back of his neck, her lips parting for him, and he didn't hesitate to accept her invitation, his palms cradling her cheeks as he took her mouth with a hoarse groan, kissing her again and again, until they were both panting, their kisses exploding with heat and desire.

"Do you feel me, Cat?" He eased a leg between her thighs, making a home for himself there. "Do you feel how much I want you?"

"Yes. Hamish, please."

"Tell me you want me." He rolled onto his back, taking her with him and settling her on top of him, his palms sliding up her back and easing her down until she hovered over him. "I want to hear you say it."

"Yes." Her head dropped back as he sucked one of her nipples into his hot mouth, his hands on her back holding her still as he slid his tongue over the taut peak, his tongue flicking and teasing. "I want you, Hamish."

His eyes closed at her words, his long, thick lashes brushing his cheeks before he slid his hands down to her inner thighs, tracing patterns on her bare skin before brushing his knuckles against the damp curls there.

She curled her fingers into his chest, a whimper falling from her lips. The way he touched her . . . she could live a dozen lifetimes, and she would never have enough of his hands on her skin.

"Hold on to me, *leannan*." He sat up, shifting beneath her so she was straddling his hips. He pressed a hot kiss to her throat, then slid a finger against the aching bud between her thighs, letting out a ragged groan. "So wet for me, Catriona. So eager."

She gripped his shoulders and arched against his teasing fingers, his touch both too much and not enough at once. "More. I—I want you so much, Hamish."

He gazed up at her with eyes as dark as midnight. "Do you know how often I've dreamed of you like this, bared to me, the light and shadows playing over your body? So many times, love, but I never could have imagined how beautiful you are."

She reached for him, her hands cradling his face. "I love you, Hamish."

"And I love you." He let out a desperate groan as he slid gently inside her, his forehead meeting hers. "You're mine, Catriona MacLeod. Forever."

There was no need for any more words, after that. The bedchamber filled with their soft gasps and cries until they fell onto the bed together, sated, damp, and breathless.

Then they slept, with her curled in his arms, his lips against the back of her neck, and his face buried in her hair.

In the end, they got a rather late start that morning. By the time they arrived at Dunvegan, the sun had long since set, and the stars were twinkling like diamonds in the dark sky above Castle Cairncross.

As soon as Hamish brought the carriage to a stop at the top of the drive, Cat leapt out. "Listen, Hamish." She reached for his hand as he came up beside her. "You can hear the murmur of Loch Dunvegan from here. How I've missed that sound!"

"It does grow on one, does it not?" He wrapped his hands around her waist and turned her to face him. "Are you pleased to be home, love?"

"Oh, yes! So pleased. But where are my sisters? I would have thought they'd hear the carriage."

"They can't be far." He pressed a kiss to her forehead. "I do hope Sorcha didn't finish Callum off with that blade of hers. It might prove a bit difficult to explain to the rest of Clan Ross."

"Oh, dear. I hadn't thought of that." When she and Hamish had left the castle weeks ago, Sorcha had not been reconciled to Callum and Keir's presence. "I suppose we'd better find out."

They went into the house but paused in the entryway. "Goodness, it's dark in here, isn't it?" She moved to the bottom of the staircase and called for her sisters. "Freya? Sorcha?"

There was no reply. The castle was eerily quiet.

"How strange. Do you suppose they're on the roof?"

"It's a clear night tonight, which is rare enough in December. Perhaps they're taking advantage of it." He took her hand in his. "Shall we see?"

He led her up the stairs, but the tiny seed of fear that had sprouted in Cat's chest grew with every step. By the time they reached the turret, her heart was thudding uneasily.

Something was wrong. The castle was too quiet, too . . . empty.

The roof was deserted, as were her workroom and her father's study. Even Athena and Artemis were gone, their box perches empty.

"I don't like this, Hamish. If they were here, they'd have heard us by now."

He turned in a slow circle in the middle of her workroom, his brow creased. "It is a bit odd, but they may simply have retired to their beds already."

"Perhaps, yes." But as they made their way back down the stairs, her fingers clutched tightly in his, she knew they wouldn't be there.

The entire castle was dark. A musty smell hung in the air as if it had been weeks since a window or door had been opened, and there was a thick layer of dust on the railing.

It looked as if no one had been inside the castle for some time.

Sorcha and Freya's beds were both neatly made, their coverlets smooth and the pillows carefully plumped, but they weren't there.

They weren't anywhere. "Hamish?"

She tried to hide the tremor in her voice, but he heard it. "Wait here, love, and I'll check the guest wing for Callum and Keir."

"Yes, all right."

Cat waited, the darkness becoming thicker with every tick of the grandfather clock, until it was pressing down on her, stealing her breath, suffocating her.

What had happened? Where were her sisters?

When Hamish returned, he was alone. "There's no one there."

A dozen panicked questions flew through Cat's mind. Had another lugger come? Had there been some sort of conflict between Sorcha and Callum? Had the villagers finally lost patience with the MacLeod witches and chased them out of Dunvegan?

The tears she'd been holding back welled in her eyes.

"Shhh, *leannan.*" Hamish caught her against his chest. "We'll find them, I promise you. I won't rest until we do."

She nodded, curling her fingers in his coat, but she didn't dare speak or the tears burning in the back of her throat would burst loose.

If they could be found at all, she and Hamish would find them.

But where to start?

Freya, Sorcha, Callum, and Keir had disappeared without a trace.

Epilogue

Somehow, they found their way to the top of the castle, some unspoken agreement between them urging them up the narrow staircase winding around the turret to the pitched roof beyond.

Cat's hand slipped from his, her feet silent against the worn stones as she drifted toward the perimeter wall and stood staring out at the still waters of Loch Dunvegan. The sky had grown darker, the bright pink and orange streaks that had lit it up like a brilliant watercolor now a deep, moody violet.

Hamish didn't speak. He didn't follow her, or attempt to take her hand again, but stood silently, watching as the velvety darkness pressed closer, wrapping her in its familiar embrace. She was so still, so quiet, her edges fading in the waning light until he could only just discern her silhouette, a motionless shadow against the darkening sky. If it hadn't been for the lock of her hair floating in the breeze, he might have believed she'd become a part of the night itself.

How many times had she stood thus, gazing at the dark water, the only sound the rhythmic wash of the restless waves against the rocks below? Dozens of times? Hundreds?

But this wasn't like all those other times. This time, she wasn't alone.

She had him. She would always have him now.

"I'll never forget the first time I came up here." He chuckled, shaking his head. "You were wearing only your night rail with your cloak thrown over the top of it, and your feet were bare."

"I remember." She turned, the moonlight falling across one side of her face and revealing the sheepish smile on her lips. "You must have thought me mad, wandering about this old drafty castle in my bare feet."

"No." He closed the distance between them, his arms slipping around her waist, his eyes closing as she melted against him, the tense line of her back relaxing as he settled her against his chest. "I was too enamored of your toes to think of anything else."

"My *toes*?" She turned in his arms. "Why on earth would you be enamored of my toes?"

"Are you not aware, Miss MacLeod, that you have the sweetest, pinkest toes of any lass in the Scottish Highlands? They quite took my breath away. I'm afraid they chased every other thought from my head. I was captivated by you even then, which is rather pathetic, really, given I still believed you'd poisoned me."

She laughed, her warm breath caressing him through the layers of his shirt and waistcoat. "I don't remember much about that night, aside from our skirmish with the smugglers, but I do remember trying to hide my toes underneath the hem of my night rail so you wouldn't see them."

"Why should you wish to hide such delicious toes?"

She gazed up at him, a twinkle in her green eyes. "You'd have me reveal my naked toes to the dashing Marquess of Ballantyne? Why, what could be more scandalous?"

He dropped a kiss on the top of her head, the loose wisps of her hair tickling his lips. Surely there wasn't a lady in all of Scotland who had softer hair than hers. "You told me all about gout."

"Gout?" She let out a groan. "Oh, no."

"Yes, indeed. Do you not remember? Gout and Wood Betony,

and Lemon Balm, and all manner of other things. If I recall correctly, you went on at some length about venomous spider bites, as well." He grinned down at her. "It was quite the treatise on potions and cures."

Her cheeks colored, and she hid her face in his chest. "Goodness, what you must have thought of me!"

He touched his fingers to her chin, raising her face to his. "What I thought, Miss MacLeod, was that I'd never encountered a lady as clever as you. The passion with which you spoke, the flush in your cheeks, and the light in your eyes was . . . well, I was utterly mesmerized by you nearly from the moment I laid eyes on you."

The green eyes he loved so well had grown brighter as he spoke. "Y-you were?"

"I was, I am, and I always shall be. You won't ever be alone again, Cat. I'll never leave you. I won't leave you." Of all the things he most wanted her to understand, it was this that was the most important. "I'm yours, forever."

"And I'm yours," she whispered, her hands coming up to cradle his face. "I only hope you won't live to regret it. Alas, fate has decreed that misfortune will follow the MacLeods."

Her face clouded, and he knew she was thinking of her sisters.

"We'll find Freya and Sorcha, Cat. I promise it." They would, because they had to. Anything else would break Cat's heart, and he wouldn't allow that. She'd turned her lovely, open heart over to him, and he'd take care of it, no matter what.

She sighed. "I know we will, it's just . . . where shall we even begin, Hamish? There's no note. We haven't a clue where they've gone, and the house looks much as it did when we left weeks ago. It's as if they walked out the door, and vanished."

"Something happened, that much is certain. Tomorrow we'll go and see the Duffys and find out if there was any disagreement between your sisters and the villagers. Wherever they've gone, you can be certain Keir and Callum are with them." His friends had promised to protect Freya and Sorcha, and they'd keep their word.

"I wish we could go tonight. Right now."

"Tomorrow is soon enough. We'll only upset the Duffys if we appear on their doorstep at this late hour. You need to sleep now, love." She didn't seem to notice it, but he could see how exhausted she was by the slump of her shoulders and her pale face.

"I know. Just a few more minutes, all right?" She rose to her tiptoes to press a sweet kiss to his lips, then turned to face the water again. The wind had picked up as the sky had grown dark above them, and he pulled her more tightly against the warmth of his body, wrapping his arms around her when she shivered.

They remained there for some time, neither of them speaking.

Was it strange that he should feel such peace in this moment? Their return to Castle Cairncross wasn't the joyful homecoming either of them had anticipated. They were hovering on the edge of another wild escapade, and tomorrow would come sooner than they were ready for it.

But as they stood there together, with the chill wind sneaking under their cloaks, he felt nothing but happiness, and hope.

Somehow, between the smugglers and the luggers, the monkshood poisoning and the gold coins, the phosphorescent paint and the haunting of Castle Cairncross, they'd found each other. She was here, with him, safe and warm in his arms, and she was everything he'd ever wanted.

He had her, and nothing in the world mattered more to him than that.

She stirred then, turning in his arms, a soft sigh leaving her lips. "Take me to bed, my lord."

"With pleasure, my lady." He brushed the loose waves of her hair back from her face, his heart swelling with joy at the softness in her eyes. "With pleasure."

Author's Notes

Bampfylde, Margaret. Recipes and Remedies: An eighteenth-century collection by Margaret Bampfylde of Hestercombe. White, Philip, ed. The Hestercombe Gardens Trust. https://www.hestercombe.com/uploads/pdf/Margaret-Bampfyldes-RECIPE-BOOK_GUIDE-BOOK-2006.pdf

The recipe for the Strangeway Drops that Hamish is so curious about in Chapter 9 appears in Margaret Bampfylde's book *Recipes and Remedies*. It's a fascinating read, with weird and wonderful eighteenth-century recipes and cures, as well as a thorough index of healing plants and cooking and medicinal terms.

Castelow, Ellen. Smugglers and Wreckers. History Magazine. Historic UK. https://www.historic-uk.com/CultureUK/Smugglers-Wreckers/

The frightening appearance of the legendary Ghostly Drummer of Hurstmonceaux, who terrorized the inhabitants of Sussex in the eighteenth-century is believed by some scholars to have achieved his ghostly glow with a creative application of phosphorus paint.

Castle Varrich, Tongue, Scotland.

> There are conflicting accounts concerning the history of Castle Varrich as it concerns Clan Mackay. Some dispute that the castle ever belonged to the clan, putting it instead in the hands of the Bishop of Caithness. There is general agreement that the castle was abandoned sometime in the mid-eighteenth century, but I couldn't find any reference to a specific year. For the purposes of this story, I've assumed that the castle was abandoned by the time Hamish and Cat visited the ruins in 1775, but I cannot confirm that this date is precisely accurate. For some stunning and detailed pictures of the ruins, please see https://www.tripadvisor.com/Attraction_Review-g319814-d7274666-Reviews-Castle_Varrich-Tongue_Caithness_and_Sutherland_Scottish_Highlands_Scotland.html

Chambers, Vanessa. The Witchcraft Act Wasn't About Women on Brooms. The Guardian. January 2007. https://www.theguardian.com/commentisfree/2007/jan/24/comment.comment3#:~:text=So%20the%20law%20wanted%20to,well%2Dknown%20politicians

Hansen, Bert. Hennig Brand and the Discovery of Phosphorus. Distillations Magazine. Science History Institute Museum and Library. Philadelphia, PA. July 2019. https://www.sciencehistory.org/stories/magazine/hennig-brand-and-the-discovery-of-phosphorus/

> Phosphorus was discovered in 1669 by Hennig Brand, an aspiring German alchemist. As a scientist herself, Cat would likely have known of Brand's discovery. Regarding Catriona's brilliant use of phosphorus paint in Chapter 11, the author has taken a creative license regarding the com-

posting of plant matter to create the phosphorus powder. Although it is possible to create the powder from plant processing, I could find no evidence they knew about composting in eighteenth-century Britain.

The Hidden History of Smuggling in Scotland. The Scotsman. Edinburgh. August 2016. https://www.scotsman.com/whats-on/arts-and-entertainment/the-hidden-history-of-smuggling-in-scotland-1472813.

Lawson, Revered R. Places of Interest About Girvan. Smuggling in Carrick. https://electricscotland.com/history/girvan/chapter35.htm.

Mackay, Angus. Book Of Mackay. Edinburgh: N. Macleod. 1906. Accessed via The National Library of Scotland. https://ia600209.us.archive.org/8/items/bookofMackay00mack/bookofMackay00mack.pdf

MacQueen, Douglas. Search for Bonnie Prince Charlie's Gold Lost from Ship Le Prince Charles Stuart. Transceltic Blog. Entry dated February 2021. https://www.transceltic.com/blog/search-bonnie-prince-charlie-s-gold-lost-ship-le-prince-charles-stuart

Myatt, L.J. An Eighteenth-century Sea Battle in the Kyle of Tongue. Caithness.org. Caithness Field Club Bulletin. April 1983. https://www.caithness.org/history/articles/eighteenth centuryseabattle/eighteenthcenturyseabattle.htm

Platt, Richard. Smuggling in the British Isles. The History Press. February 2012. http://www.smuggling.co.uk/gazetteer_scot.html

Shakespeare, William. Macbeth. Wordsworth Editions. 1992.
Thomas Numismatics. Tnumis Magazine. Meylan Cedex, France. https://thomasnumismatics.com/en/blog/louis-dor-coin/

> The gold Louis d'Or ten-pieces referenced in the story were not among the monies sent by Louis XV via *Le Prince Charles Stuart*. The detail is an invention of the author, for the purposes of the story.

The Witchcraft Act of 1735. Wikipedia. https://en.wikipedia.org/wiki/Witchcraft_Act_1735.

Witchcraft, Women & the Healing Arts in the Early Modern Period: The Witches Flying Ointment. The University of Alabama at Birmingham. December 2022. https://guides.library.uab.edu/c.php?g=1048546&p=7609204.

> One of the most persistent falsehoods concerning witches was that they had the ability to fly, and frequently flew to far-off lands to commune with the devil and other witches. Monkshood is known to be a strong hallucinogenic, and it was an essential ingredient in witch's flying ointment.